The Private Papers
of Eastern Jewel

D0928821

The Private Papers of Eastern Jewel

MAUREEN LINDLEY

BLOOMSBURY

First published 2008

Copyright © 2008 by Maureen Lindley

The moral right of the author has been asserted

No part of this book may be used or reproduced
in any manner whatever without written permission
from the Publisher except in the case of brief
quotations embodied in critical articles or reviews

Bloomsbury Publishing Plc, 36 Soho Square, London W1D 3QY

Bloomsbury Publishing, London, New York and Berlin

A CIP catalogue record for this book is available from the British Library

ISBN 978 0 7475 9116 0

10 9 8 7 6 5 4 3

Typeset by Hewer Text UK Ltd, Edinburgh
Printed by Clays Ltd, St Ives plc

The paper this book is printed on is certified by the © 1996 Forest Stewardship
Council A.C. (FSC). It is ancient-forest friendly. The printer holds
FSC chain of custody SGS-COC-2061

FSC
Mixed Sources
Product group from well-managed
forests and other controlled sources
Cert no. SGS-COC-2061
www.fsc.org
© 1996 Forest Stewardship Council

To Clive, Daniel, and Liberty, with love.

Author's Note

The Private Papers of Eastern Jewel is a novel based on the extraordinary life of a Manchu princess whose striking image, that of a beautiful girl in men's clothes, caught my attention when she appeared momentarily on screen in Bertolucci's film, *The Last Emperor*.

Eastern Jewel is fascinating in the way in which all women who have the courage to step outside the mores of their time and make their lives an adventure are fascinating. At a time of loss and emotional turmoil in my own life, I sat in the beautiful old reading room of the British Library and became lost in hers. The facts of her life as I read them presented her as a one-dimensional woman, thoroughly bad. I don't accept that she was and as I believe historians to be just as partial as novelists, I set out to bring to life through fiction what I imagined had made Eastern Jewel into the woman she became. The bad is there, but so are courage and love and a measure of loyalty and loss.

A handful of the characters in the book are loosely based on real people and I have followed the known dates and the historical facts as faithfully as I could.

The written account that follows was discovered at Peking Number One Prison amongst the private papers of the prisoner Eastern Jewel. Also found amongst her papers were a copy of a poem by Chikamatsu, an empty jar of brilliantine, a small bottle of chrysanthemum oil, a scented letter signed from a 'true friend', a half-eaten box of dried lychees and the receipt for a black pearl purchased from the Sincere department store on Nanking Road, Shanghai.

Snake and Chrysanthemum Soup

In 1914, at the age of eight years, I was caught spying on my father Prince Su as he made love to a fourteen-year-old girl. The girl had glycerine eyes and marvellous lips that had no bow but were the shape and colour of a segment of blood orange, a soft, sanguine red.

I watched from behind a carved screen as he removed her silk shoes, then dipped her tiny feet into his bowl of tea before drinking from it. The girl sat motionless and completely naked on a plump floor cushion. There was not even a comb in her long hair, which shone like laurel leaves. Deep into this amorous ritual my father pressed a sweet almond between her toes, lowered his lips to it and slowly ate the nut as though it were the most delicious thing he had ever tasted. She remained silent even as he mounted her, reaching his climax with groans of ecstasy. When he had finished and rolled away from her, she gave an exaggerated sigh of pleasure and whispered something to him that made him smile and look proud. After a little time had passed she rose, filled a bowl with warm, scented water and carefully washed between my father's legs. Then she slipped into her doll shoes and, with her robe unbuttoned, she fluttered from the room.

Under her shoes and bindings the girl's feet would have been putrescent and fetid; yet crushed into the shape of a lotus flower so that, as legend had it, her lord could enjoy 'eating the gold lotus

I

while driving his jade spear into her jade gate until the moment of clouds and rain', it hardly mattered. To please one's master was all.

I was destined never to experience this ritual, this passion brought on by the sight of those childlike feet. It is not customary for Manchu women to indulge in the practice of foot binding. We were the lucky ones. In those days in China, women's lives were ruled by the whims of the men who were their lords. Bound feet kept them from straying too far, like ducks on a domestic pond. At least we Manchu women could run away on our big feet.

I was a Manchu princess named Eastern Jewel, the fourteenth daughter of Prince Su, one of the eight Princes of the Iron Helmet in the old Imperial Court of Peking. Like my father I am a direct descendant of Nurhachi, the founder of the Manchu dynasty, and a distant cousin of the boy Emperor Pu Yi. Yet despite my heritage, I am female and considered by Manchu men to be less than them, an unimportant person hardly to be thought of at all. Yet, by my actions I make them think of me all the time. I have always believed myself a match for my brothers and made them angry by not kowtowing to them. Ninth brother said I must have been a warrior in a previous life.

I was discovered at my spy hole by Jade Lute, the thirteenth of my nineteen sisters, the daughter of my father's second and most jealous concubine. My own mother, a poised, elegant woman, was Prince Su's fourth and youngest concubine. She was thought to be of Japanese descent and considered to be the second most beautiful woman in my father's household. For the sake of good manners his wife accepted the compliment of being the first. My mother was named Yuzu after the prized citrus fruit of that name. She had a sweet, oval face with eyes as dark as muddy pools, rosy lips and a tiny provocative gap between her front teeth. Like most concubines she had an obedient nature but there was a streak of fun in her that sometimes overtook her at inappropriate moments.

I was so completely spellbound by what I was witnessing through the intricately carved screen that I did not hear thirteenth sister coming. She pulled at my hair, screaming, 'I have found a nasty little spy, a horrid little worm.' She shrieked and held on to me until the whole household came running to see what all the fuss was about.

My father was outraged by my behaviour and had me confined to my mother's rooms. For hours he paced the halls and courtyards of our house, calling my mother to his side and going over and over my many misdemeanours. Her shame was deep and painful, made worse by the pleasure taken in her disgrace by my father's wife and concubines. I vowed to myself that I would one day poison them all. Meanwhile, I took my revenge in dreams where Jade Lute, made half Gorgon half girl, was pursued by demons and devoured.

It was fortunate for my mother that she had already given my father a son, my brother Xian Li, otherwise she might have been cast out for burdening him with me. She was accused of being a woman without character, on whom her daughter's outrages reflected badly. My father said that it was unheard of for a daughter to be so vile, so without modesty or honour.

'Since Eastern Jewel burst into the world covered in blood, straining at the wet nurse until she had nothing left to give, you have allowed her will to succeed over your own,' he told my mother coldly. He reminded her that it was I who had made sexual overtures to his servant boy Pao, causing him to be flogged and given away to a less generous master. The truth was I had only asked to see Pao's snake because he was always boasting of its size and I wanted to prove him a liar. I had inspected and even touched at least two of my brothers' members and couldn't believe that a servant might have a finer one. I had thirteenth sister to thank for that betrayal too. It is irksome in the extreme to live in a house of women where the air is cloyed with envy and bitter with the smallness of their lives.

My mother, bent double with humility, tapped along beside my father in his rage, her murmurings of regret barely audible. I had

3

gone too far this time and she knew better than to make excuses for me. While other concubines had daughters who busied themselves in feminine pursuits, I was a wild and uncultured girl who was openly interested in sex, capable of cruelty and rebellious to the point of stupidity. Although she loved me I was my mother's burden and her shame.

The days passed and my father's anger cooled, but I was still confined to my mother's quarters without even a servant for company. Lonely and bored, I resorted to small mischiefs. I ate a whole box of fragrant dried lychees, which were my mother's weakness, I wasted her precious supply of rouge papers, colouring my face a bright peony pink and dancing madly around her room. Finally when I had run out of things to occupy me and my screams and kicks on her door no longer brought my mother to my side, I braided my hair into two long pigtails and, using her bone-handled fruit knife, I liberated one of them. It lay on the floor like a small, dark, dead serpent.

When she saw it my mother moaned and put her fist into her mouth to stop her cry lest she be heard by anyone listening at her door. She spent hours searching in her book of medicine for a concoction that would both speed the growth of my hair and cool my temper. She settled on a snake and chrysanthemum soup which, although delicious, had little effect on either. In her distress she made the mistake of seeking comfort by confiding in third concubine. And thus my fate was sealed.

This time my father did not shout but was alarmingly quiet in his rage. His concubines talked in whispers so as not to provoke him further. Finally, when it seemed that his anger would never reach its peak, he called the women of the household into the central courtyard and sent word to my mother to bring me to him. They all knelt, humble and expectant, as I stood before him. As though he was catching a cat by the tail he lifted my remaining pigtail so high that the pain of it made my eyes water. Then he cut it off and threw it to the ground.

4

Some of my sisters gasped while second concubine sniggered in the moment before my father silenced them all by raising his hand. He pushed me towards my mother, who was hot with embarrassment, and addressed his audience.

'It is my misfortune to be the father of Eastern Jewel,' he said. 'This unimportant daughter continues to disgrace her name with her ignoble behaviour.' He looked towards my mother and continued, 'She is like an unlicked cub, which perhaps is not her fault. I have no inclination to bother with these irksome concerns. Eastern Jewel will be sent to Japan to the house of my blood brother Kawashima where she will be taught the manners fit for her station in life, which is high, but still only that of a woman. Go about your business in this house as women and do not let the news of your small affairs reach my ears again.'

Minutes after his declaration, my father accompanied by his running servants left the house on horseback, shouting for them to keep up. A great sigh of relief was heard as the women began to chatter and gossip, knowing that my father, having made his decision, would eventually return home with his mood restored. I was led away by my dry-eyed mother to the hostile hissing of my sisters. I never saw my father again.

I could not believe that I was to be sent away to this strange place called Japan. My father's 'blood brother' sounded as scary as the dragons I had heard of in the stories told to me by third concubine, who had a vivid imagination and suffered terrible nightmares populated with the legendary creatures. Filled with a fear so strong that I couldn't eat or sleep, I begged my mother to keep me with her.

'Please, Mother, save me from the blood man,' I pleaded. But with sadness in her eyes she said that my father was not to be approached further and that I was to make the best of the situation I now found myself in. At the thought of losing my mother, as well as the only home I had ever known, my heart felt hollow. I was frightened by what lay ahead of me, but strangely, accompanying that fear a run of excitement at the thought of the unknown kept my blood singing.

Each night for a week I slept in my mother's arms as she cried herself to sleep. I breathed in the scent of her hair and grieved for her as though she were already lost to me.

During that time my father did not call my mother to his bed once. From dawn of day to dusk she busied herself with the packing of the chests that would accompany me to the Kawashima household. She told me that Kawashima Naniwa was a great man. He was the son of an ancient family, the head of a large merchant empire and was involved in Japanese politics at the highest level. She knew nothing of the women or children in his household but felt sure they would treat me well and that I would prosper. Later I was to discover that Kawashima, finding me a pretty child, had requested of my father that I be given to him to be raised in his Japanese household two years before thirteenth sister betrayed me. However, my father chose to justify my banishment, it had always been the case that whatever my behaviour I would be given to Kawashima merely because he had requested it. Of my nineteen sisters and ten brothers, I was the only one to be given away.

Ours was a rich home filled with fine silks, the most delicate of porcelain, soft blankets for winter nights and rosewood furniture intricately inlaid with ivory and jade. We had many servants, stables full of horses, kitchens that were well supplied with the best noodles, the finest rice and such superior cuts of meat that they hardly needed chewing. We were never short of sugar cakes or frosted apricots, and even the servants ate meat dumplings at least once a week. I wondered what I would be given from this wealth of luxuries to accompany me on my journey. I was then as I am now a greedy person, but, I should add, not an ungenerous one. In my opinion greed is not a bad thing, it spurs you on, makes you good at living. What is the point of life if nothing is demanded from it?

As the trunks began to fill with gifts of exquisite linen, embroidered silk runners and delicate rolls of calligraphy that were to be

6

presented to the Kawashima family, so I came to know that I truly was being sent from my mother and my home. There was to be no last-minute reprieve.

Carefully, in the chest set aside for me, my mother placed my favourite rice bowl, a pair of her coral and silver gilt earrings, a good luck charm of a bee caught in amber, a fine leather writing case engraved with my family crest and a box of dried lychees. She said the lychees would sustain me and remind me of her until I had eaten the last one and then it would be time to forget her. I asked her if it would be easy to forget her. She said that I was not like other daughters so perhaps I would not find it hard, whereas it would break her heart to part with me. She said that she would never forget her beautiful, rebellious girl.

I stored the precious box of lychees in my writing case and determined that however hungry I might be I would only eat half of them. I did not want the memory of my beautiful mother to fade before I could return to her.

'Surely I will see you again, Mother?' I said.

'Only if that is your fate, Eastern Jewel,' she replied. 'You must be brave, little daughter, and remember that the stronger the wind, the stronger the tree needs to be.'

I left our house for the first part of my journey in a plain sedan accompanied by a fat servant woman with blackened teeth and a sweet smile. The luggage followed behind with two male servants cursing their luck that they had to leave my father's comfortable house to go on a long and difficult journey with his disgraced daughter. As we clattered through the gate of our courtyard a beggar banged on the sedan's door expectantly, only to be disappointed at the unpromising sight of a skinny girl with her fat servant woman. I took a coin from my pocket and threw it at his feet. I have always delighted in confounding people's expectations of me, and in any case it is good luck to give alms to the poor.

I looked back hoping to catch a last glimpse of my mother, but all I saw was one of our cooks carrying the pot of snake and chrysanthemum soup from her quarters back to the kitchen. A great sadness spread through my body, my mouth went dry and I was sick over the skirt of the servant woman.

I wished I had been able to show my mother that I loved her, but something in my nature finds it hard to give people what they want. I don't believe she ever knew the depth of my affection for her, ever knew that it was she who made me capable of love. The cruel gene inherited from my father was more urgent in me and often drowned my mother's gentle one. All the same, I should have overcome my nature and left her with assurances of my love and gratitude. With hindsight, I imagine that she lived her days with a brick in her heart from the loss of me.

As we bumped along the potholed roads I determined that I would not allow myself to indulge in such sadness again. After all, if one is to live a healthy life it is only natural to be the most important person in it. To feel sadness at the loss of others is like choosing to be ill when you could be well. Yet whatever we may determine, the memory of a loved mother accompanies us for the rest of our lives.

My journey to Japan was a long and exciting one on which I discovered the world was a larger place than I could ever have imagined. We went by train to Shanghai and then across the sea to Yokohama. I enjoyed the adventure of being at sea and the unusual things that happened on board ship. One morning the deck was completely covered in jellyfish that had landed there during a night storm. The captain said that it was a bad sign when the creatures of the sea were not content to stay in their own element.

There were three Europeans on the ship. They were tall and white and almost as translucent as the jellyfish. I had never seen a foreigner before and I thought them very odd. Everything about them looked out of proportion, especially their noses, and I felt very glad to be Chinese. When they spoke they sounded as though they were moaning, but I liked the blue of their eyes and the way they slapped each other on the back in greeting.

8

The other passengers spoke of a war just begun in the land of these lofty aliens and I tried without success to picture those pale giants in battle. They were always stumbling about as though their heads were too far from their feet so it was difficult to imagine them wielding swords.

All three of my servants suffered terribly from seasickness and spent the journey being sick or lying on the deck moaning. I was ashamed of them, especially as, like myself, the foreigners were fine sailors.

We were tired and dusty by the time we arrived at the house of Kawashima, only to be greeted by the colour of death. White lanterns hung on either side of the tall gates and fluttered from the trees in the gardens that surrounded the house. A watchman, shaking his head as though he were praying for the dead, ushered us along a narrow footpath that was edged with swept shingle. The house, a large traditional timber-built residence, was circled by a stone wall with a western-style wing built on at one end where the garden sloped to a carp-filled pool. Half hidden by winter plum trees a wooden shrine sat on one side of a deep pond and was reflected in the water.

I followed a servant into the dim interior of the house, leaving my own to follow with my possessions. The scent of camellias hung thick in the air, their ghostly blooms staring from vases arranged like sentries along the length of the hall. Because their flowers drop so abruptly they are thought to symbolise death, yet how beautiful they are in the brief time they have to prosper.

Kawashima's mother had died the previous week, and arriving as I had at a time of death was a bad omen for me. So it was from the moment I set foot in the house the women thought me unlucky and therefore did not seek my company.

The servant beckoned us on. We passed a long room half screened with white muslin drapes where a small elderly woman, tightly wrapped in a grey kimono, was bent over a table, fat with delicious-looking food. Softly outlined against the pale drapes she appeared like a ghost at the banquet but was probably a cook or a servant of some kind. Hunger rumbled in my belly and I remembered the last proper meal I had eaten in my father's home, fish cooked with ginger, little honey dumplings and ground almond paste wrapped in rice paper as thin as tissue. I darted to the end of the table and grabbed a rice ball that was dripping in a glossy, plum oil. The old woman hissed with shock at my savage manners. My Chinese servant woman, whom I had named Sorry, because of her habit of constantly apologising, mumbled an appropriate excuse for my forgotten manners. She pulled me from the room, wiping my hands on the hem of her skirt.

The two male servants who had accompanied us from China were to return to my father's house. Sorry was to remain with me in Japan as my personal servant. I was glad of it as I had come to care for her over the course of the journey, just as she had decided to love me as best she could, and to be loyal.

We were shown to small quarters on the north side of the house that overlooked a narrow strip of garden. Although it was summer there were no flowers, no roses or peonies, nothing to sweeten the air or stir the senses. It was a garden of stones, flat and uninteresting. Compared to the spaciousness of my mother's quarters the small rooms felt like cells. Even Japanese as rich as Kawashima did not live in quite the same splendour as their high-ranking counterparts in China. Sorry went in search of food for us and to take her leave of our servants, who would enjoy a much-needed sleep before returning to Peking.

Left alone in the three almost empty little rooms, I felt sad and frightened. Compared to the noisy hallways of my family home the house was silent and full of melancholy. I ached for my mother and I wondered what would become of me without her. I missed my brothers and sisters and wondered who would there be in this house that I could play and fight with, as I had done with them. I was a person without family, banished in shame from my home. It dawned on me then for the first time, but by no means the last, that perhaps I was truly an unlovable person. I think that unconsciously I chose to live up to that expectation of my nature rather than to change it. That was a mistake, as have been so many things in my life.

I was deep in my musings when one of the household servants, a woman as skinny as a stick, came to tell me that the Kawashima family could not greet me, as they were visiting the shrine of their ancestors to pay their respects and to seek consolation. They were to return in a day or two. The stick woman gave me a cricket in a brass box pierced with tiny breathing holes. She said its chatter would keep me company. When she left I opened the box and let the cricket out. It hopped dismally to the corner of the room and sat in the dust looking as forlorn as I felt.

As in most of the difficult times in my life, all I could think to do was to sleep, so I curled up on the lowest bed with my back to the wall and slept. I had no idea how much time had passed when I was woken by Sorry bearing a bowl of egg noodles and some uncooked white fish. I knew that she had been gone a long time because the light had changed, but the news she returned with was worth her long absence. My Japanese family, she told me, comprised Kawashima Naniwa who was to be my new stepfather, his father Kawashima Teshima who was in his seventieth year and in deep mourning for his recently dead wife, my stepmother Natsuko and her unmarried half-crippled sister Shimako. Kawashima and Natsuko had two sons, Hideo and Nobu, and six daughters, one of whom had an unlucky birthmark marring her face. All the Kawashima offspring had the strawberry birthmark somewhere on their body. It was usually a small stain on the foot or hand; only their daughter Itani was disfigured by it.

To my amazement, Sorry told me that there were no concubines in the house. The cook, who was a great gossip, had confided in her that Kawashima took his pleasures away from home in the teahouses and brothels that flourished in the streets of Tokyo. He often went away for long periods of time to Osaka, the great merchant city, where he was said to keep a geisha in enviable luxury. This geisha was rumoured to have a hundred kimonos and many jewels which Kawashima lavished on her because of her various and delightful ways of welcoming his snake into her pit. Sorry laughed with pleasure at the vulgarity of this and apologised to me for the language she used. She said that Kawashima did not love his wife and this was Natsuko's tragedy as well as the fact that she had given him more daughters than sons, which displeased him greatly. Although Kawashima did not desire his wife he did have great respect for her, for she was the daughter of a most influential and refined family. It was whispered in the house that Natsuko's grief for her mother-in-law was false, a show to impress her husband. Kawashima's mother had been a difficult woman to please and had treated Natsuko badly, implying that her daughter-in-law had fooled her son into believing that her womb would be rich in sons.

I thought that Sorry had done well to gather so much information in so short a time. I loved gossip, it made me feel at home and I always felt safer when I knew what was going on around me. I told her that she would make a good spy. She laughed and said that we had come to a household where the servants were indiscreet and we would be wise to keep our secrets to ourselves. I knew that I would not find being secretive too hard as I had been brought up with concubines and their competitive daughters and thus had an untrusting nature.

It was to be six weeks before I met Kawashima himself. His wife and her sister Shimako welcomed me formally and without warmth on my fourth day in their home. Their coldness filled me with gloom and I was glad I had Sorry to discuss them with. I told her that I did not like them at all and she said even though it would be difficult, I must try to please them, if only to make my own life easier. She advised me to pretend that my mind was as young as my body, for they would find my knowledge of life vulgar in a girl of my years.

But whatever I said or did I would not gain the affection of my stepmother Natsuko or her sister Shimako. They were set against me from the start and the best I could hope for from them was indifference. They were an odd pair, quite different in appearance but devoted to each other. Natsuko's great beauty, her long dark eyes, high cheekbones and rare smile, belied her nature. Shimako was plain with a broad face and a bent body and seemed made by the gods to mop up misery. It must have been hard for her to live in the shadow of her beautiful sibling and her charmed brother-in-law Kawashima.

The only person I could truly rely on was Sorry. She was always on my side even though there were times when I tested her patience to breaking point. Her loyalty to me never wavered and without her my early life in Japan would have been very bleak.

After a few months I settled into the rhythm of the house, my homesickness faded as I grew out of my shoes and out of my misery. I discovered in that long house with its monochrome garden a place for myself that was more interesting and complex than the one I had occupied in my Chinese home. It took me some time to get used to a house without concubines. At first I had thought it novel, but I soon realised that I missed the chatter and the constant dramas that a house confining thirty women is bound to host. But my life was freer and more independent in my new home as no one other than Sorry seemed to be in charge of my welfare, and I grew more autocratic and more determined to have my way than ever before. Sometimes I found myself in the company of the women of the house but I never felt myself to be one of them. I had a secret desire for Natsuko to favour me but I could not bring myself to court her, and so instead I became the adversary she had from our first meeting taken me to be. While Shimako mostly ignored me, Natsuko broke my heart with her sarcasm and coldness. The Kawashima women never relented in their dislike of me and my own contempt for them was confirmed as I grew up an outcast amongst them. It was not in my character to be a victim and so I set out to shock them by being their opposite in both morals and manners.

As the years passed I wove myself into the fabric of the Kawashima family life while never losing sight of the fact that my thread was of a different colour to theirs. Japanese society was unlike the one I had known in China. It was not my heritage but I liked it better, especially as I had no predetermined place in it.

With Sorry more in my charge than me in hers, I had the freedom to expand boundaries and to take my pleasures in a variety of ways that would never previously have been allowed me. As neither true daughter nor guest, I may have thought of myself as special, but in hindsight I think that I was simply abandoned. I was the daughter of a prince, high born and equal in status to my adoptive family, but I know now that to Kawashima I was just a novelty with a good dowry.

Unlike China, Japan was coming to terms with the modern world, but in the Kawashima household old traditions still held sway. Had Kawashima's daughters been born just a few years later, they would have been educated at a ladies' seminary, shopped in department stores and enjoyed a life outside the home. As it was, they were on the cusp of that time and spent their days perfecting the tea ceremony and enduring hours of calligraphy lessons.

No one questioned that I chose not to join the women in their delicate pursuits. Sometimes though, when I heard their soft laughter or saw Natsuko's head close to one of her daughters as she explained a stitch, I felt a pain as real as toothache.

Like my father Prince Su, Kawashima was not much interested in me, that is, until my body ripened and my face became the sort that excited men. Unlike my father, though, he allowed me an education. I shared lessons with his sons and, like the women warriors of Japanese legend, I was taught judo and fencing. I picked up languages early and had adjusted to Japanese. Along with Hideo and Nobu I was instructed in the English language and quite soon I overtook them in my knowledge of it. I never questioned why Kawashima's blood daughters were not offered my opportunities, I just believed I was special and not cut out for their predetermined lives.

On the rare occasions that I came to Kawashima's attention he seemed mildly amused by my boyishness. He knew the women did not like me and that their shunning of my company had turned me to his sons for companionship. He was entertained by my swaggering and indulged my extreme naughtiness with his indifference to it. In common with many of the men of his generation, Kawashima was half in love with western culture and I convinced myself that he had chosen me over his daughters as the one to take advantage of the liberation of the new century.

Firmly rooted in the traditional camp, Natsuko was outraged by me, my very existence in her world unsettled her. I knew that she resented her husband's interest in me and was on the lookout for a good enough reason to have me sent back to China. Although her sister Shimako said little to my face and was always polite, I knew that she encouraged Natsuko's animosity. Bitter with grief for her crippled body which made her unmarriageable, Shimako loved intrigue and constantly whispered in her sister's ear, exaggerating everything and keeping the household in a state of tension. Secret enemies are always the most dangerous and despite her slyness, I knew Shimako to be mine.

I liked the old man Teshima well enough and often ate with him in his rooms, but over time his insistent fondling became boring and I began to seek excuses to avoid his company. I had a friendship of sorts with Natsuko's third daughter Ichiyo, who was eight months older than me. Ichiyo spied for me, partly for the pleasure of sharing secrets but mostly because she was afraid of me.

I liked to win and having my father's superior traits I naturally and enthusiastically adopted the Japanese code of conquest and courage into my own philosophy of life. This, Natsuko said, was so unfeminine that men would be repulsed by it.

By the age of twelve I was wandering the house and grounds at will and had found my way out into the winding back streets of the city. The life of Tokyo spilled into those streets, thrilling me with its smells and colours, its endless noise and its parade of people. I saw geishas being carried to their assignations in rickshaws, business-men making their way to their places of work, busy tea houses run by the mama-sans in their crude-coloured kimonos and the women of pleasure calling to each other from dark doorways and painted balconies. Once I saw a man in an alleyway force a girl to her knees before him. I was close enough to smell his sweat and desire and her fear, and to experience a wrench in my stomach so powerful that I found it hard to breathe. A few days later I tried to find the alleyway again but it had been reduced to dust and rubble. There were building sites everywhere as modern Tokyo emerged from the ancient city. New hotels and offices sprang up almost overnight amongst the little traditional shops and wooden temples, and whole streets were demolished in a single day.

Once, during a bitterly cold winter, I discovered the beggar who stood daily outside our gate frozen to the iron pillar he had watched over since his youth. His body was bent with his right hand still cupped in the begging position. The air was so cold that winter that carp froze in the water and in the dawn hours birds dropped frozen from the sky. Sorry worried that my blood would turn to crystals and wrapped me up in so many layers that I could hardly walk. At night she put hot stones in the bed and brought me only cooked food. Unlike our gate-beggar we survived that bitter season, but ever since I have dreaded being cold; it is too close to death for my liking.

In the company of Kawashima's sons Hideo and Nobu and their newly found college friends, I would sneak to the cellar beneath the western wing where the sake was kept. We would make a fire and heat the sake in an iron pot, dropping crushed ginger into it as it came to the boil. I loved the way it would fizz and heat me up in a thrilling way moments after I had downed a glass. I had first heard of the boys' 'Secret Sake Club' through Ichiyo who had discovered it while spying in my service. At first Hideo was furious that I had found out their secret, but, suspecting that I would make a dangerous enemy, he allowed me to join, as a junior member. The price of my entrance to this male ritual was to allow the boys to touch my breasts and to rub their hands between my legs. Nobu said that as an initiation the boys had cut their fingers and mingled their blood, but he thought that too harsh a rite for a girl. The first time Hideo approached me he clumsily unbuttoned my jacket and put his sweaty hands on my breasts. I knew that he was excited by the way his body trembled but he wouldn't look me in the eye and so I could not share the moment with him. One of the students, a fine-looking boy with a thin nose, said that he could have the servant girls from his father's household any time he wanted and that he had no interest in me. He was the only one to decline the childish game of feeling the Chinese princess.

The initiation was a small price to pay as I enjoyed it as much as they did. I especially liked being half naked while they were buttoned to the neck in their student uniforms. It may be that it was in the dim cellar, full of warm sake and the scent of masculine sweat, that I developed my passion for dressing as a male myself and for men in uniform. I hugely enjoyed what I considered was my private fun, but nothing much remains secret in a household where servants go too quietly about their business and delight in trading gossip. Ichiyo told me that her mother and her aunt, hearing of my exploits, thought me wild and uncouth. I didn't care as I felt only scorn for their diluted experience of life. It seemed to me that they were trapped in the past, conditioned like geishas to live on their knees, rarely grasping the truth, which is that we are alive only in the dangerous moments.

I secretly longed for Natsuko's affection but I could not bring myself to behave in a way that might have secured it. I never pardoned my own mother for being so powerless and I didn't dare trust another to take her place. Yet Natsuko's rejection of me affected me powerfully and led me through my life to value, even above passion, the true friendship of women.

If the women in my life at that time were unsatisfactory, I had no trouble with Japanese men. In their arrogance and unquestioning use of power I admired them even above their Chinese brothers. I thought of Kawashima as a great man who knew how to live his life and make the most of his opportunities. I believed that I would have made a better son for him than either Hideo or Nobu.

That freezing winter that our old gate-beggar died I was officially adopted by Kawashima. I became a Japanese citizen and was renamed Kawashima Yoshiko. Japan was to be my new country and I felt overwhelmed with happiness. If a mother's acceptance was no longer possible for me, at least I could belong here in Japan. Sorry celebrated with me, even though she was not sure she approved of my new nationality. She continued to call me Eastern Jewel when addressing me formally, but Little Mistress was her usual and more affectionate choice of name. We ate a celebratory dinner and lit a firework that rocketed to the stars. Memories of my Chinese family, strong at first, began to recede as my new life took precedence. Occasionally Sorry would cook me a Chinese dish to remind me of my heritage. She would oversee everything in the kitchen to make sure I had the finest rice and noodles and the choicest fish and meats. Despite her fussiness she was well liked by the other servants for, as she often said, she was a humble person with a most interesting mistress.

Although I was delighted to be officially Kawashima's and Japan's daughter, it was an honour Natsuko begrudged me. She had me moved to the western wing of the house, the nearest she could get to banishing me from her sight without incurring her husband's anger. The wing, more generously proportioned than the main house, had been built mostly for show. I think that the Kawashimas found its European furnishings odd and uncomfortable and Shimako described it as being fit only for barbarians. It suited me very well though as the rooms were spacious and the furnishings deliciously foreign. I slept in a bed carved from ebony and walked on floors scattered with Persian rugs. The thing I most loved about it was that it was linked to the main house by a narrow hall with a sprung wooden floor that sang like a bird when walked on. I always knew when someone was coming and became expert at recognising people by their footsteps.

In those years of my youth life progressed well enough. I was often at odds with Natsuko and Shimako, but I had friendships of varying sorts with the children of the house. I was always occupied and never bored. I indulged my passion for food, my interest in sex and my need for information. I took life on without fear, but I could not control the terror in my dreams, which were filled with death and the cold and images of me alone in a barren landscape.

I learnt early that to know other people's secrets was to have power over them. Sorry procured information that was to ease my path through life and allow me to bargain to my advantage. One spring she told me that Natsuko had been soaking sponges in bitter green tea and putting them inside herself to stop her conceiving. A fortune teller had predicted that she could now only conceive girl children. Six daughters was shame enough and Natsuko, deeply in love with her husband, was terrified that he would find out and never call her to the marriage bed again. Shimako had suggested that eating live stag beetles had been known to reverse the trend, but desperate as Natsuko was she had a horror of all insects and could not summon up the courage to do it. So when she threatened to tell her husband of my behaviour in the cellar, I said that in return I would tell him what she had been up to with the sponges and bitter tea. At first she was furious, her lips went white at the edges where they were unpainted, she said my behaviour was so low that she could hardly believe I was a girl of high birth. When I stood my ground, bending her will to mine, she became confused and crumbled before my eyes. She began to weep and begged me to keep her secret.

'My husband will be furious if he finds out. A good marriage is essential to a woman's happiness, Yoshiko, you will come to understand that one day. Please do not betray me.'

I was not one to be touched by another's tears, but Natsuko's affected me deeply. I had no intention of telling Kawashima of his wife's pathetic secrets; that would have been a betrayal of my hidden affection for her. Yet I enjoyed my power and I wanted to pay Natsuko back for never accepting me as a daughter in her house.

'What can I give you?' she cried, reaching into a chest elaborately painted to resemble bamboo. 'Take this perfumed rice powder, Yoshiko, it is pounded twice to make it the softest you will ever feel; your skin will glow more richly than gold.'

I did not move to take it.

'Give me your black pearl,' I said simply.

Natsuko stiffened, a tiny nerve flickered in her forehead, but her hand fluttered to her neck to release the pearl that seemed to me to have more lustre than ever before. She held it out to me tentatively as though she was feeding a tiger. I should have said, 'Oh Natsuko, save me. Do not give me the pearl. Give me your love instead.' But I didn't. I hung the dark globe on its silken thread where it lay between my breasts, a good-luck charm to remind me that information is power. I was twelve years old.

When Shimako, getting fatter and plainer as she aged, found out about Natsuko's gift to me she said, 'A black pearl to complement your nature, eh, Yoshiko?'

A year later I began my monthly bleeds. Sorry told me that I was becoming a beauty of the kind that did not need fine silks or hair combs to be noticed. She stood me in front of a mirror and told me to look at myself. 'What do you see, Little Mistress?' she asked. I looked and saw a girl with eyes the shape of the sloes that bear fruit in winter, a soft pink mouth and small teeth that were very white and even. I had my mother's skin, paler than that of my Japanese sisters. Like my mother's my breasts were round and well matched. I had slim hips not made for childbearing, and beautiful unbound feet with toenails like pearlescent shells.

I no longer trailed after the boys but left them to their own devices. In no time at all they began to seek my company and instead of me playing their games they began to play mine. They offered me full membership of the 'Secret Sake Club' but I declined the offer, saying that I had grown out of the childish games they played. To test my powers I would set them against each other, showing Hideo more affection than Nobu, delighting in their misery and their competitiveness. Just as they had negotiated my entrance to their rituals by the intimacies they took with me, I now took payment in kind from them. An ivory letter knife might secure a second of my tongue in their mouth, a goldfish fashioned in jade the run of my hand along the length of their member.

Sorry sold my trophies to the shopkeepers in the back streets near the house, and I gave her a share of the proceeds so that her old age might not be too hard. She often bought opium from the Chinese shopkeepers and I frequently smoked it with her. The Japanese do not care for opium and most never enjoy the pleasure of an opium dream. For me it has been a lifelong delight, its musky smoke redolent with memories and the promise of oblivion.

My life in the household continued as though it would never change. I spied on the Kawashima family and prided myself on knowing their secrets. I allowed the brothers their privileges, sparred with Natsuko and occasionally crossed swords with Shimako. I smoked opium with Sorry and Turkish and American cigarettes when alone. I listened to western music on a record player that I bought second-hand from a college friend of Hideo's. Hardly a day passed that I did not venture into the labyrinth of Tokyo's streets. I did not think of myself as an ambitious person, only as one with an enthusiasm and lust for life.

21

Kawashima was a member of Japan's prestigious intelligence network and often entertained visitors who came to discuss politics with him. Through his numerous connections he distributed patronage to those prepared to further his own cause, which he claimed was to sustain the glory of Japan. The men who came were themselves powerful, with strings of their own to pull and information to share. Like Kawashima they came from the Samurai class and included politicians, businessmen and the odd high-ranking officer, usually from the Imperial Guard. I loved their talk of honour and the way they linked the ideas of courage and loyalty to Japan, rather than to their families. I suppose it made me feel more like them, less like the orphaned outsider that I now realise I was.

With no thirteenth sister around, spying on the meetings was an easy matter. I would conceal myself between the bamboo-and-paper wall screens, or behind the fruit trees in summer when the screens were open to the fine weather. I was rewarded with news of the outside world that never failed to thrill me. The fate of emperors and the progress of revolutions informed me that, despite my adventurous nature and my escapes into the city, I lived in a small confined world.

The war in Europe had ended with Japan claiming the German concessions in China for themselves. I heard that China was weak and stood by too helpless to do anything about it. I felt proud when I heard Kawashima say that Japan would continue to bite chunks of China to fatten its own empire. I had developed feelings of shame about my Chinese origins and I once bit Hideo's hand, drawing blood, when he referred to me as his Chinese sister.

My distant cousin Pu Yi had been restored to his rightful place as Emperor of China, but I had no wish to claim kinship with him. Kawashima called him the Son of Heaven, and laughed. I envied Pu Yi's wealth and power and wondered how he spent his days in the delightful Forbidden City that I remembered from my childhood. I did not know then that his power was limited to his immediate surroundings and his wealth was finite.

I discovered in myself a passion for knowledge of the world. I wanted to understand its history, and to understand too the emotions that powered revolutions and wars. Battles excited me, and I longed for the freedom men had to pursue their ambitions and to claim what they wanted from life. I never wanted to be a man, only to have the privileges of men.

Kawashima and his cohorts would talk late into the night and sometimes I would fall asleep between the screens and wake stiff and cold, urgently needing to relieve myself. I would be so frustrated at having missed the conversation that I taught myself to stay awake by keeping hungry and pinching my cheeks so hard that they bruised. As the men talked, they drank bowls of tea and shots of sake served to them by the geishas who came to the house with the men who had 'adopted' them. It was called adoption, but in my eyes it amounted to a master–slave relationship. Most of the Japanese men I have known tend to disguise their ownership of women in a form of language that speaks paternally of care and guardianship, but however they choose to term it, it is the woman who is on her knees. I have never understood how any woman can bear to be owned by a man, which in effect they were, like a horse or an ornament. The geishas heard much but said nothing. Although mostly young, they could be relied upon to be discreet, as they prided themselves on the trustworthiness of their profession. Of course, they knew that the slightest betrayal of confidence would see them thrown onto the streets to end up as common prostitutes.

Personally, I would have preferred the freedom of a prostitute to the rule-bound life of a geisha, but in general geishas, particularly young ones, are a timid lot who take refuge in the customs and protections of their trade. Like western nuns, geishas are pumped with the idea of service, of sacrifice to a master who they hope will act benignly towards them. Still, at least they have sex, while nuns, ecstatic with the denial of it, save themselves for the God to whom they are impotently married.

23

Kawashima often overindulged in drink, but at those meetings he liked to keep his wits about him and would sip his sake frugally. He took pleasure in observing the weaknesses and subsequent indiscretions of his colleagues. I admired him greatly for his cunning and his intellect. Sometimes, one of the men would seal a daughter's fate by arranging a marriage to another's son. They disposed of their womenfolk more casually than they did of their stocks and shares. I was sick at the thought that one day I might hear of my own destiny decided in this way; I knew that despite the indulgences shown to me by Kawashima, he would never allow me to choose my own path in life. Notwithstanding his flirtation with western ideas, he believed, like Confucius, that women, although human, were lower than men and that it was the law of nature that they should be allowed no will of their own. Also, and more to the point, I came with a large dowry, which was his to dispense where he would. I knew that one day he would use it to seal a deal, or receive a favour, and I might find myself with a husband not of my choosing. If that was to be the case I vowed that I would not be a compliant wife.

More than seven years of my life passed following this pattern until on a day when she was far from my mind, I was told that my mother had died in great pain from taking bad medicine to bring about the abortion of a child caught in her fallopian tube. My hurt at the news was so deep that I could not weep and wail as people do at the death of a heroine in an opera. I was too like Prince Su in nature for that. I dug my nails into the palms of my hand until they bled and I cursed the gods for their cruelty to so sweet a subject.

I have never been able to bring myself to throw away the half-eaten box of lychees with their promise of reunion, for we cannot know in this life which of our ancestors will greet us in the next; I pray that it will be my gentle mother.

Persimmons in Honey
and a Bowl of Golden Tea

On the eve of my fifteenth birthday, just when I thought the day would pass without event, two things happened that I will never forget.

Dusk had fallen when the old man Teshima sent for me saying that he wished to present me with a gift in celebration of my auspicious day. Sorry brought me the message grudgingly.

'Not all gifts are to be welcomed,' she said darkly. 'This may be a favour you would wish from someone other than this Japanese grandfather.'

I went to Teshima's quarters and found him sitting on a wooden sofa, his feet raised from the floor and placed apart on a long stool. At each foot a young peasant girl no more than twelve years old knelt on a straw mat cutting and smoothing his toenails. The room was infused with the smell of the sandalwood incense he favoured. It thinned the air and caught at the back of my throat. Teshima was wearing a long cotton coat loosely tied and draped across his knees leaving his legs bare. I could see the blue run of his veins through his old man's skin, which was as white as rice paper. His thin hair oiled flat against his skull gave him a skeletal appearance, and he looked as though he had rouged his cheeks to mimic youth, but it might have been the effect of his high blood pressure. Between his fingers a fat handmade cigarette rolled in black paper sent a snake of smoke into the air. The girls completed their task by massaging coconut oil between his toes and into the weak muscles deep in his calves. Teshima seemed unaware of me as he rested a hand on each girl's head and rocked back and forth, sighing with pleasure. When they had finished they sat back on their haunches and waited for his dismissal. He lifted his hands from their heads and shooed them from the room. Then he beckoned me to the vacated mat and as I sat by his oily feet he handed me a small cedarwood box with an iron key in its lock.

'I have waited a long time to give you this, Yoshiko,' he said, looking at me enigmatically with his small dark eyes. 'I think that you are ready for it at last.'

I opened the box and saw nestled against each other on a bed of dark-green silk a pair of woodcarvings of a phallus and a vulva.

'They are ancient and carved by a master,' he said, reaching across me and picking them up. 'A most suitable present for a young woman on her fifteenth birthday.'

He showed me how the two pieces fitted into each other and became one entwined piece. From the age of eight years I had known how a man and woman fitted each other and I laughed out loud at this ancient man who thought that this old lesson would be new to me. Teshima smiled and laughed with me.

'Don't be embarrassed, little Yoshiko,' he said. 'You are old enough to know of these things. Soon you will have to pleasure a husband, better you know how than to go to him afraid and ignorant.' We sat in silence for a while, then he laid my gift back in its box and placed it on the floor.

'Give me your hand, Yoshiko,' he said.

He took my fingers into his mouth and licked them one by one until both my hands were wet with his saliva. Then he guided them under his coat to his phallus and moaned when I tightened my grip around it. It was as thin as young bamboo, unlike his eldest grandson Hideo's, which was of a more generous girth.

Teshima clasped his hands over mine and began to slide our four hands along the length of his member. After what seemed like a long time it became thicker and he led me to his bed and told me to undress and lie down. And I did as he asked without objection. I was both fascinated and repulsed by the old man's desire. I liked the feeling that was gurgling through me like gingered sake. I didn't like his fish breath or the softness of his skin, yet I was thrilled at last to be a participant in this familiar ritual.

He lifted his coat and mounted me in a sitting position, pushing into me slowly and telling me to relax. When I struggled a bit, half changing my mind about liking it, he growled at me to be still and I was. Taking a twisted stick from the chest at his bedside, he dipped it into a honey jar and dribbled it across my lips, sucking the stick noisily himself before placing it back in the jar. Then he bent down and put his tongue in my mouth. As he came panting to his climax, he pushed deeper than I thought it was possible to go inside another person, and his moaning became one long hum as though he were in agony. So that I would not cry out and that I would always associate the act with sweetness, he released his own mouthful of honey into mine at the same time as the pain pierced me. I was surprised that there was pain, I had never heard a concubine complain of it or heard a whimper from the bound-footed girls my father straddled.

'Better it was me, Yoshiko,' he said, leaving the bed and clapping his hands for his servant girls. 'I have been gentle with you, which is something that a young husband might fail at. I can promise you that it will never hurt as much again.'

There was a tiny trickle of blood on the sheet, which Teshima said I should be proud of as it proved I was now a woman. He returned to the bedside to scoop a finger of honey from the pot, clapping his hands and shouting for his servants on the way.

As I left his room feeling strangely sad and out of sorts, I passed his peasant girls hurrying to his side with water and soft cotton towels. Despite the pain, I had enjoyed the act, although given the choice I would not have chosen Teshima as my first lover. I have never blamed my greed for sex on that odd coupling, even though after it I could not wait to lie beneath a man again. Although I felt important, chosen, I think that in some hidden part of me, I knew that I had not only lost my virginity, but also my claim to be a child of the Kawashimas. Once again, but this time in a new way, I was being excluded from the care and support of a real family.

When I returned to Sorry, I showed her the present and laughed at the old man's foolishness. I said that we would do well to sell it as Teshima had implied that it was an original, and worth quite a bit. She asked me if there had been blood and I nodded. We decided to eat early as I was tired from my experience and Sorry thought that I looked pale. But in her secret way Shimako had decreed that no head in the Kawashima household would lie early on the pillow that night.

By the time the moon was waking and the house lanterns were lit, I had been served a good supper of chanko-nabe, the nourishing stew given to sumo wrestlers before an encounter. As a sign of respect on my birthday, Sorry added a bowl of steamed rice and red beans, the usual dish for auspicious occasions. The day had been an eventful one, for apart from Teshima's seduction of me, there had been an unusually long earth tremor just before the sun had set blood red. Sorry interpreted this to mean that my life was not destined to be a tranquil one, and I thanked the gods for that.

Later that night as I lay on a rug reading and smoking an American cigarette, I heard a thin, high-pitched wail from Natsu-ko's rooms. It was a dreadful sound, mournful as the call of a lone whale in the night sea. Sorry went running towards it and as I followed her, I felt excitement coursing through my blood at the thought that this special day had, it seemed, still more to offer.

Shimako had been found by the night watchman hanging from a beam in the wooden shrine near the carp pool. In the thin light of the moon, as he made his first round of the grounds, he had seen her body swaying gently over the Buddha shelf and had run to

28

Kawashima with the news. Kawashima ordered that Shimako be cut down and taken to her own quarters where she could be laid to bed before Natsuko be allowed to see her.

At first the body did not look like hers for she was dressed most strangely, appearing more like a geisha than Natsuko's plain sister. Tightly wound into a ceremonial kimono, she had oiled her hair into three large rolls pierced with numerous hair sticks, her lips were painted crimson, her face rice white. She smelled of rose oil and might have looked serene had it not been for her tongue, which was the colour of a bruise and protruded rudely from her mouth. I was already familiar with death's strange stillness, yet I was transfixed by the sight of Shimako's dead body. It was hard to believe that she was gone, for lying on her bed so painted and peaceful, she looked complete. I began to shake and Sorry tried to pull me from the room but I refused to go.

Natsuko's wailing was awful, I begged her to stop but she did not hear me. It was only when surrounded by her children that her howling finally descended into a low moan.

It transpired that Shimako had retired to her rooms before the evening meal, complaining of a headache. She must have dressed in her finery and made her way in the dusk to the shrine knowing that she would not be seen while the family were eating. She had hung herself with an obi sash the same colour as her stained lips. As the beat of life had left her body, the wooden sandal from her good foot had fallen to the earth floor, its partner swung on her misshapen one as if to draw attention to it.

Natsuko was beside herself with grief. Swaying back and forth she knelt on the floor by her sister's bedside weeping and moaning, her eyes red and swollen from crying. Her daughters fluttered round her like a cloud of moths, making strange sibilant noises of shock. Kawashima was visibly shaken by the odd sight Shimako made laid out in her gorgeous robes as if merely asleep. She was dressed and painted in a manner so out of character that it seemed shameful for us to be spying on her unfamiliar body. Kawashima considered her act of suicide to be one of extreme ingratitude, but he tried to comfort Natsuko with kind words.

'Perhaps she did not wish to leave your dead mother lonely,' he said, patting her lightly on the shoulder.

His wife, dutiful even in the face of such a tragedy, gave him a ghost of her old familiar smile and bowed briefly. It hurt my heart to see Natsuko in such terrible pain, but cut off from me as she was by her daughters, I was excluded from her circle. I walked with a weeping Sorry back to my rooms where we drank sake and whispered of the terrible drama of Shimako's act.

That night I dreamt that I watched Shimako as she stepped into the carp pool to swim. I could not bring myself to point out to her the dark shape of the shark waiting in the opaque water that devoured her before I woke. In all of my dreams of Shimako since that night I am in some way to blame for her death. Sorry said that I shouldn't feel guilty, I may not have loved Shimako but I had not wished her dead and that is no more than the truth.

Natsuko told her daughter Ichiyo that she was not surprised that the tragedy of her sister's death had taken place on my birthday, for I surely had the stench of bad luck about me. She said that I was fortunate that only women could smell it, otherwise my beauty would have been of little use to me. Natsuko was an old-fashioned woman full of such notions.

I thought Shimako's death by design an unnatural thing, like trees dropping their leaves in summer. No animal that I know of would choose to end its own life, even those caught in traps will leave a limb in order to break free and survive. Shimako had been as damaged in her heart as she had been in her body, a woman who had been filled with envy and anger. Well, it is a truth that we are all flawed in some way, yet still we must do the best we can for ourselves. If we sit back lamenting our fate we forget that we can influence it. She came from a wealthy and influential family. She could have managed her life better if she had been possessed of a bit more courage. When I went to Natsuko to formally offer my

30

condolences I said something of my views to her, suggesting she pray that Shimako not be punished for her contempt of the gift of life. She was furious, her eyes narrowed and she could hardly bear to look at me. She said that even though Shimako had lived in a cold world she had achieved a pure death, with all debts honoured. She told me that if I had been truly Japanese I would have understood the honour in Shimako's act.

'You like to think of yourself as Japanese, Yoshiko,' she said. 'But your Chinese blood will always give you away. I know that you do not grieve for Shimako, who outshone you in life. How did you come to be so heartless a person? You do not take after your mother, who they say was a gentle woman.'

I wasn't angry with Natsuko, but she was wrong, I did grieve for Shimako. I missed the place she had occupied in my life. There is something uniquely sad about losing an adversary.

'Natsuko, my character has been formed by different forces than your own has been subject to,' I replied. 'While you experienced a loving father, I was given away by mine, simply because another man asked for me. I saw my mother's life made miserable by the jealousies of her fellow concubines, much in the way that you and Shimako attempted to affect mine. You rejected me even before you had met me.'

'Yes, all of that is true, Yoshiko,' she said. 'Yet you are a clever person, you could have made us like you.'

I told her that I had thought about that when I first came to Kawashima's house, but even then, all those years ago, it wasn't in my nature to beg for love.

'Ah yes, I see,' she said. 'By then you were already made.'

She may have been right, for to this day I cannot bear to court love. It seems to me that unless it is given freely it is worthless.

As often happens in families, a person's character becomes transformed by death. And so the legend of Shimako began, according to which she had been a person of infinite kindness, a shining example of purity and selflessness and one who delighted in

31

peacemaking. For myself I would miss Shimako's deviousness, her skill at setting the household at odds with itself, and the soft dragging sound of her step which allowed you to know that she was coming.

In the days and weeks after her death the truth of Shimako's life emerged. In her head and heart she had been a geisha. The chests in her rooms were found to contain the most exquisite kimonos and obi sashes of every colour. She had dozens of silk hair ornaments, phials of camellia oil, hair wax and pots of white and crimson make-up paints. In one cabinet, eight pairs of high okobo sandals of the kind she was wearing on the night of her death were found, unworn and in pristine condition. By her bedside in a stone jar she had kept crushed nightingale droppings, an ancient tool of the geisha class used to whiten the skin. Under her pillow she had secreted a bound book of her flower paintings. They were most delicately drawn, each page more perfect than the last. I remember a lily so purely depicted that you could almost smell it. A fat bee hovered over one of the flower heads, dropping little globes of pollen into the trumpet of the flower, and under this fertile coupling Shimako had written Kawashima's name. Although it had never occurred to me before, I thought then that she must have loved him. I imagined Shimako locked in her rooms at night performing the tea ceremony, conjuring up the image of Kawashima sitting opposite her, a smile of approval on his samurai face. Perhaps she dreamt that she was beautiful and desirable and that he loved her. I was surprised that I had known nothing of Shimako's night games. I told Sorry that Shimako's personal servant Junko certainly knew how to keep a secret. Sorry said simply, 'Junko loved her mistress.'

Once again the Kawashima household took on the colour of death. It was almost time for the maples to turn gold, and so the flower of Shimako's funeral was the white chrysanthemum. They were placed in front of the alcoves where the scroll paintings hung and made into bouquets with black and white ribbons. Special notices were sent out and condolence gifts of money began to arrive. Natsuko kept a proper account of each present knowing that a gift of equal value must be sent back. She set the green and yellow china lion dogs that had come as part of her own dowry at either side of Shimako's door to guard her dead sister's body. A week after the funeral a memorial service was held. So it was that by her own hand Shimako had decreed that the seasons would continue without her, she would not taste the new year's rice cakes and Natsuko would be left, the loneliest of sisters. In her haste to be gone she had not thought to make arrangements for her faithful servant Junko, who, left without a mistress to serve, was turned out of the house.

Soon after Shimako's memorial service, I became aware of feeling grown-up, with little if anything of the child left in my nature. To point this out to the Kawashima household I went to the newly opened beauty shop in the Ginza Hotel and had my hair cut short in the western fashion. In the following months I began to dress in men's clothes. Not only did I find them more comfortable but also more exciting. They had a sort of glamour about them that made me feel daring.

Natsuko told me to my face that she found the look disgusting. Imagine the contrast of my riding breeches and favourite knee-high boots to her traditional dress. I delighted in shocking Natsuko, perhaps because I knew that I would never win her love and it was a way of engaging with her. It was to be a difficult year for Natsuko. She was lonely without Shimako to spend her days with, and she did not like Taeko, the spoilt girl Kawashima had chosen to be Hideo's wife. Soon this indulged creature would be in her home, while one by one the daughters she loved were leaving to become part of their respective new husbands' households. Kawashima no longer made his way to her bed and Natsuko took on the faded look of a forgotten wife. Without her sister for company, or the affection of the husband she was so much in love with, Natsuko's days were miserable. And so it was that I came to observe at first hand that a dutiful life does not necessarily bring rewards.

Determined not to follow in Natsuko's obedient footsteps, I embraced the modern way wholeheartedly, hoping that it would lead me to a more exciting life in the world outside. But I knew that any freedom I obtained would not come easily. In the heart of the house and of the men in it, old Japan held sway, women had little say and whatever their desires were they could be thwarted with a single command.

I was not without optimism though. Kawashima had always been indulgent with me, and I hoped that he might allow me a portion of my dowry to travel a little before marriage. I hoped too that I might have a say in the choice of husband for myself. But if that was not to be the case, I was determined that whatever life Kawashima had planned for me I would eventually break free and go my own way. I began visiting the shrine by the winter plum trees, asking the gods not to let me be bartered like a chattel into an arranged marriage.

It wasn't long before I discovered that my cropped hair and boyish clothes thrilled Kawashima in a way that I could not fail to notice. I knew that he had always found me attractive, but I had never before had such attentions lavished on me. He would visit my fencing lessons, never taking his eyes off me, grunting with satisfaction when I lunged theatrically and laughing when my fencing master's sword caught me out. Perhaps in breeches and boots I had stirred in Kawashima those homoerotic fantasies rooted in the warrior tradition that Japanese men are said to be prone to. It made for better soldiers if women didn't have to be taken into account. Kawashima came from samurai stock who, when they ruled supreme, were said to despise women as inferiors, useful only to produce their offspring.

I had watched Kawashima make love to both men and women, and on the whole I think that he preferred men; he was certainly more vigorous with them. Once as I looked on from my hiding place he had roared with such pleasure as he took a young soldier that the boy went quite white. I have seen him both cruel and tender with men, but never indifferent with them as he can be with women. I have lost count of the boys he has lain with but have only counted eleven women. They include Teshima's girls, a colleague's geisha offered to him as a gift and his monthly coupling with Natsuko, which appeared to me to be an act of duty with nothing of the animal in it. I risked a lot spying on Kawashima, knowing that if caught I might be sent back to China. With both parents dead I wondered which sibling would bother to claim a disgraced sister. But I could not stop myself from living vicariously through his sexual exploits, and I longed to be one of them. I suppose that at some level I had always known that eventually he would make his way to my portion of the house, to complete what had been between us since the moment he had asked my father for me all those years ago.

Teshima had been wrong when he said that sex would never hurt as much again, for with Kawashima it was always as painful as the first time he took me. He would arrive in my rooms sweating and full of sake, but never drunk and stupid with wine in the way that I had seen his sons in the cellar. His preference was to take me standing and from behind, he said he could feel the length of me better that way. He didn't speak much and was rough and heavy-handed, leaving me bruised and sore with bite marks adorning my body. Thus I discovered that it was possible to enjoy pain. I never received a compliment or an affectionate word from him, however; after that first time it was a rare week when he did not visit me at least twice. I found an unexpected comfort in Kawashima's caustic lovemaking, and sex with him was exciting and dangerous too, for I never knew how I would look or feel after it. Sorry would wince at the sight of my bruises and treat them with a thick paste she made from the tobacco plant.

My life had taken a new turn and I found myself thinking about Kawashima all the time. I loved the smell of him, the suppleness of his skin, the way he filled my rooms with life. But most of all I loved that I had become part of the routine of his life, that I seemed to belong at last. When he began sending a string of politicians, soldiers and businessmen to take their pleasure with me, I didn't object, but something in me broke with the pain of not being special to him. I was aware that his blood daughters were not used in this way, and that hurt. But I had to remind myself that I was, after all, the daughter of a concubine and had from a young age thought sex a natural occupation for both men and women. I recalled my mother was always waiting for my father's summons to his bed, and when it came she glowed with the honour of it. If it ever occurred to me that I was damaged by the encounters with the men from Kawashima's circle, I buried the thought. I did not care to think of myself as a victim and, in any case, I had no choice in the matter. I enjoyed the presents and the news of the outside world that the men brought to my quarters and sex for me was always satisfying, no matter how cruel or how inadequate the lover. Yet despite the pleasure I took in it there were often times when I was left with a hollow ache, as though without someone actually inside me, I was as alone as an orphan.

I was frequently irritable with poor Sorry, who never carried a grudge, and always forgave me. Sometimes I would have such dark days that I would lock myself in my bedroom and escape to a better place with opium. The drug-induced dreams that came were magnificent; in them I was a goddess, able to fly across continents, free to wander the earth.

Sorry worried when I locked her out. She said that even though I appeared to be a warrior, in truth I was a sad motherless girl who should never have been sent from China and from her family. In her eyes I was a daughter of China struggling in a foreign land. But the notion that all things admirable were Japanese had been instilled in me and I never for a moment regretted my citizenship of that country.

Kawashima and his friends despised China. They often joked about it and thought Chinese men weak and cowardly. I was told by a politician who visited me that my relative, the pompous little Emperor, had married Wan Jung, she of the beautiful countenance. They were not allowed to leave the Forbidden City and the Emperor commanded so little respect that his eunuchs stole from him and threatened his life. It was said that Pu Yi kept a club by his bedside and as his Empress was the only one he trusted, he set her to watch over him while he slept. I feigned disinterest, but I was ashamed to be even distantly related to a man who was afraid of eunuchs and needed his wife to protect him. He was sixteen years old, the same age as myself, old enough, I thought, to have grown some courage in his nature.

My way of life in the Kawashima household continued as I have described until the inevitable happened and I found myself one morning retching into a bowl held sympathetically by Sorry.

'You are with child, Eastern Jewel,' she whispered.

I knew before she spoke it. I think I had known for some days but the idea was so dreadful to me that I couldn't bear to think it. If I gave birth to a child now its father would be unknown. I would be relegated with Sorry to some poor lodging to be hidden away for the rest of my life. The child would not be recognised by Kawashima who would never speak of me again. He would keep my dowry to compensate for the years he had fed and housed me. My life would be lost to me and I would become an unimportant, unmarriageable person. In China I would have been just another concubine with child; in Japan I would be worse than a street whore.

I had always taken great care to avoid conception by inserting a small sponge into my vagina before each encounter. After lovemaking I would put a tube inside myself and wash with a disinfectant made by steeping locust leaves in boiled water. Sorry said that all the concubines she had known had used this method when they couldn't face another birth. She added that it only worked if the gods were willing. In my experience the gods are rarely willing. Their purpose is about erecting barriers, mine

37

has always been to demolish them and that is what I set about doing.

I sent Sorry to the herb doctor in the Chinese market to buy me a liquor that would expel the seed from my womb. She returned with a bile-green concoction, which against expectation tasted sweet as if flavoured with rhubarb. The herbalist said that if it was to work it would do so within six hours, otherwise something more powerful would be required. After the time had elapsed with no result except an excessive amount of stomach pain, Sorry tried a recipe of her own. She remembered hearing about it in my father's household when two young concubines became pregnant at the same time. The more devious of the two, wishing her child to take precedence over the other, boiled a copper band in water and as the mixture cooled added two drops of snake venom. She sweetened the mixture with honeyed tea and served it to her opponent. The copper would expel the child, the venom still its heart. Thus the job would be twice done.

'Did it work, Sorry?' I asked. 'Yes, mistress,' she replied, 'they say it is foolproof.'

The herbalist agreed with Sorry that it was indeed a good recipe but warned it should only be one drop of venom. 'Two will surely kill the mother too,' he said. The price for the venom would be high, the copper band, which should be green, he would throw in for good will.

Sorry boiled the brew until only an inch of liquid remained. Then as the water cooled she carefully dropped the venom in, making sure not to spill any of the precious fluid. I gulped the sticky serum down followed by a cup of sweet pomegranate juice to erase its bitterness. For two days I vomited up a hateful glue while the seed remained embedded in my womb.

Days passed and I devised a plan that involved telling Natsuko that I was pregnant, and persuading her to help me with a more scientific abortion. I knew that in a house that thrived on secrets, without her on my side, I had little chance of keeping Kawashima ignorant of my plight.

I would be taking a huge chance confiding in her. She hated me and would delight in having me banished from her home, so I had to find a way to secure her silence as well as her help. I was risking everything, relying on my belief that I understood Natsuko's nature better than she did herself, but I had no choice and besides, the jeopardy of the situation thrilled me.

On the day I went to her I dressed carefully in a black kimono with a dark blue obi sash. In Japan wearing black is said to be the sign of a moral person and I did not wish to annoy Natsuko with my usual attire. I powdered my face pale and attempted to disguise the provocative pink of my lips by staining them with asparagus juice. I wanted to convey the impression of humility and regret. Natsuko looked surprised to see me in so modest an outfit and was intrigued when I said I had come for her help. At first she was full of joy at my news: at last there was a way to be rid of me for good. But when I told her that the child was Kawashima's her face drained of colour and she gave a little moan. There was a long silence as she worked out what this would mean to her own life. The fear that her hated adopted daughter might bear her husband a child, perhaps even a son, was more than she could bear. She asked me how I could possibly be sure that it was Kawashima's child. I told her that not only did Sorry keep a record of my bleeds but that for some months Kawashima, being infatuated with me, had kept me entirely to himself. I said there was no question that the child would be born with the same strawberry birthmark that stained all of Kawashima's offspring.

Natsuko shuddered at the thought of the distinguishing pigment adorning any child not born of her; I could tell by the way her body slumped in the chair that she believed me. She struggled for a long time with the choice of helping me or telling her husband. But in the end I think she could not bear a child of Kawashima's born from my womb to live in the same world as her own children. And so for once, and for a brief time only, Natsuko became my ally.

Between us we made a plan that would take place during Kawashima's next trip to Osaka. The visits to his geisha were as frequent as ever and Natsuko was consumed with jealousy that both at home and abroad her husband chose other women's beds over her own. It is a fallacy that Japanese women are happy for their husbands to own geishas. They are the same as women the world over and cannot bear rivals. She may have been able to bear more easily the convention that he kept a geisha, but that in her own home he chose my bed tore her heart to shreds.

It was agreed that Natsuko would tell her doctor that she had a favourite servant who she wished to keep about her. The foolish girl had become pregnant by a man who was not free to marry her and wished to rid herself of the baby. If she had the child she could not work and would surely starve, a fate Natsuko would like to save her from. Of course, Natsuko did not expect such a distinguished man as Doctor Mura himself to perform the operation, but if he could suggest someone she would be eternally grateful. She told him that her husband would be furious if he found out and she feared the girl would be flogged half to death, so secrecy was of great importance. Doctor Mura said that although the girl probably should be flogged for behaving like a Tokyo street cat while under the care of such a fine mistress, he understood that Natsuko was acting from a kind heart and approved of her feminine tenderness. He recommended a recently qualified young man from the suburbs, and assured Natsuko that she could rely on his discretion.

A few hours after Kawashima had left for Osaka, Sorry set a dried sea horse over the door as a charm against evil. She burnt orange incense to invigorate the air and made me sip strong black tea. When the doctor who would not tell me his name arrived, I noted that he was neither young nor, I suspect, from the suburbs. As he leaned over me I could smell his sweat, which was as unpleasant as his breath. He smelled sour, as though he never washed, which was peculiar as even in the meanest of circumstances the Japanese are a clean race. I took it as a bad sign that he did not wash his hands before beginning even though Sorry had brought him a bowl of steaming water and clean linen towels. It was a bad sign too that he called for saki and only removed the cheap local cigarettes that he chain-smoked from his mouth to drink deep drafts of it.

To distance me from the pain, Sorry talked to me throughout the brutal procedure, reminding me of favourite poems and episodes from childhood. I bit into a cushion so that my cries would not give me away to the household. Just as I felt that I could not bear his exploration of my womb for one more minute, the nameless doctor finished, quickly rinsed his hands in the cooling water and, without a word to me, left the room.

Days of fever and bleeding clotted blood followed and in their wake came an infection that made me delirious for a week. I remember being conscious twice in that time, once when the sky was grey and then again when it was the pale gold of evening and the crows were in flight.

The inept doctor called once to check on my progress. He said that I would be well in ten days but that the infection had left me sterile. I would never again be with child, which he considered the practical bonus of his butchery.

Natsuko could not disguise a hiss of satisfaction at such welcome news. As for me, I would never be a mother, never nurture an infant or experience the friendship of a daughter or the support of a son. Before this time I had not consciously desired motherhood but the fact that it was now denied me seemed shocking.

With her customary parsimony Natsuko left me to settle the doctor's account. Sorry was heartbroken on my behalf and fussed around me with broths and strengthening foods. She said that with each new wound another layer thickens our carapace and strengthens our defences. In time all traces of the deed were removed, and I tried to remove myself from it too. But in sleep my mind went its own way and I suffered a recurring dream that disturbed me so much that I began to fear sleep. In this dream I would watch myself from a distance looking into a mirror that was marked with age and seemed to be running with water. Although there were people around only I was reflected in the silvery glass, and as I gazed at myself I knew without doubt that it was a stranger looking back at me, a stranger of whom I was afraid.

The week I lay recovering from my abortion, Tokyo was hit by a massive earthquake of such force that after the last tremor had faded every family knew someone who was a victim of the catastrophe. We were lucky to live so close to the commercial centre as it was one of the few areas left standing. Our gas supply was severed and we returned to candlelight and charcoal burners. I liked the mysterious quality the soft light lent to the house, which reminded me of my early years in China when I would lie in my mother's bed watching her braid her blue-black hair.

Natsuko believed that we were saved from the fury of the earthquake by the gold fish in our carp pool. She said they were of an unusually bright hue and were very lucky. 'Tokyo will never be as beautiful again,' she said sadly.

I could hear more than the pain of the loss of the city in her voice, see beyond the tears in her tea-black eyes. I know that Natsuko felt that she was powerless in her life, that she had suffered too much loss to ever regain the happiness of her youth. I wanted to tell her that she still had the power to choose where to love, that she could choose me. But as always when faced with Natsuko, I never spoke the words I wanted to; I was as locked in my nature as she was in hers.

How quickly things can change. One minute the landscape you know is there, the next it is gone. Kawashima, arriving back from Osaka after the earth's revolt, said that he felt that he had come to an alien city.

Once again Tokyo began to recreate itself with buildings to match the progress that electricity had brought. There was a buzz of energy in the air and everywhere you looked modern structures were going up.

A new breed of young woman seemed to have emerged too, secretaries, shop girls, beauticians and dressmakers who made cheap copies of popular western styles. Young women were needed to staff the hotels and business houses of the remodelled city. They came enthusiastically from their rigidly traditional homes to the equally strict conventions of the workplace. I think I envied them a little, although it has to be admitted that a princess seeks a different sort of freedom to that of a secretary or a shop girl.

At the beginning of the winter of 1924, when I was eighteen years old, Kawashima sent the young officer Yamaga to me and I discovered what it was to fall in love.

Yamaga's skin was the colour of copper, his eyes clear and unclouded, his lips as firm as apples. He was tender and arrogant in equal measure and it was not always easy to please him. I was half afraid of him yet I could not stop myself from loving everything about him. I adored the strength of his coarse dark hair, the uneven gap between his teeth, the way his uniform smelt of the black Russian tobacco he smoked. That bittersweet scent has the power to stir me to this day. I both loved and feared the churning feeling in my stomach that came whenever I saw him, a combination of elation and dread. I loved too the way he called me Yoshi and the way he danced me around, pulling me to him before kissing my lips or my hair. His touch emptied me of common sense.

For the first time in my life I loved someone more than myself and although it was unsettling, it intoxicated me and kept my blood singing. I could not eat and did not sleep much, but when I did I dreamt of little else but making love with Yamaga.

Sometimes we would lie together the whole night without making love, just holding each other and talking and sleeping. I think that I felt more loved on those nights than I ever had before, and more confident of his love. He never brought me gifts and it could often be weeks before he visited again yet I always believed that he would return to my rooms. I excused his long absences. I told myself that building a military career took time, and I was convinced that his dedication to his profession would carry him to the top. We were alike, he and I, and I believed that his feelings for me were as strong as mine were for him.

I told Kawashima that I did not want him to send me anyone but Yamaga. He shrugged his shoulders and said that I would soon tire of the boy and that he himself would find it no hardship. I was insulted by his indifference, as despite wanting only Yamaga my body missed the habit of my stepfather's cruel lovemaking, and I was surprised that he did not care about losing mine.

It was always a celebration when Yamaga came. He usually stayed the whole night, giving us time to eat and bathe together, to tell each other the stories of our lives and to laugh at the rest of the world. We made love and ate the good food that Sorry brought us, always apologising for her intrusion. We played cards for money and sometimes we fenced a little dangerously. Yamaga liked to win, it was important to him and, apart from myself, I have never since met anyone so competitive.

Those nights we shared were precious to me and I could not bear to waste them in sleep. I would watch Yamaga as he slept and delight in his even breathing. In an agony of love I would wake him with kisses and cry when he made love to me, so different was it to anything I had ever experienced before.

It seemed that the gods had at last smiled on me and sent the most beautiful and brave man in all of Japan to accompany me through life. There is nothing more splendid than a Japanese man at the peak of his powers. With my rich dowry and unusual beauty I thought that I would be as good a catch for him as he was for me. Freedom was no longer my aim. To be with Yamaga was all I desired. Marriage to him would be no sacrifice; he was a modern man, we would be equals. I liked the idea of choosing my own husband and decided that I would declare my love to him and suggest that he ask Kawashima to give me to him in marriage. After all, Kawashima had sent him to me and that must mean Yamaga had influence and was a person to be indulged.

On the day I proposed to Yamaga I woke in the dying dawn to the muffled sounds of the servants going about the house. Above the city the sky, a white vault streaked with pink, housed a solitary hunting hawk. It was cold, with a trail of snow in the air. I sensed that this was the day that Yamaga would come and even though I knew it would not be until nightfall, I was full of the disquiet of longing. Sorry served me a breakfast of persimmons steeped in honey, and a bowl of golden tea. I was too restless to eat, but I drank the tea and smoked two Turkish cigarettes. I went to the market and tried to occupy myself but I could not think straight and bought neroli oil instead of the rose one I wanted to scent my rooms. Neroli is too astringent a fragrance for lovemaking, while the soft musk of rose oil is perfect. The day passed slowly, as it will when every second is counted, and by dusk I was aching for Yamaga.

Before dark I began to dress, choosing a deep-blue under-kimono of silk, embroidered with a border of white clover and red poppies. I took great care with my appearance, brushing my skin with pumice and sweetening my breath with liquorice wood. I softened my body with a peppery chrysanthemum oil that made my skin glow and hung Natsuko's black pearl between my breasts. At last Yamaga came, brushing the snow from the shoulders of his uniform, his hands stiff with cold. I sent Sorry scurrying to bring a foot warmer while I served him a shot of sake to heat his blood.

Our first lovemaking that night was passionate but over quickly, leaving us breathless and laughing at our haste. Later we shared a bath so hot that it made me dizzy. Yamaga bathed me, lathering my breasts with a green soap that smelt of ferns. His hands were firm and confident and as I mounted him in the water he pulled me close. I clasped my feet behind his buttocks and he moaned with pleasure. We fitted so well together, as perfectly as the carving that old man Teshima had given me on my fifteenth birthday.

Sex with Yamaga was unlike any that I had experienced before. Lips on lips, tongue on tongue, our arms around each other, our appetites equal, I could find no fault in him. I felt complete, a new experience for me, as usually after lovemaking I was ready for the next lover to fill the void that had previously accompanied me through life. I didn't doubt for one moment that Yamaga was as eager to spend his life with me as I was to spend mine with him. When he told me that I was so special that the world had only space for one Yoshiko, my confidence that he would agree to our marrying could not have been higher.

We ate a supper of chicken and peppers and marvelled at how delicious food always tasted after lovemaking. I fed Yamaga the almonds preserved in salt that he loved and we shared one of my Turkish cigarettes. He always laughed when I smoked, saying that women smoking looked wrong somehow, like monkeys swimming.

I thought briefly that I might tell him of the abortion and grieve with him over what had become in my mind our joint loss, but we were so happy that I could not bear to spoil things. Against reason, I told myself that doctors are not always right and that women have a great capacity to heal. For once in my life I looked to the gods to shower me with luck and to so repair my past that it might never have been.

That night, as we lay together in my rosewood bed, I suggested that we should begin the plans for our marriage. Yamaga must go to Kawashima and formally ask for his permission. I spoke of my large dowry and joked that he would be getting a princess from a noble family, and I would be getting a soldier who would one day be a great Japanese hero. We would have a successful and wonderful life together in the new Japan.

Yamaga's body tensed and he rolled away from me and left the bed. There was a long, confusing silence only broken when he gave a short embarrassed laugh.

46

'You must know, Yoshi, that Kawashima would never agree to a marriage between us. It would be pointless to ask him,' he said.

'No, he will agree,' I cried. 'He cannot keep me here for ever, he must choose a husband for me, so why should it not be you, Yamaga? He admires you and desires your friendship. Why else would he have sent you to me?'

Already at a distance from me, Yamaga put his hands in front of him like a barrier between us.

'I do not love you, Yoshiko,' he said with a cutting honesty. 'Even if I did, I could not marry you. You are delicious and I desire you, but you are too brazen to be my wife. You are notorious in Tokyo and to marry you would bring shame on my father's house and break my mother's heart. I have obligations I intend to meet, and to do so I will marry a modest woman.'

I froze at his words, unable to move. My skin felt painfully thin and transparent. Yamaga must surely see my heart breaking, my blood pounding, veins, tendons, liver, all shrinking. Must surely take pity on me. He did not love me and suddenly, like Tokyo after the earthquake, the landscape of my life had changed. I had revealed myself to him and he had rejected me. He wanted a subservient wife who would defer to him in all things.

'How can it be that I am notorious?' I sobbed. 'I am Kawashima's daughter.'

Yamaga shook his head. 'Kawashima has not used you well,' he said. 'From the moment you were given to him, his plans for you were not those of an honourable father.'

I knew he spoke the truth, I knew too that my nature was different to that of Kawashima's daughters, and that despite being used by him I would not have wished for his daughters' powerless lives. I said as much to Yamaga and he smiled.

'Never underestimate the power of respectable women, Yoshiko,' he said. 'Those wives in Tokyo whose husbands come to you know it and despise you. You are too high born to be a geisha, and if not a geisha then what are you? To them you are the shame in

Natsuko's household. They pity her and will never accept you into Japanese society.'

I sank to the floor. A few minutes before I had been truly happy, now I was only too aware of how thin the membrane is that divides bliss from misery. In that terrible moment all the pain I had suppressed in my life flooded my body and I was wracked with sobs. In Yamaga's rejection I relived the separation from my mother and my father's abandonment of me. I had always believed I was happy to be beyond the conventions of society, but now I knew that I was a victim of them. The wounds I had seemed to suffer so lightly in the past came back to burn like vitriol, and I felt that I would never recover. I had never before cared that, unlike Natsuko's daughters, I was not introduced to the visiting daughters of their guests. I had felt only relief at my exclusion, believing myself to be so much more sophisticated than those shy, proper young women. Now I knew that I had been perceived as unfit society, a soiled creature inhabiting the foreign wing of the house beyond the dark man-trodden passage.

In his eagerness to placate me and to remove himself, Yamaga dressed quickly, his haste twisting the pain in me. His voice took on a hateful tone of pity.

'Look, Yoshi,' he said, 'I am going to tell you something that Kawashima should have told you himself. You are already promised to Kanjurjab, a prince and therefore your equal. You will go to him in Mongolia. He knows nothing of your reputation here and he will not judge you by it. It was a diplomatic choice made many months ago and should suit you well. We have had our fun and now it is over. You are a strong woman, I know that you will make the best of it. A prince for a princess will be an equal match.'

'And what of love?' I cried.

'What of it?' he said. 'It has nothing to do with us or with marriage, it is a thing apart and must not intrude on life's serious purpose. Stop thinking with your blood, Yoshiko, use your mind and prosper.' He picked up his hat and moved towards the door. 'Have a fortunate life, Yoshi, be a dutiful wife and accept your fate. At the end of the day you are only a woman, there is no other way for you.'

He was wrong in that, there are always other ways for those prepared to risk them. But I was so wounded then that I could not take relief from that conviction or from my mother's words, which Sorry kept repeating like a mantra: 'The stronger the wind the stronger the tree.' I had never desired anything or anyone as much as I desired Yamaga, but in loving him I had forgotten my vow never to care for anyone above myself, and I was paying a high price for that lapse.

I would say goodbye to that day, put it behind me for ever. From now on I would date the things that happened to me to be before Yamaga or after Yamaga. He remains for me a splendid, deathless man, the only one I was to love in the way that can leave you feeling disembowelled. He left an ache in me that can be accessed far too easily for my liking, and one that still erupts on shadowy days in what I call my little deaths. Yet I have never regretted my time with him. It is proper to experience true love at least once in your life.

Sorry brought me an opium pipe to remove me from my misery, but I refused it. I could not bear the thought of waking from a sweet dream to such morbid pain. I lay deathly quiet, fearing to move in case I broke into pieces. Through those dark hours I made no attempt to soothe Sorry, who was curled on the floor at my bedside, crying my tears for me.

I could have licked my wounds and tried to change, but that is more easily said than done. In any case I knew that my appetite for sex would overpower any attempt I might make at ladylike celibacy in the future. I was not a hypocrite, nor did I want to impose on my nature those things that Japanese men require in a wife. Even though I was branded shameless, I refused to stand in anything but my true colours. Yet had I been more like Natsuko, diffident and submissive, Kawashima might not have been tempted

49

to use me in the way that he did. I thought it useless to fight my nature for it would take alchemy to achieve a metamorphosis; my fate, though, was a different matter. I do not share the Chinese attitude of resignation to fate, I believe that, even unknowingly, we make our own. I made a vow never again to be the victim of my senses. I would keep that giving part of me, once offered to Yamaga, separate. It was possible I would love again, but never so deeply, or at the cost of myself.

Natsuko took a sly pleasure in telling me that Yamaga had become engaged the month after he had met me to the youngest daughter of a family with spectacular ancestry. This girl, she said, was so exquisite that she had been likened to the legendary Chinese beauty Xi Shi. It was said of Xi Shi that she was so delicate she could dance on a lotus leaf without sinking beneath the waters. Natsuko said the fortune-teller had forecast that Yamaga's wife-to-be would give him many sons and fill his heart with music.

I tried not to let her see the pain her news gave me but she knew it instinctively, like an animal in a fight knows its opponent's weaknesses. I let her have her victory. Poor Natsuko, taking so much pleasure in a triumph that was not of her own making. From that time on, I understood that there are two kinds of women, those like Natsuko and Yamaga's chosen one, who give up the adventure of their lives to live safely and well thought of, and women like me who live as we choose, whatever the price. Much as I longed for Yamaga to love me, he had convinced me that I could never be the sort of woman he would be happy to take as a wife. It was useless lamenting the experiences that had made me. It was done and that was that.

I waited until I could speak without weeping before tempting Kawashima back to my bed. I played the whore for him, the boy for him, and let him mark me with bites and bruises. But it was too soon for the pleasure of the pain he gave me to erase the deeper hurt of Yamaga's rejection.

As Kawashima never spoke of the marriage supposedly arranged for me with the Mongolian prince, I began to hope that Yamaga had been mistaken. But soon whispers surrounding my forthcoming betrothal began in the house. I went to Kawashima and asked directly if it was true that I was betrothed to Prince Kanjurjab. He said that it was and that I should celebrate the engagement as it would be a fortunate union for me. He told me that Kanjurjab's family were highly thought of by the Japanese and it was an honour that I had been chosen by them.

I was outraged at the idea that I would be sent like a sack of good rice to this stranger thought to be my equal, and I did all that I could to persuade Kawashima to allow me to break the marriage agreement and remain a daughter of his house. He became furious and ordered me to be silent and never to speak of disobeying him again.

'It was my duty to find you a husband, Yoshiko; don't be so ungrateful as to question my choice.'

He was ordering my fate in much the same way my father, Prince Su, had done when I was eight years old. Yet little had changed in the eleven years that had passed since then, I knew that there would be no reasoning with Kawashima. I was a woman and it was unthinkable that I should have ambitions of my own.

'You will go to Kanjurjab in two months' time at the winter's end,' he said. 'The spring sun will lift your spirits and allow you to see how fortunate you are. In the meantime we can enjoy our lives as we have always done.'

Natsuko rejoiced in Kawashima's choice of Kanjurjab for me, a union she would not have wished for any of her own daughters. Yet with me gone, whom would she have to blame for the bad luck that dogged her life?

Sorry was old now, and didn't feel strong enough to accompany me to Mongolia, but neither did she wish to return to China. She had heard that nobody knew who ran China any more. The number of poor had increased and were dying on the streets from starvation.

51

'I have lost touch with my family and have lived here in Japan too long to fill my stomach with old water, mistress,' she said.

I would miss her terribly but I didn't insist she come with me. Instead I went to Natsuko to request she allow Sorry to remain in her home as a kitchen servant. That way she could at least live amongst familiar faces and have a roof over her head. Our years together had secured Sorry enough money to indulge herself in the small luxuries she enjoyed and the opium she loved above food. I wanted her to have an easy old age. Natsuko listened politely to my request, her pale face expressionless.

'Tell me why I should do you this favour, Yoshiko?' she asked.

'Why should you not, Natsuko?' I replied. 'It is such a little thing. An act of kindness from a benevolent lady to a humble servant.'

She smiled coldly, relishing the silence while she kept me waiting for her answer.

'It is as you say, Yoshiko, a small act of kindness. Yet that is something you have never shown me. However, I am not one to harbour grudges so I will keep your servant in my household. There is, though, a price for this insignificant favour.'

'Well then, Natsuko,' I said, 'name your price.'

'Give me back my black pearl,' she said quietly.

Without hesitation I untied the cord from around my neck and handed her the dark globe, still warm from my body. She didn't thank me but I heard the faintest sigh as she reached up and secured the pearl around her own neck. It did not flatter her as it had me. Her skin, soft with time, made a poor setting for such a fine gem. And so it was that I was able to buy for Sorry a sheltered old age. Years later in Shanghai I purchased a similar jewel of a better quality, but it lacked the potency of Natsuko's pearl and had no history to it.

Spring came gloriously with glazed blue skies, a profusion of pink and white blossom in the orchard, and the starry white flower of the garlic scenting the air. Then nature, fickle as the gods, changed her mind and an unseasonal snow froze the blooms, turning them to the colour of tea before felling them to the ground.

Natsuko complained that fruit would be scarce that summer and the household expenses sure to rise. She had a mean-spirited streak that I despised. Money is for the living after all. What use will it be to any of us in the afterlife? Our wits, I am sure, will be a better currency.

Two weeks before my departure, Teshima requested to see me. With watery eyes he said that he would miss me. He called me by his dead daughter Satsuko's name and apologised for the great age that barred him from making the journey to my wedding. I thought that he must have entered his dotage, his mind seemed clouded and he had begun mixing up people and places. I knew that his daughter Satsuko had died of food poisoning in the year before Kawashima had been born, and seeking to hurt him I bluntly reminded him of this. He just looked at me quizzically and said, 'You must be a good girl, Satsuko, and show your husband honour by giving him many sons.'

Even in senility, Teshima assumed the right to lecture me. Standing before me dressed in his loosely tied cotton coat and little else, he reminded me of how he had prepared me to be a 'good wife'. He reached towards me with a bony hand and began to fondle my breasts, closing his eyes and sighing. The gesture, so filled with ownership and expectation of my compliance, was hateful and filled me with anger. My own desire, so much more discerning now than in the days when Teshima had used me, remained unstirred at the sight of his thin veined hands and stained skin.

'Don't speak to me of honour, old man,' I hissed at him. 'What honourable man would seduce his own granddaughter?'

He turned from me and began feeding the little caged bird that lived its days in the shadowy corner of his room.

'Satsuko is a hawk come to eat you,' he sang, poking his fingers into the cage. The songbird hopped soundlessly about its perch, its tiny eyes dulled in resignation to its captivity. As I left the room the two young peasant girls Teshima had owned since the day of their birth entered carrying bowls of soup and rice. One began spooning soup into his mouth while the other mopped his chin with a length of damask. I thought that he had already forgotten our conversation, but in a moment of lucidity he called out my Chinese name.

'Eastern Jewel,' he said contemptuously, 'we are not of the same blood, you foolish girl. It's blood that counts, after all.'

It occurred to me then that even though I hated the idea of living in Mongolia, and intended in one way or another to escape it, I would not be sorry to leave this house that ate the lives of women. I felt a creeping sympathy for Natsuko who, suffering loneliness from the neglect of her family, had retreated sadly to her shady rooms. I knew that the men would continue to prosper. Teshima in his old age would have his every wish fulfilled by the serving girls whose lives were his. Kawashima and his sons Hideo and Nobu would continue their lordly lives as rich powerbrokers. In those last days in his house I felt that I had little to thank Kawashima for, other than my Japanese nationality of which I was proud. I couldn't know then that years later, when it would mean life or death to me, he would deny me even that.

With her daughters married, except for her birth-marked girl Itani, who Kawashima had set up in a junior branch of his house in Osaka where her brothers would stay on their trips to that city, Natsuko was bereft. Soon she would be left with only her spoilt daughter-in-law Taeko for company. Taeko was to marry Hideo in the summer when the white anemones would be in flower. It was said that Taeko, although beautiful, had a mean nature and rumoured that she beat her servants when they displeased her.

I imagined that the ghost of poor Shimako would always accompany Natsuko in the shadows of the house, but a dead sister is poor company in difficult times. Ichiyo, herself now married to a wealthy industrialist twice her age, told me that

54

Natsuko thought Hideo's wedding date too close to the festival of the dead to be a fortuitous one. I wished Natsuko many grand-children to liven her days. I could not bring myself to be so pitiful as to hold a grudge against her for all her little acts of cruelty. After all, I had performed so many of my own. In any case, it is a waste of energy to harbour ill will against the unlucky. I was pleased to discover in myself an affection for Natsuko that defied all that had been between us. I was ready to leave, but I would miss her familiar cool smile and the ordered home that she ran with such dedication.

On my last night in Kawashima's house I dreamt that I needed to relieve myself. Every pot or hole I approached was cracked or had a snake in it. Try as I might I could find no place that was suitable and I awoke exhausted. I lay in bed watching the sky lighten, thinking that I would never again view the dawn from the bed I had shared with Yamaga or hear the singing of the hall's wooden floor as Sorry brought me breakfast.

For the first time since I had heard Kanjurjab's name I allowed myself to wonder what he might be like. He had sent me a garishly coloured portrait of himself. It showed him posed on a high-backed chair, dressed formally in dark-blue silk with a spiked fur hat on his big head. On a desk beside him sat a clock painted to forever read the mysterious hours of noon or midnight. The backdrop of the painting displayed sprays of gore-red anemones which appeared to be growing from his shoulders. I was not optimistic about our union. If his nature echoed his appearance it would make life too peaceful for my liking. I wondered what he expected of me, duty, beauty and humility, I supposed.

Sorry told me she had once met a Mongolian outside the walls of the Forbidden City. He had smelled of mare's milk and horse urine. His skin was weathered to leather, his teeth were as grey as oysters and, although she stepped aside for him, he did not smile once. She added optimistically that he was probably not a prince, so I could hope for better.

That morning, my last in the western wing, I enjoyed a breakfast of cuttlefish and garlic with a thimbleful of five-grain wine that Sorry said would protect me against the north wind. She was unsettled that I was to fly in a plane on my journey, and sad that the time had come for us to part, but I noticed something of relief in her bearing. I knew she loved me, but perhaps I had become too much for her, and she was looking forward to a quieter life. I asked her to hug me as though I were a girl again and then to let me go. I told her to remember me only if it didn't make her sad.

'After all,' I said, 'memory is given for survival, Sorry, so remember only those things you need to.'

'I will, little mistress,' she said. 'I always do as you say.'

Although I had cried at the loss of my blood mother it would have been inappropriate to cry at leaving Sorry. I was ready to let her go. Everything has its time and life lived without change is bound ultimately to be unsatisfying. I had learnt from Sorry that if you set your mind to it, it is possible to love a bad person as she had loved me. In any case I could not believe that I would never see her again. I was not superstitious as Natsuko was, but something inside me knew that I would see Sorry again.

The years I had lived amongst the Kawashimas had taught me things that I would never forget. From Kawashima I learnt that power is useless if you do not use it and that one should always have something to barter with. From Teshima I learnt that selfishness has many rewards and from Natsuko that virtue guarantees none. From Shimako I came to know that it is possible to be two people at one and the same time, also that an inner and secret life has more influence on us than the one we choose to show the world.

Although the weather had turned for the better, Natsuko caught an infection and took to her bed. She frequently suffered bouts of beriberi for which Dr Mura gave her vitamin injections, but this time she said it was influenza. It may have been a ploy to keep her from having to attend my wedding, although she did lie pale on the pillow.

When the time came for me to go she took her leave of me with her customary formality.

'I would wish you fortune in your marriage, Yoshiko,' she said, 'but that would be foolishly optimistic for someone born in the Year of the Tiger. Tigers are never satisfied, nor do they ever give up hunting.'

I couldn't resist the urge to fence with her one last time. 'Natsuko,' I said, 'your husband's geisha was born in the Year of the Tiger. If rumour is to be believed her life has been excessively fortunate.'

She smiled pityingly at me. 'In Osaka,' she said, 'the unlucky year is that of the ram.'

My rooms in the western wing looked lifeless without my belongings to decorate them. While living my life there I hadn't noticed that the walls were crumbling and in need of painting, or that the mirror I gazed into every day was leaden with age. Yet, somewhere steeped in the plaster and in the still air of the rooms there remained a trace of the excitement, the misery and the sexual encounters they had hosted. Yamaga was there too and that was a memory that could never be pure, it would always come with pain attached to it. I took up the cup he had last sipped sake from and let it fall to the floor; it broke into three shards, I stamped on them, powdering them to dust. I would take no memento of him to distract me from living. I knew, though, that his image and my pain would return unbidden no matter what I left behind me.

I wanted to live my life as it happened, not lost in nostalgia or anticipation. I didn't expect to be happy. It seemed to me that happiness was only found in those moments when time is occupied with something that takes you out of yourself. I determined to live day by day in my life, and avoid the long-term pursuit of happiness. I would let the pleasure principle guide me through my allotted time, so that when death sought me out it would find me still living life to the full.

Bone Stew and Mare's Milk

Kawashima and Nobu accompanied me on the journey to Port Arthur where I was to be married before travelling to Mongolia. Hideo was to remain at home as temporary patriarch as his grandfather was now too old for such duties.

My trunks, filled with clothes and wedding gifts, had gone before me, but in my precious writing case I carried on board the half-eaten box of lychees now shrivelled with age, my bee in amber and my mother's coral earrings.

We flew from Tokyo across Korea to the beautiful peninsula of Port Arthur in a military plane as the guests of Admiral Ube Sadamu. The Admiral, an influential and aristocratic cohort of Kawashima's, had helped to arrange my marriage to Kanjurjab as part of Japan's effort to make as many footholds in Mongolia as possible. It is a pity that power rarely comes with beauty, for the Admiral was as ugly as he was powerful.

We had news that China's weak Emperor Pu Yi had fled the Forbidden City under the protection of the Japanese. With Peking in turmoil his Imperial Majesty's safety was at risk. On a grey February morning in 1925 he had been secreted out of the city in the company of his tutor Reginald Johnston to set up home in Tientsin, the birthplace of his wife Wan Jung. Admiral Ube had a hand in the matter, and I could tell by the way that Kawashima deferred to him that he was a powerful man. Nobu told me that the

Admiral was at the centre of Japanese affairs and was a personal friend of Crown Prince Hirohito.

The journey was thrilling, especially the take-off, which was doubly exciting for me because of Nobu's obvious fear of flying. I told him I was determined to fly a plane myself one day and he laughed, not only to annoy me but because he was genuinely amused. Nobu enjoyed making me angry to compensate himself for the many humiliations he had suffered in his youth at my hands.

'You will be a wife, Yoshiko,' he jeered. 'Wives do not fly planes, they lie on their backs and breed.'

Nobu had grown into a handsome man whose strong looks belied his weak nature. He told lies to ease his path through life and always took the line of least resistance, relying on his charm to get him what he wanted. I liked him well enough, though, he had a good sense of humour and I once saw him delicately release a panic-stricken butterfly from a spider's web. His true ambition was to be a poet, but he didn't have the courage to speak of it to Kawashima. I doubt he had the talent either. Despite his prodding, I think that he admired me, even though I had, over the years, frequently exposed the frailties of his nature. I did not blame him now for taking a little pleasure in my situation.

Although he did not know it then, Nobu was to marry the daughter of our host Admiral Ube. The girl was high-born and the marriage pleased Kawashima, but she was sickly and suffered many stillbirths. She delivered Nobu only one living child, a girl who, having no brothers to compete with, grew to be not only decorative, but also scholarly.

We had taken off in what the pilot had described as excellent flying weather; the air was perfectly still with a clear bleached sky and good visibility. As we descended in an inky light, one or two stars appeared in the sky and the faint outline of the moon looked red. Kawashima took a silver flask from his pocket and offered us a shot of malt whisky. It was my first taste of any spirit other than sake or Chinese wine. The strange flavour brought to mind temples and tobacco and left my throat hot. I thought the taste interesting and admired the silver flask. But Nobu, who strove to appear unimpressed with everything, said that sake was better and Kawashima and Sadamu nodded in agreement.

I was informed by Kawashima that Port Arthur had been captured from China by Japan and was now Japanese territory. It was therefore a most suitable place for the marriage to take place, particularly so as Kanjurjab had no wish to cross a sea to meet his bride. Kawashima said that when I reached Mongolia I would be expected to promote my country in all things. As a daughter of Japan I must never forget the debt I owed to my adopted land. I could not believe that the country I so loved could truly wish me to give my life to the cold plains of Mongolia. Surely Japan had higher things in mind for me?

Kawashima had arranged for us to wait for Kanjurjab's arrival in a large house built like its neighbours in the western style, with an overgrown garden at the back, full of oily laurel and bleeding snowberry. Designed to sit comfortably in an elegant semicircle, it was painted white and guarded at its entrance by iron gates wrought with dragons and peonies. The interior was decorated in the Chinese style and overfilled with dark furniture and uncomfortable seating. My rooms were on the first floor at the front of the house, and despite the many servants they were untidy and a little dusty. The air in the house was heavy and sweet, which brought to mind decay, and the sofas and cushions were a little damp.

The house overlooked a coastline shadowed by ragged cliffs that met a grey strip of sand and shingle at the water's edge. From the back of the house the prosperous city of Port Arthur fanned out in rows of similar homes sitting in green lagoons of gardens that were lush with bamboo and magnolia. The broad streets lined with acacia trees were well kept but lifeless. I much preferred the area we had driven through from the airfield, where the poor lived around the dockyards and under the dripping bridges. There the narrow dark lanes, hung with washing and littered with everything from food remains to dead cats, had a sense of danger about them as though at any moment you might collide with adventure on their mean streets.

From the ice-free port great steamers plied their way to Shanghai, and around the aged wooden piers sampans crowded together selling fish and vegetables. You could be tattooed or drink tea served to you by women who themselves were for sale. I have always thought it a pity that wealth and position remove us to the top of the hill, away from the real life of the teeming streets where boredom is rarely a problem.

My bridegroom wasn't due to arrive until the day of the ceremony, which gave me two days to settle into the house. I thought this lack of urgency displayed a reluctance on his part to commit to our union, a reluctance which I certainly shared with him. Kawashima said that the timing was quite proper and was intended so that I would not feel rushed and would have time to prepare myself.

On our first night in the house we were served a splendid banquet at which Kawashima, Nobu and myself were the only diners. Admiral Ube had travelled on to Manchuria for some supposedly secret meetings. There were fried dumplings in a spicy broth and shredded lamb with capers. Course succeeded course, until the memory of the earlier ones had left us, but I do recall some good pancakes stuffed with winter radish and an apricot pickle made from the hard fruits usually kept for making dye. I enjoyed everything and ate voraciously.

After the servants had retired to their kangs, the little raised platforms of bricks laid side by side in the yard at the back of the house, things quietened down. I could hear the sea lapping the cliffs and the occasional call from ships far out at sea.

Nobu prepared himself to visit the 'flower girls' in a local brothel that Admiral Ube had recommended to him. The Admiral had told him that the girls in this house were the best you would find anywhere. They were mostly Chinese and had so many ways of pleasing a man that they were uncountable; no desire would be left unfulfilled, no request denied. Ube had confided in Nobu that for himself, only girls of fourteen or younger would do. After that age, he said, the scent of youth left their skin and their expressions became sour. Nobu and I laughed at the thought of the fat little Admiral making love. He was as broad as he was short with low-hanging buttocks and a pompous little swagger. Only his eyes, which were deep set, bright and serious, saved him from looking ridiculous.

I asked Nobu what he would choose from the uncountable list.

'First, I will take a bound-foot girl with white teeth,' he said excitedly. 'Just so that I can see for myself what the Chinese make all the fuss about. I will put the whole of her tiny lotus foot into my mouth as though it were a little breast. I hear that the girls with the smallest feet are the most exciting, because they are used to pain and are humble. When you have finished with them, they bathe you and feed you honey from their fingers.' As he spoke Nobu became flushed with anticipation.

'After the bound-footed girl, who I hope will be a virgin,' he continued, 'I will try the Polish girl they have at this house. Ube says she is ugly but it will be something to remember that I once mounted a girl with gold hair, and I need not look at her face.'

I envied Nobu his freedom to take off into the night and do as he pleased. I approved of his choices and would have accompanied him happily, if only to watch. For a moment I thought of running away and starting a new life. But something in me told me to wait. It was not time yet. My escape would need to be well planned and I would know where I was running to.

The moment I put my head on the pillow, I slept and dreamt of a house of colours so gorgeous that I felt strangely ill, as though I had feasted on food too rich and wine too heady. Walls of exquisite turquoise dripped with fringes of pure gold. Purple ran through violet to pink across ceilings so high that eagles nested in their corners in glittering eyries. Great cascades of silk coursed around me in luminous swathes of palest green through the spectrum to verdigris, while reds of every hue poured from huge glass bowls into pools of silvery mercury. Pearls the colour of the pinkest azaleas bejewelled every surface. As I ran through the rainbow rooms, I became aware that I was being hunted by my birth father in the guise of a huge black dog. He intended to kill me before I could disgrace him further. I ran into a small windowless room where the orgy of colours had changed into a muddy brown of the kind you create as a child, when from your paint box you mix too many colours and lose them all. In this room a race of warm blood coursed around my bare feet and a hot pain woke me and I found that Kawashima had entered me from behind and had one hand over my breast, the other covering my mouth.

'Be quiet, Yoshiko,' he whispered. 'Your cries will wake the house.' He promised to leave no bite marks that night as he thought it only good manners to hand me to Kanjurjab without a mark on my pelt. Instead he contented himself with pulling on my hair like a rein, and thrusting into me cruelly. No marks on the outside, but sore for days inside.

When he had finished he gave a satisfied grunt and rolled off me. 'I will miss our coupling, Yoshiko,' he said. 'You have such an interesting flavour, both salty and sweet.'

I smiled and leant over as though to kiss him, but instead I bit deeply into his lip until my mouth was filled with his blood. He pushed me from him and threw me on the floor.

'You taste only of salt,' I said.

I left my mark on him with a scar he would carry home to Natsuko. Yet, despite the pain involved and the disservice it had done me, I always found sex with Kawashima exciting. Since I first lay with him I was spoilt for tenderness. Lovers who are too kind leave you drowning in molasses.

Next morning, angry at the sight of his swollen lip, Kawashima grudgingly put out the gift of money I was to place at the shrine while offering up a prayer. I was about to become a wife, so I had to follow the tradition of praying for happiness and prosperity with my new husband. I was a good enough actress to fool Kawashima into thinking that I had accepted his choice of life for me, I feigned obedience and agreed to go. I had hidden my own money in the lining of my trunk and had no intention of telling Kawashima of it. I was determined to keep my money and to add to its reserves whenever I could.

I bathed in a stone bath lined with smooth pebbles to stimulate the blood and added salt to heal me from Kawashima's excesses. As I relaxed in the steamy water I took sips of whisky from the silver flask I had stolen from his pocket as he slept. Then I ate a breakfast of milk and fried eggs and made my way to the temple.

I could smell the musty scent of incense before the shrine appeared out of the gloom, and was reminded of how uneasy I always felt in such places. I prayed neither for happiness nor prosperity. Instead I asked for an exciting life that need recognise no counsel but my own. If I had to offer the gods something in return, they could make my life a short one if it pleased them.

I returned to the house to open the gifts that had arrived from the Kawashimas and the little linen bags of money, presents from rich Tokyo and Osaka families attempting to impress Kawashima with their generosity. The bags would be presented to Kanjurjab's father as part of my dowry.

Ichiyo had sent the embryo of a monkey preserved in alcohol as a fertility charm. It was horrible. Hideo sent a small jewelled dagger with a note to say it was for handling the tough meat I would have to get used to in Mongolia. I suppose he thought that was funny. There were gifts from Itani and from Hideo's betrothed Taeko, who sent an uninteresting pair of mother-of-pearl earrings. Hidden in my luggage, Sorry had wrapped a box of dried lychees with a letter she must have paid to have written for her. She said the lychees were to remind me of the journey I had taken with her long ago from China to Japan. She advised me not to drink Mongolian milk as it came from yaks, who were dirty animals. She said it was just as well that I was demanding of fortune, for I may have difficult times ahead of me. Then, apologising for giving me advice, she signed it with a cross.

Apart from the wedding kimono that Natsuko had chosen for me and sent in a cedar box, she gave me a small lacquer chest locked with a gold key in a jade bolt. The interior of the lid was decorated with old Satsuma work displaying boughs of trailing wisteria. The box housed two compartments lined with silver enamel. One was filled with the honey of April, the most perfumed of all honeys, the other a May conserve heavy with the scent of limes. Both compartments were sealed with a thin translucent cover of beeswax. It was magnificent.

Kawashima remarked that Natsuko, queen of her own hive, was sending some of its sweetness with me on my nuptial flight. He had forgotten that Natsuko herself had been given the box at the birth of her third daughter by her hated mother-in-law with the words, 'I chose such a fine gift in the expectation that you would deliver my son a boy, but it seems you are done with that. You may as well have it as the sight of it will only remind me of his disappointment and my own disgust.'

By passing the box on to me Natsuko was sending me a cloaked message, one she knew I would understand. At one and the same time it communicated her dislike of me and reminded me of my barrenness. For a brief moment she became splendid in my eyes. I was reminded that women make more interesting enemies than men because of their subtlety and their ability to inflict exquisite, rather than brutal, pain. I think it was on that day, as I held Natsuko's gift, that I first realised that I truly loved her, despite knowing that she would never love me.

The night before Kanjurjab arrived I slept alone in my bed. Kawashima didn't bother me, but said that I should enjoy my solitude as it would be the last time I would lie unstraddled. That night he took a young male servant to his bed, a beautiful, deathless-looking boy.

Shortly after dawn, Kanjurjab, his parents, siblings, concubines, dogs and unpaid servants arrived in a noisy and unselfconscious manner. As I spied on them from an upstairs window my heart sank at the thought that by nightfall I would be one of their number. Despite the finery of their clothes, they looked rough, too weathered and unrefined for my taste. Kawashima had not done well for me in his matchmaking. I had harboured the view that I was in some way special to him, but I had been mistaken.

Kanjurjab's portrait had been a flattering one. Now, dressed in a western suit with dusty shoes and a cap made from felt, he looked a little lost amongst his tribe. He was taller than most of the Japanese men of my acquaintance, but he looked plump and boyish to me. With his hair hanging lank and his shoulders slumped, he was not at all like the wild Mongolian that Sorry had described meeting by the walls of the Forbidden City.

The woman I took at first glance to be his mother turned out to be his concubine Mai. She was homely-looking, rotund and ruddy as the plums she was named after. Having a sweet and uncomplicated nature, Mai had a simple trust in life that eased her path through it. His mother Xue, named after snow because she was winter born, was a religious woman whose life was made more complicated than necessary because of her strict adherence to Lamaism, the religion of the Kanjurjab family. Xue was dressed in a silk topcoat the colour of sulphur with an elaborate headdress of silver and gemstones. She moved quickly, as though time was running out, and no matter what the company, she always seemed to be standing in a space of her own. She had a thin mouth and slits for eyes but her long dark hair woven through with silver beads was impressively thick. I came to know that she was possessed of a native cunning, but not a great intelligence.

Kanjurjab's father Tsgotbaatar was also dressed in western garb. It was to be the only time that I saw either of them in those suits. Perhaps they had been purchased specially for the occasion, for

66

neither man looked at ease in them. Tsgotbaatar was a man who communicated with few words, mostly grunting his refusal or acceptance of offerings. He had the capacity to remain completely still and I thought then without knowing him that he would have been happier in a wilder place than Port Arthur. Later I came to understand that his stillness was actually bewilderment; in strange surroundings he would sniff the air as though searching for some lost, predestined path.

The kimono that Natsuko had chosen for me was of deep-red silk, the colour for weddings. It was embroidered with yellow circles to remind me of China and edged with a border of green satin. The under kimono felt light and soft against my skin, but once its topcoat was added and wound several times with an obi sash it became bulky and uncomfortable. I hated the elaborate wig I was expected to wear to cover my fashionably short hair, and indulged the idea of hanging geisha hair bells on it and painting my eyelids red to annoy Kawashima, but decided against it. I would go through the marriage service with good manners and think of it as a stepping stone to my freedom.

Shortly before the ceremony, Mai, Kanjurjab's concubine, came to my room with a spray of wild orchids as a gift. She wished me many sons to play on the grasslands with her own, and daughters to comfort me in my old age. She said that Kanjurjab and his family were honoured to have such a high-born and modest young woman as a wife for their beloved first-born son. Obviously Kawashima had sold me with a fake pedigree.

After the old man Tsgotbaatar and Kawashima had exchanged family gifts, a simple ceremony took place and the deed was done. I stood beside Kanjurjab while the wedding photograph was taken, smelling the musty odour of his clothes and looking down at the curled-up toes of his felt boots. He had changed into traditional Mongolian dress for the ceremony, which suited him better than the western suit he had looked so uncomfortable in. I wondered what sort of lover he would make. I suspected that his body would be soft and his energy far from infinite. But then, even a poor meal can taste good if you are hungry enough.

At the banquet that followed, the men and women were separated by low paper screens framed in black wood above which you could just about see. Most Eastern men do not like to see women eating. Women were, I suppose, expected to live on air like the delicate creatures of legend. But Mongolian men are far more robust than their Japanese brothers and take it as a healthy sign if a woman eats well. I dined with Kanjurjab's mother, his two sisters Alta and Nandak, and an assortment of female cousins and friends. His father's concubine Kara, named after the great sea, was meant to be amongst our number, but she had wandered off distractedly before the first course was served. I had noticed her distress during the ceremony. She seemed to be having some kind of fit and Alta and Nandak had to hold her down by her arms. Mai did not join us, as she was busy in the kitchen checking Kanjurjab's food and making sure he was served good portions.

Kawashima had fourteen guests. They included Admiral Ube and five high-ranking army officers, there to impress the Mongolians. Tsgotbaatar's guests looked like an anarchic lot who appeared to care little about how they were viewed by anyone. Amongst their number was Jon, one of Kanjurjab's brothers-in-law, who had positioned himself so that he could stare at me through a space in the screens. I had been aware of his interest all day and had noticed the flush that coloured his cheeks whenever I caught his eye. Throughout the long dinner, at which he hardly ate, his eyes rarely wavered from my face and I wondered why his wife Nandak, sitting next to me, appeared oblivious to the attention her husband was giving me.

We were served five-snake stew, an ancient recipe supposed to contain dragon, tiger and phoenix, but in our case made from snake, cat and chicken. It was followed by little mounds of coagulated blood taken from the backbones of young chickens and allowed to half dry in the air. Lastly came oysters, each one with a pearl held fast in its glutinous membrane. 'A small token,' as Kawashima so elegantly put it, 'from Japan to its most esteemed allies.'

When the meal was finished Nobu came to take his leave of me. He wished me luck and said that if I had been his blood sister he would have been sorry for me, but as it was he thought I would do well in the country that bordered the one my ancestors had ruled. 'Life will be less interesting without you,' he said kindly.

As I waited alone for my new mother-in-law to take me to my husband, Kawashima entered my room smiling. He stood behind me and cupped my breasts with his square hands, squeezing them until I moaned with desire and pain.

'Never again, Yoshiko,' he said. 'What a pity.'

I put my finger to his still-swollen lip and pressed until he winced with pain. Nothing more was said. After all that had been between us our goodbye was to inflict pain on each other. As tenderness had never been an ingredient of our lovemaking, I did not expect or miss it in our farewell.

Mai came in Xue's place to tell me that Kanjurjab would not lie with me that night as the journey had tired him and he did not wish to disappoint me. Her little moon face was flushed red and her eyes would not hold mine.

And so, on our wedding night my husband chose over me the comfort of his plump little concubine who treated him more like a son than a lover. I thought it showed a lack of adventure and did not bode well for our future intimacy. Despite Kawashima's prediction, that night, as on many others to follow, I slept alone and unstraddled.

I found my new home Suiyuan, the blue city, so named because of its skies, a poor place compared to Tokyo. It was called a city, but in reality it was the size of a large village. Appearing out of a frozen plain in a mass of squat, sloping-roofed houses and half-covered animal shelters, it hunkered like a fort against the wilderness. At its heart stood a handful of plainly built decaying temples, from which rows of muddy lanes fanned out depressingly. Dusty little shops displayed herbs and potions that looked as though they had lain on the shelves for centuries. There were brothels run by Chinese, whose whores were girls of peasant stock from the towns belonging to China that bordered Mongolia. Amongst their regulars were the lamas, the holy men who were supposed to be celibate. There were two saddle makers in the town who worked from dawn until dusk, as did the jeweller who sat at a table made from stone, fashioning and repairing the headdresses and ornate necklaces that all Mongolian women wore for special occasions.

We arrived in Suiyuan in a blizzard, the sky leaden, the ground a slippery frozen mud. The wind was so cold it made my eyes ache and dried out my tongue. I could feel the veins on the back of my hands swelling as my lips went numb. I had hoped that it might not be too bad a place, but so alien did it appear that I could not imagine even after a hot meal and a night's sleep that it would seem any better. We had left Port Arthur with a thin sun warming our heads, lifting even my spirits. Kanjurjab had told me that it was already spring in Mongolia. It might have been, but it was not spring as I knew it.

My new husband seemed embarrassed by my presence and ill at ease in my company. His way of dealing with me was to tell me what he thought I wanted to hear. This effectively dismissed me, and saved him from having to prolong any discussion we were engaged in. Like a child who has been told he must play with a stranger when he would rather be with his familiar friends, he was distant and formal and could not wait to release himself from any congress with me.

Mai, his kindly concubine, had whispered in her strange husky little voice that the weather would not be clement until a few weeks later in May. Even then, she said with a laugh, the wind would come carrying the promise of snow. She was a simple woman who could be relied on to tell the truth, because she was without guile and had no desire to manipulate events. She reminded me a little of Sorry, although she did not have Sorry's deference or her intelligence.

Built out of the ruins of an old monastery, Kanjurjab's house missed being modest due to its long, shapely roof and ornately carved door. It had one huge half-moon courtyard at the front of the house that was crowded with gers, the circular Mongolian tents of his tribe, while the back was open to a strip of muddy land looking towards the town. The entrance hall, used mainly as a store for saddles and winter animal feed, was the largest space in the dark house. The windows had no glass but were fashioned with double wooden panels stuffed with felt and camel hair to resist the wind. All the rooms were long and narrow and led warren-like into each other without doors; there were rugs and furs scattered around, which softened the otherwise austere interior. In the room where I was to sleep, a huge brass bowl sat on the floor filled with muddy-looking water. I wasn't sure if it was for drinking or washing. The furniture looked Chinese but had lost its lacquer and even the nacre inlay looked dull and lifeless. There was, though, an exquisitely carved chest big enough to sleep in, which housed a few pieces of felt and a bundle of wooden poles. I learnt later that it had come with Xue as part of her dowry and was carved with twin fish to symbolise marriage harmony. Etched solidly at each corner of the chest, the symbol of the endless knot of Buddha's entrails performed a complicated dance. Something about the grand presence of this remarkable piece amongst the otherwise rude furnishings made me want to weep. Like myself, it had come down in the world and was meant for a more superior home than the one it was in.

Apart from a couple of poorly trained servants who could never be found, I was the sole human occupant of the house. A pair of the ubiquitous shaggy dogs that were everywhere in the camp roamed the house at will, leaving their hair and their rank odour on everything. My mother-in-law Xue suggested that I should stay in the house until I felt ready to move into my husband's ger. She told me that the family preferred the gers because of their spaciousness and their connection to the earth and assured me that they were more comfortable than the house. She said that once my memory had let go of the image of my old home, I would come to prefer them too.

I asked her if she remembered her own childhood home in China.

'Of course,' she replied. 'It had two courtyards and I lived in the corridor of the concubines with my mother who gave my father three sons before she died. My father was the youngest son of an ancient banking family, favoured over his brothers for being the only one to present his father with grandsons.'

'Do you miss your birth home, Xue?' I asked. She said that she didn't because she was on the path that had been chosen for her and she was glad to be well along it and did not care to waste time looking back.

'Life is about the journey we have to get through. It only slows us up to look back,' she said. 'Perhaps if you could accept the journey chosen for you, Yoshiko, you would find contentment.'

'What makes you think that I am not content?' I asked her.

'I have seen the colour of your water,' she said. 'When it becomes the same yellow as butter you will have settled.'

However good Xue's advice might have been, she herself appeared not to have taken it. I think she was the least content person I have ever known, always fussing with the future and quite unable to live happily in the present.

I was surprised to learn that with uncharacteristic kindness Kawashima had advised my father-in-law Tsgotbaatar that I would need time to adjust to a lifestyle so different to the one I had known in Japan. I almost wept when Xue told me of his act of consideration. I should have hated him for banishing me from a civilised life, but I longed to return to his familiar, if partial, protection.

From the moment of arrival in Suiyuan I had realised that it would not be an easy place to escape. The temperature alone might fell me and its remoteness was frightening. I was ill with home-sickness and suffered a wrenching urgency to be back in my western wing of the Tokyo house where the floor sang and the air was perfumed with the smoke of Turkish cigarettes.

Kanjurjab shared his ger with Mai and their twin sons, Otong-bayaar and Batbayaar, so named because they had been born smiling. Mai was six weeks pregnant with their third child and would eat only mutton and milk because she thought such a diet produced sons. She lived to please Kanjurjab and knew that he would take pride in presenting his parents with another grandson. Whenever Mai spoke of her pregnancy she made a point of wishing me many sons with Kanjurjab. I believed that she meant it, as she bore no resemblance to the envious concubines that I had known in my father Prince Su's household. I was disturbed by her attitude because I enjoyed her sweetness and the friendship she offered and did not wish to hurt her when Kanjurjab eventually came to my bed, as I knew he must.

It was impossible to be unaware of Mai's obsessive love for Kanjurjab. She was both mother and lover to him, leaving no desire unfulfilled, no need outstanding. Her life revolved around his care and comfort. I had seen her rubbing his stomach when he had eaten too much to help him burp or break wind. When he returned from riding, which he excelled at, she would unselfconsciously open her robe and warm his hands against her breasts. She would wipe his mouth after he had eaten and cool his tea with her breath. I am sure that in their lovemaking everything was done for his pleasure in the same way. He in turn was very physical with her, his hands always about her body somewhere, his eyes seeking hers to share some secret intimacy between them. Their bodies communicated so well that words were hardly necessary and were used sparingly. I have never before or since seen such oneness between a man and a woman.

Mai was so content that I could not pity her, but I did not desire her subjection as a way of life for myself. There was something horrible to me in being so enslaved to another human being. When Xue had travelled from China to marry Tsgotbaatar, the six-year-old Mai had come with her in her entourage. She had known and cared for Kanjurjab all of his life and it had been no surprise to anyone when he chose her for his concubine. Like Xue, she preferred to be thought of as Mongolian, not only because the people of her adopted land did not like the Chinese, who had always attempted to subdue them, but also so that she might close any divide between her and the man she loved. Mai said that in fairness to Mongolians, it was widely acknowledged amongst them that China produced fine horses and beautiful women. Kanjurjab had told her that no Mongolian woman compared favourably to her in beauty or sweetness of nature. Although Mai's nature would have been recognised as generous anywhere in the world, in Japan, at least, her looks would have been considered unfortunate.

In those first miserable days in Suiyuan it was a mystery to me why Kanjurjab had agreed to our marriage. Money hardly seemed to matter, but then that is never truly the case and my dowry was large. There was no doubt that he was a prince of a rich family, for although the day-to-day living was mean, the women wore gold jewellery and spectacular headdresses while the men owned many finely crafted saddles and feisty little Chinese horses.

Perhaps it was simply that tradition cannot be snubbed and no matter how happy you might be with a concubine, it was customary to marry someone of equal rank. Sadly for Mai, a prince could not marry a peasant. It was, though, a problem for my husband for he needed no one but Mai. She was mother, sister and wife in one plump little bundle. I had no doubt that I could seduce Kanjurjab if I needed to, but he would always love Mai and I did not grudge her the love I did not want.

My mother-in-law Xue was a cold personality who never showed affection to anyone. She was well mannered towards me but her stare was critical, she was indifferent both to my company and to my suffering. Always at some altar or other, worshipping the gods of the temple and those of the river and trees, Xue in the way of many devout women heard only her own inner voice. Guided by earth, fire, and water, she was thought to be good at diagnosing illnesses, and spent much of her time concocting medicines from herbs and minerals, and the putrid organs of dead animals.

Looking back now with more knowledge than I had then, I suspect that Tsgotbaatar probably suffered from syphilis. He was slowly going blind and although still capable on a horse and good at wrestling, his mind wandered and he was rarely lucid. Xue diagnosed him as having too much water in his body and treated him with brimstone and blood letting. I don't believe that she had lain with her husband for some years for she displayed none of his symptoms, while his concubine Kara seemed as distracted as he was and was often in a foul mood with her master, a rare thing for a concubine, even a Mongolian one.

Xue had conceived Kanjurjab in the first week of her marriage to Tsgotbaatar. It had been a difficult pregnancy and the pain in her back was so bad that she could not stand. When the time came to follow the livestock to pasture, she had to be taken on a cart and cried out at every bump in the road. Her labour lasted three days and left her weak and forever prone to periods of exhaustion. Her next two pregnancies were even more difficult than the first. She bled heavily and this left her anaemic with no pink in her mouth or eyes.

Xue's eldest daughter, Alta, looked like her but her youngest, Jon's wife, Nandak, seemed possessed of only Mongolian blood and was darker-skinned and shorter than her mother. Mai said that Xue might look strong but that she had never made up the blood lost at the births of her children, and that life in the grasslands was too hard for her. She added in a whisper that she would be surprised if Xue made old bones.

Xue's history allowed me to feel a connection with her as well as a certain amount of sympathy for her. She was a hard woman to like and I never managed that, but I could see how she had been made. We had both been banished to this ungenerous land, given to men by other men who did not value us. Although it had made her bitter and difficult, she had accepted the hard life chosen for her and had turned to religion and superstition as her salve. Unlike Xue, I would never accept that Mongolian life was my fate and I was determined to escape it, no matter what the cost.

It was bad luck for me that Kawashima had settled on Xue and Tsgotbaatar's son for my husband, for unlike some other scions of Mongolian royalty, Kanjurjab hated to travel from his beloved grasslands and had scant knowledge of the world. Indeed, he had little interest in anything except Mai, archery and horses. I think that the journey to Port Arthur had been the furthest both in miles and experience that he had ever travelled. It had not whetted his appetite for adventure; he needed so much less of it than I to enjoy his life.

In those early months of our marriage I lost heart and had difficulty in even imagining how I might plan my escape. It was to be some time before Kanjurjab finally called me to his bed, but in the meanwhile the only comfort I could find was in the company of Mai. I looked out for Jon to flirt with but I only ever saw him in Kanjurjab's presence or in that of Alta's husband Boria, a stern man who seemed to disapprove of me.

When not riding or honing his archery skills with his brother-in-law, Kanjurjab spent most of his time with Mai in his ger. It provided everything he needed in a home and was spacious and splendidly decorated with colourful wall hangings and mounds of fur skins for bedding. Mai cooked traditional Mongolian food on a stove housed in the centre of the ger which burnt wood and dried animal dung. The air always smelled of meat and milk. There were brass pots as well as clay ones on low wooden shelves, and now a wedding photograph of Kanjurjab and myself hung askew above them in a silver frame. Kanjurjab used his saddles as chairs and would lounge on them, laughing at his boys as they, like all

Mongolian children, wrestled endlessly. The painted wooden door of the ger faced south as was traditional. It was carved with a swastika for good fortune, and of course there was the ubiquitous altar on the back wall and the usual mangy dogs about the place.

Whenever I visited the ger I sat with Mai to the right of the door under the eastern protection of the sun, Kanjurjab usually sitting to the left under the western protection of the great sky god Tengger. It was warmer than the house and I liked the way the light filtered through the small hole in the roof, but I could not envisage a time when I would willingly forgo my privacy to share it with my husband, his concubine and their noisy children. But through the long dark nights in my room I suffered a self-pitying loneliness. I was so cold that I took to sleeping curled up with the dogs as near to the fire as I could get, away from the wall that was damp and as cold as ice.

Apart from the extreme cold, which was the worst thing for me, I had to adjust to many other difficulties. Even on the shortest of walks, great pyramids of animal dung drying for fuel had to be skirted, while the art of walking on frozen mud was one I never completely mastered. Camels spat their foul juice at will, and the fetid smell of the horses and oxen was at times unbearable. And then there was the vastness of the Mongolian sky, with no visible horizon, which seemed to trap me more securely than any jail. Kanjurjab still insisted that it was spring, which made me tremble at the thought of what winter might bring.

The food was so awful that quite soon after my arrival I suffered a bout of poisoning so violent that without Mai to nurse me, I think that I might have died. She shared my bed, warming me with her fleshy body, and fed me boiled water on the hour that she had infused with bitter herbs. It made me pleasantly light-headed and soothed my stomach. No mother could have been kinder and I felt I had found a new Sorry and was comforted.

To appease one or other of her gods, my mother-in-law Xue built an obo shrine at the door of the house. It was a simple pile of stones with a hollow space for offerings. I guessed that some unpalatable food or animal part would be a suitable gift to lay in it as there seemed nothing sweet or pleasantly perfumed to be had anywhere in my new home.

As Mai fussed around me, Xue told her that my illness was because of my reluctance to accept my life on Mongolian soil. She said that I must eat only dried cheese and that I should dip a finger from my right hand into a glass of milk, flicking it once towards the sky, once into the air, and once into the wind; in that way I would acknowledge the gods of the land and a calm would descend upon me. Xue did not want to lose me in the first months of my marriage to her son in case Kawashima thought I had been intentionally poisoned. I expect she thought that if I died he would require the return of my dowry and that Kanjurjab would have difficulty in finding another wife. Under Xue's instructions, Mai supplied a bowl of jaundiced-looking butter and helped me to the door with my offering. It was a still night, but so cold that the frigid air scalded my lungs. The sky was beautiful, full of constellations and falling stars and the moon hanging huge and white. I was filled with sadness at the thought that the immense sky sheltered a land so wide and hostile that I would never be able to navigate it on my own.

I was beginning to understand that my escape would not simply be a matter of running away. It would need careful planning and the help of someone who knew the land and how to survive it. To get to Suiyuan we had travelled from Port Arthur on a long train journey, then in oxen-drawn carts across miles of frozen earth, while the wind burnt any bit of skin left exposed, and the iron wheels thumped against the impacted ground. Without help to retrace the steps of the journey, I had no idea of even which direction I should go in. I had ached for a week after we arrived and knew that I would have to go through something similar again if I had any hope of escaping this place.

I recovered from the food poisoning and tried to adapt to the only diet available to me, that of bone stew, meat broth and mutton fat. There was Russian tea with salt and mare's milk, a nostrum surely contrived by a sadist. But luckily there was plenty of vodka. I drank mine neat like sake, declining the sour milk that Mongolians liked to add to theirs. There was always plenty of the fermented liquor airag, made from mare's milk, but I could only drink it if I held my nose, as its rancid smell turned my stomach. The children sucked liquorice root, which I imagined would be sweet like aniseed, but when I tried it it was bitter and so rough on the tongue one might as well have sucked wood.

It took some time, too, to get used to the terrible smell of my new family. Compared to us Japanese, who bathe and perfume ourselves, Mongolians have a more natural smell. It is not hard to understand why, when to wash you must first break the ice on the water, while to remove your clothes any time other than between the months of June and August is, to say the least, foolhardy. The furs and felts of the tribe secured the smell of blood and fish; not even the winds from Siberia could remove their rankness. I thought that my perfumed body must smell false to Mongolians, who have a habit of breathing you in when first introduced to you, but as I had no intention of removing even one layer of clothes before the weather improved I knew that I would soon smell just like them.

Boredom was a problem, as I had no occupation other than to please myself, which was difficult with so few pleasures at hand. I sought my usual refuge in sleep, but one can only sleep so much in the day before one is robbed of it at night. There is nothing as depressing as those solitary Mongolian hours with only the dog's snores for company. In search of occupation I set about making the house more to my taste so that I might take some pleasure in being in it. Sorry would have wept to see my poor efforts, but I discovered that it didn't take much to please me when there was no excess of comfort. I rearranged the scant furniture and pushed the pile of furs that was my bed to the corner of the room. Mai said she thought it very strange to move things around, as in the ger everything had its own place and was never changed. She was very impressed with Natsuko's parting gift to me and brought Xue to see it and to taste the honey that had solidified in the cold. Xue said that honey kept better in a clay pot, but that it was a very attractive thing. I soon forgot the insult attached to the gift and found the sweetness of the honey a welcome addition to the bitter Russian tea.

I hid the preserved monkey embryo from Ichyo in Xue's wedding chest and hoped never to see it again. Amongst my other presents I had my knife from Hideo, the lychees from Sorry and a cashmere blanket from Itani, my birth-marked stepsister. I put my leather writing case on top of the chest so that I would not forget to take it with me when the chance of escape came.

Most of my clothes were unsuitable for the weather, so to cheer the place up, I hung them around the walls of my bedroom as Mai had hers in the ger. Luckily my riding breeches were warm and did not look out of place in my new home. I wore them with the del, a Mongolian knee-length tunic belted at the waist with a coloured sash worn by both men and women. Dels were padded with felt and buttoned to the neck to keep out the cold.

Mai got caught up in the idea of decorating and brought some lengths of red and white felt which she hung on the walls around my bed. The colours disturbed me, calling to my mind blood and bandages, and soon they began to inform my dreams. In one of them I was being swept away by a fast-flowing river, while all the women from my life stood along the bank dressed in lengths of fabric that flapped in the wind like tattered fragments of the Japanese flag. I frantically called to them as the water dragged me relentlessly down its cold reaches, but my voice was silenced by the thundering juggernaut of the river. I was desperate for Sorry to see me, but she was lost in an opium sleep on the river's bank and did not stir. My birth mother was looking away from the river towards my father's house and I knew that she chose not to see me. Natsuko and Shimako stood side by side holding hands like children. They smiled coldly as I passed, their painted lips blood red against the whiteness of their powdered faces. Mai tried to help me but was distracted by her children and I was swept away.

In my waking hours I prayed for summer to come. Mai said that I would be amazed by the blueness of the sky when it did arrive. She said we would spend our days warmed by the sun and our evenings in the light of a hundred fires. Her favourite time was in the summer when they left Suiyuan to follow their stock as they grazed the vast grasslands. She thought I would enjoy the nomadic life for apart from never having met anyone who hated the cold as much as I did, she was sure that I would not be bored. I looked forward with Mai to those approaching months more than she could have imagined. I knew that nothing would go well for me until my blood warmed and I could walk without kowtowing to the wind.

In the first month of our marriage a celebration was arranged so that all of Kanjurjab's people could offer their congratulations to us. An evening of feasting, songs and storytelling was to take place in the gers of Kanjurjab's family. Xue said that it would mark my transformation into a true Mongolian wife. I had spent only the briefest of times with my two sisters-in-law yet it was enough to know that I had no desire to be like them. Jon's wife Nandak had sweetness in her nature but no sense, while Boria's wife Alta was too like Xue to appeal to me.

On the night of the festivities along with Kanjurjab I was to visit each ger to be formally greeted and to sample the food and entertainment. As most of his tribe was related to him, it would be a long night, one that Mai said would not end until the last star had left the sky.

Xue for once seemed content and involved herself in the preparations. She brewed me an infusion of nutmeg to heat my blood and presented me with the gift of a black jade pendant. The ornament, a token from her mother, had been given to her when she had left Manchuria to marry Tsgotbaatar. She did not seem at all sad at the loss of the necklace but handed it over quickly and without ceremony as though she were being relieved of a burden.

'Take it, take it,' she said, pushing it into my hands and waving away my thanks. She said that when the time came I in my turn should give it to the bride of my firstborn son. Xue appeared to be hurrying through her life ticking off tasks from a great list that she felt obliged to complete. It was as though she had a secret desire to fulfil all her obligations, so that she might be free to die and enjoy a happier reincarnation. Perhaps the handing on of the pendant represented an important task on that list.

I must say that in its extreme simplicity the jewel was splendid. It was polished to a fine sheen with the sacred lotus Nelumbo carved at its heart. I had never seen a jade so dark, but it made me sad to think that I would not have the son Xue wished me. I have never found a place in which to hide the pain of my sterility from myself and have often wished there was a time limit on memory. As I accepted her gift, I felt sorry to deceive Xue and was astonished at the depth of my guilt.

I sensed that it stirred some pride in her that her only son had taken a wife who, like herself, had been chosen from China's soil. I could have made an alliance with Xue, but she was a difficult woman to get along with. I respected her stoicism, a quality akin to courage, but her sense of duty was so strong that I could not imagine her understanding or forgiving my escape when I made it. She believed that we should accept our fate, but what mother would feel sympathy for the wife who deserts her son? I think that Xue had always been unhappy in Mongolia. Filled with duty and religion, she had spent her days in medicine making and prayer, defending her heart against the very idea of pain. She was a living reminder of what could happen to me if I did not act on my desires.

I thanked her for the beautiful pendant and hung it on its silken thread around my neck where its weight between my breasts reminded me of Natsuko's pearl. I wondered if my stepmother thought of me when she wore her claimed-back treasure.

As though she had been reading my thoughts Xue said, 'Your life is here now, Yoshiko; it is better not to think of the past. It will only make you sad to remember the family you may never see again.'

I asked her how it had been for her to leave her family behind and take up such a different way of life.

'Well,' she said, 'one is always on display in Mongolia; I miss the comforting shadows of my Chinese home. I am a woman who does not smile much, and people like you better if you smile.'

It was the nearest Xue ever came to admitting her misery to me.

Before dusk on the evening of the feast, with her cheeks whipped to red by the wind, Mai blew into the house. She said she had come to take me to Kanjurjab, who would lie with me before the festivities. She seemed very excited about it and explained to me how I should go about pleasing him.

'Don't worry, Yoshiko,' she said, 'you cannot remain a virgin forever and nothing is as bad as we imagine it to be in our fears.'

Although I understood better than most the place of a concubine in a man's life I did not wish to hurt Mai and I said as much to her.

'I am glad it is you,' she said. 'I always knew he would take a wife. It is good we are friends. I will help you as much as I can and you will soon learn all you need to know and become used to it.'

I wished briefly that I had been that innocent girl of Mai's imagination, but only briefly. I knew that my escape would be born out of my experience, and that innocence was the last thing that would be of use to me when the time came to leave. But once again I was disturbed by how affected I was by these simple, too easily deceived people of Kanjurjab's tribe.

Mai said that Kanjurjab was not a hard man to please because his heart was open. He took his pleasure in covering a naked woman and although it was cold, I shouldn't be concerned because we would lie on fur near the fire and I would be well covered by my husband.

'He has a fine big body,' she said with pride, 'so you will not lose too much heat.'

I did not want to lose any, but the anticipation of intercourse with Kanjurjab excited me. I had been celibate for too long and it would surely be the most pleasurable thing available to me in Suiyuan. My healthy appetite for scx, food and adventure had been starved for too long. I remembered my brother, all those years ago in China, telling me I must have been a warrior in a previous life. Things would certainly have been easier for me if I had been born a man, yet, given the choice, I would not relinquish those senses and experiences peculiar to a woman. A man will never know that mysterious sisterhood we have with nature, or the exquisite touch of silk against a heavy breast, or the power that comes with knowing you are beautiful. And then again, who would give up the vanilla-scented skin of a woman, a fragrance so delectable that no distillation of oil or nectar could match it? I envy men their power and their freedom, but not their minds or their bodies.

Mai advised me not to talk too much while lovemaking, in case Kanjurjab thought he was not pleasing me. 'In any case,' she confided, 'no man likes a chattering wife.'

She gave me a scarf made from thick wool to keep my head warm when it was time to go from ger to ger. I thanked her and said, 'It is a day for presents, Mai, and this is a very practical one.'

'Well, your ears could freeze without it,' she said, 'and it will hide your short hair.' She took my hand and led me, bending in the wind, to my husband's ger.

Kanjurjab was sitting on a saddle at the back of the ger in a space usually reserved for honoured guests. Mai left quietly as he beckoned me to sit beside him on a deep fur rug. I couldn't help noticing that this positioned me below him so that I had to look up to speak to him. It has been my experience in life that men, whatever they may say, prefer a woman in this position, and can be encouraged to pity or generosity better while we look up

84

to them. Lucky for us, I suppose, that such simple ploys often reap generous rewards.

Mai was right: Kanjurjab was a large man both in height and weight. He was a good four inches taller than most Mongolian men, who only looked big when on their small horses. He had huge hands with dirty nails and a surprisingly benevolent face. Although we were of a similar age, he looked younger and reminded me a little of Hideo when he was pretending to be not the least bit interested in me. His expression was nervous and irritated at the same time, like a fish when netted but still in the water.

We sat in silence for some minutes and then without looking at me he said he would like some tea. I offered him vodka from the flask I had stolen from Kawashima, but he made no reply, waiting instead for me to get up and serve him the tea he had requested. When I did, he handed it back to me without tasting it and said that I had forgotten the salt. I generously laced the milky brew with the preserve and placed it into his hand.

'Thank you, Yoshiko,' he said. 'I hope you will learn my tastes before too long. I cannot be expected to explain every little thing to you.'

'I hope so too,' I replied. 'I have always been a quick learner and would not wish to bore you with the tedium of becoming my teacher. Boredom is surely one of the worst things in life, don't you think?'

Silence fell again as he sat slurping the horrible tea and looking into the distance. Despite his pomposity I liked him. He had a boyish sweetness that he couldn't disguise and on that evening at least, in the forgiving firelight, I found his lack of pretension and the rudeness of his ger exciting. Even though I would have preferred a little more danger in his make-up I reminded myself that there were things about him that I did admire. He was known in his tribe for his skill at mounted archery and no one could deny his fine horsemanship or his tenderness with Mai.

85

It occurred to me that Kanjurjab, used to having everything done for him, was waiting for me to prepare myself for him by removing my clothes. Perhaps he wanted me to lie at his feet and wait to be mounted. I had no intention of undressing in his near freezing world, so I decided to take matters into my own hands and show him that with a little imagination a fully clothed woman can be as exciting as a naked one. I knelt before him and released the silver buckle of the Russian belt that he always wore at his waist and it fell clanking to the floor. Slowly, one by one, I undid the loops on the buttons of his long del and, except for his thick leather boots, I found him naked underneath. I began to softly bite and lick my way up the insides of his legs, taking my time and placing my tongue where past experience had shown it would give the most pleasure. Behind the knee I knew to be a particular favourite, and the shallow cup where leg meets groin in a tender run. The muscles on his legs were hard from a lifetime of riding and contrasted strangely with his plump skin, which both smelled and tasted of butter.

He made no sound but set his legs apart on the saddle, tightening his grip to balance himself. I reached his member, took it into my mouth and licked him to a full erection. He began to moan alarmingly and I released him, but he grabbed my head and guided me back to finish what I had started. After a little I rose, pulled up my del and held its hem in my mouth while I undid my breeches, then I squatted on his lap allowing him to penetrate me fully. As we rocked on the saddle I dug my feet into the thick fur of the rug and held my hands above my head in the way that I had seen him do when riding without reins. He grasped my buttocks, pulling me closer at each rock of the saddle until there was no space left between us. As I pushed my tongue into his mouth, caressing his with little darting movements, I ran my nails down his back and moaned his name. I took satisfaction in his noisy climax, for I would have been surprised not to have been able to lead the boy to wherever I wanted him to go. Throughout the satisfying bout I had kept my del on and the scarf Mai had given me around my neck. It was the warmest I had been since arriving in Suiyuan.

It was some time before Kanjurjab spoke a word. He busied himself with his buttons and his belt, then finally he said, 'How did a young girl like you know so well what would please me, Yoshiko?'

I told him that in Japan we were shown in sketches how to give our husbands variety and pleasure in lovemaking, so that they would not tire of us before making their children. I often surprised myself with how easily I could make a good lie. It would be true to say that lies have always been a useful currency to me. One must be careful though, as used without caution a lie will sometimes reveal a truth.

Kanjurjab grunted in a questioning way at the novel idea of having to be taught sex. He slipped the flask from my pocket, poured me a shot of vodka into the cap and took a long swig from the flask himself.

'I hope you saw a lot of sketches, Yoshiko,' he said.

We laughed together and at that moment became friends. I knew that I would never desire him enough to choose to spend my life with him, but he did slip into my history retaining my friendship and goodwill. I doubt though that I kept his.

'We will have a good life and many children together,' he said. 'You were made to produce strong sons, Yoshiko. Your hips may be a little lean but your spirit is strong. Mongolia is a country blessed by the gods; you will be happy here now that you know your duty.'

There was no true answer I could give him either about duty or the tribe of sons he expected me to produce for him so I changed the subject.

'Will you teach me to ride?' I asked him.

'If you think you need it,' he replied, and we both roared with laughter.

When I next saw Mai, she asked tentatively if I was all right. I said that I was and that I had done my best not to chatter.

'You will be a good wife,' she said.

I told her that no one could be as good a wife as she was a concubine. She giggled at the flattery, but my conscience was not eased.

Airag and Russian Tea with Salt

I would say that most of the Mongolians I have known would be lost in any society other than their own. Their sky, earth, rivers and mountains are as much a part of them as any family member and are treated with equal respect. Land and family are one and the same thing and Mongolians rarely question their place in either. On the vast plains of their inclement realm, surviving the elements breeds in them a kinship with nature and each other that transcends the daily struggle of their lives. While I, permanently seeking escape, felt subdued by the vast acreage of the Mongolian sky, they regarded it as Father Heaven's blanket. Their frozen earth was a mother who bore their weight without complaint. Locked in a symbiosis of blood and soil, Mongolians need their tribes, their elemental gods and their testing land more than any people I have ever known.

And so it was remarkable that my brother-in-law Jon put this oneness, the only life he could imagine, at risk because of his desire for me. This desire, persistent in him as hunger, set him at odds with himself, and eventually turned him from a loyal family member into my faithful creature. Since my wedding day I had been aware that he was attracted to me and although he had done his best to avoid me in Suiyuan I had often felt the heat of his concentration. There had been times when his focus on me was so intense I was convinced it would not go unnoticed. Yet apart from a greeting or two we had hardly spoken.

Only an hour after I first had intercourse with Kanjurjab I settled on Jon as the one who would guide me from Suiyuan to civilisation. We were in his ger drinking the awful airag and listening to a long and dreary story about Mongolians crushing their captive enemies beneath boards as they feasted on top of them. Tsgotbaatar was wandering around in a daze telling his own unintelligible story in a low mumble, while Xue sat next to her daughter Nandak, sipping tea. The ger was steamy with the heat of bodies and panting dogs. Mai kept smiling at me as though we were sharing a delightful secret, while Kanjurjab with his hand on my shoulder listened to the story intently, as though he had never heard it before.

I became aware of Jon's stare and as our eyes met and held for the briefest moment I knew that an opportunity had opened up to me. I knew too that my choosing him as my accomplice would be his downfall. Yet despite my not wanting to hurt him, he was my chance, perhaps my only one. I believed then as I do now that we should act on our desires or pay the price in bitterness and disappointment. You cannot blame the fox for killing chickens, he is just being a good fox. We are all animals and to survive well should be each individual's aim. I have often wondered why nature included guilt in our make-up; perhaps it was a joke.

Sensing that it would take no time at all to seduce Jon, I reminded myself that I must take things slowly or I might just as quickly lose him. An appetite fulfilled too soon is easily forgotten. Far better that I should linger over the preparation of his seduction so that the uniqueness of the delicacy he desired would remain with him long after his sexual possession of me. My boredom with Suiyuan receded as I began to plan my seduction of Jon. Because the cost to him would be so great, I knew that I would more easily achieve what I wanted in the name of love. This lesson I learnt from Yamaga. I had to become mistress of Jon's feelings so that for my sake he would risk everything that he had previously held dear. Such sacrifices are usually made in the courts of attachment or loyalty and can take years to mature. But love, if the circumstances are right, can succeed just as well.

Although still young by the time Jon came into my life, I had lost count of the men I had made love with. Some were more easily called to mind than others, but I was, I believe, a fair judge of men's strengths and weaknesses. I knew Jon to be a good enough man, but I recognised in him a run of unsteadiness that would make him pliant and easy to manage. His sexual prowess, however, was something one could not guess at accurately. It does not follow that handsome men make good lovers or ugly men bad ones.

Jon was neither plain nor handsome. He was short with a slim, muscled body and skin as brown as tobacco. He had lean lips, a strong jaw line and eyes as dark as raisins and as clear as a baby's. Without those eyes you would not have picked him out of a crowd.

Like Kanjurjab, Jon was a fine horseman, good at wrestling and archery. Although they were close friends, when it came to sport and riding they were as competitive as brothers. Despite the difference in their height and bulk, their wrestling matches were never a foregone conclusion, as Jon frequently conquered Kanjurjab's stature with his agility.

He was married to Xue's youngest daughter Nandak, a hardworking girl, popular because she danced rather than walked about the place. Nandak seemed to enjoy the company of everyone she came into contact with and could often be seen tumbling around with the younger children or running with her dogs. I think that she was a simple girl who didn't have the sense to be critical about anything. I never once saw her without a smile on her face, which was a pretty one with a tiny squashed nose and soft plump lips. As a couple, she and Jon appeared no more than content with each other, but then none of us outside such unions truly knows what goes on in them and there may have been love. Jon had two concubines of about the same age as Nandak. He had three daughters with his concubines and no child as yet with Nandak. I couldn't tell which daughter belonged to which concubine, but it hardly mattered as they were, all five of them, inseparable.

And so it was that on the same night my husband first took me to his bed I began to plot my escape from cold, cold Mongolia. It had been an eventful day in more ways than one. I went to bed tired but optimistic. Rolled in a fur with a dog at my side, I drifted into a deep sleep and dreamt that I was sitting by the carp pool in Kawashima's garden. There was a delicious basket of fruit at my side and my fingers were stained pink from the ripe cherries I had been eating. I was wearing the mother-of-pearl earrings that Hideo's betrothed had given me and on my finger, set now in a ring, was my lucky bee in amber. Natsuko was picking little blue plums from branches that she had to stretch up her arms to reach. She was wearing her pearl which looked so dark and beautiful nestled against the shimmering silk of her kimono that I longed for it all over again. Fluttering nearby was the most gloriously co-loured butterfly. It settled on the cuff of Natsuko's robe and I knew that it was Shimako. She was happy now, transformed into colours more elaborate than the kimonos of even the most indulged geisha. She was the Shimako of legend, benign and beautiful, admired by all who looked on her. My body felt relaxed and totally at ease in the warm sunshine. As I reached into the basket for a perfect apricot, Natsuko gave me the sweetest smile I had ever seen.

I woke full of longing, knowing that even if I did escape Mongolia, I would never be able to go home again. The fire had gone out. The room, dank and cold, was gloomy with shadows. I tried to comfort myself with the truth that I had never found domesticity in life as satisfying as in my dreams. But I could not quite throw off the peculiar emptiness that homesickness inflicts on our hearts.

The following day I started riding lessons with Kanjurjab and from that time on I took every opportunity that I could to be near Jon. He would often be in the corral when we returned the horses after our ride, and while he spoke with Kanjurjab I would brush against him as if by accident. Sometimes I would bend to stroke his dog and careful not to stare too brazenly, I would look up to him and hold his gaze for a moment. I never forgot to touch the pulses on my wrists and the little cup at the base of my neck with chrysanthemum oil so that even when not in his sight he could sense me nearby. Once I discovered him breathing me in, an expression on his face as though I were the essence of attar of roses. I liked the way his body became still in my company, as though he were not quite sure what to do with it, and the way he couldn't help showing off to me when he rode in my line of sight. Sometimes he would ride out with Kanjurjab and me, pointing out little things to me in the way you might offer the sweetest meats imaginable to a favourite relative. As far as I could tell, Kanjurjab was completely unaware of Jon's interest in me. I think the idea that his brother-in-law wanted his wife was something that would never have occurred to him.

Boria, my other brother-in-law, would occasionally be in the corral when we returned the horses there. His greeting to me was always given unsmilingly, as though he was addressing a child who might at any moment become too familiar with him. He was only a little older than Kanjurjab but appeared more severe, as though he took life and its burdens too much to heart. He seemed content enough in his marriage to Xue's eldest daughter Alta, who was as serious in nature as her sister Nandak was light-hearted. Boria's concubine Dokus was the only truly beautiful Mongolian woman I ever met.

I often wished that it had been Boria and not Jon who desired me, as I found his indifference and lack of sentimentality attractive. Jon was a boy compared to him and always looked diminished in my eyes when standing next to Boria. But men like Boria never put love above honour, so he would have been of no use to me. Still, one cannot help desire, it will settle in the most useless places. Perhaps I was attracted to Boria because he reminded me of Yamaga with his hard body, thick sensuous lips and the shock

93

of dark hair that complemented his eyes, which like my own were the purple-black of sloes.

As the weather grew warmer the sky changed from grey into startling cobalt blue. Great fountains of clouds turned pink at dusk and the moon appeared whiter than ever. Xue said with resignation that it was a sign that summer was upon us and soon we would be on the move. Already the single-pole travelling tents were being stacked on the carts, while mounds of shapeless lumps of soap to supply our summer needs were being fashioned from acrid butter. As the days became warmer, the preparations increased and Mai said that I should select the furs I would take to sleep on. She made me a pair of light felt boots and advised me to take my honey cask as she thought that its sweetness in my tea would compensate me for the irritations of the nomadic life.

But Tsgotbaatar died suddenly, and our plans to leave for the short summer on the grasslands were put on hold. Nandak found him by the south well stretched out on the ground as though he was asleep. Only moments before he had seemed his usual self and had been seen urinating by a pyramid of dried dung. Nandak realised she had come across a grave situation, but she couldn't disguise her excitement at being the centre of attention with her news.

Xue later said that Tsgotbaatar's blood had become so rich that a clot must have reached his heart and stopped it beating. She was certain that he would have been felled without pain, and she hoped her own end might be as merciful. She advised me not to say his name for some days, as around the time of his death she had seen a sudden spark in her fire which meant that Tsgotbaatar was not yet in the lower world and might be looking for the soul of a loved one to take there with him. She said that if we did not weep his name nor grieve too deeply he would soon settle.

I went to see him laid out on his finest white fur, his dogs quiet for once, sitting beside him with downcast eyes. His face, which in life had expressed bewilderment, in death had settled into a replica of Kanjurjab's spoiled one. No one could find his concubine Kara, but as she often disappeared for hours at a time, that was not unusual. Xue said that it was a good thing that she could not be found, for had she been there she would have been as confused as an old dog looking for a bone long since buried. Sometimes Kara's mind settled in the past so that she could not deal with the present. It was to be hoped that she would stay away long enough for Tsgotbaatar's soul to start on its voyage to the lower world, as her weeping would only delay his journey. She added gloomily that the company of ghosts, no matter how loved and respected the dead person had been in life, was unsettling.

It was impossible to know what was in Xue's mind as she gazed, seemingly emotionless, at the still body of her husband. I could not stop the mental picture of her ticking off the final and heaviest task on her list. I believe that had she known about it, Xue would have taken to heart the Indian custom of *suttee* where the widow, having in the absence of a husband no further purpose in life, throws herself on the funeral pyre. I always had the impression of Xue that death could not come too soon for her. Her stoicism and sense of duty acted as a warning to me. I had no wish to find myself widowed and waiting for death in Suiyuan with no colour in my mouth or eyes.

An hour or so after Tsgotbaatar's death, Kanjurjab called Boria and Jon to his ger. The women were excluded as they huddled together tending their fire, crying themselves blind in their lamentations. For the first time since I had known him I heard Kanjurjab's voice hard with anger as he sent his boys packing for laughing at their play.

In every society that I have lived in, it is the men who make decisions and organise the formalities of death. It would seem that it is for women to give in to their weaker natures and to wail their grief. For myself I do not like to join in with the ebb of life, it collides uncomfortably with my instinct to live it.

Mai invited me to sit with Xue and Boria's wife Alta, but I was restless and wanted to walk. As I left them crouched around the fire in Alta's ger it occurred to me that Tsgotbaatar's wife and daughters had not shed a tear. The camp was droning with sobs from every other ger, but Tsgotbaatar's home was almost silent. Mai's little eyes were swollen with crying, but I think her tears were more for Kanjurjab than for Tsgotbaatar. The truth was that Tsgotbaatar, both as husband and father, had left Xue and her girls long before his death and they were already used to his absence.

Some hours later I came across Kara at the back of my house. She was banging her head against the wall, calling Tsgotbaatar's name over and over, pulling wildly at her matted hair. Her face was covered in blood and as I eased her away from the hard stone wall she sank to the ground, moaning softly. I wondered how she had learnt of Tsgotbaatar's death. I don't think anyone had told her; perhaps she knew it instinctively, like her master's dogs knew it. I took her inside, cleaned her wound, gave her vodka from my flask and left her to her grief.

That night a pale moon drifted high in the dark sky. It lit Suiyuan in a ghostly light and set the dogs barking. Mai said that it signified that a pure heart had left the earth that day. She told me that every Mongolian had a small piece of the great god Tengger set in the crown of their heads, and that that little piece of pure energy had a counterpart star in the heavens which at death goes out. She said that she could tell that Tsgotbaatar's star had left, and pointed north to where the sky seemed full of stars. Then she put my hand on her stomach so that I could feel her baby moving. When I said the child seemed to be very strong she agreed and told me that was because it was a boy.

Our departure for the grasslands was put off until the funeral rites had taken place and Tsgotbaatar's family had performed the proper prayers and made the appropriate offerings. In an unexpected stroke of luck Kanjurjab, busy with arrangements and shocked that he was now head of not only his family, but also his tribe, asked Jon to ride out with me. He explained to Jon that although I was fearless on horseback, I was without skill and did not yet understand a horse's nature. And so it was that through Tsgotbaatar's death my episode with Jon found its beginning.

At first Jon was polite and formal with me. He showed me none of the same kindness that he had when Kanjurjab had been with us. I expect that he was doing his best to resist the pull in my direction, but he might as well have fished in grass, for he did not have the steel in his nature to resist me. He knew that a liaison with me would break the ties of both family and friendship for ever, but I knew he would not be able to help himself.

I welcomed the warmth of the summer in the hope that it would be my first and last one in Mongolia. I was determined to be gone by the time winter set in. If I waited too long my journey out would be even worse than the one that had delivered me to Suiyuan.

On one of my longer than usual rides with Jon, we came across a tall octagonal tower that sat surreal and elegant in the newly green landscape. Jon said that when he was a boy he and his friends held races around this charming old pagoda, and once he had fallen from the top of it and been knocked unconscious. I asked him if he had been badly hurt and he said that he had broken his arm and that to this day it was still a little twisted.

'Let me see,' I said.

He pushed his sleeve up and showed me his arm, which turned, as though offended, from his body. I ran my finger slowly down the length of it pausing on the pulse at his wrists, and he moaned softly and took a step backwards.

'I'm sorry to offend you, Jon,' I said, as though hurt at his withdrawal.

He looked at me for a long time, then he said quietly, 'Nothing about you offends me, Yoshiko. My head and heart are full of all the things about you that do not offend me.'

'Don't you know that it is the same for me,' I said. 'My head and heart are always full of you, Jon.'

'Simply by speaking, Yoshiko, we betray your husband and my friend,' he said sadly.

'Yes, that's true,' I said, 'and betrayal is hard, Jon, even for me who did not want this marriage. If women could choose I would not have chosen Kanjurjab. I can hardly bear my life here. I think that I will die young with the harshness of it.'

'Don't speak of death, Yoshiko,' he said, taking my hand and placing its palm against his cheek. 'I cannot bear to think of your death, although I suspect that you may be the death of me.'

I laughed to distract him from the idea, saying that I would never choose to hurt him and the thought of his death was too dark a thought for such a light summer day.

'I will speak of it only once more,' he answered, 'for I must tell you that even before I met you, Yoshiko, I knew you; that is why I couldn't take my eyes from your face on your wedding day. You came to me in a dream on the night that I married Nandak.'

'You dreamt of another woman on your wedding night, Jon!' I teased him.

'It was not the sort of dream you think,' he said. 'I did not see your face in this dream, but the moment I set eyes on you in Port Arthur I knew that you were one and the same person.'

'What sort of dream was it?' I asked.

He told me that I had come to him disguised as the shadow of a woman with short hair and beautiful breasts. As Nandak slept beside him, I had taken a knife from my sleeve and mortally wounded him. As he lay dying, I had stolen a clot of his blood and put it in a phial that hung around my neck. He had called to me as I left his ger, begging me to stay, but I went without a backwards glance. He remembers feeling strangely sad to see me go. When he woke, Nandak told him he had been weeping in his sleep.

'What a horrible dream. How you must fear me, Jon.'

'I both fear and love you, Yoshiko, and between this fear and love I have never felt more alive.'

That same afternoon I made love with him on the hard earth at the base of the pagoda. He said that the scent of me was like no other woman he had ever known and that my fragrance would have the power to wake him even from the sleep of death.

Jon was a sensual and romantic person who despite his rough appearance had a heart to match the most sensitive of Japanese poets. He had spent his youth trying to hide the softness of his nature in a society where it was not considered masculine to show emotion or be quick to tears. Sorry would have liked him and been sad at how I intended to use him. Natsuko, of course, would not have been surprised at my cruelty, while Kawashima would have been amused.

A truthful woman will admit that to be made love to by a man who loves you so much more completely than you do him is a most seductive and heart-warming experience, comparable perhaps to looking into a mirror and discovering yourself to be not only beautiful, but also alive with the sort of power that darkens your eyes and makes your skin glow. The feeling was new to me. Neither Kawashima nor any of the men he sent to me, including Yamaga, had been in love with me. I had often experienced feelings of sexual power when men addicted to my lovemaking would return time after time. But I had never before experienced this giving over of the whole self to the other, as Jon had given himself to me. I was delighted that my plan to get him to love me had worked so quickly and so well. Perhaps, though, he had loved me at first sight so that my task was accomplished even before begun. I have read of such things in Japanese literature and I believe that I loved Yamaga from the moment I first saw him. In Jon's love for me I was reminded of my own feelings for Yamaga and of the sickening pain I had suffered at the loss of him. I sensed that Jon would not have my powers of recovery, but of course he would live. In truth I was not the shadow woman of his dream and he would not be mortally wounded. Eventually we all learn that in the core of love lies the worm of tragedy. It is the way of attachment and cannot be avoided. Even Mai and Kanjurjab will be lost to each other at the end, for when love is established so is the seed of its eventual conclusion. Most people long for love and feel less than complete without it. They cannot settle until their twin is found because they are not enough for themselves. Since Yamaga I have done my best to avoid love, but then I am quick at learning life's lessons.

After that first time, not a day passed without our making love, usually by the pagoda, but sometimes in the green meadows where the grass smelled clean and made tiny cuts on our skin as we rolled naked on it. Jon was a considerate lover but too conventional to be exciting to me. I could have taught him how to please me better, but I wanted him to think me unskilled in such matters. In any case, Kanjurjab was proving an adept student and had called me to his bed several times since Tsgotbaatar's death. I think that he was eager for me to conceive, so that his father's star might be replaced in the heavens. If I had been able to, my life may have found its place on those bleak plains of Inner Mongolia. They say that women born in the Year of the Tiger make good mothers.

Meanwhile, Jon found caution hard and I worried that we would be discovered before my plan could be put into action. Throughout the day he would seek me out, talk to me with his head bent to one side, as though everything I said deserved his complete attention. It was as though he could not bear to have me out of his sight. Such captivation was what I wanted from him, but it did put us at risk. Sometimes, late into the night when everyone was sleeping, Jon would come to the house, quieten the growls of the dogs and cover me with his body until the thin dawn light seeped through the cracks in the shutters. I asked him what he told Nandak and his concubines about his night absences. He said that he didn't need to tell his concubines anything and that Nandak believed that since Tsgotbaatar's death he found it difficult to sleep and felt the need for solitary contemplation.

'Does she really believe that?' I asked doubtingly.

'How would I know?' he said. 'Her smile disguises everything she feels.'

I often saw Jon full of nervous energy, striding up and down between the gers as though he might explode with the knowledge of us. He was like a boy who had discovered in himself an unsuspected capacity for love and adventure and was fired with the thrill of it. He told me that he felt as though his blood was shouting and that he couldn't concentrate on even the simplest task. It surprised me that no one seemed to notice Jon's behaviour, but I thought it wise to draw him into my plan before his changed personality gave us away.

I chose my time well, waiting until just before we made love. Close at his side against the pagoda wall, I said that if I couldn't have him forever as my one true love, then I couldn't bear the torture of having to be near him every day. I would run away and be lost to him, even if it meant spending my life in misery.

'Where would you run to, Yoshiko?' he asked.

'I would run to China, Jon,' I said innocently, as though I had just thought of it. 'I could make a life there, although it would be a poor one without you.'

'You would die on the plains by yourself,' he said, touching my cheek lightly. 'For you, even summer nights in the open would be a burden. Without me to read the stars for you, how would you navigate?'

'Then come with me, Jon,' I said, 'take me out of Suiyuan so that we can have a life together. I cannot bear it here and when we are discovered, as we are bound to be, things will be the worse for us.'

Surprisingly, Jon put up no resistance to the idea of us leaving Suiyuan together. I think that at first the idea was like a fantasy that he enjoyed imagining and talking about. All true lovers dream of a future with the object of their desire and the idea of escape allowed Jon to imagine what his might be with me. It wasn't long before he came to believe that not only had it been his idea, but also that it was our only chance of spending our lives together. He said that he had the courage of love and was prepared to give up everything for the passion he believed to be ours. Although he was sorry to desert Nandak and his children, he was more ashamed of betraying

Kanjurjab. Despite the pain the severing of such strong ties would cause him, Jon would have paid any price to be with me.

With his blood up, he made a plan for us to slip away on the first night of the summer grazing. We would simply go on a ride and never return. The camp would be busy with the putting up of gers and preparing the first meal. It would be dark and we would have a few hours' start before anyone thought of looking for us. If we stayed longer, it would be impossible for us to be together at all, as Kanjurjab would resume his rides with me and I would be expected to sleep in my husband's ger.

Any plan we made would have its hazards, but Jon said that he would risk all three of his souls for me and that he loved me more than the stars in the heavens, more than Tengger himself. I echoed his words back to him but could not think that he believed them; they sounded empty and passionless to my ears.

People think me cruel, and they are right. I can be very cruel, but I am not without sympathy for my victims. I liked Jon, but I felt impelled to act on my own behalf. I readily confess to selfishness, something that we all repeat many times in our lives.

One morning Boria decided to ride with Jon and me to the pagoda. He had never joined us before and Jon was uneasy about it. Of course, Boria, who never did anything impulsively, had his reasons and we should have taken more care with where we led him that day than we did. Looking back I think perhaps he had noticed Jon's unnatural behaviour, or maybe he was suspicious without really knowing why. All he said was that it was a fine day for a ride and that he would enjoy the company.

When we reached the tower Jon and Boria raced around it as they had done as boys and in a light moment Boria encouraged me to join in. It made my head spin and I had to dismount and lie on the ground with my eyes closed until the sky had stopped dancing. I looked up to catch Boria staring at my prostrate body, and then at the young nettles flattened to the ground where Jon and I had lain the afternoon before. His mood changed abruptly and I knew that he had guessed our secret. He dismissed my offer of vodka and rode home between Jon and me without speaking.

If it hadn't been for Boria, I would have made my escape with Jon and left him in Port Arthur to make what he could of his life. I had already begun sewing my money into the lining of the del I planned to wear on the journey into China. Jon was deciding on which horses would be best and which dogs to take with us. We would probably only need to sleep one night in the open, two at the most. It depended on how far the tribe travelled on that first day before settling on a camp. The dogs would keep us warm as we slept and would warn of intruders. Apart from the horses and dogs, Jon would take the three nuggets of gold that had come to him as part of Nandak's dowry, and for luck a small statue fashioned in silver of Maitreya, the Buddha of the future. He gave me the three gold weights and said that I should hide them on my person. As Nandak would notice the missing Buddha he would bring it with him on the night of our escape. I did not tell him about my own money but said that I would take all the jewellery I possessed, including the jade pendant that Xue had given me. Jon said, 'Leave the pendant, Yoshiko. Kanjurjab should give it to the woman destined to be his true wife.'

With our plans made and only a few days to go before we started our journey, I was confident of success. I decided that I would return the gold nuggets to Jon when we were safely across the border. He would need them to finance his new life, wherever he chose to make it. Before I left him I would place them on the pillow next to his as he slept; it would ease my conscience and save me from having to see his pain.

I told Jon that with so little time to go before we would be together for ever, we shouldn't risk our plan with the chance of discovery. Boria may have had suspicions but he had no proof of anything. Jon agreed and we decided to stop the rides, and his nightly visits to the house.

But he couldn't keep away and one night after we had made love and he lay sleeping, slumped across me, the dogs gave a low growl and I opened my eyes to find Boria standing over us. He didn't say a word, just stared for a little, then turned and left the room as quietly as he had come.

Jon slept on but I lay awake, anxious that by morning Boria would have sought out Kanjurjab and informed him of his wife and brother-in-law's betrayal. Yet something told me that might not be his way of dealing with the situation. Boria was not the sort of man to rush into things without thinking them over first. He would have no fears for my punishment, but he was fond of Jon and would not wish to see him disgraced and banished from his family and friends. It was likely that Jon and I would be gone before Boria decided what to do with his newfound knowledge. In any case, it would be pointless for me to appeal to him to keep our secret. He alone would decide and no amount of pleading from a mere woman would affect his decision.

When Jon woke I didn't tell him of Boria's visit. Instead I sent him back to his ger with a kiss and the scent of my chrysanthemum oil lingering on his skin.

As it happened, Boria, who looked like a man who'd had a sleepless night, made his intentions clear to me that same morning. I was sitting on a pile of furs, smoking one of my hoarded Turkish cigarettes, when he came striding into the house. Without even the formality of a greeting, he told me what his plans for my future were.

'It was an unfortunate day that Kanjurjab settled on you for a wife,' he said coldly. 'Unfortunate for my family and I suppose for you too, Yoshiko.'

I nodded in agreement. 'Blame me if you will, Boria, but you cannot fashion love out of the air. I do not love my husband, nor do I like his way of life, and those two things will never change.'

'Only because you will not let them,' he said. 'You are too determined for a woman, too without duty and humility. You will cause trouble wherever you go, Yoshiko, because it is not in your nature to accept your fate.'

'I agree, Boria,' I said. 'But what is to be done about it, especially as I have no desire to change my nature? Whatever you plan to do about it, I will not spend my life in this desperate place. Jon is the only one who will help me escape it.'

'You care nothing for Jon,' he said scornfully. 'You will use him and desert him without a thought.'

'I care, Boria,' I replied. 'But I am desperate. I will do what needs to be done to avoid living in your frigid world. It is my nature to free myself, just as it is yours to be bound by duty.'

Boria snorted in disgust. 'No matter how clever you think you have been, Yoshiko, you have simply overwhelmed a less devious nature than your own. Jon is too good a person to believe that anyone could plan what you have without love being the spur. I am angry with him for being such a fool, but I won't let you use him so badly.'

'You can't stop Jon helping me,' I said. 'We will find a way no matter how difficult you make it.'

'I know that,' he said flatly. 'But I can save Jon from a life he would find not worth living. When you leave, Yoshiko, it will be without him.'

'But my dilemma is that in order to go, I need Jon to take me.'

'Jon is not the only one who can take you out of Suiyuan. I have a plan that will help you leave tonight without his knowledge, one with a greater chance of success than you would have had with him.'

I was suspicious of Boria; he was a clever man, sure of himself and determined. I could see myself as the victim of his plan.

'So it will be the honourable Boria who helps me to leave my husband?' I asked quietly.

'It will be me,' he said. 'Not because I care what happens to you, Yoshiko, but because it is the lesser of two evils.'

'Still, Boria,' I said, 'I am Kanjurjab's wife, and you put yourself and your family at great risk by assisting me.'

'Like you, Yoshiko, it seems I have no choice. This way only Kanjurjab's pride will be hurt, but without his family Jon's life will be a poor thing not worth the living, Nandak's heart will be broken and my family will be damaged beyond repair. So, providing you do exactly as I say, you will get what you want so badly and in time we will all recover from the disgrace of our connection with you.'

'It seems that I don't have much choice, Boria, so tell me your plan and perhaps I will agree.'

'Firstly, Jon must not come to you tonight, you must make certain of that. Be ready to leave as soon as it is dark, keep the fire going and the dogs in as normal so that no one's attention is drawn to the house. If you do as I say and make no goodbyes to anyone, my plan will work.'

'I will be waiting for you, Boria, but if you let me down it will be you as well as Jon who pays the price,' I warned.

'Bring only what you can carry with ease,' he said, ignoring my threat. 'And remember, nothing is accomplished yet. We will be in danger until the moment that I return here unseen and without you.'

After he left, I felt excited by the thought of where I might find myself when the sun next rose. Somehow I knew that Boria was right when he said his plan had a better chance of success than Jon's would have. He had a cool head on his shoulders, whereas Jon's, hot with passion and romance, was blind to the true danger of our situation.

I believe that Boria cared for Jon a great deal, but his willingness to help me stemmed more from his fear that his whole family would be torn apart if Jon ran off with me. In Kanjurjab's small tribe, the chain of family and honour was linked by blood and loyalty and these two were considered paramount to a decent life. The stain on the family from the chain breaking in such a fashion would humiliate them all for years to come. By helping me, Boria sought to avoid that humiliation. I would be the only miscreant, a woman without loyalty who had deceived them.

They would hold my foreign blood to blame and never return to Japan for a bride.

That afternoon under a deliciously hot sun I rode to the pagoda with Jon. He said that he found me distracted, so I told him that my mind was full of our plans and that it was excitement and not distraction that he sensed. I said too that he should not come to me that night as Mai had told me that Kanjurjab intended to visit me himself. I knew that Jon would fret his night away thinking about it, but I could not risk Boria's plan. Seeing the pain on his face, I kissed him tenderly and told him that Kanjurjab meant less than nothing to me, but we should not risk our future together for the sake of one night. We made a sad sort of love and held each other close. Jon could not know that I was saying goodbye to him, but when he looked back on it he would understand that it was my farewell, even though a little later we made a second more vigorous coupling. As we left the pagoda I leant across the divide between the horses and locked hands with him; we didn't let go of each other until Suiyuan came into sight. I was full of pity for him, but my resolve to be done with all things Mongolian was as strong as ever. As we were dusting the horses down he put his hand possessively over my breast.

'Remember, Yoshiko,' he said pleadingly, 'think only of me tonight.' I took up his other hand and slipped it under my del onto my naked breast and promised him that I would. I wanted to comfort him, to postpone his misery for one more night.

Mai was sitting outside my house watching her boys play. Her stomach and breasts were swollen with her pregnancy, she looked tired out, as though the child in her womb was using her up. She greeted me and said she had come to ask me to comfort Kanjurjab who was still sad at the loss of Tsgotbaatar. He was in his ger and nothing she could do seemed to cheer him at all. I put my arm around her and told her that I would do my best. I would like to have taken a good leave of her, but as that wasn't possible, I contented myself with a sisterly hug. I told her to rest on my bed for a while but she said she had to help Xue pack up her medicines, as we would be leaving for the summer grazing in two days' time.

I didn't find Kanjurjab sad, although he did seem eager to be distracted. 'Turn the page of your picture book, Yoshiko, and show me something new,' he said.

For the first and the last time in his presence I stood before him and slowly removed my clothes, leaving only Xue's pendant hanging heavily between my breasts. Kanjurjab was wearing a long unbuttoned del, he was smoking one of my Turkish cigarettes, watching me with interest. I took the cigarette out of his mouth and drew deeply on it before throwing it onto the fire. Opening his coat, I pressed my naked body against his half-clothed one, putting my hands on his buttocks and pushing us together so that I could feel him stirring. He said he was surprised to find my body so perfect. He had thought I must have some small deformity hidden beneath the clothes I was usually so unwilling to remove. After he had stroked and admired me I rubbed him between my breasts till he was hard, bending my head to lick his member, knowing that I would never experience his peculiar taste again. Then I lay on my stomach at his feet, arching my body over his saddle so that he would know to enter me from behind. His thrusts were strong and without thought for me, which I didn't object to. I moaned out his name until he became so excited that he climaxed too quickly for my pleasure, but I had enjoyed our last coupling and quite forgot to think of Jon. Later, when he was sleepy, I sat naked on his buttocks and massaged him with my hands curled into fists. I licked him under his arms and in the crease at the back of his neck, as I had once seen Teshima's peasant girls do to him; Kanjurjab seemed to like it as much as Teshima had. When I had finished, I built up the fire and lay with him naked beneath a fur cover, letting him sip vodka from my mouth until the flames of the fire and the vodka made us so hot that we had to throw off the cover. He told me that I would have made a better concubine than a wife.

As I left his ger, I wondered briefly if he would miss me more than hate me once I was gone. But then how can you truly miss someone that you do not know?

Once back in the house, I finished sewing my money into the lining of my del and put on all the jewellery I possessed. I filled a small felt bag with my writing case, Natsuko's honey box and the three gold nuggets that I reasoned Jon would want me to keep. I concealed Hideo's knife in the top of my boot and filled my flask with vodka. Taking off the jade pendant, I placed it on top of Xue's wedding chest where she could not fail to see it.

After darkness had fallen I waited two hours for Boria to come. Just as I was beginning to despair of him, he entered the house so quietly that even the dogs did not stir. In a gesture of silence he put his finger to his lips and beckoned me to follow him through the back door of the house. I picked up my bag, covered my head with the scarf that Mai had given me and took a last look around the room that had been mine for the few cold months of my marriage. I prayed that I would never see it again. On an impulse, I took back the jade pendant and slipped it into the pocket of my jodhpurs. Xue would not care, she had already ticked it off her list.

As we made our way stealthily from the house I froze with fear at what I took to be the howling of a wolf. Boria whispered that it was only Tsgotbaatar's old dog keening for his dead master. A bitter wind blew from the east as though to remind me of the hostility of the landlocked country I was fleeing. It rocked Suiyuan with the frigid air I had come to loathe. I could not wait to be done with Mongolia, that land between Russia and China whose way of life would not have been out of place a thousand years ago, and whose people, if you were not careful, would steal your heart and keep you captive.

Soon we had left the gers behind us and were weaving our way through the narrow streets of Suiyuan where the poor excuses for houses rose from the hard mud roads like squat tea boxes. The little town was silent, shut tight against the keen night. We saw no one on the streets and apart from the occasional cough and the short bark of a dog, it would have been possible to believe that Suiyuan was entirely deserted.

Boria's stride was long and it was an effort to keep up with him. Once, as he turned a corner well ahead of me, I thought that I had lost him. I was breathless by the time we reached the small Chinese quarter where, in the second lane, without knocking, he opened the door of a house indistinguishable from that of its neighbours. The padded felt door shut behind us with a soft thud and for a second or two until my eyes adjusted to the gloom the room appeared completely dark.

I heard light footsteps on the stone floor approaching the room and assumed them to be those of a woman. But Boria was greeted by a tiny Chinese man dressed in a drab brown coat, wearing a fur hat so large that it made his body appear more that of a doll than of a man. He had long dirty nails and shoulders that slumped forwards as though he suffered from a curved spine. There were white bristles sticking out of the three little rolls of fat beneath his chin, and his turned-up nose looked as though it had not grown to a proper size. At one and the same time his appearance gave the impression of slyness and humility.

We were in a small, poorly stocked shop that had bunches of herbs hanging so low from the ceiling that they touched the top of Boria's head. In the far corner of the room below an empty birdcage there was a fat barrel of mouldy-looking rice. Dotted about on the uneven shelves pots of five-grain wine and clay jars of juniper berries gathered dust. A chipped glass bottle, half-full with the bitter gum of myrrh, was seeping its contents into a sticky puddle. Dusty and unlit, the shop was heavy with the unpleasant smell of old rice. I hoped that Boria was not going to leave me there alone; indeed, for one unsettling moment I thought that I had been brought to this charmless place to be murdered. But I didn't really believe that Boria thought me worthy enough to lower himself to such an act.

We were ushered through to a narrow corridor off which three rooms, each lit by a single candle, stood doorless in a line. Two of these chambers were occupied by what I recognised to be flower girls and their customers. From the room furthest away, a man was grunting with such pleasure that Boria, filled with embarrassment, would not catch my eye. He tried to drown out the sound by stamping his feet and clapping his hands together as though to warm them from the cold. He did not like it when I laughed.

I caught the familiar fragrance of opium and thought of Sorry. Suddenly in that mean little brothel I felt more at home than I ever had in Kanjurjab's house or his ger. I felt that nothing would happen to me there that I could not control or change by bartering.

Boria told me that the shopkeeper Wu Yang had planned to travel from Suiyuan later that summer to his homeland in China where he would buy a new whore and fresh supplies for his shop. For the right price he was prepared to leave before dawn on that very day with me hidden in his cart. He would take me to the Mongolian city of Baoton, where I could board a train on the newly built railway that would take me to the coastal towns of China. Once there, I would have the choice to stay or to return to Tokyo as I pleased. Boria knew that I could not return to Kawashima's household, and said that if I had any honour left at all, I would change my name and disappear into a world peopled with my own kind. I wondered what sort of creatures he considered to be my own kind, but I didn't bother to question him on the subject.

In a high little voice, Wu said that his price was only for getting me to Baoton. After that I was on my own and he would take no further responsibility. He would accept either money or jewels and didn't care which, so long as he was paid well. I thought I might regret letting him know that I had money so I offered him my mother-of-pearl earrings. He laughed and said, 'I would not risk my dog for those.'

Turning to Boria, he whined that he would do it for a fair sum because he was an old man whose heart had grown as soft as his body, but he was no fool and the earrings were an insult.

'You have better ornaments, Yoshiko,' Boria said bluntly. 'Let us get on.'

'Take the earrings or nothing,' I said to Wu. 'They are more than generous for a ride in a cart.'

'One risks a lot smuggling princesses,' he replied, as though it were a regular occurrence for him. 'I would be a fool to bargain with my life for such paltry baubles.'

'Then don't,' I replied. 'I will find someone else to take me.'

'Give him what he asks,' said Boria darkly. 'There is no going back now.'

Sensing that Boria's anger was barely contained and that the plan might fall to bits if I pushed too far, I offered Wu the smallest of Jon's nuggets on the condition that he threw in a pipe of opium. I intended to do the cart part of the journey in the sort of sleep that would protect me from the ruts in the road and from the cold of the east wind. Wu accepted the nugget so quickly that I knew it was more than he had expected. He said that we would leave in an hour and went into the unoccupied room to set up the pipe for me. I turned to take my leave of Boria who had already reached the door of the shop.

'Wish me luck, Boria,' I called.

'If you ever come back, Yoshiko,' he said, 'I will kill you myself.'

'Don't worry, Boria,' I replied. 'If I had to return to Suiyuan, I would let you.'

After all my fearful imaginings, the journey out of Mongolia proved to be so much easier than the one that had brought me in. I slept my opium sleep in Wu's cart and dreamt that I saw Xue in the light of a huge fire. It was night, the sky was dark and starless, with a wind that fanned the flames and sent them higher than her ger. She was burning Tsgotbaatar's belongings, one by one. Each time she threw something into the fire she became thinner. As the flames grew and devoured every last remnant of Tsgotbaatar's life, Xue, as thin as a stick, her face as expressionless as ever, turned into a hawk and flew away. In the light of the fire I watched her dark wings merge with the black sky until she became invisible.

I woke to Wu shaking me to tell me that the train was about to leave. 'If you want to be on it,' he said laughing, 'you must board immediately.'

The sun was at that place in the sky that tells you it is well past noon. My mouth was dry from the opium and I felt dazed from my long sleep and dazzled by the brightness of the sun.

'Why did you let me sleep so long?' I asked him.

'I do not often get the chance to gaze on such a sleeping beauty,' he replied, with the faintest hint of sarcasm.

'Are you boarding too?' I asked, grabbing my bag and jumping from the cart.

'No,' he said. 'It would be an honour to accompany you, but I take a different path to the one that is best for you.'

I paid the Chinese guard for my ticket from a few yen I had put in my boot for such expenses. As I settled myself into an empty coach, the train pulled away and I saw Wu sitting on his cart waving to me. Under his huge hat his three-chinned face was creased into a smile that looked triumphant.

Twenty minutes into my journey I was awake enough to notice that Xue's pendant and the two remaining gold nuggets were gone. There are some things that you are just not meant to keep. I wished Wu bad luck of them as I patted the reassuring bulk that lined my del, and fingered with relief the Su family crest etched into my mother's precious writing case.

I closed my eyes and allowed myself to imagine a bath filled with steaming water and perfumed with my favourite chrysanthemum oil. I intended to make my way back to Tokyo under an assumed name, to make contact with Sorry and to make a life for myself that would be neither conventional nor boring. But for a few days I would enjoy the comparatively civilised amenities that China could offer. I needed time to make a better plan than the one I had in my head. I wanted new clothes and to eat delicately prepared food that contained neither mutton nor butter.

It was hard to believe that I was free. I would remember 1926 not only as the year of my twentieth birthday but also as the year of my liberation.

Life-prolonging Eggs and Goose Testicles

The inn called The White Syringa in Port Arthur stood above the pier where the steamers departed for Shanghai. There was a syringa tree in the inn's small garden, not white as in its name, but suffused with the more usual lilac flowers. If I left the shutters of my room open I was overcome by its scent, a fragrance which, like that of ripe strawberries, was so heady as to be reminiscent of decay.

The house, a single-storey building, had airy rooms, low beds and light that entered as though filtered through a prism. The wooden structure, a little damp from being so close to the sea, was half-painted white, as if someone had tired of the work and given up. To this day if I smell syringa, I am reminded of the feelings of excitement and regret that I experienced in that charming half-painted house, and the joy I took in being clean, perfumed and warm.

The day I arrived, I went to the bathhouse and spent hours washing with a ball of finely milled soap that smelled of chestnuts. The steam was comforting, the heat quite wonderful, but I was full of sadness. I could do nothing but sit hugging myself as salty tears streamed from my eyes. Unbidden, the vision of Mai's plump little face came to my mind and stirred my heart with loneliness for her. It seemed I was destined to lose everyone I loved. My own fault, of course. Boria was right, I was headstrong and unable to compromise, but that didn't mean that I was without doubt or regret.

There are bound to be those in every life who capture your affection, whether you want them to or not. Mai was one of those people in mine. I can still picture her perfectly, remember well the little mole shaped like a berry at the corner of her mouth, the comforting cushion of her breasts, and her front tooth, clipped at an angle, which she broke while biting on a coin to help her through the birth of her twins. If I concentrate I can summon up the cracked tones of her strange voice and hear her husky childlike laughter. My tears were for Mai, for letting her down and for the loss of her.

I found myself wishing that I had not taken Xue's pendant. If only in the secret part of her, I wanted Mai to think well of me. I determined that in future I would not be grasping where wealth was concerned. Money comes and goes but memories can be coloured for ever by one venal act.

The inn served excellent food and for the ten days that I was there I made the most of it. I gorged myself on little clams that just resisted the bite, mussels steaming in their sea juice, silky oysters and hearty stews of sea turtle. I ate freshly boiled life-prolonging eggs and goose testicles braised to a delicious goo with rice that tasted of almonds. In my heart I am Japanese, but I am Chinese in my stomach and love every kind of food. After the deprivations of Mongolia I was excited by so much variety and indulged myself in everything that took my fancy. I bought myself a huge box of preserved plums and a jar of ginger in syrup to eat in my room between meals.

I formed a plan to travel to Tokyo by sea in the guise of a sophisticated Chinese woman, a young widow perhaps, or the daughter of a wealthy merchant family. I set about changing my look so that even Natsuko would not recognise me, at least not from a distance. Although I loved my jodhpurs and boots, they were in a poor state, and so much my trademark that I would have been instantly recognised in Tokyo. I threw them out and chose for myself a collection of high-necked dresses that buttoned on the side and emphasised my figure. They were cut from lengths of rolling satin that caught the light. I selected the most gorgeous colours I could find, a floral pink that lit my face, a luminous amethyst that reminded me of the Mongolian sky, and one for evenings of the most delicate ivory piped with gold. I bought satin shoes with little heels, and jade earrings that danced above the collars of my dresses and turned my eyes to the colour of damsons.

Port Arthur was full of treasures. I secured lip paints and perfumed oils, pencils of kohl to outline my eyes, sake and Russian tobacco, and just for fun some chewing gum flavoured with cherries.

I had my by then shoulder-length hair styled with a permanent wave, copying the Eurasian girl pictured on cigarette packets who contrived to look inviting and sulky at the same time.

I knew that I had caused a stir in Port Arthur, as any young woman on her own was bound to do. But apart from one night when I visited the Polish flower girl that Nobu had slept with, I spoke only to the manager at The White Syringa Inn and to the shopkeepers.

I went to the house of flowers because I wanted to see the foreign girl's golden hair and look at an occidental woman's body. I had to pay highly for her time, but it was worth it if only to discover that golden hair is more like straw in colour and texture than gold, and in the Polish girl's case was not replicated anywhere else on the body. Her limbs were big and round, her thighs seemed out of proportion to the slimness of her waist. It confirmed my prejudice that oriental women are not only the most beautiful, but smell the best too. Her scent was milky, but I liked her round blue eyes and her straight nose. She told me that she remembered Nobu because he had made her listen to his poetry, which she did not understand.

While I was there I took a pipe of opium and was massaged by a blind woman in her fiftieth year who in her youth had been a popular flower girl with ugly men who told her that they were handsome and that she was lucky to be chosen by them. She said although blind she could always tell if a man was ugly because of the way he took a step backwards on introduction.

At night in The White Syringa Inn, I would lie on my bed with the shutters open, watching the stars. I smoked Turkish cigarettes, drank sake and usually fell into a drunken sleep a few hours before dawn. My dreams were of overgrown gardens full of dark shrubs, and lowering trees where oily laurel pressed against snowberry, and bindweed coiled its way through black wisteria. Every night in those domestic jungles I fought for air as the advancing plants threatened me with their motionless breathing.

I always slept late into the morning, waking to a delicious breakfast brought to me by a serving woman who never caught my eye. I took time over my dressing, luxuriating in the feel of hot scented water on my skin and the caress of satin as it slipped over my body. I learnt to walk on shoes with heels and to sway in the dresses that only allowed short strides, lest they split at the seams. I revelled in being a free and independent woman about to start at last on the adventure of my own life.

One day I purchased my ticket for a berth on the boat that would take me to Yokohama, and looked forward to the long journey.

The day the boat pulled out of the port, I stood on deck and glanced up to the house on the cliff where I had first met Kanjurjab; it looked lonely and uncared for. At eye level the teeming port was alive with people, noise and life, and I felt at home. I believe that I am more suited to live at eye level than on top of the hill. I don't think that is something that can be said of most Manchu princesses.

Two days later in the port of Kagoshima I left the boat to walk on land and to look at new faces. Kagoshima, unlike Port Arthur, had few shops and was hardly cosmopolitan, but I managed to buy soap and fresh supplies of sake. In a small, open-to-the-sky restaurant on the dockside, where you had to stand to eat, I took a bowl of plain steamed noodles to settle my stomach. It felt good to be walking on true Japanese soil again.

When I returned to the boat, an elegant young Japanese woman, dressed in an ankle-length skirt and, despite the fine weather, a jacket with a fur collar and matching hat, had boarded. She was leaning against the handrail smoking what I knew by its scent to be French tobacco. She wore shoes with the highest heels I had ever seen, and at her feet sat a small, expensive-looking snakeskin suitcase. Her blue-black hair was cut into a sleek bob and outshone the dark fur of her hat.

She greeted me with the American 'Hi', and offered me a cigarette from a crumpled blue packet. Introducing herself as Madam Hidari, she asked me in Japanese if I spoke English.

'Yes, I do a little, but I am out of the habit,' I said, accepting the cigarette. 'But you are Japanese, why do you wish to speak English?'

'Oh, only to p-practise,' she said with a slight stammer. 'I love everything American, their language, their fashion, their music. Oh, just everything. I would like to speak English p-perfectly.'

'I love most things Japanese,' I replied. 'But I am happy to practise English with you.'

She laughed, lit my cigarette with a silver lighter and then, as though we were already on familiar terms, she put her hand on my arm and told me that she thought me beautiful and looked forward to my company on the trip.

From the moment I first saw Tamura Hidari posing on the deck as though she were acting in a film I sensed that we would be friends. I liked the way she dressed, the way she chain-smoked, always lighting a fresh cigarette before the old one was half finished, and the way she held my eyes when speaking as though I was the only person in the world of interest. I liked too the feeling of excitement she created around herself, as though ordinary everyday things when happening to her took on more colour, more drama than when happening to others. Tamura possessed that quality, rare in Japan, of glamour. She was a beauty in a most individual way and, like most beautiful women that I have known, she sometimes looked so plain that it made you question why you had ever found her attractive. There was nothing pretty about her face, but it had a clean elegance that spoke of independence and modernity. Individually her features were undistinguished, but arranged together they were surprisingly arresting. She emphasised her too-small eyes with a smoky shadow smudged beneath her lower lashes, which lent them mystery. She had a delicate nose and wide lips that were always pale because she never wore lip paint. Her body was straight and slim like a boy's, and she smelled of jasmine, her favourite fragrance. She ate little and was hardly ever still. She always stuttered when pronouncing the letter P, which I found endearing. And conversely, there was about the frailty of her body a hint of the strength of mind that mirrored my own.

Tamura was the widow of a businessman who had died young, leaving her with an infant daughter, a couple of small businesses and some properties in the Chinese student quarter in Tokyo, which she rented out mostly to students and shopkeepers. She had been in Kagoshima to inspect the small import company she owned and was in the process of selling.

'Business is a man's world,' she said. 'But it is surprising how well, given the chance, we women can do at it.'

Tamura told me that she was alone in the world because she did not speak to or trust her husband's family. They kept her daughter from her and would not let her see her. She said they had tried to steal the business from her too, but because her husband had included her name in the ownership papers they had not succeeded.

'But they will never give up,' she said. 'If I stay in Japan it will eventually be the worse for me.'

Tamura's father-in-law had been struck down by a stroke so he could not move or speak or take Tamura to the courts to reclaim his son's business as he would have wanted.

'It's woman against woman at the moment,' Tamura told me, 'and I am a match for my mother-in-law, but soon, when she

120

realises her husband will not get better, she will enlist the help of her son-in-law and I could lose everything.'

They wanted her to live in their house under her mother-in-law's watchful eyes, a fate that would have driven Tamura to suicide. Her husband had been the only son amongst seven daughters. His mother had doted on him and could not bear his young widow to have any happiness.

'They would have p-preferred it if I had been the one to die,' she said in a matter-of-fact way. 'Lucky for me, it is the gods who choose.'

Recently Tamura, not at all concerned with reputation, had begun a venture introducing café girls, the newly popular rivals to the geisha, to businessmen and politicians. She said that in these modern times young men found geishas boring, while older men were keen to indulge in something new. Café girls wore western clothes, permed their hair and could dance in the American style. They smoked in public and were exciting companions for men who neither wished to adopt a geisha nor to endure the mannerly courtship geishas were trained to expect. Café girls accepted money, gifts and favours, they offered their bodies readily, but unlike common prostitutes they were educated, modern and often well connected.

'I don't care that I am no longer respectable,' Tamura said. 'One day soon I will sell everything I own, gather up my little daughter Sachiko and go to New York. In America I will be respectable, I will educate Sachiko and see that she makes a good marriage. I hope her husband will be an American. My husband was rare amongst Japanese men in treating me as his equal. I would like Sachiko's husband to consider her his equal.'

As the boat progressed to Yokohama, so my friendship with Tamura was cemented. I confided my story to her, and she was amazed to learn that I had lived as the wife of a Mongolian prince. When I spoke to her of Jon, she said that I shouldn't feel bad about him as at least I had made his life interesting and given him a more varied history than he could have hoped for before knowing me.

'A p-princess and an adventuress will make good friends,' she assured me. 'You and I will be as close as sisters, Yoshiko. I know it, and when I am this sure I am never wrong. We will come to trust each other with our secrets, because even though you are a p-princess, we are fashioned from a similar cloth.'

She was right. Not that we were really alike in little things, but more that we had the same determination to make our own lives, whatever the cost. Like me, regardless of tradition, Tamura ignored class and convention and took the path most enticing to her.

The journey passed quickly in her company and on the last day as we passed Mount Fuji I pointed it out to her, saying, 'How beautiful it is, Tamura, the snow so untouched. It will be as cold as Suiyuan at the top.'

'I don't care for mountains and open views much,' she said. 'I am only at home where buildings etch the skyline and the streets are full of p-people.'

'You would hate Mongolia, Tamura,' I said. 'There is nothing but space there.'

I knew what she meant by open spaces being frightening, but despite my love of cities and my unhappiness in Mongolia, nature still had the power to touch me without fear. For all her strength, Tamura did not entirely trust herself with her own survival. She believed that money solved every problem and that without it life was a dangerous thing. But money, while useful, will not solve every problem and it would have been of little help to her at the top of Mount Fuji.

Perhaps having a child made Tamura more vulnerable than me. While I was sure that I was the safety net in my own life, Tamura thought hers was wealth, but despite that, she was one of the bravest women I have ever known. I had no doubt that she would be happier in America, where money could buy you any life you wanted. In that land of giants the rules were not made by old men whose chauvinistic traditions were bred in the bone. It was easy to picture Tamura swinging on her high heels through the streets of New York, wafting the scent of jasmine around and standing out in the crowd.

Before the journey was over she had offered me one of her smaller houses in the students' quarter, which she said was a very lively area. If I agreed to accept the men she sent to me, she could assure me that in no time at all I would have enough money to establish my own household, or even to join her in New York. I had no desire to go to America, Japan was my only family, but I accepted her offer. It solved my problem of where to live, and I knew that the men Tamura would introduce me to would be of the highest rank and that my life would not be boring. It would suit me very well until it was time to move on.

That journey from Port Arthur to Tokyo remains with me as one of the most delightful trips I have ever made, and the day I met Tamura Hidari remains one of the most fortunate of my life.

My twentieth birthday was celebrated in Tokyo, just as I had hoped it would be all those months ago on the cold plains of Mongolia. It was thrilling to be back in my home city, and I loved the house that Tamura set me up in, not least because every room spoke to me of her. It stood three storeys high with two rooms on each floor and had windows hung with shades the colour of parchment. It was painted pale yellow and wisteria grew against the front walls, reaching almost to the roof. The first floor had a wooden veranda where in the evening, in the cooling air, it was pleasant to sit and listen to the crickets chatter. A long staircase with a turned handrail rose through the house like a tree heading for the light. Every room was warm, which endeared the house to me more than any other of its numerous advantages. At ground level there was a kitchen that smelled of rice water and vegetables. It had two sinks, one at kneeling height, the other sunk into the stone floor. There was a low table bleached white by the summer sun which filled the room from dawn to noon. Three or four sleeping mats were rolled neatly by a door that led out to a walled yard, empty except for a large smooth stone for washing clothes.

I took up residence at the top of the house where in the slightest breeze the roof whispered small complaints to itself. My bed, a low wooden frame with a thin mattress, had a blue cover made from a silk as crisp as paper. It was embroidered with white honeysuckle and single-petal peonies. Behind a tall screen, there was a jug and a basin for washing as well as a square basket filled with cotton towels. Shards of sunlight channelled their way through the thin fabric of the blinds, showing up motes of dust in the lit air.

The rooms on the first floor were mostly used for entertaining, although if I felt tired in the afternoon I would sleep in one or other of them. They were furnished with bamboo furniture, which Tamura liked better than dark wood. She said the gloominess of rosewood and ebony reminded her of her mother-in-law's house. Delicate drawings of storks and weeping fig trees in painted frames lined the walls. There was an oil painting of a girl with long hair carrying an open fan. She was taking tea with an old man who looked like the three-chinned Wu, only not quite as sly. Both rooms shared the veranda and when the wisteria was in flower they seemed cooled by its fragrance. One had a western-style daybed draped with an old kimono and there was a gramophone, which stood on the floor, accompanied by a stack of popular dance and jazz records. By the glass door that led to the veranda, a small painted chest housed not only sake and vodka, but also the newly imported gin that looked like water, smelled of juniper and tasted of sloe. Tamura had generously filled a cedar box with Turkish and French cigarettes, enough to last a month.

The second room was longer and more traditional in style. It had a low Japanese bed which stood only an inch above the floor, a paper screen that hid a large Satsuma-ware washing bowl, and a low bench where tea could be made and served in plain white bowls fashioned from such fine porcelain that you could see the tea glowing through.

I loved the house for being mine alone, and for the way it sat anonymously between similar houses, allowing it the privacy of the undistinguished. My dark days receded in those sunlit ones and it seemed easier to fight my demons when they came.

Tamura sent me a diminutive maid called Miura. She was fifteen years old, worked hard and did what was asked of her without being in the least subservient. Miura would have been startlingly pretty had it not been for a birth deformity that challenged her otherwise enchanting little face. She had been born with a drooping eyelid that almost covered the whole of her right eye, so that she appeared to be permanently winking. Her mother, in desperation to help her daughter, had sold her hair to a wigmaker to pay for a doctor to repair Miura's eyelid. The doctor was in his sixtieth year and suffice to say he would have made a poor seamstress. Miura's eyelid had been only marginally lifted and now it had an uneven scar along the length of it.

I let her sleep in the half-open-to-the-sky room next to the kitchen, which she said was a great luxury for her as she would have been perfectly happy on the kitchen floor. She didn't have a change of clothes and wore shoes two sizes too large for her which she fastened by tying rags around them. She kept a caged canary that she called 'Baby', and talked to it constantly in her own birdlike voice.

Every day I sent her to the market for fresh flowers, as I hated to see even the smallest sign of decay on the lilies and the sprays of orange blossom that I favoured. I cared nothing for the extravagance and in any case I think that Miura sold on the day-old flowers to a nearby hotel that rented its rooms by the hour. As far as I was concerned she was welcome to the few coins she made from the transactions. I have always thought it a good policy to be a generous mistress. Envy and deprivation are the enemies of loyalty, after all.

In no time at all, I became familiar with the complex run of streets, little squares and dead ends that made up my new habitat. It was a busy area where both Japanese and Chinese students in their smart uniforms thronged together as they made their way to their lessons. There were plenty of shops, a few small hotels and a reliable laundry. Two streets away there was a bathhouse that was known for its pure water and scented steam.

Wealthy Chinese families had begun sending their young bloods to Japanese military academies, to be trained in the tradition of discipline and instilled with the determination to rid China of the communism that threatened their privileged way of life. Dressed in uniforms that reminded me of Yamaga, they came in their time off to socialise in the streets of my quarter where they could speak their own language and eat their native food, cooked on the pavement by other scholars funding their own education.

I was glad to see Chinese families recognising the superior qualities of a Japanese military training, not only because usually Chinese soldiers are merely untrained drifters without a trade or land, but also because communism is alien to human nature. The strong will always succeed over the weak, oil will always rise above water and there's an end to it. Be it emperor or dictator, both require an underclass to rule over. The language may differ, but the common man's life will always be formed by hands other than his own.

I enjoyed the sight of the students strutting around, but for me they did not compare with their Japanese counterparts who, although usually shorter in stature, had a stronger measure of iron in their blood.

I would have loved to have worn such uniforms myself, but Tamura advised that I would be better disguised as a mysterious high-born Chinese, rumoured to be of royal blood. She thought that Japanese men would flock to such a creature and would pay well to be entertained by a woman of a higher class than their own. I pointed out to her that such a disguise was not too far from the truth of my origins and she said that she knew that, but it was not

Eastern Jewel who I was attempting to hide, but Kawashima Yoshiko.

So I stayed in my elegant dresses and took to wearing elaborate make-up and imported shoes with heels as high as Tamura's. I smoked my cigarettes through a long ivory holder and wore fresh flowers in my hair. I called myself Yang Fuei Fei, the name of a legendary Chinese imperial concubine who, like Helen of Troy, was said to have brought about the ruin of an empire. I would have preferred more comfortable clothes, but I had to agree with Tamura that not only did I look beautiful in the clothes she urged upon me, but also my disguise was thus complete.

I only entertained men who appealed to me. They did not have to be handsome, but as Tamura sent me only rich ones, my wealth increased at a satisfactory pace. Occasionally, for my own pleasure and excitement and at no cost to them, I would take to my bed one of the numerous uniformed boys who filled the streets and who were themselves looking for adventure. I had no objection to sharing my couch with older men, but no one wants to dine on fish alone and variety has always pleased me.

Tamura told me that my reputation as a woman of royal blood, talented in the art of lovemaking, was spreading, and she had more requests from men who wanted to meet me than it was possible for one woman to fulfil.

'You will make us both rich,' she said. 'No matter how much I ask for an introduction there is always a waiting list of eager suitors ready to pay the price.'

'Let's make the most of it,' I said. 'Next season they will want only virgins or peasant girls.'

'Then we will give them what they want,' Tamura said confidently.

I knew though that the life I was living would not suit me for long and eventually something new would take my fancy. In any case, Tamura had already begun to sell off her businesses and would soon have enough money to live the life she desired for herself and her daughter in America. I thought that she should go sooner rather than later as, despite the effort she made to appear happy, I could tell that she was pining for her daughter Sachiko.

I asked her how she intended to claim her daughter back from her in-laws, for they were unlikely to just hand the child over. She said that she had everything planned and that nothing would stop her, certainly not her disagreeable mother-in-law, who was a stupid woman without imagination or wit and who was easily deceived. Tamura still had a key to her husband's family home and she said she intended to enter their house in the hours before dawn when everyone was in a deep sleep. She would take her daughter, and within the shortest period of time she and Sachiko would have begun their journey to America.

'What if Sachiko cries out?' I asked her.

Tamura laughed. 'She won't,' she said. 'Sachiko is used to my visits; I go into that house and her room several nights a week. The moment I wake her, she smiles and wants to play. She knows that I love her and will come with me willingly. She is a clever girl and has kept her promise to keep my visits secret.'

I worried about Tamura stealing into her in-laws' house and shuddered at the thought of her being apprehended. For a week after she had told me of her nocturnal visits, all my dreams concerned flight and capture and I could not sleep easy knowing that she put herself at such risk. If Tamura was discovered, her mother-in-law would remove Sachiko to one of her daughter's houses where Tamura would find it impossible to see her. She could be arrested or even confined to an institution for what would be considered her unnatural behaviour. An independent woman willingly divorced from her family is likely to be thought mad in Japan.

I knew that she had already begun to convert the money from her businesses into dollars. She would have enough to make the journey and set herself up in America before summer came again to Tokyo. She often tried to talk me into going with her to New

York, but much as I cared for her, I could not imagine myself there.

Time was passing quickly, as it always does when life is full. I often thought of my Japanese family who were close to me in distance yet might as well have been a million miles away, barred as I was from their company. Yet one overcast, humid day as I was entering a hotel to have lunch with Tamura and a new client, I almost collided with Kawashima as I walked through the revolving door into the lobby. He was leaving with a colleague who, like him, was dressed in a western suit with dark shoes, carrying a leather briefcase. He glanced at me with interest but without recognition, and gave a little bow of apology as I turned my face from him. I was so shaken by this brief encounter that I had to sit in the lobby until my heart stopped racing.

It gave me a thrill to notice that the small, jagged scar I had inflicted on his lip was still there, permanently etched white against his florid lips. As I watched him through the glass door taking leave of his companion, I felt weak with desire for him. I longed to stand with him behind me and feel his desire and anger as he entered me in the rough way that rarely varied in his lovemaking. I could smell him where he had brushed against me, and I savoured once more the scent of his sweat and the familiar fennel soap that he always used.

That same night my companion, one Doctor Atarki, was the beneficiary of all the passion Kawashima had stirred in me. Atarki, a respected Tokyo surgeon, liked to play the victim, the princess's servant. He enjoyed me ordering him to my bed to be my plaything. But that night it was my pleasure that was paramount. I blindfolded him so that I could impose in my mind Kawashima's face in place of his. Although he enjoyed being commanded by me, I don't think Atarki was comforted that night, and feeling that I had used him more than he me, I refused his gift of money, which embarrassed him.

'You must let me give you a present, Princess,' he said. 'Maybe some jade? I know a craftsman who works in a stone so pale it is almost white.'

'You may owe me a favour and that will be the end of it,' I dictated, and he agreed.

It was at this point that I decided it was time to make contact with Sorry. I knew that I could simply wait for her at dusk by the opium seller's door where she came at least once in every three days to replenish her stocks. But instead I positioned myself across the street from Kawashima's house, disguised in my dress and high heels with a fan for extra concealment.

I hoped that I might catch a glimpse of Natsuko, which was unlikely as she rarely left the house. I cannot explain my love for Natsuko. I stole her husband, brought trouble to her house and unsettled her boys. I never once gave Natsuko a reason to love me, but against reason I longed for her affection. I did not see her that day nor was I ever to see her again, but I remember her whenever I see black pearls or extra bright carp. She lives in the shadows of my life, in my dreams and in my worst fears. Who would have thought that Natsuko would come to occupy such a potent place in my heart?

There was something different about the house that I couldn't at first work out. Then I noticed that there was no watchman at the gate, a sight from my youth that was no longer common in Tokyo. I felt proud that I had lived on that cusp between the old and the new world. I had spent my childhood in a land where women practised the tea ceremony for their masters, where girls were not properly educated and where men took all the decisions that mattered. A few years earlier, Kawashima as good as owned the watchmen he allowed to guard our gate, who would have starved without his patronage. Now, although there were beggars on the streets still, there was plenty of work in the factories and small rooms could be rented cheaply. Modern Tokyo had risen amazingly quickly out of the earthquake that had seen off not only the old buildings, but many of the old ways too.

My heart ached that I could not enter my old home. I would like to have strolled around the western wing and stood quietly by the shrine where Shimako ended her life. I longed once again to hear my wooden floor sing with the sound of Kawashima's footsteps, and smell the scent of the food Sorry brought to my rooms. So much had happened to change me since I was last a daughter of the Kawashima household, but I believed that for as long as that house stood there would be a part of me in it that I could never reclaim.

I stayed until the fireflies came out, but Sorry didn't appear; I had to wait three more days before she emerged from the house. When she did, I followed her down the familiar streets to the opium seller's door and then I called her name. I was shocked that she recognised me right away and that to her my disguise was completely transparent. She told me that it was my voice that had given me away. Face to face, she said I looked so different from little mistress that even had her eyesight been as good as in her youth she would not have known me. She looked the same sweet old Sorry, but she had developed a chronic cough and her old hands trembled a little. She had the pallor that comes from overindulging in opium, and her once-lively eyes were dull.

I took her back to the little yellow house where we sat on the veranda and drank sake, which made her face red. She knew I had run away from Kanjurjab and told me that Kawashima had been informed of it, and in disgust had said that I was dead to him now and my name was not to be mentioned in his house again.

Sorry was happy enough in her old age but she said without me she could never feel completely at home anywhere. Since my departure there was no one to bring the servants' gossip to, no one who truly understood the workings of a Chinese mind. She was eager to tell me everything about the Kawashimas and her eyes sparkled with joy at sharing news with me once again.

She told me that Natsuko was content to have my name banned and that she had given my rooms to Hideo and his cruel young wife Taeko, a girl who was full of complaint and spent extravagantly.

Teshima's mind had gone. He often had to be reclaimed from the streets, where he wandered with no idea of where he was going. His peasant girls secretly taunted him with tepid soup, cold-water baths and massages too strong for his old bones. They let his toenails grow and never cleaned his teeth. At night they slept either side of him in his bed to wake him on the hour so that he did not pass water on his mattress. Sometimes they would fall back asleep, leaving him on the pot for hours. 'He has a wild look,' Sorry said, 'as though his mind is in a place of torture.'

I did not feel pity for him. After all, he had owned those girls since their birth and they only became what he made them by example.

'They have a good life now,' Sorry laughed. 'It is they who get the best food and he the scraps. Of course, they would be beaten if Kawashima ever found out, but they are as crafty as Teshima was in his sane days and protect themselves from discovery.'

After our first meeting Sorry came to see me every afternoon. I loved being with her and hearing all the Kawashima news. As in the old days she cooked for me, bought my opium and each evening before she returned home she would brush my hair. She taught Miura some of her Chinese recipes and told her stories of what an adventurous child I had been. I was the heroine of Sorry's tales and in them I always triumphed over adversity.

Sorry told me that Natsuko was kind to her and would often give her little presents of fruit. Occasionally they would walk together in the garden and Natsuko would reminisce about happier times spent with her sister Shimako. She never mentioned me or spoke of my time in her house, but she treated Sorry well and I was grateful to her for that. Whatever Sorry said about missing me, she had found a good home in which to spend her last years.

Kawashima had adopted a new, younger geisha in Tokyo who Sorry said pleased him greatly. The one in Osaka was left with her hundred kimonos to dream of happier times.

In 1926, at the beginning of winter, Tamura sent me a politician called Sesyu Hanaoka. Sesyu came from a wealthy, established Tokyo family who for a century had dealt in wine, tea and salt. He had the whitest teeth I had ever seen and dark hair with eyes to match. He was ridiculously generous and even though he had paid Tamura an unusually large bonus to put him at the top of her list for me, he still showered me with presents. In no time at all the little house began to fill with bolts of silk, gold cigarette lighters, imported perfume, strings of pearls and endless supplies of tobacco and alcohol.

Sesyu was a man who enjoyed having fun. He would take me to the latest American films and to dinner in the private rooms of the best restaurants. He gave parties at my house where his friends would come with their café girls and stay until dawn. Although he was a member of the diet he never talked politics with me, but would sometimes speak about his family business.

Like most of his friends who came to the house, he had married into his own class. He had four children, all boys whom he loved and indulged. Tamura told me that his wife was ten years younger than him and quite pretty, but Sesyu himself rarely mentioned his family. It suited me not to talk of them with him. He had his life with them which had nothing to do with me. I knew they would be with him long after I had left him and that was how it should be. It was easy not to be the jealous lover for I did not love Sesyu, although it was impossible not to like him for his sense of fun and his generosity, which bordered on madness. It was not confined to me alone; he gave Sorry and Miura presents of money and once he bought Miura a beautiful metal cage for her canary to replace her ageing wooden one. She was speechless with gratitude and cried for hours.

During our lovemaking, he liked me to keep my high heels on and sometimes he would paint my nipples with honey and at the height of his passion lick it off as though it were the nectar of the gods. The smell of honey and sex would always remind me of Teshima, and my fifteenth birthday.

I enjoyed the way that, after sex, Sesyu would lie on my bed and smoke with me, telling me jokes and seeking my opinion on things.

133

As far as Japanese men go he was less traditional in his views on women and more relaxed than any I had known before him. Like Tamura, he admired all things American. He bought me nylons and pretty suspender belts so that he could slide his hand up the silky length of my legs and make love to me as I leant against my bedroom wall, wearing nothing but them and the shoes that made me taller than him.

Within a few months of knowing me, Sesyu made Tamura the offer of a huge financial settlement so that he might be my only lover. Tamura, by then almost ready to leave for America, accepted his offer and honourably gave me half of the money. I secretly continued to see Dr Atarki, not only because by his neediness he had found a friend in me, but also because I did not wish to be owned by Sesyu.

In autumn of the following year, when the trees were bare of leaves and the evenings dark Sesyu told me that he was madly in love with me. He said that he wanted to buy me a bigger house where I could live elegantly with servants and where he would feel more at home. Although it was a tempting offer I didn't consider it, not even for a moment. I was already bored with life in the little yellow house and I knew that when Tamura left Tokyo there would be little to keep me from moving on. I had no intention of spending my life as Sesyu's girl only to end up like Kawashima's Osaka geisha, alone and dependent on his favours. I told him that I would consider his offer, which was a generous one, but needed thought. He was not happy, but feeling sure of my eventual acceptance he granted me the time. It was lucky for me that I did not love him or my fate would have been sealed under his exclusive protection. I would have been condemned to the life that Sesyu ordained for me until my looks began to fade and he to tire of me.

I had a fancy to go to Shanghai for a while. I had heard that life was exciting there and that women were not as confined by tradition as they were in Japan. Sesyu himself had told me that

Shanghai was considered to be the Paris of the east and was full of foreigners, imported goods and American marines. His enthusiasm was infectious and increased my desire to go. Japan was my true home, but I could no longer live there without the recognition I so craved. I would need to do something noble so that I would eventually be able to return to my homeland as a welcomed daughter, with my reputation restored. Perhaps in Shanghai I would think of a way of doing that.

A cool spring followed that winter but by May Tokyo had become hot and humid. Sesyu continually pestered me to move with him to a larger house and I told him that I would, but that I wanted a few weeks in Tamura's house to pack up and to give her time to find a new tenant. Sesyu, impatient as ever, bought the house anyway and, generous as always, presented the deeds to me as a gift. He reluctantly agreed to keep his word and not expect me to move in until the summer's end.

As if in slow motion, those last few weeks crawled by in long, humid days and short, rain-drenched nights. My time was taken up with a series of pleasures made more delightful because they were coming to an end. I entertained Atarki in the mornings when I knew that Sesyu would be working. Most days I had lunch with Tamura who, almost ready for flight, was full of nervous energy and could never quite settle to a conversation, or sit still for long. I caught something of her excitement and began in my head to make my own plans for departure. In the afternoons I slept on the daybed on the first floor, covering myself in a silk shawl. In my dreams I would find myself in intimate conversations with Natsuko, or watching Teshima's girls giggling together at his discomfort. I would wake just before Kawashima was about to enter me and be filled with disappointment.

I didn't look forward to telling Sorry that once again I was leaving Tokyo. I knew that it would make her sad. She had struck up a touching friendship with Miura, who had found another mother in Sorry. The pair of them would come to my bedroom full of excitement, as I dressed for the evening. We would drink gin flavoured with the juice of sloes and smoke the French cigarettes that went well with it. Miura would help me to bathe and get my clothes ready, while Sorry, finding it hard to bend or to move quickly, would sit on the bed and explain to Miura how I liked things.

I usually dined out with Sesyu and his friends in one or other of the popular restaurants where, because they spent like emperors, they were treated like royalty. Once he took me to the Kabuki theatre, where all the female parts were played by men. They clicked around the stage as though on bound feet, their faces slyly painted into characterless masks that mocked real women. Despite the make-up and the exaggerated movements, some of them contrived to look more beautiful than one would have thought possible.

During the performance I saw an old lover from my Kawashima days. He was sitting with a café girl half his age, his thick hand resting in her lap. He was a member of the Wakatsuki Reijîrô cabinet, a brutal lover and, as it turned out, a friend of Sesyu's, who he greeted enthusiastically. I thought that he hadn't recognised me, but as he took his leave he whispered, 'Your secret is safe with me, Yoshiko.'

The day after our visit to the Kabuki theatre, I told Sorry that I intended to go to Shanghai and that she could come with me if she wished. I wasn't surprised when, giving the excuse of age and habit, she declined. She said that Natsuko had told her of the civil war in China, and that she had no wish to be a communist. I didn't bother to explain that Shanghai was untouched by the struggle; it wouldn't have changed her decision. Through tears of regret she prepared me an opium pipe, saying she would share it and we could go to the place of opium dreams where we would always be able to find each other.

No one prepared the pipe quite like Sorry. She trimmed the wick to perfection, using the best lamp oil and heating the spindle just so.

I loved the way her body leant in an arc over the bowl at just the right angle as she warmed the pellet over the flame, crooning to herself as though pacifying a baby. Like me, Sorry had never had mother's milk to give, but I felt like a child being offered the breast whenever I smoked opium prepared by her.

In the month before I was ready to leave Tokyo, Tamura came to take her leave of me. She said that one night very soon she would collect Sachiko and they would depart for New York and never return to Japan. If I ever wanted to find her there I should look her up in the telephone directory under the name of 'Mrs Jasmine'. She assured me that I would always find a home with her and that she would never stop hoping to see me at her door. She had sold my house to a mama-san who she said had a fine business brain and a good enough heart. It had been agreed that I could stay until the end of the summer. I kissed her on her unpainted lips, staining them with the red of mine. I wished her good luck and told her to be careful.

I was relieved when news reached me that her plan had been successful and that she and Sachiko had made their escape before her mother-in-law could foil it. It was odd to think that only a couple of days later she would be making her way in what she called the land of opportunity.

With Tamura's leaving, the life went out of Tokyo. I felt the same sadness I had experienced on leaving Mai in Mongolia, but without the sense of guilt that had accompanied that parting. Despite understanding her reasons for going, I felt abandoned by Tamura, and shocked at myself once again at how deeply I had misjudged the strength of my attachment to a female friend.

I had dreams in which I would find babies in the city and hide them in the cellar of a house that was familiar but not mine. I always forgot where I had put them and would search in a panic lest they starved to death. Miura said that I often cried out the name Yoshiko in my sleep, as though I was searching for a girl of that name. I told her that it was the name of an old school friend who I sometimes missed.

Suddenly everything around me was changing and although much of the change was of my choosing, my black days returned to plague me once again. Japan was going back to its old ways and was becoming increasingly anti-western. It reacted to the trouble in China with a prudishness that was making it a difficult place for a woman such as myself to live in. A ban against permed hair was introduced, and one against the teaching of English in schools. Geishas, representing the more traditional way of life, came back into favour, while the little progress that women had made was wiped out in an orgy of nationalism and a return to those ancient values that Japanese men felt at home with.

It was time for me to go, but before I did I found time amongst the planning and packing to speak to Atarki about Miura. I wanted him to repair my little Miura's face. With surgery she would be a beauty who might find herself with better choices in life than those she had at present. When I told her what I intended she said that she was happy enough as she was. She didn't trust Atarki, whom she had once seen dancing as though his limbs didn't belong to his body. The thought of such a man wielding a scalpel terrified her. After a few days, though, I managed to convince her of her beauty. Her vanity got the better of her and she agreed to him being asked.

Atarki said that it was not his field but he knew of someone who would do it and he was glad to be of help to me. He said that he would pay for the operation and make all the arrangements. He was as good as his word and Miura's eyelid was operated on by one of Tokyo's top plastic surgeons. When the time came for her bandages to be removed we were both surprised and delighted at how well the procedure had worked. She couldn't stop looking at herself in my mirror, and hoped that with her newfound beauty she might aspire to the more lucrative life of a prostitute. I thought that she would do well in that profession. Her delicate body, narrow hands and tiny feet would attract a great many clients.

In gratitude for a job so superbly done, I gave Atarki an hour or two of the peculiar type of pleasure that he enjoyed so much. I ordered him around and made him bring me vodka, which I threw in his face, telling him that I had requested sake. I beat him with a cane while I sat on top of him and insisted that he lie still as I did what I wanted to him. I bit his lip as I had done Kawashima's, and drew from him blood and a deep moan of satisfaction. I think that he enjoyed that evening more than any other in my company, and was, I thought, well repaid for his favour to Miura.

I did not tell Sesyu that I was leaving him and Tokyo. I could not be bothered with the battle or the pleadings that I was bound to reject. I had no doubt that he would easily survive my going and it would not be long before he found a girl to live in the pleasure dome he had bought for me. Sesyu was a man who needed to think himself in love, to have someone other than his wife to lavish presents on. For someone as generous as him, a new passion would not be hard to find. I knew that I would not break his heart, as surely as I knew that leaving him would not break mine. If I stayed with him, I knew with certainty that I would live to regret it.

Before I left, I gave Miura money and secured her a place with Tamura's 'good-hearted' mama-san. Sorry said that if she couldn't have me, she would give what affection she had left to little Miura, whom she had come to love. It pleased me that I had brought two such unlikely friends together.

I cut my hair short, returned to wearing jodhpurs and boots, and packed only a few clothes and those things that were precious to me. Not wishing to repeat the mistake I had made by taking Xue's jade pendant, I left Sesyu the deeds to the house on the pillow of my bed.

As Miura slept I took my leave of the yellow house and left the city before the morning mist had evaporated. I passed the copper roof of the Imperial Palace, coloured with verdigris, just as the sun rose above the dark pinewood that surrounded it. I pictured

Hirohito, the Emperor of Radiant Peace, asleep in his gilded bed and wished him and Japan good fortune. I was leaving too early for the maples to colour, but the abundant white anemones waved me goodbye.

It had been interesting, an interlude in my life that had allowed me to spend time with Sorry, and to see Tamura fulfil her ambition. I was satisfied that Miura would have a better life than she could have hoped for before she knew me. As for Doctor Atarki, he would miss me and enjoy his misery.

I felt that I would never see Sorry again and, as it happened, I was right. In the spring of the following year, she died from the vicious influenza virus that carried off many infants and aged in Tokyo. The news of her death reached me on an overcast day in Shanghai when I was already feeling gloomy. I had lost my sweet, sweet Sorry.

I rarely prepare opium without thinking of her, or eat dried lychees without the scent reminding me of the times I spent with Sorry as a girl, gossiping and nibbling them as we sat on the bed, she and I against the world. I never found another Sorry to look after me, for she was irreplaceable.

Longhua Peaches and Sake

There is a saying that, regardless of any other factor in our lives, it is the one of timing that seals our fate. Nothing proved the saying more for me than the time I spent in Shanghai. In those teeming streets where fabulous wealth and extreme poverty collided, where there was a price for every cruel pleasure and murdered children were the debris of the rivers, I became greedy for experience and lost what there was of goodness in my nature. It seemed to me then that I had been fashioned for that particular city at that exact time and no warning that I would be seduced by its grasping decadence would have affected me then.

The day I arrived in Shanghai I booked into the Central Hotel on Nanking Road and took a walk along the foreshore known as the Bund. By the time I returned to the hotel for tea served in the British fashion my head was buzzing with the myriad images of Shanghai that have stayed with me to this day. I came to know the city so well that if you asked me now, I believe I could draw a map of it from memory. I fell in love with it completely. I think what overtook me was its unique combination of virtue and vice that hung like the scent of opium in the air, imbuing it with the promise of bliss.

In the crush of Shanghai's streets, I rubbed shoulders with rich old men who strolled with their beautiful Russian mistresses. I smiled at the sailors hurrying to 'Blood Alley' where the Cantonese girls who serviced them were called saltwater sisters. I admired the speed of the running rickshaw boys, and the shiny new black automobiles that ostentatiously cruised the narrow roads. I flirted with the red-turbaned Sikh police who shouted at the cars and hit the rickshaw boys with their truncheons. And after that first day I learnt to turn my head from the 'honey carts' filled with human excrement from the international settlements as they made their way to the reeking night-soil jetty. The stinking cargo was loaded on boats and taken up the rural creeks to the farms. So rich was the living for those with money in Shanghai that Chinese farmers prized the waste from their bodies as being especially fertile.

Every kind of human being was to be found in Shanghai, not just different nationalities, but the good, the bad, the rich, the destitute, those with religion and those without, the whole and the crippled and of course the dead, who had to be constantly cleared from the dirty Huangpu River. Beggars ended their days in the sewers, or had to be stepped over as they expired on the streets. So poor were the peasant Chinese of Shanghai that infanticide was a common crime that never came to court. The sale of children was so prevalent that I have heard foreigners say that the Chinese ask more for a pig than a child.

You could buy anything you desired in Shanghai, exotic foods, imported spirits, the latest French fashion, powder to kill bedbugs, strawberry jam to stir into your tea, delicious Longhua peaches and wonderful furs from the Siberian Fur Store. There were bookshops and beauty parlours, teahouses and theatres where you could see the latest American and Chinese films. As well as a hundred dance halls, there were seven hundred brothels. Opium dens were never more than a few yards away and there were clubs and whorehouses run by Korean gangsters.

On my first walk I bought myself a box of black Russian cigarettes; they had gold bands around their filter and looked darkly glamorous. I must have been approached a dozen times by beggars and people trying to sell me everything from tickets for the Peking opera to crickets in little wooden cages.

The only other thing I bought on that first day was a guide to the 'flowers' of Shanghai. It listed the hundred most popular girls, the more refined courtesans, the Japanese geishas and the boy actors who often doubled as prostitutes. The most expensive of the 'flowers' were the virgin courtesans whom only the richest men could afford to deflower. When summoned, these girls were taken to their assignations on the shoulders of their pimps, so that the dust of the street would not defile them before their customers did. They were very young girls, some no more than ten years old, but painted like dolls, their tiny mouths as red as blood. They seemed already to have lost their innocence.

The thrill of Shanghai entered my bloodstream like nicotine and kept me addicted to its peculiar but easily acquired taste. Only the most confident, the most brazen, survived well in Shanghai. I was determined to be amongst their number.

Within a month or two, I had found myself a small circle of acquaintances made up from fellow guests met in the busy international bar of the Central Hotel. Following their lead, I dressed up for dinner and drank gin and tonic before and brandy after. Most of my new companions were transient foreigners, American and British journalists, French salesmen and Chinese and Korean entrepreneurs. But a few others, attracted like myself by the city's air of excitement, took up more long-term residence.

One of these companions, a plump but elegant woman who claimed to be the daughter of an Indian maharajah, took a fancy to me and drew me into her circle. She gave her name as Rajkumari, which I later discovered means princess in Hindi. She told me that like her other friends I could call her Mari. She had a huge circle of acquaintances and could often be found drinking with European aristocrats or Japanese playboys, as well as with the White Russians who always claimed to be princes or counts no matter what their true origins. Although she had a superior manner and modelled her accent on the English ladies who took tea at the Astor Hotel, she wasn't above being seen in the company of the most brutish of gangsters.

I can't imagine that even in her youth Mari would have been thought beautiful, but she had an energy about her that was attractive. She was an inch or two above being considered short, rather puffy in the face, with dark shadows that ringed her huge eyes. She had dyed black hair, as well as an inflated belief in her own beauty. Mari had a penchant for the demi-monde. She never slept before dawn and never left her suite until after lunch, which she took in bed from a tray. She believed the morning sun to be damaging to her skin, which was the colour of burnt toffee and smooth as an olive.

Her excessive tidiness amused me, but was a burden to the hotel staff. She couldn't bear anything to be out of place or dusty and was constantly calling on them to clean her rooms. She liked to be in control of everything and everyone, and the slightest hint of chaos really upset her. I think she suffered a constant fear of death which, no matter how much she organised her world, was of course the one thing that she couldn't control.

Like me, Mari enjoyed being a woman who made her own decisions, and said that she intended never to marry and have to answer to a man for her actions. She was a silent partner in a nightclub owned by a couple of Korean brothers, who also ran brothels and the lucrative night-soil business.

They were good-looking in a hard sort of way. The younger had a thin scar that ran the length of his right cheek, which spoilt his otherwise perfectly balanced face, but added to his roguish appeal. The elder brother was thickset with sensuously full lips and watchful eyes. He had a suspicious nature, but could be generous to those he liked and he seemed to like Mari.

Mari never went into detail about where her money came from, but behind her back everyone who knew her said it came from crime. I believed them, because although she told me she received a small allowance from her father, she spent like an heiress, denying herself nothing and living in the most expensive suite the Central had to offer.

The brothers enjoyed her contacts and her company, were themselves good company, but I wouldn't have trusted them for a moment. They supplied Mari with the pretty girls she preferred to men, and took her gambling at the Chinese Jockey Club, out beyond Hangkou Park. Mari was a compulsive gambler and lost a fortune on those so-called 'china ponies', which were imported from Mongolia. She borrowed money from her Koreans to pay her debts, and ended up doing them favours of a kind she said would probably shock me. Mari often boasted that if she was ever desperate for money she had enough information on those brothers to insure her an income for years to come.

Through her I made a lot of interesting contacts myself, and learnt that it was who you knew in Shanghai that determined how successful you would be. She took me to cocktail parties at the houses of the rich French who lived on Avenue Joffre and to the homes of the more sedate British at the residential end of Nanking Road, whose gardens, she said, were based on those of the stately homes of the British aristocracy.

I still wore my jodhpurs and boots and whenever we were out together the contrast between them and her beautiful saris always caused a stir. The fashion for Chinese women in Shanghai was a seductive version of the Manchu cheongsam which, influenced by western taste, had become shorter and tighter, revealing more of the female shape than the modest flowing folds of the original. I liked them and bought a couple, but I tired of them quickly. I was looking for a different image to the familiar one of a Chinese beauty. Under Mari's guidance I was influenced into French chiffon dresses and shoes with straps that wound sinuously around my ankles. I more often wore my jodhpurs, but I will never forget the feel of that silk chiffon against my skin, or the way those shoes made me feel potent and desirable.

Mari hated the way the men flocked about me, 'like jackals around a kill', she would sneer. She was never one to give a compliment easily. She said that it was just that I was 'fresh meat'. She was wrong, of course. I never had trouble attracting men and I always found generous ones prepared to support my lifestyle.

But it wasn't a truly satisfying life. I had little idea of what would be. Intoxicated with the heady variety and uniqueness of Shanghai, I chose to ignore the little island of emptiness within. I told myself that it must be homesickness. I certainly thought of myself and of my home as Japanese and still planned to return to it in glory one day when the chance offered itself.

So, when the Chinese in Shanghai became anti-Japanese there was no question of whom I sided with. They resented Japan for harbouring Pu Yi and suspected the Japanese of trying to claim Manchuria for themselves. But they were cowardly in their hatred and the Japanese were able to walk the Shanghai streets without fear of attack.

Time passed, and in 1931 a week or so before my twenty-fifth birthday I was contemplating whether to take up with a German industrialist who had been pursuing me, when an Englishman called Harry Sanger bought me a drink at the bar of the Central and became for a while my friend and lover.

Harry was without doubt the best-looking European I had ever seen. Each feature of his face was perfectly proportioned, from his blue eyes, so dark they were almost navy, to his slim nose and full lips. He had brown hair and was tall even for a European. He wore linen shirts and brogue shoes, and sometimes a panama hat with his Garrick Club tie fastened around its brim in the noon sun. He had a warm scent about him that reminded me of oranges and a deep laugh that was always close to the surface. Harry wasn't the first European I ever made love with, but I discovered in him a run of passion that belied the cool exterior that he, like most Englishmen I have known, presented to the world. He enjoyed having fun, loved good food and never said no to a drink. It was Harry who introduced me to wine, which I didn't enjoy, because it tasted ancient and the smell was reminiscent of wet fur and mould. When I became used to it, he tried to teach me the difference between a good wine and a great one, but I never got it. I preferred the instant way that spirits heated the blood.

Harry constantly teased me, which at first I didn't understand for it wasn't an oriental way of behaving. His practical jokes could be cruel, as he was quick at noticing what others tried to disguise about themselves and couldn't resist making them squirm. For instance, Mari had a problem with hair on her upper lip, and like a man she shaved it daily. Noticing the shadow, Harry quipped that she was changing into the man she had always wanted to be. As Mari didn't like her preference for girls to be spoken of and was conceited about her looks, she was very offended. I think his habit of embarrassing people was a way of keeping the spotlight off himself. I suspected he was not everything he made himself out to be. He told me that he was getting married to an English girl called Jenny, whom he loved because she had an uncomplicated nature and would willingly climb mountains with him. He said she was a tall girl with green eyes and strong hands and to his delight she rode a horse like a man. His engagement meant nothing to me. Harry was fun and that was enough for the present.

In any case, I could not claim to be exclusively his. As well as sleeping with him, I frequently took the younger brother of Mari's gangster partners to my bed. He was a man who, like Kawashima before him, not only believed he was superior to any woman, but was also pitiless in bed. Although he never mentioned it, I think that Harry knew and didn't object. Like most men in Shanghai he was caught up in the idea that any sexual fantasy could be gratified and that he could have whatever he desired. Perhaps he found it exciting to share his lover with a gangster. It would give him something to remember in the long winter nights ahead of him in England, as he sat by the fire with his green-eyed wife.

147

Harry was in Shanghai to do business for his family company, which dealt in porcelain. He found it amusing that he could sell china in China, and that the expatriate English thought his product superior in style and quality to local porcelain.

From our first meeting I was as comfortable with Harry as though I had known him all my life. In the months I spent with him before he returned to England we managed a lot of fun and made memories of things that could only have happened in Shanghai.

One midnight, dressed as a servant boy, I went with him to the glorious Shanghai Club, the so-called headquarters of the British community in the city, whose members were supposed to be the pillars of the Establishment. No Chinese were allowed, but Harry said he had a connection, and as it was late and I was disguised as a servant we would get away with it. It always seemed odd to me that the British were so anti-oriental, mainly, I suppose, because I felt superior to them.

We filled my flask with brandy and although it was only a short distance from the Central we took a rickshaw to the Shanghai's impressive main door. Harry gave only the briefest of acknowledgements to the night porter, who obviously knew him, and without even glancing at me, said, 'Good evening, sir,' and returned to reading his book.

We walked through a small library where Harry paused briefly at a circular table littered with newspapers to read the headlines of the *North China Daily*. Then he turned, pulled me to him, put his tongue in my mouth and gave me a long, long kiss. I tasted the strange curdled taste peculiar to Europeans and wondered what I tasted of to him. Taking my hand he led me down some steps to the echoing halls of the basement and on through double doors that opened into a columned room housing an elegant swimming pool that shimmered in dim light.

Two naked men were embracing in the water, one of them whose face I could not see had his back to me; his legs were wrapped around the other's waist and they were kissing passionately. The movement of their bodies in the water made delightful little slapping noises, which echoed around the room. Their skin, turned to the colour of limes by the reflection of the pool's tiles, appeared in the pitchy light to form one strangely shaped animal. They took no notice of us and went on embracing as though we didn't exist. I expect they thought that Harry was of their own persuasion and that I was a paid-for short-time boy. The scene, framed by the Grecian columns and gold-leafed walls of the spectacular pool, would have made an exceptional painting. I said as much to Harry and he replied, 'In a peculiar sort of whorehouse, maybe.'

Even though he professed to disapprove, I think that, like me, Harry was excited by their sport. He pushed me behind a pillar and kissed me in an urgent sort of way and told me that I looked delicious dressed as a boy, and then assured me that it was just a joke, for he was all man when it came to women. We took our clothes off in one of the cubicles housed along the side of the pool. It had half doors like those of a stable, so that the legs and the heads of the occupants could be seen from the outside. When we emerged naked, the pool was empty.

Harry practically threw me into the water and then performed a perfect dive and came up beside me. I teased him that perhaps he had only found me attractive in the first place because of my jodhpurs and boots and the fact that I had short hair like a boy's. I was laughing, but for once Harry wasn't. He shoved me against the side of the pool and told me to shut up. We swam a couple of lengths not touching, then he pulled me to the steps, and as we left the water I could see that he was already hard. We made love in the cubicle with me standing on the narrow bench with my back against the wall, so that Harry, who was at least a foot taller than me, could stretch his arms out to each wall and enter me with ease. He looked like the painting of Hercules holding up the pillars of wisdom that I had seen in the club's entrance hall.

Halfway through our coupling, I heard two splashes and an odd high-pitched laugh. Harry cursed and held his cries in as though he thought that in silence we would not be noticed. His thrusts became quicker, as if he couldn't wait to finish, and as he did he told me I was a good boy and then cursed again.

I told him that he made love beautifully and he said that what we did was fucking, not making love. I liked the word, but I was used to oriental euphemisms and when I tried it out it sounded strange on my tongue and made Harry laugh. He said that it was a man's word anyway and didn't come out right when a woman used it.

I remember thinking that night that Harry's wholesome moun-tain-climbing bride would get more than she bargained for with him as a husband. I hoped for her sake that, like myself, she had a certain boyish charm that would keep him from wandering down amongst the boys.

As we were leaving, I noticed that one of the new men in the pool was the star of that season's popular Peking opera *The Drunken Beauty*. We had seen it with Mari at the Lyceum the night before and had thought him exquisite. He still had his performance make-up on, which in the dim light of the pool looked oddly threatening. I recognised his partner as the wealthy German who could be found most nights at the Casanova club, a girl on each arm, a fat cigar in his mouth. He was a huge pink-skinned man in his fifties, with fingers like sausages, and the coldest eyes I had ever seen. He had his young lover pushed firmly against the wall of the pool and was entering him from behind with such force that the water splashed over the edge in choppy waves. The boy had to hold on to the side so tightly that his fingers were white with the effort of it.

I wondered briefly what those English wives, with their white gloves, reserved voices and rigid rules, would have made of what went on in the club's pool after the midnight hour.

We were making our way through the famous long bar with its high stools and gleaming mirrors when Harry suddenly picked me up and sat me on its polished surface. We served ourselves a generous measure of whisky from a cut-glass decanter, linked arms and drank it down in one go.

'Let's fuck again,' he said, unbuckling his belt and practically dragging me to the floor. I knew his lust had been stirred by the rough coupling of the fat German and his slight oriental lover, but whatever the inspiration, I always enjoyed Harry's enthusiastic lovemaking.

'That will help you to remember me, if I can ever bring myself to leave Shanghai,' he said. I told him that no woman ever forgot her most passionate lover, which seemed to satisfy him. He needn't have worried. He compared well to all of my lovers, and not only did I never forget him, but over the years I have often thought of him with tenderness and a degree of regret at his absence.

I believe that in Shanghai Harry found a way of being that satisfied the shadowy side of his nature, probably kept hidden in England. There were nights when he was nowhere to be found and times when his bruises spoke of a more desperate sort of sex than the kind we shared. Had he stayed in Shanghai, perhaps he would have indulged that side of his personality too much and lost that part of himself that was full of happiness and light.

A few years later the Shanghai Club would be occupied by the Japanese, who would shorten the legs of the tables and chairs for the convenience of their bantam-sized officers. I expect they behaved in the same way as the English club members did, only the language of their hypocrisy would have been that of honour, as opposed to that of manners. As night became day, did samurai kiss samurai in the love pool of the British club, I wonder.

I never lost my attraction to Japanese men, but after Harry Sanger my taste where lovers were concerned became more liberal. I grew to like not only the creamy smell of Europeans, but also their generosity and sense of humour which, once you are used to it, colours your way of thinking forever.

On the way out of the club, Harry stopped at the night porter's desk and openly offered him a large note which he took without once looking at me. He said to Harry that on such a muggy night he supposed a midnight swim was very refreshing. Harry replied that it had made him feel like a new man. We went on to the Venus Café and ravenously ate beef stroganoff and paskha, a delicious pudding of cream cheese and dried apricots. Then, with our stomachs hot with vodka, I took Harry to the opium den around the corner from the Astor Hotel for his first taste of the poppy. Six hours later, he told me that he thought we had only been there for a few minutes, although he remembers dreaming that he was on a beautiful beach made of flat white pebbles that were soft to the touch. The water was as tender as velvet and his playmates were his old school friends whom he loved and admired.

During Harry's last week in Shanghai the air was heavy with humidity and high winds that whipped the street's litter into doorways and rattled the ill-fitting windows of the Central Hotel. Everyone said that a typhoon was on its way and that it would be the last one of the summer before winter was upon us. At night the leaden air made it hard to breathe and turned my dreams into nightmares where I watched myself walking down empty streets without even thoughts for company. When the storm finally broke, it wrenched the tiles from the roofs and sent them crashing to the street. It littered the Bund with sea debris and flooded the drains so that the roads ran with water so high that it lapped at the rickshaw boy's knees.

I was in the Nanking Cinema with Harry watching an American movie called *Forty Winks* at the time. We had been drinking sake from Kawashima's flask and smoking Harry's English cigarettes. The torrential rain on the roof drowned out the soundtrack of the film, so we left and ran back to the hotel for our last night together. By the time we got there we were completely drenched and shivering. We shared a hot bath, drank a lot more sake and made love twice. Harry asked me to slick my short hair back like a boy's and to wear the high heels, suspender belt and black stockings that Sesyu had given me. He liked me half boy, half girl; it satisfied all his needs, I suppose. Later, when I sat on the floor playing cards with him, dressed in that way and smoking one of my black cigarettes, he told me that if he ever had a reluctance to make love to his wife he would picture me as I was then and he was sure it would solve the problem. I observed that he called it making love and not fucking and I felt a little envious of his bride to be.

Next morning we went for breakfast at the Chocolate Shop on Bubbling Well Road. Harry ate eggs and pancakes and I had ice cream, which I had never eaten before. He gave me money, and a St Christopher coin on a chain. He said St Christopher was the patron saint of travellers. He told me that he worried about where I would end up, and that it wouldn't harm me to have a saint on my side. We left the Chocolate Shop arm-in-arm and went to the Siberian Fur Store where he bought me an astrakhan coat and two silver fox collars to keep me warm through the winter months. The dark little eyes of the pair were fashioned from tiger's eye; there was a brocade loop that held their tails in a symbiotic knot and their feet hung realistically over my shoulder.

We walked back to the Central Hotel along the crowded streets, where we had to press ourselves against a wall to allow an elaborately decorated bridal sedan to pass. It was covered in fresh flowers and accompanied by musicians and the bride's family. Harry shouted out 'Good luck', but they ignored him. He asked me what I thought of marriage and I told him it was probably a good thing for a man. He laughed and said that he would let me know.

I could tell that he was sad to be leaving, but he said that he intended to come back and that I hadn't seen the last of him. I didn't believe him. I thought that he was just one of those people who hated goodbyes. In those days no one who had once sampled the delights of Shanghai could believe that they would not do so again. But after that time I never saw Harry again.

I felt strangely empty without him, as though I had no idea of what I should be doing. I took a bath, missed lunch, and I suppose I missed him too, at least for the rest of that day. But Shanghai was a difficult place to be lonely in for long.

Mari, pleased to have Harry out of the way, took me over once again. She had a jealous nature and hadn't liked me moving away from the intimacy of her connections. She couldn't bear her friends to wander or to have experiences that she wasn't a part of. When I told her about swimming at the British Club, she said that she had done a similar thing in India, only with the wife of a colonel in the Indian Army. I often felt annoyed with Mari and it would be a lie to say that I liked her, but she was a useful contact and kept me company in the months leading up to that New Year's Eve, when things were to change dramatically for both of us.

It was Mari who found me the beautiful villa on Rue Lafayette, at half the price of my room at the Central. I moved in that December, when Shanghai seemed to forget that it was Chinese and celebrated Christmas as though it was the most natural thing in the world. Weeks before Christmas Day there were decorations and artificial snow in the windows of the stores. Along the promenade of the Bund the trees were hung with shiny glass stars, and there was a Christmas tree in front of the Shanghai Club. The Chocolate Shop served Christmas pudding with ice cream and on the Avenue Foch you could buy gold and silvered almonds in boxes tied with red satin bows.

It was colourful, fun and foreign, and Mari who had experienced European Christmases before was even more excited about the season than me. She took me shopping for presents and to a different party every night. We bought flesh-coloured lingerie edged with pale lace, and chiffon dresses that floated like gauze in the slightest breeze. In a rush of excess, Mari bought me a ring set with a huge moonstone and we drank champagne at every stop we made. In the early hours of the morning, I would return to my rented villa exhausted and sleep until after noon the next day, when we would start the whole thing over again. Sometimes Mari would come to the villa to pick me up. She would talk to me while I bathed in the delightful marble-floored bathroom that had mirrored walls and brass taps. Sitting on the edge of the bath puffing on Camel cigarettes, she would fill the small room with smoke and gossip. The bathroom had stone shelves on which I kept my chrysanthemum oil, and a chandelier above the bath where I hung Harry's St Christopher's coin on its silver chain. Camouflaged amongst the crystal drops I forgot it, and have a fancy that it is still there, swaying in the humid air of that scented room.

On my first night in the villa I dreamt that Miura's little songbird was caught up in the room. It flew about in a panic, dashing itself against the walls, getting tangled in the folds of the chintz curtains that hung at the long windows. When I finally clasped it in my hands, I saw that it had the face of poor Shimako and thinking that it would fly away, I threw it out of the window, only to watch it fall to the ground.

It doesn't matter how lightly we may choose to travel; in the shadows and in our dreams the company of ghosts is always with us. Shimako often comes to me in mine in the form of a flying creature, perhaps because I like to think of her free at last from her dragging leg. I think Natsuko would have been surprised to discover that even in death her sister accompanies me, stirring my longing for home.

With Harry gone my dark days came more often. They were deep and disabling and I dreaded them. I knew when they were about to overtake me because nothing would be right, not how I looked, how I felt nor how I related to others. I would dwell on my life's disappointments and relive the feelings of those painful times in a self-indulgent wash of misery. The loss of my mother, Yamaga's desertion, Natsuko's coldness to me all seemed to be alive in the present and no amount of socialising could console me. I would take to my bed, get drunk on sake or lulled by opium until the dark hours passed. And they always did, leaving me light-headed and longing for company.

On one bright morning during those weeks of Christmas festivities, I woke with the dreaded hollow ache and knew that it would not be a good day. The pain made no sense to me. There were painful memories from the past, but my current life, although lacking direction, was interesting and, I thought, hopeful. But that day, the gloom was so deep that I didn't have the energy to go to my favourite opium house. I started drinking early to deaden the pain and to dull the sense I had of being completely worthless. I could not wipe the picture of my sweet mother's face from my mind, or lessen the sound of Shimako's voice telling me, when I was just twelve years old, that her sister's black pearl matched my nature.

I missed my appointment with Mari and she came to the villa, furious with me for letting her down. She said that my depressions were a luxury that I gave into too easily. 'Sometimes, Yoshiko, I feel a little tested by life myself, but it is foolish to lose the day. You know that I can't bear to be let down. I waited in the Virtue teahouse for almost an hour.'

I apologised to her and determined that I would not allow the next dark time that came to possess me in the way it had done that day.

Perhaps I was too free, too unbounded to feel safe. I was as alone as an orphan and frustrated in my desire to be a true daughter of Japan. The Kawashimas may have rejected me, but in my heart I felt that my country never would. I needed to find a way to serve it that would give me the recognition and purpose I so craved. Much as Shanghai had captivated me, I wanted to be taken back into the fold, cherished and treasured by the only parent left to me, Japan.

Dismissing my melancholy as indulgence, Mari was interfering and full of advice. She said that I was a determined person and could help myself if I really wanted to.

'Try a girl for a change, Yoshiko. I swear it would lift your gloomy moods in a way no man ever could.'

Just for the sake of experience I agreed, although I had my doubts that I would enjoy it. I felt odd and unsettled at the thought of it, as though I was about the business of building a house on a swamp.

A few days before, Mari had met an interesting Russian girl in the French Jew's pawnshop on Nanking Road. Trying not to catch Mari's eyes, she'd had tears in her own as she handed over a rather fine diamond brooch, and took in return a small wad of used notes. The pawnshop was a familiar haunt for Mari, who was always running out of cash because, as she said, her father had so many daughters to support that he often forgot to send her funds. I didn't believe that her father sent her anything, and as she usually reclaimed her treasures from the pawnbroker within weeks, it was obvious that she had a secret means of obtaining money that she did not want known.

Under Mari's sociable front there was something dark and unreachable. It showed in the way that she suspected any act of kindness, and in the restlessness of her nature. It was as though if she sat still for too long she would be overtaken by her demons. I think that she hid what she thought would revolt others under a cloak of sophistication and the pretence of gaiety. Though I could not bring myself to like her, I was attracted to the air of danger that hung around her.

In her usual way of collecting people, Mari had made friends with the Russian girl and discovered that she had been the lover of an heiress in Cairo, who for the sake of respectability and to secure her father's fortune had married a high-profile politician and given up her lesbian lover. She had arranged a small fund to secure her lover's silence, on the provision that she left the country and never contacted her again. According to Mari the girl had set about a world tour and had fetched up in Shanghai, low on funds and friends, but full of charm. She claimed to be a countess, of course, one who, fleeing the Bolsheviks, had arrived in Egypt alone and almost penniless. Mari said that she was a cold-climate beauty with narrow grey eyes and pale skin as matt as paper. She had only been in Shanghai a few weeks and was already pawning her jewellery to pay for the undistinguished room she had taken in a small hotel near Yanglingbang Creek, on the edge of the French concession.

When my mood returned to normal, Mari brought her for dinner at the Central and introduced us. 'Call me Valerie,' she said in her light, evenly pitched voice. It was a name she liked and had chosen for herself. Her real one, she said, would have given away her royal connections and put her in danger from the revolutionaries that she said were everywhere in Shanghai.

As the city was full of people claiming to be from foreign royal ancestry it was hard to be impressed by Valerie's story, but she certainly had something of the patrician about her. No foreigner in Shanghai liked to be thought ordinary. I did not blame her any more than I did myself for promoting the most glamorous image that she could. Valerie was a year or so older than me, but she contrived to look younger. She always dressed in white, like the American naval wives who shopped at Hall and Holtz, and mimicked the accents of the English upper class. She used a man's cologne that smelled of lime and basil and was never seen without her string of pearls, which she said lit the paleness of her skin.

She liked to give the impression of being more cynical than she actually was, but I discovered her to be quite tender in her nature. She gave money she could ill afford to beggars and loved children, especially those of the poor. I didn't care much for her air of moral superiority, but she had a quality of goodness in her nature that encouraged friendship. There was something trustworthy about Valerie that put people at ease. Perhaps it was the confident way she moved or her childlike acceptance of everyone she came into contact with, but whatever it was you could not walk with her without linking your arm through hers, or stop yourself from taking her hand as you crossed the road.

Mari thought that we would make good companions and, in a desire to be in control of everything and everyone, she encouraged me to become Valerie's lover.

And so it was Valerie who introduced me to the games that women play in the bedroom. And that was what they were for me, just games to while away the long afternoons when Shanghai slept. Valerie was too gentle in bed to satisfy me, but I found comfort in being touched by her and never suffered those moments of loneliness I experienced after sex with men. Her pale skin, delicate bone structure and air of fragility were so feminine that I could not think of her as a lover even though I always had wonderful orgasms in her company.

I think that Mari's lovemaking must have been quite different to Valerie's. She had once shown me a leather dildo that had been fashioned for her in India and I remember thinking that, if she enjoyed that, how much more she would enjoy the real thing. When I said as much to her she replied that she was the one who used it on the girls who came to her bed, never the other way round. Valerie relied on a more sensuous style of lovemaking that did not involve toys. I enjoyed the strange perverseness of it, but then I enjoy a good massage or a dish of sushi, both of which I can live without. I discovered that sex with a woman is like being hungry for meat and being given soup; you do not starve but it isn't quite enough.

Valerie didn't agree that sexual love between women was perverse. She said that she believed that whatever existed in nature was by definition natural, and that God had chosen for her to be as she was.

On Christmas Eve, a few days after my first sexual encounter with Valerie, I was looking for fun and agreed to share a flower girl with Mari at the house of Sure Satisfaction where the male clients, taking us for prostitutes, handled us familiarly, one of them saying he would take both of us for the night. When they discovered we were about the same business as themselves some were amused, but most were disgusted. I have never understood why men feel so challenged by a woman's sexual appetite when they don't seem to mind other kinds of greed too much. Perhaps it clashes with their notion that the seed of a woman's lust should not set itself, but be planted by the one perfect gardener.

For myself I never felt ashamed of my choices, yet I will say that from the first time I slept with Valerie, I lost something earthed in myself and became with her, as with every other woman I coupled with after, a good actress. I knew that Valerie was being faithful to herself and her true nature, while I was going against mine and seeking comfort under false pretences. I found it unsettling and began to experience feelings of disgust with myself. I didn't want to end up like Mari, indulging in too much of everything and excited by nothing. In the sleepless reaches of the night, I was taken down strange paths where, although I was lying still, unnamed fears made my heart race. There were times in those boundless days in Shanghai when I longed to be back with Natsuko and Sorry, unaware that as well as excitement and fun there was a high price to be paid for freedom. As a child I had wanted to break the few boundaries that held me. As an adult I mourned that there were none left.

But despite my misgivings, Valerie turned out to be one of the better things in my life, at that time at least. She was interesting and generous and I enjoyed her cool company and the way she tapped her way lightly through life. The best thing about making a woman your lover is that she will become your intimate confidante and closest friend. And so it was with Valerie. The lovemaking became nothing more than an aperitif to the sharing of confidences and the companionship that grew between us. She did not mind that I had other lovers and told me that her own plan was to marry a rich man so that she would never have to worry about money again. But despite her venal plans, there was something puritanical about her. And though I liked her well it was hard to love her because she kept a portion of herself in reserve.

I had expected to see Mari at the Christmas Eve party at the American Club but she didn't turn up. It was odd, because I knew that she was looking forward to it. I thought that perhaps she was still at the House of Sure Satisfaction, where I had left her asleep in the arms of the doll-like prostitute she seemed so taken with.

Christmas Day was spent in bed with Valerie, recovering from the excesses of the night before and discussing how unlike Mari it was to miss the fun. So after a rest and a good dinner, Valerie and I went to the Central to see what had happened to her. I asked for her at the desk where they said that she had checked out without leaving a forwarding address or a return date. It was hard to believe that she would have left so suddenly without taking any leave of us. I went to her rooms and found them completely empty of her things. The bed was made up, its cover smooth, its pillows plumped. The vacant wardrobes smelled of her perfume but nothing else spoke of her occupancy. Even the cedarwood linings were gone from her drawers. There was only the faintest scent of Mari to suggest that she had spent the last five years in those tidy rooms that looked as anonymous as any other unoccupied suite at the Central.

I questioned the doorman of the hotel who told me that he hadn't seen Mari leave, but that she had sent friends for her belongings. He wouldn't tell me who the friends were, even though I tipped him generously. I could see that he was scared and I didn't push him. It wasn't hard to work out whose names he could not bring himself to say.

When I checked with her Korean partners, they told me that she had gone back to India. I had seen her only the day before and she had said nothing to me about leaving Shanghai. I knew that she had intended claiming back her stake in their club, and putting the money into some shares she had been given a tip about. I couldn't help feeling that that was at the root of things and it disturbed me. It had only been a week since she had commissioned a diamond bracelet to be made for her by the talented Russian jeweller who worked from a tiny shop in the so-called Nevsky Prospekt. She had spent a long time over its design and put down a large deposit on it.

161

It seemed unlikely that she would have left without her money or the bracelet.

I waited two days before informing the police of her disappearance. I didn't really expect her to suddenly turn up. They said they would make enquiries, but they stressed that people came and went in Shanghai as they pleased. As she had checked out of the Central of her own free will there wasn't much they could do.

Valerie told me not to worry. She said she had met women like Mari before and they rarely put down roots. She had probably tired of Shanghai and had left wanting to avoid a fuss. I couldn't take comfort in Valerie's view of events. For one thing she hardly knew Mari and for another, I knew Mari well enough to know that she was still in love with Shanghai.

I don't know why Mari's disappearance bothered me so much; after all, I felt little if any true attachment to her. But I did suspect that something in her life had gone badly wrong and I felt that, had she been planning to leave, I would have been amongst the first to know. It was unsettling and I would have wanted her to enquire after my well-being if I had disappeared. There is, after all, an unspoken obligation of care in every friendship.

Years later at a time when I had nothing to do but think about my past, I remembered that at the time of Mari's vanishing, I had come to a crossroads in my own life. I was aware that my nature was reckless and that if my spirit was to remain basically good, I had to rein it in. But my instinct led me to explore the shadows of my nature and I chose the darker path and let go of Mari. I should not have given up the search so easily, but as I was to discover, whatever I did would have been of no use for I believe Mari was dead even before I reported her missing.

I slept only once more with the sly-eyed Korean partner of Mari. I had grown tired of his brutality and his peasant's nature, which was greedy and desperate. As in other lovers that I chose because they reminded me of Kawashima, he turned out to be like all imitations, a poor one. I knew without proof that he was respon-

162

sible for Mari's disappearance and after we had made love and he had drunk a third of a bottle of gin, I asked him to tell me what had happened to her. All he would say was that perhaps some poor farmer would get more with his night-soil delivery than he had bargained for, and that I would be wise to forget Mari and stop asking about her.

Mari had run up huge gambling debts which she had demanded the Koreans pay for her out of the club's profits. Perhaps she had threatened to expose the brothers' illegal dealings and was becoming a nuisance to them. It was likely that rather than allow her to retrieve her money and continue to meddle in their affairs, they had murdered her and disposed of her body.

Such was the ethos in Shanghai in those days that I was not particularly surprised. I knew that given the passing of a few weeks, Mari would be completely forgotten. It frightened me to think that if I upset the wrong people, what had happened to her could easily happen to me. It was tragic that Mari, so fastidious and obsessively tidy in life, should end up mingling her blood with the pungent ooze of Shanghai's night soil. I dreamt of her lying at the bottom of a lake, her dark hair tangled in weeds, her huge eyes translucent and hopeless.

Perhaps I should have left Shanghai then, when I was still afraid and still able to be shocked. Instead I bought myself a small pearl-handled revolver, and although I felt a little ashamed not to be pursuing justice for Mari, I went on with my life. I whiled away the next couple of days in the company of opium and an assortment of unexceptional men and agreed to go with Valerie to the New Year's Eve party at the Cathay Hotel.

By the time we arrived at the Cathay's splendid ballroom it was crowded to capacity with Shanghai society, the orchestra was in full swing and Valerie and I had to shout at each other to make ourselves heard. The singer, a Chinese boy, polished to perfection, looking like a ventriloquist's dummy in a western tailcoat with white tie, was crooning a song about the moon and love. His hair was slicked back and glossy to match his shoes and I remember noticing that he wore make-up. The huge ballroom was extravagantly decorated with hundreds of tiny lights strung around the floor-to-ceiling mirrors, which were set in ornate plaster frames. White lilies garlanded the malachite pillars that supported the domed ceiling of the vast chamber in which no space had been left unembellished.

Shanghainese, White Russians, the British, of course, and quite a lot of Japanese who looked bemused by it all lined themselves three deep at the bar and crowded the dance floor. There were stars from the new film studios, dressed in satin evening dresses and wearing spectacular faux jewellery, their eyes dark as ink in their overpowdered faces. American sailors in white uniforms that looked too small for their big bodies stood heads above everyone else. Beautiful Chinese and Russian girls with their gangster lovers flaunted their imported dresses and freshly permed hair. There too, attempting to look as though they were enjoying themselves, were the mournful-eyed Jewish Russians who drank too much and took snuff. I saw the manager from the Venus Café with his exquisite half-French, half-Chinese boyfriend and the girl who had dressed my hair that afternoon in the beauty parlour in the French concession.

By the time I had drunk two vodkas and the best part of a bottle of champagne with Valerie and some others we had picked up at the bar of the Central, I was feeling lively and looking for fun. Amongst our party was the pink-skinned German who had been in the pool of the Shanghai Club. This time he was with a Chinese girl dressed in a tight gold cheongsam as bright as Natsuko's lucky carp. Mari's two Koreans joined us with their new partner, a fat little Russian who chained-smoked and had a habit of polishing his bald patch with his hand every couple of minutes. They were drinking malt whisky and flirting with Valerie who looked wonderful in an evening dress of cloudy white chiffon that she had bought in Cairo in more affluent days. I had chosen chiffon too, but a sea-green one with silver shoes. I had silk wisteria in my hair and I was wearing the moonstone ring that Mari had given me. Valerie said that she had never seen me looking more beautiful.

It was well into the evening before I noticed the taller-than-usual Japanese soldier who was leaning against one of the pillars, staring at me. He had a huge head, a thick, straight moustache and was wearing high boots that needed polishing. He wore the uniform of a Japanese line officer with the jacket flung over his shoulders in the American fashion. Despite the crush there seemed to be a space around him, as though people didn't care to get too close.

For reasons that I can't remember now I went over and introduced myself to him as the Princess Eastern Jewel. Perhaps I wanted to impress him, wanted to stand out amongst the glittering guests at the Cathay that evening. It was an odd thing for me to do, because I always wanted to be accepted as Japanese, especially when in their company. I had grown to despise the subservient nature of the Chinese, who I rarely claimed as my kinsmen. As it turned out it didn't matter how I introduced myself. Captain Tanaka Takayoshi already knew who I was. He knew everyone who was important or interesting in Shanghai, as you would expect of the director of Japan's secret service in the city. I had heard of his arrival in the city some months before but hadn't come across him. We had moved in different circles and I particularly avoided Japanese officials, fearing that Kawashima or Kanjurjab would discover my whereabouts.

Tanaka found us a table and we drank and flirted for the rest of that evening. Every so often someone would make their way to the table and thank him for some favour or ask his opinion on something. I could tell that he was considered important and I enjoyed being in his company. I was surprised to discover that the Captain knew about my life in Kawashima's home and about my marriage to Kanjurjab. He was amused and impressed at my escape from Mongolia and told me that he had been watching me for some months, knew where I lived and thought the villa too secluded for a Japanese woman living alone. It pleased me that he considered me Japanese. I commented that I was rarely alone, and he nodded knowingly. I was disturbed that he knew so much about me when I had not the slightest suspicion that I was being watched.

I was so fascinated by him that I left Valerie to fend for herself and allowed him to take me home in his car, which he drove himself. I was sure Tanaka desired me, but try as I might on that first night to entice him to my bed, he refused on the grounds that he was not my social equal, as I was a princess and he a commoner. He took sake with me and told me to be more cautious about locking my doors and suggested that I consider moving back to the Central.

'The Chinese are like a thousand flies buzzing about with their irritating insurrections,' he said. 'If they continue, we'll teach them a lesson they won't forget, but you should be careful.'

He left me his card and said that if he could ever be of use to me he would deem it an honour to assist me.

For days after our meeting, I couldn't get him out of my mind or forget the scent of him, which was as warm as ripe quince. I recalled that he hadn't smiled once in the time we had spent together, although I had felt his approval. I was hugely attracted to him and the fact that he was a spy quite thrilled me. I waited as long as my patience would allow for him to contact me, but eventually I took matters into my own hands. I think that had I not, Tanaka would not have come to me and an eternity might have passed before his desire would have overtaken his inverted class snobbery. Valerie said that I would be better off without the friendship of a man like Tanaka. But I had the bit between my teeth, and what did she know of him anyway?

Remembering Tanaka's offer of help if I ever needed it I called at his apartment and asked if I could borrow one hundred and fifty American dollars from him. He gave it to me without hesitation. I offered to pay him back in his bed but he wouldn't hear of it. So I devised a plan that eventually not only seduced him, but also released him from the boundaries of social class he had imposed. Ours was a pairing of like with like, and I know now with hindsight how dangerous such a union can be. A saint and a sinner would work well for each other, but two sinners are a volatile mix. It would have been better if we had never met, for once united there was no way that we could survive each other intact.

I began to call on him daily, always requesting money, which he never refused. The amounts I borrowed got bigger and bigger until one day he told me that I would have to wait a little as he didn't have that many dollars on him. I told him that I could wait forever but that he didn't have to.

'Tanaka, I may be a princess,' I said, 'but I am also a woman who needs your protection. See how small my hands are compared to yours, your body could crush the breath from mine without effort. Where I am weak you are strong. How can you deny this compatibility when it is so obvious?'

I slipped off my dress and let it fall to the floor. Then I turned my back to him, bent over and slowly undid the little buckles of my ankle-strap shoes, so that I was left standing in just a suspender belt and the sheer-seamed stockings that Valerie had given me for Christmas. They were so fine that as I undid them from the clasps that held them they slid down my legs like a silken snake and drew a sigh from Tanaka. I sat on his bed and told him that he must take me or I would forever be in his debt, something that a commoner should not allow a princess to suffer. I am not sure whether it was my nakedness or my appeal to his honour that finally brought an end to our fencing with each other. But under his mosquito net that smelled of camphor, Tanaka took me for the first time.

He was a huge man in every aspect, enjoyed sex as much as I did and in its throes he could be cruel and tender, master and slave, never scared of hurting me, never scared to be gentle. His skin tasted of lemons and salt and I liked the way his dark hair slipped through my fingers.

He was secretive and daring and loved danger for its own sake. His hunger for information was endless, his memory so extraordinary that he never forgot a name or date, and could remember conversations verbatim. I had met my match, but too late in my life to be satisfied with one man, or to be able to take a subservient role in his life. Besides, I had left a large portion of my heart with Yamaga, and I had vowed never to love again.

Tanaka's sexual tastes knew no boundaries other than that of gender. He had never made love with a man, even though he enjoyed it when I dressed as one. He liked me naked, liked me in silk, liked me dressed as a boy, dressed as a girl, liked me in high heels and particularly in boots. He regularly visited a Cantonese prostitute in a bordello where he also gave private banquets for like-minded friends. The woman was rumoured to be tiny in stature and to have the smallest bound feet in Shanghai, but she could satisfy not only him but also as many of his guests as he wished to treat. Girls with bound feet were not usually to the taste of Japanese men, but in my experience the idea of a woman physically altered to appeal to a man heightens their appetite. Think of the painted face of the geisha, her red lips signifying the passion her naturally pale ones might deny, or the dark, kohl-rimmed eyes of the concubine, which mimic the lust of sexual arousal.

After that first time under his mosquito net in the sparsely furnished room that smelled of camphor, we began to spend more time with each other, and although it wasn't always my bed that Tanaka's boots hung over, it didn't matter as neither of us was sexually faithful to the other. I cared nothing for his infidelities and Tanaka, apart from the occasional lapse into jealousy, seemed not to mind my adventures.

He was for me the combination of lover and protector that I had been seeking all my life. I think that for him I was a force of nature that simply overtook him. And this developed a bond of loyalty that was somehow tied up, not only with each other, but also with Japan and its ambitions. We saw ourselves as children of the new Japan, the Japan that would conquer the world and share with us the respect and privilege that came with power.

Valerie began to draw away from me, for she did not like Tanaka. But I was so caught up with him that I let her go without a fight. It was the first time in my life that I had a man who accepted and knew me for what I was. I believed that whatever happened in our lives, it would never be finished between us.

In those early intoxicating months of our relationship we would often have sex several times a day. Sometimes we would share a lover or we would go our own ways for a few days to return refreshed. We grew closer and closer, without the usual sentimentality that goes with such intimacy and I came to know that the dark side of Tanaka's character was as out of control as that of my own. He liked to hear of my exploits, but every so often there would be one lover who fuelled his anger and put him into one of his long sulks. He would threaten to have the man killed unless I gave him up, and on occasion I was tempted not to, just to see what would happen, but it never came to that. Despite our straying, the passion between us seemed boundless, our loyalty unshakable. Before I met Tanaka, lies came easily to me, but if I lied to him it felt as though I had betrayed myself. There was nothing I couldn't be honest with him about; he was the one person who understood the good and bad in me and liked them both. But I always knew when he was lying because his body would go still and he would look me straight in the eye, something people don't usually do in general conversation.

Tanaka's connections in Shanghai were myriad. He had access to places that I had never been to and wherever he went he was treated with great respect. I don't recall him having special friends, but he had so many acquaintances that he gave the impression of being popular. In fact, people were afraid of Tanaka and ill at ease in his company. He took comfort in our partnership; I was his one true friend and he enjoyed showing me off.

We would go to the boxing matches at the Sokols, the Russian sports club, to watch beautiful young men pit their strength and skill against each other. I preferred it to Sumo wrestling as the contestants were better-looking, the audience more interesting, and the smell of blood and vodka quite intoxicating. Valerie came with us once, but she hated what she called 'the cruelty' of it, and I know that she didn't care for Tanaka's company much. Like Mari, Tanaka loved horse racing and would take me to the Shanghai Race Club on Nanking Road. He preferred it to the one way out beyond Hangkou Park that she had favoured. Mostly we lost money, but on the occasions that we won we would celebrate with sex and champagne. Sometimes we would take over the Ambassador Club and invite everyone that we considered important to drink with us till dawn. Tanaka paid the cabaret girls to sleep with his guests in the dark little rooms above the lushly decorated club. We drank in his officers' mess, where only the best sake was served and our gambling partners were the arrogant young officers from Hirohito's cabal.

Tanaka loved good food and took me to houses in the Chinese quarter where it was cooked with reverence. For a price, you could eat rice-maggot omelette, or wild boar that had been trapped in the forest near Kyoto and drowned in honey from bees that had fed on white clover. We ate wonderful sweetmeats made from almonds and pear syrup, and invariably ended the banquet with a soup of samphire or chestnuts. The cooks were superb, but then it has to be admitted that it is the Chinese with their exceptional greed who excel in the art of cuisine.

In those narrow streets of the Chinese quarter where there was never a time free from the clatter of mah-jong, where pet finches sang at the doors of the crowded tenements and washing hung from poles between the houses, Tanaka began introducing me to his network of so-called spies, who were in reality the thugs and thieves of that district.

By the Gate of Longevity, in a house of mean appearance, I met a shrivelled old woman referred to as Mother. Her boys were legion, although not of her blood. With a nod from Mother they would obey any order that Tanaka gave them. Mother always wore a scarf tied in a knot at the back of her neck and a cheaply dyed padded jacket to protect her chest, which she said was weak. Tanaka said that she wore the scarf because she was bald and that the jacket was padded with money.

She told Tanaka that I was as beautiful as jade, but that my nature was fashioned from iron. I reminded her, she said, of herself when young, and she hoped that I would have the good luck in my life that she had experienced in her own. It was hard to imagine that she had ever been a beauty and I didn't enjoy being likened to her. I hated the idea of ageing and never allowed myself to dwell on my own mortality. You cannot enjoy your youth unless you defend yourself against the idea that you will lose it. In any case it was obvious that she was from peasant stock and, like unwatered fruit, her type dry up while still on the branch.

Mother owned a few houses in the quarter, one where she kept girls from the villages, who she sold according to their looks. If ugly, they became overworked teahouse waitresses, if pretty, prostitutes. Tanaka had his pick for free and sometimes chose the plain over the pretty.

As I became more and more involved with all aspects of his life, my dark days were fewer and the need to protect myself from boredom disappeared. And so it was strange that my dreams at that time were of the land that I stood on falling into the sea, leaving me to float in a sky so silent that I could hear the beating of my own heart.

As Tanaka learnt more of my nature and discovered that he could trust me with any secret, it occurred to him that I would make a fine spy, and before long it was I who was taking his orders to Mother, I who knew her boys by name. In an effort to make me even more useful, he sent me to the best language school in Shanghai to improve my English. He put me on the payroll of the Special Service Organ and at my request arranged for me to take flying lessons. Thus I came to fulfil my ambition to fly a plane, one that I had carried with me since that first flight from Tokyo to Port Arthur with Kawashima and Nobu. I wished Nobu could have seen me flying, he would have had to eat his words.

Under Tanaka's tutelage, I learnt the trade quickly. I learnt how to position myself in restaurants so that I could hear conversations three tables away, and how to conceal myself in powder rooms, where I often picked up surprisingly useful information. I became skilled at making friends with the most unlikely people, such as the indiscreet wives of high-ranking American naval officers, who thought it bohemian to be my friend. I would court them at the bar of the Palace Hotel where, bored with shopping, they gathered to drink pink gins or disgusting-looking cocktails laced with so much fruit that they looked more like food than alcohol.

As a general principle it seemed that they admired the Japanese, aspired to be like the British aristocracy and thought of the Chinese only in terms of servants and merchants. Their chatter was of clothes and perfume and the indiscretions of their husbands' fellow officers. They spoke of where they were being posted and what had been discussed in the mess the night before. Free to be themselves, unlike Japanese wives, they took full advantage of their liberated state, doing and saying what they wished, even to the extent of ridiculing their husbands to each other.

Tanaka said that however innocuous a piece of information seemed it could be important and lead to bigger things. He kept a dossier of who was unfaithful to whom, who took drugs, who gambled beyond their means. He put people in his debt by paying their accounts or getting them the best girls or indeed the best doctors when an abortion or medication was needed. It seemed that everyone owed him a favour or prayed for his silence. He told me that it was a dangerous position to be in as no one enjoyed having their secrets held at the discretion of others, or being in their debt, but it made him a good spy and he enjoyed living danger-ously.

It was 1931, I was in my mid-twenties and enjoying my life in Shanghai. I had a lover, a salary and a fascinating new profession. Things were going well when out of the blue one day, Tanaka's superior in the north, Colonel Doihara, made a request for me to report to him in Tientsin in three days' time. He said he had an assignment for me that I was uniquely qualified for, one where I could, if successful, further Japan's push into the north-east of China. I should be prepared to stay in Tientsin for as long as the task took and I would, he said, need clothes for mixing in the highest society.

Tientsin was the birthplace of the Chinese Empress Wan Jung. I had heard that it was an interesting city and I was keen to go. The Emperor Pu Yi, in exile from the Forbidden City, had set up home there. He lived with his wife under the control of the Japanese, in somewhat more reduced circumstances than he was used to. It didn't take much to guess that Doihara's reference to 'the highest society' meant Pu Yi and his wife Wan Jung, 'She of the Beautiful Countenance'.

Tanaka hated Doihara, who was always questioning the huge expenses claimed by the Shanghai office. He didn't want me to go, but he couldn't refuse his superior's orders and reluctantly made the arrangements for my journey to the north. He was very agitated and said that he knew that Doihara would attempt to seduce me and that he could not bear the thought. I promised him that I would not lie with Doihara, but he wasn't satisfied and made me swear on our friendship that I would not take the Colonel as my lover.

However, I was delighted to be recognised by Doihara as one of his agents and to be given a job of my own which did not involve Tanaka. It was a step towards Japan accepting me as its own. I packed carefully, choosing mostly western clothes, as well as an oriental outfit with which, despite my oath on our friendship to Tanaka, I planned to seduce Doihara.

Sour Cherries and Acacia Honey

I flew to Tientsin, taking my turn at the controls with a young Japanese pilot I had first met when taking flying lessons. He was an occasional lover of mine, a man of wit and arrogance whose company I enjoyed since he wanted nothing more than sex from me and was prepared to do me favours in return. It was cold in the cockpit and we kept warm with regular shots from a thermos of hot tea laced with sake. After a smooth flight we landed in the city of Tientsin on the day before the Colonel was expecting me. Tanaka had taught me that the element of surprise puts you at an advantage and I had a plan that I thought would not only intrigue Doihara, but also display my skills at disguise and deception.

The hotel where Tanaka had arranged lodgings for me was only a short car ride from Doihara's headquarters. It was a sturdy four-storeyed building, built out of the ruins of an old merchant house with pretensions to western grandeur. There was a dignified-looking doorman, uniformed Chinese staff, Indian carpets and rather dismal lighting. On the same road the Country Club, a grand establishment managed by the English, equalled the Shanghai Club both in style and luxury. Of course, Chinese were forbidden entrance, but I heard that an exception was made for Pu Yi and his wife because of who they were. While enjoying the club's hospitality, the great Emperor was treated with a qualified respect that bordered on insolence, which even the lowliest of the English were skilled at showing their Chinese superiors.

Tientsin was a smart city, with good restaurants, markets and theatres and a branch of Laidlaw and Company that was almost as well stocked as its Shanghai parent. The quality emporium was a favourite of Pu Yi's and was responsible for his ridiculous western outfits that included tweed jackets and plus fours, as well as the short coats that were split at the back into two tails that the Emperor wore with striped trousers and silk ties. There were department stores on Victoria Road and even a racecourse, but the city did not have Shanghai's intoxicating air, nor the power to instil into its inhabitants the feeling that they lived at the centre of the world. It did though have an international community with foreign industries and foreign troops too. The Peking Opera played there and the city boasted a modern cinema, as well as the usual opium dens and brothels.

I was excited about the adventure ahead in Tientsin, but I reminded myself of the last conversation I had with Tanaka before leaving Shanghai. Generous as ever, he had given me money and advised me not to trust Doihara with confidences that he might later use against me.

'I should send a chaperone with you, Yoshiko. I wouldn't trust the Colonel with any woman, let alone one as beautiful as you.'

I knew his jealousy had more to do with Doihara's superior rank than with possession of me. But I would take his advice and be careful not to give away too much to the Colonel.

I was very fussy about the room I chose at the hotel and made them show me three before I settled on the one with the biggest bed and the softest rugs. It had a surprisingly well-appointed bathroom with huge brass taps and a wooden tub that was half a foot thick. The main reception rooms although poorly lit had electric lamps, but the bedrooms and halls, not yet electrified, were somewhat gloomy. There were oil lamps on the bedside tables and candles in the bathroom as well as a large hurricane lamp standing on a chest at the foot of the bed. The chest was carved with dragonflies so lifelike that you could almost hear the drum of their wings as they hovered over equally realistic flag lilies. I opened the lid and the fragrant scent of eucalyptus overtook me. It reminded me of Shimako, for she had used it in her linen chests and often carried the perfume of her bedcovers in her hair. I prayed that I would not dream of Shimako that night, for dreams of her always ate into my happiness. With Shimako's habit in mind, I scented the sheets with my own choice of chrysanthemum oil and stroked some into the nape of my neck and at the pulse of my wrists. I sent a servant boy to buy me sour cherries and acacia honey and some beeswax candles to soften the blue light of the oil lamps. I had brought champagne and sake with me, and some of the black Russian cigarettes so perfect to smoke at night.

After I had slept for an hour, I bathed and dressed myself in the full-length robe of a Chinese gentleman of middle rank. Its long sleeves covered my obviously female hands, while it was buttoned so high as to disguise my slim neck. I tucked my hair into a silk skullcap and except for an obi sash that bound my breasts flat, I went naked under the loose-fitting coat.

The doorman of the hotel looked at me inquisitively as I entered the car ordered in the name of the Princess Eastern Jewel of the Su family, the title Doihara had said I should go under in Tientsin. Without a moon the sky was as dark as kohl. No stars lit our way, but the car's pale headlights beamed two bars of light along the straight road.

Tanaka had told me that Colonel Doihara was extremely ambitious and usually worked late into the night at the headquarters of Tientsin's Special Service Organ. He was tireless in his pursuit of success, and because of his contacts in Manchuria he was known by western journalists as 'Lawrence of Manchuria'. What he hadn't told me was that Doihara, if not exactly handsome, was a powerful-looking man, high born and trusted by the Emperor

Hirohito himself. I expect Tanaka hadn't wanted to present his superior as too impressive, knowing that such vigour and influence would be attractive to me. Doihara had a reputation not only as a womaniser, but also as that of a man who stopped at nothing to get what he wanted. I knew I would soon be breaking my promise to Tanaka, but with luck he would never know, and promises are merely conveniences to ease the path of life. I have never extracted a promise from anyone and I give them no value in relationships or negotiations.

To heighten the sense of mystery and excitement that I wanted to conjure for the Colonel, I arrived at his headquarters exactly at the stroke of midnight. With the lowest voice I could muster, I told the desk officer that I had to see Doihara and that my purpose was so secret that I could only reveal my business to him personally. I was searched by a young guard who ran his hands interestedly over my coat, from my neck to my feet, before looking at my face in what appeared to be embarrassment. He told me to stay where I was and he would see if an interview would be granted.

Five minutes later I was ushered into the Colonel's office, where he sat behind a huge desk, writing on a document with an expensive-looking gold pen. He was a well-built man, clean-shaven, with a broad face, a wide nose and sombre eyes. I guessed him to be in his late forties. He didn't look up at my entrance, but ostentatiously took a revolver from the desk drawer and placed it by his right hand and continued writing. Perhaps he thought that I had come to assassinate him with my bare hands or maybe he just wanted to intimidate me.

After a long silence he glanced up briefly and asked my name, fingering the revolver as he spoke. He addressed me in an elegant form of Chinese with no trace of a Japanese accent. I answered him in the same language, lowering my voice to what I thought was a masculine pitch.

'You need not know my name,' I said, 'only that I have come to be of use to you.'

177

He leant towards me, squinting as though to see me better.

'Your voice is that of a eunuch,' he said contemptuously. 'Are you from Pu Yi's household?'

'I am of his blood, but not his household,' I replied.

The Colonel leant back in his chair and let his eyes sweep me from head to toe. And then, very slowly, he stood up, fastened the top button of his jacket, replaced the cap on his pen and returned the revolver to the drawer.

'Well then, I think I know who you may be,' he said, rising from his chair and taking his sword from where it leant against the desk. 'But just to be sure, I need to see beneath your disguise.'

He came towards me, extending the sword, still holding my eyes with his. Without a change of expression he suddenly made one long graceful movement and sliced through the silk fastenings of my coat. I remained completely still as he gave a satisfied grunt, and with a small lunge split the silk obi sash that bound my breasts. As it fell to the floor I removed the skullcap and Colonel Doihara burst out laughing.

'You're a brave girl,' he said. 'One slip and I could have scarred you for life.'

'You have a steady hand, Colonel. I can see you are a man to trust,' I replied.

'Flattery is not something I have ever been susceptible to, Princess,' he said pompously. 'A beautiful woman though is something no real man can resist.'

Since the day that I lost Yamaga, I have never fallen prey to flattery myself. It can cloud the mind. Doihara was a man who would be difficult to manipulate, not because he thought himself immune to a woman's wiles, but more because he had a cunning, mistrusting nature. I knew that he had the power to promote me and to make my position in Shanghai absolutely secure. I would need to impress Doihara in every department if my star in the secret service was to rise. I suspected that his womanising was a way of feeding his vanity rather than a susceptibility to female charm, and that I would have to fatten that vanity with the sighs and moans of a whore in his bed.

He willingly agreed to my suggestion that we go to my hotel and further our acquaintance, although he took a rankling amount of time to tidy away his sword and call for his car. He said that it was rare in life to meet a true adventuress and that he would like to get to know me better, but his manner was cool and arrogant and I was beginning to dislike the Colonel.

I was sorry that I would not be able to share the seduction of Doihara with Tanaka. Discussing our conquests was a pastime we both enjoyed, but I knew that although I could manage his occasional jealousies, where it concerned his hated superior it would only highlight his deep belief that, as a commoner, he himself had no place in the bed of a princess. I missed Tanaka's camaraderie. It would have been fun to discuss my seduction of Doihara with him, but by extracting a promise of fidelity from me he had put such a subject out of bounds. From this distance I could bring myself to feel critical of him. In his company, his personality was such that no other man shone quite as brightly. He might have to play Captain to Doihara's Colonel but he was, I thought, the man's superior. Tanaka would always be a huge influence in my life, but it felt good to be the author of my own adventures once again.

As we sat a little apart in the dark interior of the Colonel's car, he shut his eyes and did not speak to me. There was that tension between us that comes before first-time sex, when you have yet to touch, yet to discover how things will be between you. In those enthralling moments the throat dries, the heartbeat increases and everything appears to be in slow motion. It is as if time actually stops. It is to experience that feeling again and again that I take so many lovers, for in its distraction I am as far from death as I can be without opium.

It took only minutes to reach my hotel in the car, which was driven by a young soldier who treated the Colonel with great respect, almost scraping the pavement with a bow as Doihara ordered him to wait and to keep his wits about him. The Colonel seemed nervous in the outside world. He had left his headquarters with a gun in his pocket and had pulled down the blinds in the car the moment he entered it.

'Perhaps it is a good idea you are in disguise, Yoshiko,' he whispered as we entered the hotel. 'Now that we are invading Manchuria, no Japanese can feel safe where Chinese roam at will.'

He followed me in silence to my room and watched as I lit the candles, pouring us each a glass of champagne. He didn't drink his, saying he thought it overrated, a drink only suitable for whores and westerners. Sake was his choice and he accepted my flask in the hope that the quality of the drink lived up to the distinguished receptacle it came in. Ignoring his criticism of the champagne, I drank both glasses quickly and agreed that sake, like all things Japanese, was superior.

Since Doihara had sliced through the fastenings of my coat, I had tied it at the waist with what remained of the obi sash. In the car the coat had separated, exposing my booted leg, which even though he showed no sign of it, I felt sure must have excited the Colonel. As I stood before him, I undid the knot of the obi and allowed the coat to slip to the floor. The Colonel told me to sit on the bed while he undressed, which he did slowly, folding his shirt carefully and hanging his jacket on the back of a chair. There was something insulting in the way he took his time, sipping his drink and staring at me as though to check for flaws. I started to remove my boots but he barked, 'Leave them.' I smiled and lay back on the bed.

Despite his reputation as a great womaniser, Doihara was a disappointing lover. He liked to be on top and laboured at it like a workman digging a trench. He was noisy too, grunting and moaning as though exhausted by the effort. He smelled cool like metal, which was not unpleasant, but I cannot say the experience of coupling with him surpassed any other that I had experienced. As he smothered me with his huge chest, covering my face so that it was hard to breathe, I found myself wishing that he had Tanaka's understanding of a woman's body. He seemed unaware that he had a living person under him. I may as well not have existed except as a receptacle for his seed. I would be able to tell him in truth that he was a true samurai, which I knew he would take as a compliment. His lovemaking was entirely selfish, so it was all the more amusing that he thought himself a great lover. I hoped that he was a better spy than he was a lover.

Doihara's scent was entirely new to me, but there was something about his body that seemed familiar, like someone I remembered from a long-ago dream. As he worked his way to his climax the sudden realisation came to me that it was my father Prince Su to whom Doihara bore a remarkable physical resemblance. It came to me too that what I had felt for my father was desire, a forbidden thing. Lust is often to be found where taboo exists. Yet how could I not have recognised those childhood aches to be desire? How odd that I should have discovered those forbidden feelings, so many years later, under the heaving body of the Colonel. I could not blame the child I had been for desiring my all-powerful father. He was, after all, the centre of the world I lived in. Only the most beautiful women lay in his bed. His concubines vied for his attention and prospered when they achieved it. As I lay by the Colonel I recognised where my desire for cruel and powerful men had its origins, and knew too that I was powerless to change those patterns bred in the bone so many years ago.

In homage to the stirred memory of the little bound-footed girl who had serviced my father and whom I had spied upon, I filled a bowl with scented water and carefully washed between Doihara's legs, all the time telling him what a masterful lover he was. He became so excited that we lay together for a second time and unfortunately he laboured at the task longer.

Doihara was as susceptible to flattery as any man despite his protestations, and the longer I spent in his company, the smaller in stature he appeared. Although I respected his office and understood that he had the power to influence my position I could not admire him. Yet, for entirely venal and ambitious reasons, I still wanted to impress him.

When we woke some hours later we ate the sour cherries and the honey, a sweet and sour combination of tastes I have always enjoyed after lovemaking. The Colonel washed his mouth out with the flat remains of the champagne, saying that was all it was good for. He told me that I was truly the horizontal delicacy my reputation had claimed but that he didn't like my short hair.

'A woman should have long hair, Yoshiko,' he said. 'It is the rope a man pulls her to him with.'

The room had chilled as we slept, the candles burnt to stubs, and the lamps still leaking their blue light shone dimly. Outside, the starless sky was coal dark and strangely disarming. I had dreamt of Jon, weeping as he lay in his wife's lap, while she, as ever, smiled her vacant smile.

I hate waking in rooms that have once been warm and ready for passion, but have become cold with reality when expectations have not been met. Not so for Doihara, who was puffed up and pleased with himself. He left the bed and dressed surprisingly quickly. He told me to come to his office after breakfast and he would inform me of the task he had in mind for me.

'I am pleased with you, Princess,' he said. 'I know you will do the job well.'

After he left, I woke the hotel's servant boy and told him to bring me soup with an egg in it, and some fruit. I knew that in what was left of the dark I would not sleep again. At dawn I saw a cluster of morning stars in the lightening sky and remembered that Sorry always thought of them as a good omen.

'There is nothing like the morning star for luck, little mistress,' she would say. 'It's a gift from the gods to the early riser.'

I am not a superstitious person but better a good omen than a bad.

*　　*　　*

My task was not as exciting as I had hoped, but as Doihara explained it was a vital one. He had mistakenly thought I was a childhood friend of Pu Yi's wife Wan Jung, and wanted me to join her and the Emperor at their villa, Quiet Garden, in Tientsin. I was to persuade the reluctant Wan Jung, whose beauty was legendary, to agree to go with her husband to Manchuria in the north-east of China, where Japan was extending its empire. There, Pu Yi would be proclaimed Emperor of that province, which was also the homeland of his – and my – ancestors. It was a bleak place, a land of hostile terrain and challenging climate.

Despite his longing to be restored to his throne and to regain his status, Pu Yi most likely would have wished that he had been offered somewhere other than the land that bordered Mongolia. Not only was there a dislike of the Chinese on those borders, but also a healthy strain of communism. Since the murder of the Romanovs by the communists, no emperor could feel easy about that particular philosophy. All the same, as I was eventually to remind Pu Yi, even China's Great Wall had not been able to keep out our own magnificent Manchu warriors. It was not without reason that those of our blood had been called the 'Eastern Tartars'.

'Perhaps, it is in the stars for a Manchu emperor to once again enter China from its borders,' I said, even though I knew that one such as he could lay little claim to our ancestors' courage. If he did achieve his ambition to restore his throne, it would be as Japan's creature.

The Sun Empire needed that Manchurian foothold in China, and under the pretence of being Pu Yi's champions they intended to make him their puppet and enlarge their own power base. Doihara was eager to fulfil his orders and remove the royal couple from Tientsin and place them where they would be the most useful for Japan. Pu Yi would live with the title of Emperor, under a big sky on a hard land, where he would come to know that it was the Japanese who ruled and not him. He would eventually know, too, that along with the privilege and power he had been born with, the Emperor of China's Qing dynasty had also been cursed with devilish luck. It may be that he would live in Manchuria more luxuriously than I had done in neighbouring Mongolia. Yet still, the climate and much of the terrain was so similar that had I been him, I would not have gone, even for a throne.

Doihara had nothing but contempt for Pu Yi; he thought him a weak man whose blood was so thin that it wouldn't nourish mosquitoes. Face to face he was deferential, but behind Pu Yi's back he decried him as a decadent and spineless man, who was the last and weakest creature of a dead dynasty. In truth, Doihara, despite being a scholar of Chinese history and fluent in several Chinese dialects, despised all Chinese whatever their rank. He warned me not to be seduced by the Emperor's fine manners. He said they disguised the true weakness of his character and that at heart Pu Yi was a spoilt child, a bully to his inferiors and a bad judge of character.

'Let me give you the mark of the man, Princess,' he said. 'When he lived in the Forbidden City, his greatest pleasure with his child concubines was to whip them until they bled, then to bathe them by candlelight while he cried in sympathy at their pain.'

Pu Yi had no concubines in Tientsin, as he was obsessed with restoring his throne and besieged by dreams of his assassination. Even though the Qing Emperor could only take one of his own clan as a concubine, he was mistrustful of everyone and saw the sword in every new face he came across. At that time, he could not find it in himself to trust even a Manchu girl. Doihara thought this state of affairs would not last long, as Pu Yi had always needed young girls to pamper his ego and to reassure him.

'His wife,' he said, 'is dull and disillusioned with him, she no longer sleeps in his bed. Wan Jung only stays because she values status above everything else in life.'

Wan Jung did not wish to leave Tientsin unless it was to depart Asia, or to return triumphant to the Forbidden City. Tientsin was the city of her birth, she had family and prestige amongst the community there. Her life was freer than it had been in the Forbidden City, and since her husband's consort Wen Hsiu had divorced him she was the only official woman in his household. In Tientsin, she could and did indulge her extravagant nature, buying anything western she could get her hands on. She spent a fortune on jewels, clothes and shoes, radios, imported tobacco and perfumes and, on one ludicrously extravagant occasion, two grand pianos.

In briefing me on the etiquette of dealing with the Emperor and his wife, Doihara told me that Wan Jung insisted on being called Elizabeth, a name Pu Yi had selected for her from a list of English names that his old tutor Sir Reginald Johnston had submitted to him. Pu Yi chose for himself the name Henry, and forever after in anti-Imperialist circles they were jokingly referred to as Mr and Mrs Henry and Elizabeth Pu Yi. Doihara said that Wan Jung was a stupid woman who wanted to go to America, where even though she wouldn't be a proper empress, she would be feted as one. He said with scorn that America was an indiscriminate country where, without royalty of their own, they fawned over royalty from elsewhere, no matter how minor. Even though I considered myself as patriotic as the Colonel when it came to Japan, I did not believe that the Emperor of China would be considered minor, wherever in the world he chose to live.

Doihara had no respect for any dynasty that wasn't Japanese. He considered western royalty pointless, as to him whether they be princes or commoners, all westerners were inferior beings. He was furious that he had to treat Pu Yi and his wife with respect and could hardly bring himself to speak normally to Wan Jung, let alone address her courteously.

'She's a weak opium addict, no longer beautiful, but she has a hold on her husband that I haven't been able to break,' he said irritably. 'As long as she resists their going, he will make no decision to leave Tientsin. You must convince her, Yoshiko, that

Pu Yi has a loyal Chinese population in the north-east who are longing for his return. Persuade her that she can resume her life as Empress there, and eventually be restored to the throne in the Forbidden City. She will trust you as a Manchu princess and a playmate from her childhood.'

I was not at all sure that Wan Jung would remember me and I didn't care for Doihara's constant references to my Chinese background. But I could see that for this task my ancestry would, as it had often done in the past, work in my favour. My own recollections of Wan Jung were faint. I remember that she once came to our house with her mother, who was sister to one of my father's concubines. I think my mother told me to be nice to her, because she had come on a long journey and was a frail child. I don't remember playing with her, although I think my sisters might have. I could just about recall a pretty little girl I would have spurned for being too similar to my own sisters. Even if I had known she was destined to be an empress I would still have been unimpressed by her. Then as now, empress meant the same to me as wife, subservient and dutiful.

I decided not to tell Doihara of my own at best vague memories of the childhood of Wan Jung. I had no idea where he had received the information of our closeness, but I hoped that Wan Jung would at least have heard of me and have the good manners to greet me as an acquaintance. I hoped that Wan Jung's opium-influenced memory was poor and that she would take my word for what special friends we had been. I had confidence in my powers of persuasion and considered myself thoroughly up to the job asked of me. If Japan had decided that the Chinese Emperor should be a figurehead in Manchuria, then I would do all I could to encourage Pu Yi to return to the land of our shared ancestors.

Doihara arranged to pick me up at dusk and drive me to the Quiet Garden himself. He would present me to Pu Yi as a companion for Wan Jung. He told me that if I could not convince her to accompany her husband to Manchukuo, Japan's name for

Manchuria, with words alone, then I was to do whatever it took to get her to change her mind. Pu Yi's decision to go to Manchukuo needed to appear to be his choice, no matter how his wife's consent had been obtained. For all his reliance on Japan and his loveless marriage to Wan Jung, Pu Yi listened to his wife and would only go to Manchuria with her agreement. In Doihara's opinion, fear would change the mind of the reluctant Empress quicker than anything else. I was to convince her that their lives were in imminent danger and that it was no longer safe for the Emperor to stay in Tientsin.

'Do what you have to,' he said. 'I want results, Yoshiko, and I need them quickly. Japan cannot be held back on the whim of this one pathetic little woman.'

Doihara said that Wan Jung slept her drugged sleep in the afternoons, appearing for dinner, apparently sober, a state that lasted for about two hours before she returned to her room and took up the pipe again.

'She sits at the table as course after course appears, but she never eats a morsel,' he said. 'The woman's as thin as a sapling.'

Occasionally, after dinner, the Empress liked to drink champagne and to play cards with Pu Yi. But lately even that wordless little ceremony had fallen victim to their growing dislike of each other's company. The Empress was a poor card player, and Doihara imagined it was a relief to Pu Yi not to have to face the nightly company of his ailing and unloving wife.

Before leaving for the Quiet Garden, I spent the afternoon shopping in the provincial but well-stocked Tientsin stores. I bought Tanaka a good watch and an illustrated book of sexual positions with complicated drawings, done by an old eunuch from the Forbidden City. I pictured the ancient artist spying through screens as I had once done, but whereas I could hardly breathe with the excitement of the scene before my eyes, he, more usefully, had busied himself with charcoal and paper. I treated myself to some French perfume that smelled of frangipani, and for Wan Jung I purchased a beautiful silver kaleidoscope, thinking that, as an addict, she would enjoy anything that distorted reality.

After a walk around the old river port where I spent half an hour in the company of a short-time boy, who was adept but not pretty, I went back to the hotel and bathed in the bathroom, which had a toilet that flushed and thin cotton towels as large as sheets. The water was cool against my skin. It smelled faintly of mud and, I suppose because I had been thinking of my childhood, it reminded me of the scent left on my hands after I had trailed them in my father's carp pools, a forbidden pleasure that allowed me the joy of disobedience. I packed and changed into the western dress that I knew Wan Jung favoured. I chose a soft wool skirt and jacket of dark blue and draped the foxes that Harry had bought me around my shoulders. I rouged my cheeks discreetly and wore lipstick, something I was not in the habit of doing, but Doihara had told me that Wan Jung had an ashen complexion and used a lot of rouge to mimic good health. I wanted her to feel at ease with me, to remember that we were of a shared and superior class and that I was someone she could trust and confide in.

Doihara took fifteen minutes to drive to the house, which although a solid enough one, was remarkably unpretentious for an Emperor. It sat squarely in gardens scattered with maple and silver-barked willows. There were shutters at the windows and twisted wisteria snaked around them giving the house the appearance of a cottage, rather like the ones the English built on Nanking Road in Shanghai. It may have been the grey evening that made the house look lifeless; the light was certainly about to go, but there was a gloomy feel to the place, as though its occupants did not care for it. The garden was well ordered with neat paths and pruned trees, but it had the dispirited look of land that is tended without love and so gives nothing back. So strong was the gloomy feeling of the place that for a moment as I stood facing it I fancied the house was quietly weeping.

Two Japanese soldiers sat on a bench outside the front door smoking and sharing a joke. Warned of our approach by a pair of squawking caged cranes, they jumped to attention, too late for the Colonel to have missed their lack of formality. Doihara was furious, his anger as cold as ice. He slapped one of them across the cheek and said they were a disgrace to Japan and that they would be dealt with later for such slovenly behaviour. His eyes were as hard as iron, his lips a thin white line. I marked how in an instant his fury could be aroused to gigantic proportions by the smallest of concerns.

We entered a hall busy with Japanese officials going in and out of the ground-floor rooms, carrying files and boxes. There were plain-clothes and uniformed officers everywhere, the sound of their shoes on the hard floors emphasising the fact that the Emperor and his wife were not the exclusive occupants of the so-called Quiet Garden.

In a later conversation that I had with Pu Yi, he told me that he had named the house himself. He had chosen 'Quiet Garden' not to mean a peaceful place, but to imply that he would wait quietly until the opportunity came to resume his rightful place on the throne of China. He was a man who all his life had waited for others to order his days and had lost the power to take control of his own life. His lack of action must have been disappointing for his wife, who had no doubt hoped for a more interesting life as Empress. It was no surprise, then, that she preferred to spend those waiting days in poppy-induced dreams, where colour and life and light filled her being with joy for as long as she slept her opium sleep.

Pu Yi and his wife occupied the rooms on the first and the top floor of the house. They lived chaotically but comfortably, in the western style, with good furniture, luxurious rugs, a gramophone and a library of American band music. Wan Jung had only one lady-in-waiting, who took care of her clothes and accompanied her on shopping trips. Their living rooms were so untidy that one guessed straight away that there were few household servants.

Because Pu Yi thought it too dangerous to open the windows, the smell of dog hung unpleasantly on the air.

The house was well supplied with fine wines, including an outrageously large stock of champagne. There were cases of expensive sherry that no one touched and the usual array of liquors. There was plenty of gin, whisky and sake, even though it gave the Emperor a headache, and Chinese five-grain wine, which Wan Jung believed had the power to keep her young.

Doihara told me that Pu Yi's only income came from pawning the jewels he had brought with him from the Forbidden City. But, since this finite source had begun to dwindle, his expensive team of advisors had deserted him for wealthier patrons. The Colonel thought their desertion to be a good thing, as Pu Yi now had fewer people whispering in his ear and was more likely to listen to his Japanese advisors.

During his time in Tientsin the Emperor had run up huge debts in the city. Those in trade were reluctant to allow him to extend them despite the kudos the Emperor lent to their business. He owed Laidlaw and Company a great deal of money for the extensive wardrobe in the western style they had supplied him with, and many restaurants and jewellers in the city would never see a penny of the money he owed them.

In his first years in Tientsin, when the numerous caskets of jewels were full and the pieces of fine jade seemed infinite, he had given generously to the old corrupt warlords who had fetched up in the city. He had trusted that they would do everything in their power to bring about his restoration. They in return had promised him their lifelong loyalty, then, one by one, they had deserted the Qing Emperor in his hour of need.

I was surprised and relieved when, in front of Doihara, Pu Yi said he needed no introduction to me. He remembered me well from his childhood as the girl who wanted to be a boy. He said that he was pleased that I had come, as his wife was in need of a female companion to share her lonely days. His own time, he said, was spent dealing with the affairs of his forthcoming restitution, which it was his duty to pursue with dedication. He bemoaned the fact that even his beloved golf had to be set aside and that he had given up going to the cinema and to restaurants, as he wanted his people to understand how much he was prepared to sacrifice so that they might have their Emperor returned to them.

To me Pu Yi looked more like a schoolboy than an emperor. He was slightly built with short oiled hair and a nervous tic in his left eye. There was an air of privileged aristocracy about him and a look of uncertainty in his eyes. Dressed in a Prince of Wales checked suit and highly polished shoes, he smelled, like an Englishman, of soap and cologne. His nails were manicured and polished to a fine sheen, his teeth, which were slightly yellow, looked too large for his thin-lipped mouth. His black hair was slicked back flat and he wore thin-rimmed glasses that made him look studious and unattractive. He was a cold-hearted man with, as I was later to discover, a secret contempt for almost everyone he came into contact with. He was full of obsessions and superstitions that he allowed to rule his life. Regardless of where he was, he would spit on encountering something unlucky, would never eat green food before white and always hesitated before entering a room, debating with himself whether he should cross the threshold with his right or his left foot. He was easily swayed in his views and frequently changed his mind depending on whom he had spoken to last. He was incapable of making even the smallest decision on his own. It would not be an exaggeration to say that it had to be suggested to him when he might urinate, or eat, or sleep. It was a wonder to me that this creature had Manchu blood in his veins, for there was nothing of the warrior in either his demeanour or his thinking.

The Colonel had advised me not to be fooled by the Emperor's seeming indifference to his wife, for although he did not love her, he trusted her passion for the Dragon Throne and knew her desire for its restoration to be as strong as his own. However, he did blame her for the desertion of his consort, Wen Hsiu, for whom he had a pale sort of affection. After her departure, Wan Jung had insisted that the girl be demoted from the rank of consort to that of commoner. It still rankled with him that Wan Jung had shown great pleasure when Wen Hsiu had been granted a divorce, something that Pu Yi had been horrified at. If a commoner could divorce an emperor, then the world was even more of a mystery to him than it had become since his flight from the Forbidden City. There had been a great deal of rivalry in the household between the two women, which Pu Yi had found amusing and had not discouraged. But since his consort's departure, he felt his home to be diminished and found his bed colder than ever before.

I was given a room on the top floor of the house next to Wan Jung's lady-in-waiting. It was comfortable, with thick rugs and walls painted the exact colour of the sanguinaria poppy print of the bedspread and curtains. The colours stirred memories of those blood-and-bandage dreams I had suffered in Mongolia. The room was dusty and cold and I sought out a servant woman and told her to clean the room and to hang up my clothes. I told her to put a hot stone in my bed, and that if I found my room not cared for again she would be beaten. From being surly she became humble, as even the worst servant will when encountering a mistress she knows will not hesitate to carry out her threats. I brushed aside her assurances that I would have no reason to complain, and sent her off to bring me tea and fruit.

I would speak to Doihara and arrange that the royal couple were given more servants and a chamberlain to oversee them. It was not fitting that the Emperor, who lived under the care of the Japanese, should reside in such chaos.

Wan Jung's lady-in-waiting told me that the Empress was looking forward to meeting me and that she would see me at dinner, which she liked people to dress for. I chose a simple black dress and wore it with the black pearl I had bought, against my better judgement, in Shanghai. It didn't match the beauty of

Natsuko's gem, which had passed between us with such feeling, but it reminded me of her, which was oddly comforting.

Pu Yi was already in the dining room when I arrived. He was dressed in a dinner jacket and black tie, his sleeves were cuffed with diamonds and he wore an expensive-looking gold wristwatch.

'I have a very fine collection of pearls myself,' he said, looking at mine closely. 'I especially like the ivory ones as they are more as nature intended, as well as being flattering to the skin.'

The Empress arrived and was introduced to me by Pu Yi, who told her that I was one of his many distant cousins.

'Yes, I know of you, Eastern Jewel,' she said in a surprisingly strong voice.

Although still young, Wan Jung appeared ravaged by the experience of her years. She walked as slowly as a woman twice her age and pulled nervously on the long rope of bloodstones that looked too heavy for her delicate neck to support. A litter of Pekinese dogs yapped at her feet, which were clad in high-heeled shoes a little too wide for her narrow feet. Despite her frailty, I could see where her reputation as a beauty came from. She had a fine bone structure, a delicate nose and a sweet soft mouth, and there was a touching sadness in her eyes that remained even when she smiled. She was morbidly pretty and so thin that when I took her birdlike hand in mine, I felt as though the slightest pressure might crush it. Opium addicts often have a livid hue, but Elizabeth was so pale that even the spots of rouge on her cheeks did nothing to disabuse me of the idea that she was seriously ill and might collapse at any moment. There were dark shadows under her eyes and her deep-red lipstick emphasised her opium-stained teeth. Every so often, with a pained expression, she would place a hand on her temple, as though she had momentarily forgotten what business she was about. Her fingers had the smudged brown tint that came from softening opium into pellets, and her hands trembled slightly so that her cigarette shook. Yet despite these handicaps, she appeared, at least in my eyes, to have an ethereal beauty that was timeless. Her features were pleasingly symmetrical and the dark eyes under the arches of her perfect eyebrows were of a luminous black.

I felt an immediate connection with her and, unusually for me, I was overcome with what felt like a sisterly desire to save her from her demons and return her to a healthy life.

'Perhaps we will be friends,' she said without emotion.

I replied truthfully that I hoped that we would, and secretly regretted that our true relationship would be based on lies.

That first dinner together, like all of those to follow it, was a tortuous event taken almost in silence. Pu Yi ate course after course, concentrating on the food greedily, while his wife chain-smoked French cigarettes and drank champagne. Occasionally Wan Jung would pick up a morsel of food and drop it onto the floor, where the sea of snuffling little Pekinese patrolled hopefully. For once in my life I found myself without appetite, grateful for the wine, which was pleasantly rich.

After dinner, Wan Jung picked up her two favourite Pekinese and invited me to her room to play mah-jong. She said goodnight to Pu Yi and he replied formally that he wished her a pleasant evening.

'I hope you sleep well at Quiet Garden,' he said to me. 'And that my late hours of working do not disturb you.'

Wan Jung's room was a touching homage to the west, which she obviously admired. In a clutter on her dressing table were French perfumes and English lavender water. A round tub of Max Factor powder sat next to a pink enamelled hand mirror that needed polishing. On every surface there were silver-framed photographs of herself and Pu Yi with western leaders and pictures too of American film stars who I doubt she had met. At her bedside she kept the works of Shakespeare and the poetry of Byron, although I had heard that she had struggled to pick up even a few words of English. The books appeared untouched and had tasselled markers at their centre. In a glass-fronted chest of drawers of the kind found in haberdashery shops were pairs of white buckskin gloves and fine-seamed nylons stacked neatly in their Cellophane wrappers. There were supplies of foreign cigarettes in gilt boxes and gold lighters and porcelain ashtrays painted with roses, which sat on the tables at her bedside. On a round mahogany table underneath a grimy window, a silver tray of gin and English tonic water was accompanied by a small dish of sliced lemons. The only Chinese influence in the room was in one corner where a low sofa plumped with silk cushions sat beside a foot-high coffer that housed everything an opium addict might need to indulge their passion.

We didn't play mah-jong that night. Instead we smoked an opium pipe and shared confidences as though we were old familiars. I felt genuine warmth towards the frail Empress, which took me by surprise, as I had not expected to like her.

Wan Jung asked me to tell her the story of my life and so I told her of my childhood in the Kawashima household. She said that it would not have suited her as she had never cared for the Japanese, finding them full of brutality and oblivious to true art. I said that on the whole I found Japanese men to be interesting lovers and that I liked their arrogance. She laughed and said that she thought that their legs were too short and their noses so poorly designed that they snorted rather than talked.

She confided to me that at first she hadn't wanted to marry Pu Yi as, even though he was Emperor, he was not the sort of man most young girls dream of as their ideal husband. But over the years she had come to value her position as wife of the twelfth Emperor of the great Qing dynasty. She said that although she had never experienced true love, she had heard that it was short-lived anyway, and she believed that it was status that would keep her warm in her old age. I didn't point out that it was her status and the life it had imposed on her that had reduced her to her present state of ill health and indecision.

It was with true conviction that she said she would give up opium when Pu Yi was restored to his rightful place in the

Forbidden City. It would be no hardship, she claimed, as she wasn't addicted and smoked merely to remove herself from the difficulties of her everyday life in Tientsin. Her longings for her old palace, she said, were so strong that without opium she would spend her days in misery. I knew an opium addict when I saw one, and Wan Jung was amongst the worst I had come across. In truth, she was dying in the thrall of the gory little poppy.

That night I slept in her room and dreamt a blue opium dream of the kind I had experienced before. Blue is the most bloodless of colours and I woke calm. Wan Jung seemed calm too, but she looked even worse than she had the night before. Her eyes were red and circled with dark smudges, her skin had taken on a greenish hue and her voice had lost its strength and was cracked and shaky. Even so, it was still possible to see in that frail fading creature how she had once deserved the name Radiant Countenance. I thought that even the most delightful photographs I had seen of her might not have done credit to her beauty in the days before she fell in love with opium.

When I returned to my room, I congratulated myself on how easily I had achieved her confidence. She had even told me that she knew that I was someone she could trust and that she actually did remember me from her childhood. She said that my name was a threat on the lips of concubines to their daughters. They would tell them that obedience would save them from the fate of Eastern Jewel, a girl who, like a tiger cub, fought and bit her way through her days and would never find a husband in this life or the next.

I knew that to stay friends with Wan Jung I would have to live two lies. Firstly, I must not appear to be on the side of the Japanese, whom she hated. Secondly, I would have to appear to smoke opium with her every night or I would lose her friendship as quickly as I had seemed to gain it. Faking would not be easy, but I would need to learn it fast or I would be as out of control as the Empress herself. Loving opium as I did, it was easy for me to understand Wan Jung's addiction. I have addictions of my own, but they do not poison my life's blood as opium will when it is your only lover.

After that first night of sharing confidences with her, I had no doubt that I would be able to talk her into convincing her husband that the imperial couple's future lay in Manchuria. But despite many weeks spent in a similar pattern, in which our friendship grew and she said that I had lightened her days, Wan Jung's determination not to go to Manchuria remained. She had a run of stubbornness in her make-up that belied her frail looks, and such a strong dislike of Doihara that she was bound to resist anything that had his stamp of approval.

'He has the poker player's trick of lying with a veiled face,' she said. 'How can such a man be trusted? In any case, it is an insult to expect us to take the advice of a mere Colonel.'

I attempted to raise Doihara in her esteem by telling her that, although she disliked him, she must believe that he did have the Emperor's best interests at heart. As for Doihara's lowly rank, I said that just as a farmer would better a prince if you wanted advice on growing crops, so the Colonel was an expert, not only in politics, but also on the north-east region of China where he had served, learnt the language and history.

But while I talked into one ear, Wan Jung's childhood tutor, Chen Tseng Shou, whispered into the other. He told her that he was not convinced that the Japanese had all three of the north-east provinces under control and that he had heard that in any case, they intended to name Pu Yi Chief Executive, and not Emperor of Manchuria. He advised her to be cautious of Doihara's promises and suggested that she warn the Emperor that Japan had not been honest with him. Chen Tseng Shou had known Wan Jung all her life and she trusted him above anyone else. It was obvious that he loved her and was loyal to her family, just as it was obvious that he despised Doihara and was suspicious of all Japanese.

Despite Doihara's view that Wan Jung was a stupid woman, I must say I found myself agreeing with her instincts regarding what

197

would be best for herself and Pu Yi. When she told me she believed that going to Manchuria would be the end of them and that they would be safer and happier leaving China altogether, I thought that she was reasoning well. Had I been Empress, I too would have left the country and let others seek to reinstate me. But of course I could not tell her that and continued to attempt to convince her to go to that harsh land, where I knew she would suffer not only the distress of the dangerous journey, but, once there, the indignity of watching her husband kowtowing to his Japanese masters.

I had to be a silent witness to my own cruel deceit of the frail Empress, which I could see was beginning to take effect. Wan Jung knew that the tide of events was against her. Pu Yi's brother, studying in Japan and impressed with the successful Japanese nation, wrote to the Emperor advising him to trust the Japanese and go to the north-east. Pu Yi himself, although still listening to his wife, was becoming more susceptible to Doihara's advice. His overpowering desire to resume the role of emperor influenced every thought in his head and often caused arguments between him and Wan Jung.

Her fears of Manchuria were visceral, her bowels literally loosened at the very thought of the journey to that place. If they were discovered by the Chinese they would be beaten to death. And she was afraid of losing home and family and finding herself powerless to escape what she believed would be a hateful situation. Although she would never have admitted it, she worried about the practicalities of feeding her opium habit in new and unfamiliar surroundings and feared the nightmares she knew would come if she could not.

She was right to worry about such things, but with me her instincts let her down, for she believed me to be her true friend. Owing to her loneliness and desire for friendship, she trusted me. And even though she did not heed my advice and knew that my presence in her house was influencing her husband, she remained kind to me. She told me that despite us not being able to agree on the Manchurian question, she believed that I was only advising what I thought best for her.

It took me years to learn, and then only under the most dire of circumstances, that it is people, not country, who are owed loyalty. In retrospect, I wish with all my heart that I had advised Wan Jung to leave the Quiet Garden with or without Pu Yi and to make her way from China to the west, where she could have played the Empress-in-waiting in safety. Instead as she slept her long drugged sleeps, I made plans to terrify her into leaving Tientsin for the north-east. I was tiring of the life I had to live in the limited house and longed for the pleasures of Shanghai.

Doihara, although a daily visitor to the Quiet Garden, had not approached me intimately again as on that first night. Despite the less than memorable sex on that occasion, I had suggested that it might amuse him to spend the night in my room, while Pu Yi dreamt of restoration in his, a few feet away. He declined, saying it would not be a good idea, for if we were found out Pu Yi would be less inclined to trust me. Wan Jung would turn her back on me and be even more set against going to the north-east.

'In any case, I like new flavours, Princess,' he said. 'But I am flattered that you would wish to eat the same dish twice.'

In my frustration, I attempted to comfort the two soldiers that Doihara had left on guard under threat of disciplinary action. But he had scared the liver out of them and despite my offer to please them both they thought it was a trick to test them and declined. So I resorted to known paths and found relief in the short-time boys that plied their trade in the dark lanes around the docks. But short-time boys live up to their name and, like weak opium, satisfy only the hunger, leaving the desire unquenched.

I decided to put all my energies into motivating the royal couple to remove themselves to Manchuria as soon as possible. So it was a fortunate stroke of luck for me when Pu Yi's old tutor, Reginald Johnston, paid one of his visits to the Quiet Garden. He had come to ask Pu Yi to write a preface to a book that he was writing about his time as the Emperor's tutor. It was to be called *Twilight in the Forbidden City*, and Johnston, describing himself as a 'faithful and affectionate servant to his Majesty the Emperor', had dedicated the book to him. Pu Yi was immensely flattered and wrote a short preface for Johnston, praising him as one not surpassed even by the best of China's native scholars.

During Johnston's visits, Pu Yi always insisted on evening banquets, where course after elaborate course was brought to table in portions that would have fed the thousands of eunuchs of the Forbidden City. The best of fish, meat and wine was consumed, while Pu Yi's ego was massaged by Johnston until he glowed with self-esteem. The Emperor and his old tutor talked together as though no one else existed. This annoyed Doihara, who did not like or trust this foreigner who had the Emperor's full attention. The Colonel would have kept all but Japanese voices from Pu Yi's ears if he could.

On one particular occasion Pu Yi, knowing them to be a favourite of Johnston's, ordered tiger prawns to be served in abundance. Less than an hour after gorging himself Pu Yi was the only one at the banquet to come down with food poisoning. He suffered agonising pains in his stomach, his skin turned green and he was violently sick for hours. I took the opportunity to persuade him that there must be a Chinese agent in the house out to assassinate him and that, from now on, all his food must be tasted before he touched it. Of course the truth of it was that, with his usual bad luck, he had selected and eaten a bad prawn. But after our talk nothing could have convinced him of that and he was so scared by my suggestion of assassins that the house was in an uproar for days while he had every member of staff, including the Japanese, interrogated.

Wan Jung was unmoved by the commotion and her husband's fears. She thought that his bad luck had struck again and believed that greed was the cause of his illness. Just as a lifetime of talking would not have persuaded the Empress that they would be safer in

Manchuria, I began to think that neither would the odd suspected attempt on her husband's life. But Pu Yi was more susceptible to fear than his fragile wife, and in his state of apprehension he began to set his sights towards Manchuria by sending presents of jade to those generals in the north-east who had submitted to the Japanese forces of occupation. Doihara thought it a good sign and said that Pu Yi was making allies in Manchuria so that he would have his own power base there when he arrived.

After a few days, though, the Quiet Garden settled back to its usual routine, and Pu Yi began once more to listen to his wife. But he was in a torment of fear and indecision, one day saying they should go to the north-east, the next that they should leave for the west until popular opinion, which he believed to be on his side, called them home to his rightful throne.

My next move was to arrange for a phone call to come to the house from one of Pu Yi's favourite waiters from the Victoria Café. We bribed the waiter to do it and threatened the lives of his children if he ever spoke of it to anyone. He was to tell Pu Yi that, wishing to protect his Emperor, he felt obliged to inform him personally that some suspicious-looking men had been making enquiries about the times Pu Yi chose to eat in the café. They had even enquired which were his favourite and most ordered dishes. He said he could see the bulges of their weapons under their coats and he feared they wished to harm the Emperor. He thought that, for his own safety, Pu Yi should not eat there again.

My plan was to make Pu Yi's life in Tientsin so bound by terror that he would be afraid to enter his own garden, let alone the city. As a prisoner of his fear, I thought that he would be more inclined to escape the house that would become his jail. But terrified as he was by the phone call from the waiter, it was to take three more episodes to set his flight in motion.

I had a meeting with Doihara and we set on a plan to have a basket of fruit with the card of a known sympathiser sent to the house with the message, 'To Henry and Elizabeth, may they prosper' forged in a hand that Pu Yi would recognise as that of his friend. Nestled under the oranges, like two sleeping assassins, were a pair of live grenades.

The house became still while those who knew the plan waited with racing hearts for the Pu Yis to discover the deadly fruits. When they did, there was a scream from Wan Jung and such fury from Pu Yi that Doihara had to calm him with the promise that he would double the guard at the Quiet Garden. The Colonel told Pu Yi that things in China were going badly for the Emperor and there were enemies everywhere. But he assured him that nothing would be received into the house again without a thorough inspection of it first.

I felt sorry for Wan Jung, who reacted to events moving too fast for her to think properly with mood swings and fury towards Doihara. She insulted him by calling him incompetent and requested that someone of higher rank be brought in to liaise with herself and Pu Yi. She brought her tutor to stay at the Quiet Garden and listened only to him. Although she was polite to me the warmth had gone from our relationship and I would sometimes catch her looking at me like a child who had been hit by a trusted mother. It hurt me to lose her affection but I could not blame her: I had trespassed on our friendship and she knew it. Her tutor told her that during my childhood in Japan, my blood had been influenced away from the elegance and loyalty of the Chinese, and was now tainted with the cold ambitious streak of my adopted nation. He advised Wan Jung that I could no longer be trusted. Her lady-in-waiting, in the pay of Doihara, told me that he had convinced her mistress that things had taken a turn for the worse on the day I had arrived at the house, and that he did not believe it to be coincidental. He truly was a good friend to the Empress and, although I had lost her confidence, I was glad she had someone on her side. I had no doubt that Pu Yi would in the end go to Manchuria, but I had a secret hope that Wan Jung might still avoid that fate.

Next in our campaign, an ugly but innocuous snake was laid to sleep under the covers in the Emperor's bed. It was placed on the sheet near to where his heart would lie and looked on first sight like a hideous piece of excrement. On its discovery both Pu Yi and Wan Jung, faint-hearted with fear, finally felt the need for flight. He still hankered for a throne, even a Manchurian one, while she still longed for the west. As they endlessly debated where they should go and consulted fortune-tellers for guidance, I got on with the final plan with which to scare them from Tientsin.

Our last and conclusively successful attempt was a plan of my making and a triumph. We engineered a series of riots in the Chinese quarter of the city from where the sound of gunfire carried clearly on the night air. The Emperor quaked at the sound and was white with fear. His eyes, behind the wire-rimmed spectacles that gave him the appearance of an intellectual, were those of a frightened child. He was told that the Chinese were getting out of hand and that martial law had been declared in the Japanese concession. For fear of a mass invasion of the Quiet Garden, the house had been ringed with troops and armoured cars. Colonel Doihara advised Pu Yi that neither he nor his Empress should show themselves at the windows, which must now be kept not only closed, but also shuttered both night and day.

And so it was that year of 1931 in the gloomy month of November, with a final assurance from Doihara that he would rule over Manchuria as a monarch and that he would retain the title of Emperor, Pu Yi requested that he be taken there without delay. Scared out of his wits and ready to accept any advice the Colonel had to offer, he agreed without argument that it would be safer for him to travel to his new empire without his wife, Wan Jung. It was promised that she would follow him within weeks, accompanied by the bulk of their luggage and their pets.

Pu Yi took a brief leave of his bewildered Empress as she stood in her nightdress in the hall of the Quiet Garden, and a better one of me, saying that when he was restored to his throne in Peking, I would be an honoured guest in the Forbidden City. As we stood at the open door, the contrast of the Emperor, disguised in a Japanese army greatcoat and cap, and his ill wife in her thin nightclothes could not have been more extreme. He dressed for travel, his mind focused on his own safety, she frightened and shivering with the cold, attempting to contain her fear. Without a shred of empathy in his make-up and used to his own desires being paramount, Pu Yi had no sense of the fear and panic his wife was experiencing. I put an arm around her shoulder and called her Empress, to remind her to have courage. She stopped sobbing and turned away from her husband, slowly mounting the stairs to her room.

The great Qing Emperor was driven from the Quiet Garden secreted in the boot of his own expensive convertible. A personal servant drove, while one of Pu Yi's advisors played passenger in the back seat. The car made its way to the dock, which sat in the British concession on the banks of the Pai River. It was a short but not uneventful journey, as the nervous driver hit a telegraph pole, causing the Emperor to bang his head badly enough for him to suffer severe bruising and concussion. Dazed, and without even the formality of a greeting, Pu Yi was hurried from the boot of the car along a concrete wharf to a waiting unlit motor launch which would take him out to sea to meet with the steamer *Awaji Maru*. Unknown to Pu Yi, the Japanese officers aboard had orders that, if they were discovered by the Chinese, they should set fire to a hidden store of petrol aboard and send the Emperor to his heavenly throne.

In the Quiet Garden, Wan Jung spent the rest of that night chain-smoking cigarettes, comforted by her old tutor. She set her lady-in-waiting to packing her clothes, even though it would be many weeks before she would be allowed to follow her husband. Shortly before midnight, she called me to her room so that she might take her leave of me. The Colonel had taken pleasure in telling her that he was sending me back to Shanghai the next morning, and that he was leaving his subordinate in charge of the Quiet Garden.

'Even though you are not my true friend you have been good company and I will miss you, Eastern Jewel,' she said. 'An empress is destined to be alone, I suppose, especially when she is married to an emperor who thinks only of himself. Take my advice, Eastern Jewel, and do not trust the Japanese. Whatever you may think, they do not consider you one of their own.'

I should have listened to Wan Jung, whose instincts I knew to be good. But she was the victim that night and I could not see her in any light other than that. I couldn't accept that there may have been sense in her advice. I trusted Japan, was zealous in its promotion and longed to serve it well. I took my leave of her with a kiss on the lips, which made her laugh, saying that I hoped to see her again.

'You must visit me in Manchuria, Eastern Jewel,' she said. 'Unless of course I have been lucky enough to die in my sleep before I go to that alien place.' I felt fearful for her, but forgiven.

In the new year when she was finally taken to join her husband, news reached me that she hated Manchuria. She suffered from the extreme climate and was subject to bad dreams and poor health.

I often thought of the ailing Empress wandering the halls of her inferior palace, ill and lonely, but proud in the knowledge that she was number one wife to China's true Emperor. She was poorly used, a victim of politics and her own snobbery, as well as of my betrayal of what, under better circumstances, might have been a rare friendship.

Doihara, with his usual ease in such matters, had lied to Pu Yi, who on his arrival in the north-east was named Chief Executive, not Emperor. He had a victory of sorts a few years later, though, when he was finally enthroned as Emperor of the Japanese state of Manchukuo in the company of his ailing and drugged Empress.

During those cold years in Manchukuo, Pu Yi was to take a second wife, a girl from the Tatala Manchu clan called Tan Yu-ling. She was sixteen years old, the same age Wan Jung had been when she married him. Tan Yu-ling died four years after the marriage, supposedly from typhoid, although it was rumoured that she had been poisoned by the Japanese so that Pu Yi would have no heir. Those who spread the rumours said that Japan wanted Pu Yi's brother to succeed him because he was married to a Japanese aristocrat, and a son from that marriage would have Japanese blood.

I took my leave of Colonel Doihara with relief. He told me that I had done a good job for Japan and that my efforts would not go unrewarded. He advised me that I should think carefully before returning to Tanaka, who he thought was a poor match for me.

'Tanaka is not the monster slayer you take him for,' he said. 'In any case, it is unfitting for a princess to align herself with someone of his class. If you want to prosper, Yoshiko, find yourself a man you can look up to.'

On my arrival in Shanghai, Tanaka told me that my stepmother, Natsuko, had died a few weeks before. He had the news through an army colleague who knew of my connection with the Kawashimas. Natsuko's heart had stopped beating as she walked in her garden under the winter plum trees, only a few feet from where her sister Shimako had hung herself on the night of my fifteenth birthday.

Tanaka was sympathetic, but he didn't understand the depth of my loss. He thought that I had hated Natsuko and, like many people who only believe what they see, he had no conception of how close hate and love are, or how much the one takes colour from the other. I sent him away and shut myself in my villa until I could bear to face the world again. Night after night my dreams were endless parades of the dead, where my blood mother and Shimako stood with Natsuko, like willows in a ghostly threesome, behind a glass door that would not shatter no matter how hard I beat upon it.

I had to let go my fantasy that one day there might be a reconciliation between my secretly adored stepmother and myself. I would never now experience a loving gesture from her or hear her soft voice speak words of forgiveness. At the news of Natsuko's death something broke inside me, something that I knew would never repair itself. The thought of not seeing her again was so distressing that the only comfort I could find was in opium. But I woke even from that happy sleep with the pain undiminished.

If Natsuko had loved me would my nature have been different? Does a love returned hold you firm like an anchor does a boat in stormy waters? So much is claimed for the power of love, but it has only ever wounded me. Not for the first time, I felt orphaned and angry. There is such hopelessness in the pain that comes from the death of a loved one. In that pain you cannot change the fact of their death, or bury the certainty of your own to come.

Bourbon and Raw Fish

For my part in the operation to encourage Pu Yi's flight to Manchuria, Japan commended me and bestowed upon me the rank of major, which I think I deserved. To celebrate my promotion, I had the full dress uniform of a Japanese officer especially tailored for me from the finest wool available. I gave instructions that the jacket should be narrowed at the waist and the collar set lower than was customary, so that my neck, which was long and smooth, could be more easily admired. I had my hair cut shorter than ever before and glossed it with brilliantine so that it shone and looked as dark as night.

Tanaka, who had been in a bad mood ever since I had returned from Tientsin, said he thought that, as usual, I had taken things too far. My promotion to major had been an honorary one, and my outrageous new look was bound to annoy those Japanese officers who were more conventional than him.

'They have trouble enough accepting a woman as a spy, Yoshi-ko, let alone having to mingle with her in the mess dressed like an operatic version of themselves.'

I didn't let his views bother me; after all, I was used to criticism, having been subject to it for most of my life. I knew that his jealousy of other men liking what they saw was at the root of his irritability. But, unlike before, he seemed unable to cast his mood aside. No day passed without an argument between us, and nothing I did seemed to improve his mood.

We made love as much as ever, but there was in our coupling a sort of desperation, as though he were seeking something that he had lost. I tried to release him from his gloom with new tricks that I had learnt from younger officers, but instead of pleasing him it only seemed to torment him more. He appeared to have lost his taste for innovation and liked nothing better than for the two of us to share one singsong girl in the afternoon and another in the night. I didn't mind indulging him, but I required more variety and would take time off from his company to please myself. When I returned to his bed he would sulk and take me without words, his hand covering my mouth so that I could not talk and annoy him further. He often chose to enter me from behind, telling me he did not want to see my face, which he wished was not that of a princess. 'A man is better off with a whore any day,' he said sulkily. Yet despite his festering anger, I liked his anguished lovemaking better than the sugared company of the singsong girls.

I was surprised that he did not ask me if I had slept with Doihara in Tientsin. At some level I believed that his displeasure with me had at its heart his jealousy of the Colonel. Yet he never mentioned Doihara's name and when I did, he feigned disinterest.

Tanaka frequently told me that I had gone beyond common sense in my indiscriminate behaviour, and that his association with me was holding up his promotion. I couldn't agree with him, as I felt myself an honoured daughter of Japan, who had achieved rank and was trusted with the highest matters of state. It was true that my reputation in Shanghai was such that everyone knew who I was, but I believed that was as much for my successes on behalf of Japan as it was for my sexual exploits. The position bestowed on me was a surprisingly modern one to have come from Japan's male hierarchy, but it confirmed my belief that any woman brave enough to take her own path in life could succeed. Most men, especially Japanese ones, have difficulty dealing with a woman's success, but I had imagined Tanaka to be above such sensitivities. In the past he had always encouraged me in my ambitions, and although I knew he was capable of jealousy, I did not like his new tendency to criticise and limit me.

Despite his ill temper, Tanaka presented me with a congratulatory gift of a divinely carved netsuke attached to a leather purse that held a rolled copy of a poem by Japan's seventeenth-century playwright Chikamatsu. The poem spoke of fidelity and honour and Tanaka's voice trembled as he read it to me.

Such a fine netsuke must have cost a great deal of money and, wanting to repay him for his generosity and to improve his mood, I told him that he was the best lover I had ever had. I also told him that, despite what he may have believed, I had not slept with Doihara.

'I know different, Yoshiko,' he responded curtly. 'I had you followed in Tientsin. In any case, do you think a man like Doihara would keep his mounting of a princess quiet when it adds so much to his reputation and takes so much from mine?'

'Why should it bother you, Tanaka?' I asked. 'Only you are important to me; he means nothing.'

He gave a bitter laugh and pulled me to him. 'I asked you not to lie with him,' he said severely. 'As far as Doihara is concerned, it was important to me that you were my princess, not his.'

Despite Tanaka's gift, which I knew was as near to a declaration of love as I would ever get from him, I could tell that he was not to be consoled by words. I put the poem into my writing case amongst the few sentimental things I felt the need to preserve. In an effort to rid him of his anger and assuage my guilt, I encouraged him towards cruelty in our lovemaking. Night after night I had bite marks down my back and on my thighs. There were purple bruises on my buttocks where he slapped me, thrusting so violently into me that I had to bathe in salt water twice a day. When his mood finally improved and he was returned to his old self, I felt like a child who had been chastised, her father appeased of his anger at last. I believe I enjoyed the releasing of his anger more than Tanaka did himself.

I could not, though, regret the presence of Doihara in my bed; it was his report on me that had secured me my rank and might achieve further promotion for me in the future. Everything worth having has its price, and sex with the Colonel was a small one to pay for such magnificent gains.

With Tanaka mollified, I was once more able to revel in the delights of Shanghai. I overspent on clothes and jewellery, continued to indulge in a varied love life and when dark days returned to me, I saw them off with sleep and opium dreams.

There are no dreams like opium dreams. Colours are like no colours you see in your waking hours, the food you eat is that of the gods and the sake you drink is smoother than the skin of seals. You are as one with tigers and those you have loved appear to you as uncritical as a twin. So seductive are the gifts of opium, that if I were not a stronger person than Wan Jung, I would have joined her in her addiction years ago.

Some months after I returned to Shanghai, Tanaka was called to a meeting with Colonel Doihara in Tientsin. He was apprehensive, thinking that he was being called to task for overspending, but he returned two days later in good spirits with news of our next assignment. Tanaka had been charged with the planning of a secret task which would, if successful, have enormous benefits for Japan. Colonel Doihara gave explicit instructions that I was to assist Tanaka and play a key part.

Between us, Tanaka and I spent huge sums of money to finance our extravagant lifestyle and he was sure that sooner or later he would be called to account for it. We often joked about expense sheets that might include singsong girls, opium and an endless string of whores. So it was good to have a big job which would allow us generous expenses.

Japan, fed up with the Chinese and wanting to warn the world not to challenge us, had ordered that we set in motion an attack on Shanghai's Zhabei district and claim the territory for our own. We were granted unlimited funds from the Kwangtung Army coffers. We were also informed that waiting offshore was a Japanese invasion force ready to send in its troops. Under the pretext of protecting the Japanese community, supposedly under attack from the decadent Chinese, we would swat the world's criticism like a fly from our food.

The attack would have the added advantage of distracting attention from Japan's efforts to claim Manchuria, under the so-called independent leadership of the Emperor Pu Yi. I don't think that my task of encouraging Pu Yi to go to the north-east would have been so successful if he had known how fragile Japan's hold in that area was. Although Manchuria lay under the protection of the samurai sword, its supremacy was challenged by the Chinese, who hated their Japanese conquerors and fought back at them in a thousand little insurrections. Japan wanted to show the Chinese, once and for all, that they were the masters.

I felt sorry for Wan Jung, who I knew would be terrified every time the Japanese were challenged. Manchu have always felt superior to ordinary Chinese, but they are aware that they are hated and might become the victims of their more numerous countrymen's revenge.

My part in the plan was to employ the thugs Tanaka had introduced me to through Mother to disrupt the Japanese community in Shanghai. Mother's boys were to burgle their homes and businesses in order to give credence to the Japanese invasion force, and I was to make sure they did it. I was thorough with my briefing and Mother and her boys did their job enthusiastically, brutally beating our Japanese brothers, destroying their homes and terrifying their families. I would not have wished such misery on them, but as Harry used to say, 'you can't make an omelette without breaking eggs'. Sometimes citizenship comes with a high price.

I revelled in being part of Japan's ambitions for the future and how, within a few days, Shanghai became full of danger and excitement. My blood sang when the Japanese marines gathered in Zhabei, the rail station district, to set about the Chinese. I loved the feeling of knowing what was about to happen and the anticipation of success that went along with it. I was so besotted with the samurai nation that it never occurred to me that Japan would not achieve its aims, or that I would ever live to regret my part in its triumphs. I watched the little war progress and felt excited and alive. As our tanks advanced along Sichuan Road, the air filled with yellow fog from their exhausts and I felt the thunder of their rolling vibrate through my body. With our blood up, Tanaka and I made love everywhere, in his office, in the back of his car, in the toilets of restaurants and once actually up against one of our tanks.

Our troops were resisted briefly by what Tanaka said was a more disciplined style of Chinese soldier than had been seen before, but only briefly. We were invincible and had the factor of surprise on our side. Tanaka was in his element and loved being at the centre of events. We would sit in his office drinking little shots of sake, receiving news of how things were going in progress reports from our headquarters. We often took western and Japanese guests to the top-floor restaurant of the Park Hotel on Bubbling Well Road, from where you could view the war safely. There was a long waiting list for tables, but Tanaka was treated like royalty and had a table held permanently for him and his guests. We ate the Park's indifferent food, accompanied by the noise of our planes and the shelling from our warships.

It took a few brief weeks for Japan to devastate the Chinese city over the bridge, and to remind the world that we were a nation of warriors who would let nothing stand in our way.

We were flown over burning Shanghai in Japanese aircraft. We could see by the destruction of the city what a great success the attack had been. I am sorry now to say that I applauded it. Many of Shanghai's residents had died in the battle, but it seemed pointless to be sentimental about their loss. Shanghai was overpopulated and most of the inhabitants of the Chinese quarter were starving anyway. If it hadn't been by Japan's ambitions, they would have been seen off anyway by famine and disease. Zhabei was razed to the ground and its inhabitants made homeless. Like water from a tap, they poured into the International Settlement and the French concession.

It was weeks before Shanghai returned to something like normal. It taught the Chinese their place, showed Pu Yi the determination of his Japanese allies and unsettled the world for a bit. But Shanghai, like the good whore she was, adapted herself to her new masters and once again prospered. We eventually withdrew our troops when the world complained, but not before our allies had used our attack as an excuse to enlarge their own settlements in Shanghai. If I didn't already know it, their opportunism taught me how to manoeuvre according to circumstance.

When the shelling had stopped and we had secured the area, I walked through what was left of the Chinese quarter in the company of some senior Japanese officers. I should not have done that, for the pity of it comes to me to this day in flashes of self-disgust. From the sky the destruction had looked like a successful clearing of the slums, but from the ground I was aware of the price humanity had paid for my country's ambitions. We had to step over the bodies of the dead and cover our mouths against the black smoke from the fires that smouldered on for months. The smell of burning flesh was disgusting and I had to avert my eyes from the human limbs that littered the streets. The little city within a city was eerily quiet, the dogs had disappeared from the streets and I missed the sound of mah-jong.

The few Chinese remaining in the district bowed low to us as we passed, but could not look us in the face. I saw an old woman raking pathetically through a pile of debris. She reminded me of Sorry and that was when the first shock of what had taken place hit me. Circumstances such as those in the devastated Chinese quarter made it hard for me to forget that my blood was Chinese. Even though my heart was so much for Japan then, I could not deny my Chinese inheritance on that day and was overcome by the misery I had helped to inflict on my countrymen. I wanted to hold on to someone, to feel the forgiving touch of a human hand, but the exultant Japanese officers would have thought me mad and the Chinese would have cringed at my touch.

After that victory there were more beggars on the streets and the price of opium rose, but the city itself seemed to retain its essence. In Mother's life, though, much had changed, for she had lost some of her boys, who had unwittingly got caught up in the battle, and was reduced to living in her one remaining half-destroyed house. To stop her whining, Tanaka arranged for her to be given enough money to help her rebuild her business, but life was never the same for her again. There were younger and stronger gangsters, who, taking advantage of the damage she had sustained, stepped in. She continued to make a living, but she had lost her prime position. There were bigger fish in her pond, it's true, but at least she still swam in the same water.

After our success in claiming the Chapei district for Japan my blood hummed expectantly for days, as though I could not believe that it was all over. I discovered what it felt like to shake the world a little, which is a disturbing combination of elation and fear. Yet despite my misgivings I believed then that the whole of my life had been a preparation for that time and that I had found my true place in the world in service to Japan. Conversely, just as I finally felt accepted by Japan, I began to experience nightmares so bad that I started to fear sleep.

In the months following what became known as the 'fake war', I lost Valerie's friendship. She said that my indifference to the suffering of my own people, by which she meant the Chinese, was so cold-hearted that it was as though she had never truly known me. I suppose I could have told her that she was wrong in that, but I think that Valerie had come to her own crossroads, and I would have lost touch with her eventually anyway. She had more of the martyr in her make-up than me and our friendship was not destined to last. It seemed that was the case with most of the women in my life, but I could not mourn too deeply for Valerie; she was no Natsuko, no Mai or Tamura to me. After our sharp parting, I would sometimes see her at the Sanjiaodi fruit market looking for bargains. She had given up the idea of catching a rich husband and had joined a French Catholic mission dedicated to feeding and educating the orphaned children of Shanghai's streets. Her pearls had gone and she no longer dressed in white, but there was a purpose in her manner that I had never noticed before. Perhaps she too had found her true reason for being in Shanghai. It didn't occur to me then, but now I see that Valerie reacted to the world she found herself in out of the goodness in her nature, while I avoided what was left of it in mine. Given the choice, I am not sure that I would choose a good heart over a selfish one: there would be too many things in life to trouble it.

In Shanghai there was a new mood amongst the Chinese of the city that made the Japanese uneasy. Secretive as ever, the Chinese were divided amongst themselves politically, but they were as one in their hatred of the Japanese. You could sense it in their silent insolence and in the way they addressed you in emotionless voices and took your money without thanks. Even Mother, whom I paid to keep me up to date with what was going on in her decimated quarter, had cooled towards me and advised me against visiting her without a bodyguard. The Chinese knew my face, apparently, because a poster had circulated after the fake war with my likeness on it. It named me as a murderer of my own kind and called for the blood of Chinese babies to be revenged with the shedding of mine. After she told me that I always made her come to me. I never visited her again in the little house by the Gate of Longevity. I couldn't trust her not to betray me and take a price for my head. She was a woman without principles and would have done anything for money.

I began to feel uneasy and isolated whenever I found myself in my villa alone. I got rid of my Chinese servant woman and replaced her with a Russian girl, who was a poor laundress, but less of a worry to me.

My dreams were haunted with the images of dead babies and I would often wake in the night thinking that I heard their mewling. In daylight, sense reasserted itself and I knew the cries to have come from the legions of Shanghai's cats whose complaints were made bolder in the dark.

As the months after the fake war passed, my dark days became more frequent and I found myself dwelling on the past. The death of Natsuko had made me uncomfortably aware of time and drawn my attention to how many of my relationships with those I had loved had gone wrong. It was no longer fine to be good enough for myself; I had not been enough for Yamaga and was perhaps too much for Tanaka, I had betrayed Mai's friendship, lost Tamura to another country and cruelly deceived the touchingly frail Wan Jung.

It is only when you look back and discover that you have the sort of history that you may not have chosen for yourself that age begins to trouble you. I was in my late twenties, mirrors still reflected my beauty, but even though time had been kind to me there were tiny lines appearing around my eyes and I seemed to have lost my love of self. Some mornings I felt newborn, as though I could start my life from scratch and become something more than I was, but as the day progressed the burden of my nature overtook me and often made the need for opium urgent.

Tanaka had been disappointed not to be promoted after the taking of Shanghai's Chapei district and returned to being moody and argumentative. We saw less of each other than ever before, but I still thought of him as my true partner in life, until one day I walked into the Park Hotel and was introduced to Jack Stone, an American journalist working for the *New York Herald Tribune*.

He was standing at the Park's bar with his arm around Lauren Brodie, a red-haired Irish reporter, one of the few female journalists in Shanghai. Jack had only been in Shanghai two days, but was already surrounded by a group of what seemed to me to be admirers.

My first sight of Jack Stone made me feel as though I were standing on the edge of a precipice and the centre of me had been thrown off balance. From the moment I first heard his name, the sound of which reminded me of the clatter of mah-jong pieces, something in me softened. He was five years older than me and an inch shorter, but I always felt that I was looking up at him. He had a delicately repaired harelip that gave his mouth a fragile, sensuous appeal, brown hair and grey eyes the colour of the sky just before it snows. Jack wasn't really good-looking, but he had a magnetic appeal and women loved him. Perhaps it was his quiet wit that drew them to him, or maybe it was the way he listened, his body still, his head slightly to one side as though he wanted to hear every word. Whatever it was, I was immediately seduced, and although he was not instantly mine, I desired him as much as I had Yamaga.

A couple of days after our introduction, Lauren Brodie came to see me and asked if I would be prepared to be interviewed by Jack. He was doing a piece on Shanghai personalities and wanted to include me in the group. I agreed to the interview and arranged to meet him in the rooftop restaurant of the Park Hotel. It was part of my job to know the foreign correspondents and to try and influence their reporting. But I dressed to meet Jack more as though I was going to a lover's bed than to a work meeting.

Jack was the sort of man whom Tanaka would be jealous of, and one that might give more trouble than pleasure. In any case, I was coming to the conclusion that giving in to my desires, as I had always done in the past, was perhaps the very thing responsible for my depressions and disquieting dreams. Yet I tried on three outfits for that meeting before settling on a shapely skirt and high-heeled sandals. I added a soft satin blouse, leaving the top buttons unfastened and powdering the valley where my breasts met. As my only jewellery, I wore a pair of tiny seed pearl earrings so that he would notice my small ears. Instead of my usual chrysanthemum oil, I chose musk for desire and touched it lightly at my throat and wrists.

I saw him in the restaurant before he noticed me and felt the same twist in my stomach as on the day I had first seen him. He was talking to the hotel manager and when he saw me he smiled and instantly came to join me. He was very business-like and probing in his interview. He pushed me on what he called my pro-Japanese stance, questioning my allegiance to a country that wanted to 'crush' my homeland.

'China was where I was born,' I said. 'But I was sent from it as a child and I don't consider it my homeland. Japan gave me a home and an identity; we belong to each other. Whatever happens, Japan will always have my loyalty.'

'America is my country,' he said. 'But we can be critical of country, surely? It's people that come first, don't you think?'

I didn't answer him. My loyalty to Japan was something that I had never questioned before and I found the subject quite disturbing.

We talked for a couple of hours, mostly about my rank in the Japanese Army and how I viewed the so-called 'fake war'. He asked me about my relationship with Tanaka, but he didn't write anything in his notebook on that subject. It felt more informal, less like an interview that way and I learnt as much about him as he did about me. I discovered that he chain-smoked Camel cigarettes, that he drank whisky, bourbon when he could get it, that he believed that wearing silk pyjamas under his normal ones would protect him from typhus, and that he was estranged from his wife, who hated him for leaving her alone so much. I asked him if he loved her and he said that, obviously, the very fact that he was in Shanghai showed that he loved his freedom more.

'And Lauren Brodie?' I asked.

'Just a friend,' he said and smiled.

I left the restaurant annoyed with him. He hadn't flirted with me or paid me a single compliment. Months later, Jack confessed that our meeting at the Park had affected him deeply and that he could hardly think straight when he came to write about me for his paper. He said that, although he was good at disguising his feelings, he had been overpowered by the look and the scent of me. He had tried, without success, to dampen the feelings of what he described as an unsuitable attraction, unsuitable not because we came from different continents, but because I loved Japan and Jack despised it.

When I told Tanaka about the meeting, he said that most of the foreign journalists in Shanghai were pro-Chinese and that westerners had a sickly sort of admiration for the underdog. He said that Jack Stone was highly thought of amongst his fellow Americans, but that I should be wary of him.

'Let him seek you out,' he said. 'And then only feed him what we want him to know.'

Six weeks passed before I saw Jack again. During that time Tanaka had received orders to report to Doihara in Inner Mongolia to assist him in setting up an independent government under the Mongolian Prince Teh. I had never met Teh, although he was a kinsman of mine through my marriage to Kanjurjab. I had heard stories that he was a fearless warrior and much loved by his tribe. I advised Tanaka not to mention his connection with me, as I was sure it would work against him in Mongolian circles.

I felt sorry for him, as I knew that he would hate working in close contact with the Colonel. He told me that he could not take me with him because my orders were to stay in Shanghai and ease the path for his successor, but I think it was more that he couldn't bear to see me in the company of Doihara. Nothing would have taken me to Mongolia anyway. I joked with him about the climate, warned him not to eat the butter and told him that he would like the Mongolian girls, who were plump and warm-hearted. They would, I said, be impressed by his size and his inventiveness in lovemaking.

On the day that he left, he told me that he hated the cold air of parting between us. He said that he would always keep the image of my face in his heart and that he would never fail to protect me in whatever way he could. He begged me to give up opium, which he thought would eventually destroy me.

'It's the only Chinese thing about you, Yoshiko, and your worst habit.'

It was true that the Japanese thought little of opium and despised the weak nature of the Chinese for using it, but I didn't agree with him that it would be the ruin of me. It was I that used opium, not opium that used me. I had smoked it since girlhood and knew how to stay on the right side of addiction.

Tanaka left me a little money, but to save face he had to pay off his own debts, which were considerable. He said that he could not guarantee that his successor would be as generous with my expenses as he had been, so he arranged for me to draw a monthly salary, something that I had never bothered to do before.

'You will have to live more carefully,' he said. 'It could be months, maybe even a year, before I return.'

In fact it was to be many years before Tanaka would leave Mongolia and he was never to return to Shanghai. I had already come to my own decision to be more cautious, if not with money then with my emotions. My meeting with Jack Stone had worked on me in a strange way and I could not get him out of my mind. I had been dissatisfied with myself and my way of life for some time and sensed that in Jack's company I might find relief. Tanaka thought that opium was the problem, but opium was only the bandage on the wound of a hollow life. I had come to the conclusion that a constant stream of lovers took away rather than gave comfort, and I was experiencing a desire to change.

Weeks passed before I was to see Jack Stone again. Meanwhile I was grooming myself to be a different sort of woman. One that would take no more lovers, less opium, and experience, as a result, more restoring sleep and contentment.

There was a night when I dreamt that I saw Jack on a bridge as he crossed the Huangpu River. I called his name and he turned, held out his cupped hands and showed me happiness lying in a glass bowl. It was a dark little kidney-shaped bean, curled as in sleep. 'We can share it,' he said. I couldn't bring myself to touch it for fear that it was not sleeping, but dead.

Tanaka's replacement, Major Muto, was a man who counted every yen and did not approve of debt or extravagance. I could see that things were not going to be easy for me under his supervision. He seemed to disapprove of my Chinese blood and declined to address me either by rank or as Princess. He didn't question the salary that Tanaka had arranged, but he was meticulous in scrutinising my expenses, which he often declined to honour, saying Japan should not have to pay for my pleasures. It was obvious he did not have Tanaka's understanding of how a spy needs to live.

Muto was older than Tanaka by about a decade. He was married and had eight daughters but no sons, which kept him poor and feeling inadequate. He was poisonously cruel to inferiors and slimy in the presence of his superiors. I disliked him at first sight and developed the habit of calling into his office only once or twice a week. I would relay to him any information that Mother had brought me, as well as what I had discovered for myself through my own contacts. The rest of the time I avoided him. This infrequent connection suited Muto, as he was ill at ease in my company and didn't know how to deal with a Japanese woman who had not only aristocratic blood, but also rank.

Tanaka wrote me letters saying that he missed me, but he felt that he could do well for Japan and for himself in Mongolia. I knew that he had an ambition to return to Japan covered in glory. I believed that he would achieve his desire. But in his absence it was not Tanaka who filled my thoughts, but Jack Stone. Even though I hadn't seen him since that day at the Park Hotel, I knew through Lauren Brodie that he was still in Shanghai.

One evening when the rain smelled of dust, I made my way to the telegraph office and contrived to bump into Jack as he arrived to file his copy. He didn't seem too pleased to see me, but in the awkward silence between us he blurted out an invitation to join him for dinner if I was free. Of course I accepted. Breathing in his scent of pine and whisky, I waited for him in the small telegraph office while he dispatched his work. I felt oddly shy with him, a most unusual experience for me. When he had finished, we took a rickshaw to an unfashionable Japanese restaurant north of Suzhou Creek, in what was known as Little Tokyo. Jack said he loved the raw fish they served and the fact that no other westerners seemed drawn to the place. He told me that he usually ate there alone, that the simplicity of the surroundings pleased him and that he had never taken anyone there before. I allowed the flattery to melt through me, sweet like honey, bypassing my usual cynicism. Even then, so early on in our relationship, I discovered in his company a less wary self.

It was perhaps the best and the strangest night of my life, for with Jack I lost my lifelong desire to keep secrets. I surprised myself with a new openness that left me feeling lighter and somehow relieved. We talked for hours about our lives, our hopes and regrets. Jack wanted to know everything about me, and so, against my nature, I allowed him into the labyrinth of my life.

I told him about the abortion, about Teshima's seduction, about Kawashima and all the other men who had made their way to my rooms in his house. When I had finished the tale of my childhood, Jack reached across the table and stroked my cheek.

'You never stood a chance,' he said. 'It's a wonder you have survived at all.' There was pity in his voice but for once I didn't object to it.

He told me about his own childhood in New England.

'It was quiet and ordered and desperately boring,' he said.

'My father was a math teacher, a subject that, to his bewilderment, I could never grasp. I think that he loved me. He taught me to fish and to play tennis and, without knowing it, instilled in me a desire to be as unlike him as possible. My mother was careful and shy with me, until the day she sank discreetly to the floor of our town library and died without fuss. A massive stroke, they said. I can't tell you how much I regret never attempting to break through her shyness. I realise now that I never truly knew her.'

Jack confided that he had always felt unsettled in life and that he had a restless nature. Usually when he got what he wanted, he lost interest in it. He had desired marriage, but within weeks of the wedding he was being unfaithful to his wife. He had felt trapped and flight had been his answer. He doubted that he had spent more than a few months of their three-year-long marriage in his bride's company.

'She's beautiful and intelligent,' he said. 'It won't be hard for her to find someone better than me to spend her life with.'

Journalism suited him. He was a good reporter and liked not having to accept any version of events but his own. The job allowed him a way of living that didn't require wholehearted commitment, either to family or to country.

It was still raining when we left the restaurant and Jack made me wear his jacket. We walked together in the rain, his arm around me, until we found a rickshaw to take us to my villa. By dawn I had told him everything about my life. I left nothing out, I wanted him to know the best and the worst of me. In the focus of his intense grey eyes, I found myself weeping. I hadn't realised that I had so much to cry about, or that I felt so deeply for the child who had made the woman that I had become.

Jack said I should take consolation from the fact that my life, given that we lived in the twentieth century, had been an extraordinary one, especially when judged by the standards of his own dull childhood. Although he had never met anyone like me, part of him was sorry that we had met at all, because now we were linked together and he would never be truly free again.

I had no food in the villa, so we made a breakfast of sweet tea and, exhausted, we fell into my bed. Jack reached for me in his sleep and I wept again, but he didn't stir.

When we woke, he said that he was going to get his things from the Park Hotel and move in with me. I liked the way he made such an instant decision and the way he forgot to ask me if I wanted him to move in. I did, of course, even though I thought that we would make an odd sort of couple. We hadn't even made love and knew little of each other's habits, yet I felt stupidly optimistic.

Shanghai, cleaned by the rain, smelled intoxicatingly of the new day. The sun was shining and I didn't need opium, or anyone other than Jack, to make me feel that life was worth living. It was true that he was a stranger to me, a man met by chance, but it was as if my body had always known his scent and touch. Nothing about him seemed unfamiliar, although he said it was the opposite for him, that everything about me was a new delight.

Jack's lovemaking turned out to be as complex as his nature. When moody, as he was occasionally, he would take me slowly, as though debating whether he wanted me at all, leaving the bed the moment it was over. Usually, with his humour restored by our closeness, he would return within minutes, two glasses of bourbon and two lit cigarettes in hand. I liked those times better than the ones when he was so distant that I felt unimportant to him, as though I was just anyone, not his girl. He liked variety, to use me when I least expected it, as though his right to me was unquestioned. Once, when I was talking to my Russian maid, he sent her from the room and pushed me to the floor, entering me without looking into my face, then leaving me there on the ground, without a word, when he had finished. After those cold couplings, he would desert the house and be gone for hours. When I asked him what made him like that, he said he thought that those times came out of resentment towards me for owning him, and anger at himself for not being able to resist me.

Mostly, though, Jack relied on humour to seduce me and we laughed a lot together. At his best he was warm and witty, full of life and passionately demanding. 'Just wear musk to bed,' he would say. He loved the scent so much that I gave up chrysanthemum oil, and can never now smell musk without thinking of him.

Often after sex he would hold me to him so closely that it was hard to breathe. At those times my old self surfaced and I felt suffocated and trapped. If I struggled, he only held me tighter, saying, 'You can't die of love, you know, Yoshiko.' I already knew that, but perhaps he was reassuring himself.

For all my resistance to being contained by him, I never once thought of deceiving him with other men. He was not like Tanaka and may not have forgiven me. I still looked, still felt the habit of desire, but I never, in those long Shanghai days, acted on it with anyone other than Jack.

I liked myself in his company, felt as though I were being restored to goodness. Strangely, he had more dark days than I did, days when he would drink and smoke to excess. He once took opium with me, but said he didn't care to repeat the experience. It had made him feel so good that he knew he must never use it again. I think he had an addict's nature and sensed that it would destroy him.

In subtle ways we changed each other, until we became that blended thing called a couple. Jack liked me to wear feminine clothes, and so I gave up my jodhpurs and boots to please him. I still kept my short hair, because he liked it that way. My lips, he said, reminded him of bubblegum, soft and pink. He thought it a crime to disguise them with lipstick, so I didn't.

Perhaps Jack was testing me, reassuring himself that if I was compliant in little things, eventually I could be brought round to his thinking on the one thing that stood between us, Japan. For myself, if I wanted to change Jack in any other way than in his views on the nature of Japan, I was not aware of it. I loved the way I could pick him out in a crowded room by the halo of his dark hair, loved the outdoor smell of his skin and his square hands, too large to be in proportion with his body. His pale skin and grey eyes, so western, so different to Japanese men's, fuelled my desire. I adored his sense of humour, the way he never repeated a joke, and I was always proud to be at his side. But I didn't care for the secret side of his nature that made him lock his desk drawers and seal his letters before I could read them. Perhaps because he had released me from the tyranny of my own secrets, I could not bear him to have any of his own.

I believe, though, that I changed Jack more profoundly than he did me. In his past life he had resented emotional ties, had always chosen flight over fight. In our shared one, he couldn't bear the idea that we would be parted; he wanted to keep me to him, and despite his fear of capture I knew that he would never willingly fly from me. I wasn't sure that I could say the same for myself.

I was surprised at how quickly people in Shanghai accepted that Jack and I were together. My new boss, Major Muto, was one of the few to disapprove, he was outraged by my association with a western journalist and told me that he had reported it to his superiors in Japan. I knew that he had also written to Tanaka in Mongolia, because I found the carbon copy of his letter in his secretary's waste-paper basket.

Tanaka wrote to me every few months. He never once mentioned Jack in those letters and neither did I in my replies to them. I received them through Muto's office and didn't feel the need to speak of them to Jack. I thought that he wouldn't understand the unbreakable connection between Tanaka and myself and there was no point in arguing about it.

Jack picked up his own mail from the Park Hotel and I learnt over the months to know when he had received a letter from his wife. On those days he would look for distraction, spending hours in bookshops and usually buying me some little token to show he

227

had been thinking of me. I suspect he felt guilty, as though by reading his wife's words, he had in some way cheated me.

Major Muto was right to be concerned about my affair with Jack. Jack often tried to persuade me to return to my Chinese roots and to deny Japan. It was one of the few things we argued about, and just as he could not be persuaded of Japan's innate superiority in the world, so I could not be turned back to China. The subject was always alive between us and was often the cause of Jack's moods. He saw China as a country bravely struggling to pull itself into the twentieth century, while I thought it would only prosper under the rule of Japan.

'Your admiration of Japan is the only vulgar thing about you, Yoshiko,' he would say.

Despite our arguments, Jack and I complemented each other to such a degree that I became fearful of how easily I could imagine life without him. Indeed it was hard for me to envisage the circumstances that would allow us to be together for ever. He often spoke of me returning to America with him and although I loved him for that, I could not see myself living so far away in a country that disapproved of Japan. Plenty of western men fall in love with and stay in the orient, but much as I wanted to count Jack amongst their number, I knew that he was not likely to be one of them.

I was glad that I never had to keep Japan's secrets from him. He already knew as much as I did about what was going on inter- nationally. Major Muto's mistrust of me meant that he rarely showed me any correspondence from Japan and only seemed to require me to report on gossip. I was less well informed than in the days when Tanaka had had his finger on the pulse. It was getting harder to find things to report back to Muto. Jack wasn't interested in my old haunts and we only occasionally went to nightclubs. He never gambled and didn't care for fancy food, preferring the Chocolate Shop's western-style menu to those of the celebrated

Russian and French restaurants. We still ate in what we considered to be our restaurant in Little Tokyo, where he was always the only westerner.

Jack showed me a Shanghai that I had never really been a part of before. The foreign correspondents were an eclectic group, held together by the glue of humour and cynicism. They were mostly well informed and intelligent, Jack said, but seeing too much of the shabby side of life left them without much optimism. But they were good fun and had a different way of enjoying life than I was used to. Talking was their thing and conversations went on late into the night, always accompanied by alcohol and laughter, lots of laughter. At weekends we would often join a party of them and hire one of the many elegant houseboats for rent on the river. The boats had western names like Daphne or Enid, but Jack would rename them Eastern Jewel or Princess for the duration of our journey.

I wasn't the only oriental in the group. The good-looking Russian reporter Misha Salmonov, who worked for *Pravda*, had a taste for Chinese girls and would take along a different one each time. He and Jack seemed to have a special connection and would debate politics and philosophy for hours.

Sailing down the creeks and through the rural areas, where scruffy farm dwellings lined the banks, we would eat delicious lunches of prawns cooked with chilli and drink copious amounts of white wine that tasted of limes. There was beer too, but I didn't care for it, although Jack preferred it to the wine. In the heat of the long afternoons we would sleep in one or other of the small below-deck cabins, making lazy love when we woke. On the journey home, drinking and dancing on the deck to the music from a wind-up gramophone, Jack was at his most mellow.

Sometimes we would go to the American Club, one of the few foreign clubs in Shanghai that allowed Chinese members. I went to a Thanksgiving party there with Jack where he got drunk on bourbon, and Teddy Black, the *Chicago Tribune* reporter, had to help me get him home. It wasn't the first time that I had needed help to get Jack home, but, as if to excuse himself, he told me it was because he missed America and that the club and the bourbon reminded him of the bars he frequented in New York.

I knew that ache, that longing to be home. I still had it somewhere in me, still knew that nowhere would ever belong to me again in the same way that Kawashima's house had. I didn't tell Jack that I understood, though. I couldn't bear the idea that he would one day return to America. He often said that he could be recalled to New York at any time, but, as I knew his going would wound me, I pushed the thought from my mind. Jack never wanted to hear about my work; it made him angry that I still worked for Japan's Special Service Organ. He never stopped asking me to give it up and he never understood my trust in and love of Japan.

When I did report to Muto, it amused me that he was so ill at ease in my company. I thought the man odious and took full advantage of being a princess. I would drop the names of Japanese aristocrats whom I had known as a child and watch him squirm in the knowledge that I was better connected than him. But despite holding my own against his relentless small-mindedness, I began to despair of ever enjoying my work again. I was still unpopular with the Chinese in Shanghai and I knew that Jack found my notoriety hard to bear. He wanted me not only to stop working for Japan, but also to denounce it publicly. For his sake I kept a lower profile than usual, but that was the most I was prepared to do.

Just like Jack, Muto would try to talk me into giving the work up. 'You have a new life now,' he would say. 'Surely it conflicts with your duty to Japan to be so close to this American?'

'On the contrary, Major,' I would reply. 'I think that it keeps me better informed.'

Tanaka still wrote to me regularly. I replied infrequently. I wanted to tell him that I had moved on, but I couldn't bring myself to write the words. He was doing well in Mongolia and often wrote of his successes, saying that when the time came for us to return to Japan, we would be feted for our services to our country. My affection for him was as strong as ever, but whatever was to happen between Jack and me, I knew that things would never be the same with Tanaka again.

I tried to imagine myself living in America with Jack. I supposed that many Japanese had made a good life there. I could seek out Tamura under her new name of Mrs Jasmine. I could make friends, be with Jack and continue our story. But however hard I tried I could not picture it. Where would we live, what would I do with my days? Jack would travel and leave me in a country I had no connection with. Often in the throes of lovemaking, he would whisper in my ear, 'Come home with me. I love you more than Japan ever could.' But America was his home, not mine. Mine was to be found in the very name Japan, which could not be separated from my heart, even though Jack now occupied a place there too.

Almost two years passed before a decision needed to be made. In that time I continued to work for Muto. While Jack wrote, my days were spent trawling Shanghai, listening to the pulse of the place and to the people who gave me insights into its hidden language. Mother was still useful, as were Mari's Korean boys, who knew everything going on in the underworld. I frequented the Central's International Bar, chatted to its doorman and gleaned as much as I could from Jack's colleagues. It was not the same life that I had lived with Tanaka. It lacked the sense I had enjoyed in those days that the world could change at any moment and that if it did I would be at the centre of the storm. But my world did have Jack in it, and that was enough for then.

Years ago, in my misery over losing Yamaga, I had vowed never to seek happiness again, but in Jack's lovemaking, the sweat from his skin printing the memory of his body onto my own, I realised that, without even knowing it, I had been happy since that first dinner with him in Little Tokyo.

Then, in a horrible coincidence of timing, Jack was recalled to New York in the same week that the Empress Wan Jung, through Doihara, sent for me to go to her new home in Manchuria. She was feeling lonely and longed to hear the gossip from Shanghai. Doihara sneeringly said that Wan Jung felt the need for some sophisticated company, which he took as an insult to the Japanese who surrounded the imperial couple, never letting them out of their sight. I was to stay in the Emperor's household until Doihara recalled me to Shanghai. I imagined that it would be a month or two at the most.

Just as I didn't want Jack to leave me, so it would hurt me to leave him, but at the same time I knew that I would go to Wan Jung. If he really wanted me to spend my life with him, he would wait. I told him that I had to fulfil this order from Japan. Doihara had said that I was needed and Tanaka, hearing of the posting, wrote to me, without any reference to Jack, and chose the words duty and honour to remind me where my loyalties lay.

Outraged that I could even consider going, Jack did everything in his power to stop me. There was a day when he wouldn't let me out of bed. Between passion and anger, he took me as though he could convince me better with his body than with words. I tried to explain to him that I had orders and must go, but he wouldn't listen to reason. In the end I resorted to my old habit of deceit and told him that if I had to finish with Japan, then it must be done properly. I spoke the words 'finish with Japan', knowing that I could never orphan myself in such a way. The ethos of honour and loyalty to emperor had seeped through the pores of my skin as I had spied on Kawashima from behind the paper screens. It had entered my blood when Yamaga had made love to me, survived through heartache and betrayal and had been, and was, the one constant in my life.

'If you stretch the ties between us too far they will break,' Jack said flatly. 'It's not country or blood that should hold us, but our love. How can you even consider parting us?'

'Will your love die if I go?' I asked.

Jack sighed. 'I'll wait a month for you,' he said. 'If you don't come to me by then, I'll know that you never will.'

Jack, who made his living from words, had finally run out of them.

'I will come,' I said. 'I promise.'

On our last day together we didn't go out; neither of us wanted to talk to other people. Jack helped me to pack, folding my clothes as if in slow motion. He sat me on our bamboo sofa and took a photograph of me wearing his favourite dress, a thin-strapped blue cotton one with a matching bolero. I never understood why he liked that dress so much; I thought that it made me look ordinary.

He was going back to the Park Hotel for his last month in Shanghai. He said that he couldn't bear the idea of living in the villa without me, it would be pointless. He wanted people and noise around to distract him from his feelings.

We went to bed and made excessive love, vowing to be together again. Jack was brutal in his lovemaking. In the end neither of us found the reassurance we were looking for that the bond between us was unbreakable. As we rose and fell together, I found that I was able to put a barrier around my desire, to limit the damage to a drop of distilled toxin that would fester in my heart. Jack said that he felt as though he were falling from a great height, without a parachute. I had no idea of whether I would see him again and could not bear the thought that I might not.

On my way to the airfield, I called into Major Muto's office to file my last report. I could tell that he was put out that I should be invited to visit the Imperial Family, even if it was only the Chinese one. But he was relieved too. My removal to Manchuria would return his days to the conventional order that he treasured.

Champagne and Pickled Ginger

I arrived in Changchun, renamed Hsingking by the Japanese, in a
military supply plane. Doihara had arranged the flight for me,
which was a smooth one. As I came down the steps from the plane
a young officer saluted and escorted me to the army truck waiting
on the runway to take me to Pu Yi's palace. It was an early
summer's day of the kind I had experienced in Mongolia. The sun
was high in the sky and there was a thin shell of snow on the
ground and on the sloping roofs of the houses.

Hsingking was a small farming city in the process of being
rebuilt by the Japanese, who boasted that it would eventually rival
Paris. Alongside the indigenous population there were thousands
of Japanese immigrants making new lives in the country that they
had been told would feed Japan, and make them rich.

It was a short journey from the airfield to Pu Yi's residence,
where in the large reception hall I was greeted by General Hayao
Tada. I knew him to be the Chinese Emperor's chief military
advisor. Doihara had told me that he was a man of great wit,
but too in love with the lifestyle of the upper-class Chinese to be
reliable in his judgements.

He addressed me as Major and welcomed me as a fellow officer,
even though I was dressed in a wool suit and draped in my fox furs.
I told the General that I was honoured that he should receive me
personally. He said that he had been looking forward to meeting

234

such a famous princess, whose reputation as a great beauty he could see now was an understatement. His flattery made me laugh, as I knew it was meant to.

General Tada was an interesting-looking man who, unusually for a Japanese officer, smiled a lot. He had receding hair the colour of iron, horseman's legs, which were slightly bowed, and a muscular physique. I noted that he smelled of the same 4711 cologne that Pu Yi used, and wondered if the Emperor gave him presents. He was clean-shaven, with a square jaw line and deep-set eyes. I was to become familiar with his habit of pulling on his eyebrows and with his unsettling stare, which I had no trouble in meeting.

Tada told me that he had heard a lot about me from Doihara, who had been promoted to Major General and was having great success in Mongolia in the company of Prince Teh. He said that Doihara referred to me as Asia's 'Catherine the Great', and I must say that, despite seeing through the flattery, I liked the reference.

'Seeing you in the flesh, Princess,' Tada said, 'it is a wonder to me that such a beautiful woman is also such a successful soldier. Your triumphs in Tientsin and Shanghai are impressive. I hope that we might spend some time together discussing them.'

As he took his leave of me, he clicked his heels together and, without even the slightest touch of humility, bowed so low that he almost touched the top of my boots.

'I should tell you, Princess, that I love all things Chinese,' he said. 'It is rare that there is an exception to that rule, and in your case, quite impossible.'

For the first time that I can remember, I was not insulted by being referred to as Chinese by a Japanese male. There was something so completely disarming in Tada's personality that it was impossible to be offended by anything that he said. He left me in the company of the palace's Japanese chamberlain, a man responsible for the household staff and expenses. With his flat face and little currant eyes, the man looked mean enough to be good at his job. Tada said the chamberlain knew the palace inside out and would give me a guided tour before showing me to my quarters.

I did not find Pu Yi's Manchurian palace beautiful. It had been remodelled out of the old Salt Tax Office and still had the air of commerce about it. Yet it was a good deal more fitting for an emperor than the shambolic Quiet Garden in Tientsin had been.

You entered the residence by any one of the four iron gates set in the fourteen-foot-high brick walls. At each of the four corners were gun towers. The spacious courtyard was bare of plants, but there was a magnificent pair of terracotta pots, taller than the Japanese guards who, like the vessels, stood at either side of the main door. The house consisted of two long, low buildings, built one in front of the other, their roofs fashioned with sloping tiles in the Chinese manner. The two mansions were connected, as though by an umbilical cord, through a wide hallway that was hung with dark red silk and carpeted with a runner of imperial purple. In the first mansion there was a large reception room that housed a vast table scattered with papers and boxes of files stamped with Pu Yi's crest. The wood-panelled walls and doors were carved with images of lions and mad-eyed dragons chasing their own tails. The ground floor of this building had numerous small rooms that were occupied by Japanese secretaries and junior officers, all seemingly about the business of aiding Pu Yi. In fact, their true function was to never let him out of their sight. They were always in earshot of even his most private conversations, and although I worked for the secret service myself, there was something about their manner that revolted me. The top floor housed the sleeping quarters of Pu Yi's Japanese butler and others of his domestic staff. The rooms there, having no fireplaces, were cold and draughty.

The second building was decorated more fussily with walls painted in the imperial yellow, to make the Pu Yis feel at home, I supposed. Its rooms had wider windows than those in the first house, but they were covered with dingy fly screens that blocked the light. Some effort had been made to make the rooms fit the Emperor's station and they were filled with lacquered furniture, embroidered hangings of orange and blue silk and low couches. In the day sitting room, there was a western-looking fireplace with a crudely painted portrait of Pu Yi in a gilt frame hanging above the mantle. It reminded me of the one I had received from Kanjurjab before our marriage. It flattered the Emperor, much as mine had flattered my husband.

When I referred to the house as the Imperial Palace the flat-faced chamberlain said that it was called the Emperor's Palace, as his Imperial Highness, the Emperor of Japan's residence was already known throughout the world as the Imperial Palace. I knew that Wan Jung would be insulted by such distinctions and ashamed that her husband, once the greatest man in China, had accepted the mean discriminations of his Japanese masters. In Tientsin, she had confided to me that she thought her husband would have made a better eunuch than an emperor. I pointed out at the time that even the Forbidden City's eunuchs used their power well and would not have wanted to trade places with the Emperor.

My quarters in the Salt Tax Palace consisted of two small rooms and an even smaller bathroom that had a tin bath in it, but no taps or toilet. There was a wooden shelf and a copper water carrier, which I guessed was used by the servants for filling the bath. In the bedroom, there were Chinese rugs on the wooden floor decorated with peonies that appeared to be carved into their velvety pile. Under the bed there were two plain white porcelain night pots. The second room had a desk, a low sofa and floor cushions made from thick black cotton. The curtains were made from the same black cotton and lined with felt. They were ugly but I thought that at least they would keep out the draughts. I was pleased to note that both of my rooms had fireplaces. Wan Jung had left a note on the desk, saying that she was delighted that I had arrived and that she would come to my rooms before dinner, so that we might greet each other in private.

237

When she came, surrounded by a cloud of the little Pekinese dogs that she loved, I was shocked at how ill she looked. In Tientsin she had been painfully thin, but now she was skeletal. Her dark hair had lost its shine and was scraped back severely from her face and set in braids. She had finally succumbed to the peculiar livid skin of the opium addict and had developed a pronounced tremble throughout her body. Yet, despite the ravages opium had wrought, to me she was still beautiful. I had expected her to be in western dress but she was wearing a Chinese high-necked coat of emerald-green silk with gold satin fastenings. Long jade earrings swung elegantly just above her shoulders and a huge silvery pearl set in a gold ring weighed down the middle finger of her left hand. In the memories I have of my blood mother, she is dressed in much the same way as Wan Jung was that day.

I greeted her as 'Your Majesty', and she smiled and said, 'In Manchuria, I will call you Eastern Jewel. We will not forget that we are Chinese, or ignore those formalities that will make us feel at home when we return to the Dragon Throne in the Hall of Supreme Harmony.'

I had forgotten how Wan Jung could never speak normally when she spoke of the Dragon Throne. Her language became archaic, while her voice took on the gravity of an actress playing the part of an empress. Yet in all other conversations, she had a delightful sense of fun and a charming naturalness.

She seemed genuinely pleased to see me, even though the smile that lit her face did not fully reach her eyes. She said that I was as beautiful as ever, but that I must excuse her colour, which was, she sighed, due to the polluted air of Changchun.

'You are lucky, Eastern Jewel, to have such beautiful skin. I suspect that it comes from your mother. Her beauty was renowned among concubines.'

I thanked her and asked her what her life was like in her new palace in the capital of Hsingking, which I noted she still called Changchun. She said that she was sick with longing for her true palace in Peking. She lowered her voice and told me that she hated everything about Manchuria, which she said was a brutal place full of peasants and soldiers.

'We are infested with rats here,' she said scornfully, as though rats were unheard of in the Forbidden City. 'Only the Japanese would call such a humble building a palace. It is so small that it is impossible even to lose your way.'

It was true that compared to her Peking home, where you were likely to lose your way in the hundreds of alleys that opened onto vast courtyards, her Manchurian home was a poor thing. She said that in the Forbidden City, you could enter the palace through fifty gates, visit a different temple every week of the year, dally on the myriad little bridges over lilied ponds, or take green tea in the Imperial teahouse while watching archery.

No Chinese likes to lose status and 'She of the Beautiful Countenance' was no exception. It seemed to me that Wan Jung was more out of touch with reality than she had been in Tientsin. She would never accept the Salt Tax Palace as home and constantly spoke of a future when she would return to the life she had lived as wife to the great Qing Emperor of China. It was impossible not to be aware of the yearning that was eating away at her. Her longing for her imperial home was so strong that it overcame her natural pessimism. I understood the ache of homesickness, but Wan Jung's had become an obsession that diminished her usually fine powers of reason. Despite her hatred and distrust of the Japanese, she nurtured the belief that they would eventually return her and Pu Yi to Peking in triumph. She told me that this belief was the only thing that kept her from drinking hemlock, although on those days when it was hard to keep her hopes alive she sometimes considered it.

After I had listened sympathetically to her news we sat informally on the floor cushions in the small study and talked of the latest fashions, while she petted one or other of her little Pekinese. I showed her my jewellery and the silk nightdress trimmed with exquisite French lace that I had bought to console Jack only days before our parting. I had never worn it. She was like a child being given the run of their mother's possessions. It was touching to watch her going through my things with such admiration. That afternoon, we chain-smoked cigarettes and between us we drank a bottle-and-a-half of champagne. I made her a gift of the silk nightdress and she told me that, when she returned to Peking, I could take my pick of anything of hers that I liked from the Imperial Palace.

Did Wan Jung truly think that everything was as she had left it in her old home? Did she imagine that her clothes, still folded with tissue, were lying in the fifty chests of her dressing rooms? Perhaps they were, perhaps the rows of her shoes, her imported perfumes and the little drawers filled with incense were waiting for her touch in the undisturbed air of her apartments, but I did not think so.

We were intimates that afternoon, gossiping and laughing at little things. She asked me what path my life had taken since she had last seen me and I told her about Jack.

'Don't weep,' she said, handing me a linen handkerchief. 'You could still have him if you wanted.'

'Yes, of course,' I replied. 'I could still have him if I wanted.'

But did I want Jack more than I wanted Japan? If I chose him over my country would I spend my life in regret, suffering the humiliations of a refugee? If I released Jack and honoured Japan would it help to dilute the venom in my heart that I felt at the loss of him?

'You are luckier than you know, Princess,' she said. 'I sometimes think that I will never have a man inside me again.'

Pu Yi never came near her, nor did she want him to, but there were times, she said, when she longed to be touched. I joked with her that she was living surrounded by men; surely there must be one amongst them whom she desired.

'The thing is, Eastern Jewel, you have never allowed your class to determine your journey in life, whereas mine holds me in a prison from which there is no escape. An empress can only lie with an emperor; anyone less would put the throne and her life at risk.'

240

'Wan Jung,' I whispered. 'If you let go the desire to be Empress, you could escape this place. There are other ways for a young and beautiful woman to live; a moment of courage and you would be free.'

'Being Empress is the last and only thing left to me, Eastern Jewel,' she said. 'Whereas you make your own fate, I have no choice but to follow mine.'

It was the only time that I was to speak of desertion to Wan Jung. I had no wish to betray Japan by encouraging her to go against their plans, yet something in me longed to release her from the awful life she was living. The thought of her dying in the hated Salt Tax Palace was unbearable, but she had a run of fatalism in her nature which made her incapable of action and there was nothing I could do about it. After our time together in the Quiet Garden, I don't think that Wan Jung ever truly trusted me again, but without her tutor whispering in her ear, I think that she was able to forgive me. I came to love those late afternoons in her company and still treasure the memory of them. She liked me to talk of Shanghai and of my past adventures, and enjoyed speculating on how Tamura might be living in America, and whether Mari was dead or alive. For those few hours, when she was not feeding the tyrant of her addiction, we shared what felt like the sweet companionship of sisters.

I didn't see Pu Yi for three weeks; he had an illness that gave him splitting headaches and made him vomit. Wan Jung said that he had lost his voice and suffered a constantly high temperature. His doctor said he had seen the illness before and that Pu Yi would recover within the month. The Empress was fearful that he had been given poison, but I'm sure she was wrong in that. Her Emperor was as unlucky with his health as he was with everything else in his life.

Thirteen days after I had left Shanghai, I received a letter from Tanaka saying that he was pleased that I was with Wan Jung in Manchuria as he thought it brought us and our plan to return to

Japan closer. Amongst his other news he wrote, 'I hear that your friend, Jack Stone, has returned to America.'

The words were such a shock to me that I had to read them over and over again, trying to convince myself through tear-blurred eyes that they could not be true. I could hardly believe it, but I knew Tanaka and he would not have said it if it wasn't true. So Jack hadn't even waited out the month, he had broken the bond between us and cut himself free. If a heart can break twice, I think that for the second time in my life, mine broke on that day. With no letter from Jack, explaining his reasons or giving any promise of his return to China, the old feelings of abandonment overtook me. The pain of it was caustic and sent me running for opium.

Yet, in fairness, despite my promise to him, I'm not sure that I would have returned to Jack within the month anyway. But love is not fair nor logical, and his not waiting inflicted a wound too deep for me to take lightly. The betrayal set me to seeking old ways of salving my pain, and I knew, with grey disappointment, that it would not be long before I sought out the bed of General Hayao Tada. Tanaka had been blind to my true addiction; it had never been opium.

Even so, that evening, after reading Tanaka's letter, I shared a long pipe with Wan Jung and sharing her heartache, too, I dreamt of the Forbidden City. It was covered in a layer of cold white frost. The twenty palaces of the city sparkled as though covered in diamonds, while its gates and ornamental bridges were hung with icicles. The moat surrounding the Imperial Palace was encrusted with silvery ice that reflected the tiles of the palace's roof in a thousand little yellow flags. In my dream, the city was so silent that you could hear the gods breathing. When I told Wan Jung of it, she said it was a sign that the Forbidden City was waiting for its Imperial Family to bring it back to life. My dream put her in a good mood for days.

On his recovery, Pu Yi invited me to dine with him and I was pleased to accept, as I had often found the dinner hour lonely in the

Salt Tax Palace. Wan Jung no longer bothered with meals; she just picked at the food brought to her apartment on a tray. Apart from her huge consumption of opium, she drank a lot of champagne and smoked so many Turkish cigarettes that her fingers were stained sulphur yellow. Given her lifestyle, it was not surprising that her waking hours were just a fraction of those in which she slept.

I dressed carefully for that first dinner with Pu Yi, guessing that General Tada would be joining us. Choosing a midnight-blue crêpe de chine cheongsam, I pinned a diamond brooch in the shape of a dragonfly above my breasts. I had bought the brooch for myself in Shanghai to celebrate my promotion and had never worn it in Jack's company. I smoothed chrysanthemum oil on the pulses at my wrist and between my breasts and, despite it not being musk, I thought of Jack. Because I sensed Tada would like it and knew that Jack would not, I smudged the outer corner of my eyes with kohl.

If it were true that Tada was seduced by everything Chinese, then I would do my best to live up to that fantasy. I had done it well enough for Sesyu in Tokyo. In any case, I would choose to play a concubine over a geisha any day. Geishas, hidden under their face paint, courtly manners and endless undergarments, make the sexual dance too complex. A concubine is there for the taking the moment she is desired.

Pu Yi greeted me with his usual courtesy, but I couldn't tell if there was warmth in his eyes, because he was wearing dark glasses. He apologised for them, saying that he had an eye infection left over from his illness and that the light made his eyes water. I knew that he suffered from progressive myopia and that he was practically blind without his spectacles. Dressed in the uniform of commander-in-chief of the Manchukuo Army, one that had no doubt been made up for him, he was covered in medals and looked uncomfortable. At his feet two huge English mastiff dogs slobbered strings of saliva onto the carpet.

'Welcome to the Salt Tax Palace and to Manchukuo, Princess,' he said, taking my hand briefly into his own limp one.

I noticed that whereas Wan Jung always used the Chinese name Manchuria for her new country, Pu Yi was happy to please his masters and use the Japanese, Manchukuo. I despised him for being such a watered-down Manchu.

Tada was standing near the Emperor attired in his Japanese dress uniform looking very smart. He greeted me like an old friend and poured me champagne. The meal was good enough, better than anything I had eaten at the Quiet Garden and I enjoyed watching Tada satisfy his healthy appetite. He took Chinese pickled ginger with his duck and refused the raw fish that most Japanese would have preferred. After dinner the three of us played poker with the senior officer of the Japanese gendarmes, a serious man devoid of humour. The gendarmes were housed in the palace and were so placed that no one could come or go without their knowledge. Pu Yi could not receive letters without them first being read by our poker companion and every household item was delivered to and thoroughly inspected by his men. They had the Chinese Emperor so under control that he could not urinate without them first lifting his robes. I was impressed, but not surprised by such attention to detail. It was part of the Japanese ethos to be thorough and one of the reasons for its success in the world arena.

It didn't surprise me that Pu Yi never questioned what in reality was his confinement. In Tientsin, I had noticed how well defended he was against the knowledge of the obvious. I think he was as deluded as Wan Jung in his belief that he would be returned to Peking in triumph and was prepared to put up with anything until that glorious day came.

During the game, we drank tall glasses of jasmine tea and ate candied orange peel. Pu Yi declined the tea, explaining that he could no longer drink it as the inferior quality of the rice in Manchuria had given him piles, which reacted badly to tea. At ten o'clock he stood up, gave his apologies for leaving us so early and said that he had much to do and that he would be working into the early hours of the morning. In a voice shaking with emotion, he said that he had made a resolution never to be lazy again. He owed it to his people to strive tirelessly for his reinstatement to the Qing throne, which would not only give them back their pride, but would also satisfy his aggrieved ancestors. As he left us, the two giant mastiffs rose and followed him out of the room. Despite his grand uniform and the impressive size of his dogs, he looked a pathetic figure.

I asked Tada what the Emperor would be working on and he said that most likely he would be reading the *Book of Changes*, which he believed would help him to think intellectually. I had dallied with the book myself but had found it too male-orientated to appeal to a woman. It was full of sentences that began with, 'The superior male' or 'The great man'. I understood, though, why it would appeal to Pu Yi.

Tada offered to take me to one of the new bars in Hsingking, where the wealthier of the Japanese immigrants in Manchukuo could drink sake and lie with Japanese prostitutes. I said that I would rather drink champagne with him in his quarters, where we might be alone. He picked up a bottle from the sideboard where they were lined up in neat rows, handed me two glasses and guided me towards the east wing of the house where he had a fine apartment furnished in the Chinese style. We drank the champagne, went back for more and then attempted to outdrink each other with shots of sake. I discovered Tada to be an amusing companion who seduced with a quick humour and a talent for cruel mimicry. He had Pu Yi's voice and body language off to perfection. I knew that perhaps not that night, but soon, we would lie together and that he would be a good lover. Of course, there are always exceptions to the rule, but I have found that men who make you laugh also make you moan in bed.

Tada told me that he had left his wife, with whom he was bored, in Osaka and planned never to return. He said that, unlike me, he was in love with China and could not bear even to think about what his life had been like in Japan. I felt sorry for his wife who had lost such a life-enhancing man and even more so when he told me that she was barren. For a Japanese wife to be barren is a disgrace that taints every minute of her life. It reflects on her husband, who without offspring cannot continue his bloodline.

Halfway through the second bottle of champagne, we clumsily undressed each other and lay naked on the bed. I wanted to make love, but Tada said we should wait until our senses were less saturated with alcohol. He asked me to tell him the story of my first coupling with a man and not to spare even the smallest of details. I could not bring myself to tell him of my breaking by old man Teshima or those that had followed him in the Kawashima household. He may have known of it, but if he did he never said.

I told him that my first lover had been Kanjurjab, but that the telling of that experience would bore him and so I would relate the story of Harry and the midnight swim at the Shanghai Club. I replaced the fat German's young male lover with a beautiful Chinese girl, knowing that Tada would find that more exciting. I modelled her on the fourteen-year-old girl whom I had watched through the carved screen servicing my father, all those years ago in my birth home. I said that the girl had long dark hair that coiled in the water like sea snakes, and that apart from a pair of silk slippers that covered her tiny bound feet, she swam naked. I described the water of the pool as the palest of blues, through which the girl's body gleamed like that of a mermaid. I said that as Harry and I made love in the cubicle, we could hear the guttural moans of the fat German as he entered his young whore, and hear too her tiny cries of feigned pleasure. By the time I had finished the tale we were both too drunk to make love and so we went on drinking until we fell asleep.

When we woke at sunrise he pulled me towards him and entered me without a word. I liked the weight and hardness of him. I tried to think of those things and not of Jack, and mostly I succeeded. I wanted to please Tada, so that he would remember me above all the other lovers I was sure he had enjoyed. It was a vanity on my part that I wanted the memory of sex with me to set the standard of encounters to follow. I accepted his tongue into my mouth as though I was savouring the most delicious oyster. Arching my body so as to give him more pleasure, I ran my nails down the length of his back and cupped his buttocks with my hands, helping him to push into me. It was not often in sex that I gave so selflessly. I wanted to leave him wanting more. I wanted too to replace my feelings of hurt at Jack's betrayal with those of revenge. Revenge is so much more pleasurable than pain.

Before I left Tada's rooms, I kissed the purple scar where his appendix had been taken out and asked him what would give him the most pleasure when I returned that evening.

'Come to me dressed as the Chinese princess that you are,' he said. 'But be as obedient as a concubine. Wear the same perfume, the same dark paint around your eyes and be barefoot.'

I liked a man who knew the game he wanted to play and I looked forward to indulging him and myself in the role. As a taster of my obedience to come, I knelt before him as he sat on the bed and took his member into my mouth, sucking as softly as I could until he came with a deep groan of satisfaction.

For what turned out to be the ten months of my stay with the Pu Yis, I never missed a night in Tada's bed. I played his Chinese whore and refused nothing that he asked of me. He was a man capable of losing himself in a woman's body in a way which, despite my little games of servitude, made me feel delightfully powerful. He loved the roundness of my earlobes, the crescent of my lips, the hollow in my throat and even the curved arches of my feet. He said that Chinese women had a delicacy of shape that could not be matched by those of any other nation. The General was in love with the idea of concubines, with Chinese legends of beauties so delicate you might crush them as they lay beneath you. His ambition was to live in China with a stable full of horses and a house full of concubines vying for the pleasure of his company between their sheets. I thought that he would be a strong master, respectfully kowtowed to by his servants, adored by his women. I had no desire to be one of them, but in his bed I came near to losing myself, to forgetting the girl in the blue dress whom Jack had said he loved.

It was lucky for me that I had my General for company, otherwise the time that I spent in Manchuria would have been very lonely. Wan Jung slept, locked in her plush bedroom, while Pu Yi wasted his days in endless meetings that were designed to keep him occupied, while Japan got on with running Manchukuo. Pu Yi had a Manchu tutor who was teaching him the language of his ancestors, but he preferred English and was attempting to make it the second language of the court. Of course, the Japanese would have none of it.

Outside the cold Salt Tax Palace, the world was full of intrigue. There was a war in Europe and Japan had allied itself with the axis powers of Germany and Italy. To the rest of the troubled globe the Qing Emperor and his number one wife must have seemed like relics from a dead past.

Tada frequently visited the nearby headquarters of the Kwangtung Army where, if Wan Jung was to be believed, he indulged what she believed was his cruel nature by devising terrible punishments for the captured bandits who challenged the Japanese in Manchuria. I believed her, but I did not judge him in the same way that she did. A General has to know how to use propaganda, as well as to be good at battle strategy. There can be no better message to a bandit than to use his fellows for bayonet practice. I never asked Tada about his treatment of prisoners; he had his work to do for Japan as we all did.

I often rode out with him on horseback and once or twice he left me to play stand-in general over a borrowed detachment of Manchurian soldiers. I chose the best-looking captains to sleep with and paid them for their services with Kwangtung gold. It was no secret to Tada that I used his men; in fact he encouraged it and would later ask for every detail, what they did and what they said. I had to make up stories for him for, strangely, when in those narrow barrack beds, I had begun to feel ashamed of myself and preferred a silent sort of union. I wanted Jack to come and save me from myself, but I received no word from him.

Heralded by the bitter winds that howled in the stairwells of the Salt Tax Palace, a ferocious winter arrived in Hsingking. The frosts were so hard that the giant pots in the courtyard cracked from top to bottom and had to be replaced with a pair of couchant stone lions. Some of the rooms in the palace were heated with open fires, but the halls were freezing and in the early morning ice could be found on the inside of the windows. I began to long for Shanghai with its central heating, hot water on tap, and streets warmed by jostling crowds.

In the summer months in Hsingking, I had taken to occasional walks in the gardens of Tatung Park, where the boys who rutted with Japanese soldiers strolled prettily. It was the only place where I allowed myself to dwell on Jack and sometimes to weep sorry tears for myself. But now, in the cold leafless season with the benches deep in snow, even that dubious pleasure was denied me. By mid-afternoon it was dark and, as in Mongolia, the white moon of winter kept its promise of nights so cold that they slowed the blood and made your eyes ache.

It was no longer a pleasure to ride out on horseback. The ground was so hard, the air so frigid that even the horses complained. I did sometimes drive with Tada to the Kwangtung Army's headquarters to play poker in the cell-like rooms of my favourite captains, where I felt obliged to reacquaint myself with them. Under their rough blankets, skin to skin in the pale warmth of their oil stoves, those friendly couplings only made me desolate.

I suggested to Wan Jung that perhaps it was time for me to return to Shanghai, but she wouldn't hear of my leaving. As I had no orders from Doihara to leave, I had to make the best of things and see the winter out in the dark Salt Tax Palace. I apologised to her for wanting to go, explaining that I had always hated the cold and that I had too little of her company for my liking.

'You should smoke with me more,' she said. 'Then your days would not seem so long.'

As it was, I was indulging in the poppy more than was safe. It kept the cold, and thoughts of Jack, at bay. Tada said that he could tell when I had smoked opium because my eyes were clouded and for days after my saliva tasted as bitter as melon seeds.

Wan Jung told me that she herself had begun to dream of the Forbidden City. In those comforting slumbers she said that she was at peace with herself, secure in the knowledge that she was the honoured Qing Empress. She slept in rose-scented linens and bathed in silvery pools big enough to swim in. In the company of her elegant ladies-in-waiting, she floated over ponds filled with water lilies of such unusual colours that she had no words to describe them other than that they were filled with light. She was so happy in those dreams that I feared her opium intake would increase to the extent that there would be no part of the day when she would be her real self. Tada said that he didn't think it mattered that much, for in his opinion Wan Jung wouldn't live for much longer; he thought she might as well spend the time left to her in a world where she could be happy. He had a way of getting to the heart of things that was difficult to argue with.

Pu Yi was talking about taking another bride, as Wan Jung, he said, was no longer fit to show herself in public. The idea of it added to Wan Jung's misery. If Pu Yi were to have a son by another consort, then she would have a stronger power base than the Empress herself. The thought of it turned the knife in Wan Jung's heart and made her more anxious and insecure.

Doihara visited only once from Mongolia. He greeted me familiarly and said that I had lost none of my beauty since he had last seen me in Tientsin.

'Your lover Tanaka does well enough,' he said. 'But I am not convinced that an officer so like his men in nature will ultimately succeed in his objectives.'

250

It seemed strange to me to hear Tanaka described as my lover. I had not seen him for almost three years, two of which I had spent with Jack. But his letters to me were frequent and they often spoke of our future together. Even though I had reluctantly made the decision to let Jack go, I could not get him out of my mind and every time I received a letter from Tanaka, I wished that it had come from Jack.

Pu Yi ordered a banquet to honour Doihara, which was attended by Tada and the senior officers of the Kwangtung Army, as well as some successful Japanese entrepreneurs doing well out of Manchukuo. Apart from Wan Jung and myself, the only other women at the meal were two geishas attending their owners. Like Wan Jung, they did not eat.

I think that Doihara, despising the Emperor's company, would have preferred to go without the banquet, where he was seated next to him, but for appearances' sake he had to attend. He could barely observe the formalities towards the royal couple and managed to make even his deep bow appear insulting. His attitude was abrupt to the point of rudeness and sometimes he would completely ignore the Emperor when he spoke, pretending he hadn't heard him. Upset and, as always, a little afraid of Doihara, Pu Yi reacted by drinking too much and resorting to the flattery that Doihara despised.

Tada had arranged for Doihara a liaison with a beautiful Japanese prostitute known for entertaining only those of high rank. In his impatience to be out of the Emperor's company and in that of the prostitute's, Doihara excused himself and left before the oranges were served. In the Forbidden City no one would have dared leave such an occasion before the Emperor and so it was not surprising that Doihara's departure filled Pu Yi simultaneously with fear and anger. When Wan Jung wished him goodnight, he told her spitefully that Doihara had left because he could not bear her company. She replied that Doihara could not bear the company of any Chinese, least of all that of the hungry-for-approval Emperor. I was pleased to see that even though her health was poor, her skill at fencing was as good as ever.

The next day I was called to a meeting with Doihara. I asked him if he had enjoyed the company of his night companion. He said that he had, and that she deserved her reputation, but she was a little too fleshy to be perfect. After the pleasantries were over, he quizzed me about the Empress. What did she talk about? How extravagant was she being? How anti-Japanese were her sentiments?

'For instance, Yoshiko, who in the house is loyal to her?'

'No one in this palace, not even the Emperor,' I replied.

Despite the fact that I was betraying Wan Jung's confidences, I was truthful with him. I confirmed to him that Pu Yi did not visit his wife's bed and he said it was a good thing that he did not, as a Qing offspring would only complicate matters. When I told him of her dreams he laughed and said that it would never be part of Japan's plans to return Pu Yi to his Dragon Throne.

'There is room for only one imperial house in Japan's territory,' he said. 'Pu Yi's usefulness will run out as soon as our hold on Manchukuo is complete. We didn't pay for it with the blood of the Kwangtung Army to make a gift of it to that pathetic creature. It is an embarrassment for Japanese soldiers to have him as their commander-in-chief.'

Wan Jung truly hated Doihara, with good cause. She felt disliked and powerless in his company. After his visit she was upset for days, going about her life nervously, as though his intention had been to assassinate her. I assured her that if he had been ordered to oversee such a dreadful act, the deed would have been accomplished before she had the luxury of worrying about it. Both Wan Jung and Pu Yi were paranoid about being poisoned. Pu Yi had a servant who tasted everything for him, yet still he would not eat the rice sent to him by his Japanese sister-in-law Saga Hiro, even though it was of the finest quality and might have saved him from his piles. Wan Jung, fearing that poison might be slipped into her champagne, never drank from an already opened bottle.

Fuelling her suspicions that the Japanese had murder in mind, a bill had been passed by the authorities naming her husband's brother Pu Chieh as the successor to the Manchukuo throne. Pu Chieh was married to Lady Saga Hiro, a relative of the Japanese Imperial Family. That way, through the maternal line at least, the throne of Manchuria would be occupied by someone from a Japanese bloodline.

Wan Jung veered between the view that, under world pressure, Japan would have no option but to return the Pu Yis to their Chinese throne, and the belief that an assassin was behind every curtain. She always locked a servant in her room to make sure that no one entered it while she was away and kept a rope ladder under her bed, so that she could escape if a fire were set under her door.

My views were in tune with Doihara's insomuch as I believed that only samurai blood was strong enough to hold and rule Manchuria as one state. I did not believe, though, that Wan Jung's life was in danger. Pu Yi might have to die, but his wife, a mere woman, childless and clouded with opium, would, I believed, simply lose status and be returned to the care of her family. I took comfort from that belief, as I had come to count Wan Jung amongst those that I loved.

After Doihara had left to return to Mongolia, Pu Yi questioned me about my own meeting with the Major General. He was angry at the way Doihara had treated him and wanted me to reassure him that all was well. I told him that Doihara's only concern had been for the Empress's health and his hope that the royal couple were adjusting to their new life in Hsingking.

Pu Yi nodded as though he was pleased, but persisted, 'Major General Doihara seemed distant in his attitude. Perhaps there was something not to his liking in the palace?'

'No, your Majesty, I am sure not. I think the Major General's mind was on Mongolia where he has important unfinished business.'

He accepted my explanation of Doihara's behaviour, but it was obvious that he remained unconvinced. Yet, whatever slights and bad behaviour Pu Yi had to put up with from his Japanese masters, he always managed the formalities and the appearance of calm. Those close to him knew that he released his stored-up anger on his pageboys in late-night beatings. The boys, chosen from local orphanages, were frequently seen with black eyes and ugly bruises on their faces. Sometimes they tried to run away, which only gave the Emperor a good excuse to give them another beating.

In Tientsin, the Pu Yis had enjoyed the freedom to shop, to visit the cinema, or to dine with friends. They had, at least in the early days, enjoyed a degree of family and social life. In Hsingking, though, they were not allowed to leave the Salt Tax Palace unless on official business. Even then they had to be accompanied by one or other of the Kwangtung hierarchy. Wan Jung complained to me that she could not even walk in the park, which she longed to do. I easily obtained permission to accompany her, and her childlike excitement at the idea of our outing was touching. But she was tired out in ten minutes and could not stop coughing for an hour. Her health was so bad that I imagined that the beautiful Empress would be dead within the year.

One evening, as we were looking through old copies of American *Vogue* and smoking pink Russian cigarettes that Tada had obtained for us, news came that the Pu Yis had been summoned to make a state visit to Japan. Wan Jung was horrified, not only at the thought of visiting Japan, but also at how difficult it would be for her there without recourse to her habitual intake of opium. She thought of the Japanese as her enemies and did not wish to appear at a disadvantage in their company. Her reputation as 'She of the Beautiful Countenance' was too hard for her to live up to any more.

Pu Yi told her that he preferred to go without her, as he would have many duties of state and did not wish to be embarrassed by her unreliability, but he insisted that she prepare herself for the visit, in case the Japanese required her presence.

A team of dressmakers was brought to the Salt Tax Palace to outfit Wan Jung with a completely new wardrobe. She was to have both western and traditional clothes. Her court robes, which were held in the keeping of one of the high consorts, were sent for and a new set of pigskin luggage arrived by air from Tientsin, along with twenty boxes of handmade shoes. In the hope that her health and looks would improve, Pu Yi had her opium intake cut drastically, but she became so ill with shaking and delusions that it had to be restored.

Our time together was spent with me attempting to assure her that she was not being called upon to attend her own execution in Tokyo. I reminded her that through Pu Yi's brother's Japanese wife she was now distantly related to Emperor Hirohito himself. He would hardly allow one of his own relatives to be murdered. I think she took comfort from that. As it happened, Wan Jung was not required to accompany her husband to Japan. Doihara had advised that she was too ill to travel and that her erratic behaviour would be an embarrassment in the Imperial Palace.

So excited was Pu Yi by the prospect of his state visit, and distracted by his preparations, that, yet again, he failed to take proper leave of his wife. He made his farewell in the company of Japanese officers without so much as touching her hand. Wan Jung was left in the cold Salt Tax Palace as she had been left in the Quiet Garden when Pu Yi had fled in fear from Tientsin. She told me that she knew when the time came for her to die that he would not be at her side. She had no expectations of him as he had never been with her when she had needed him.

'He makes much of loyalty,' she said. 'But he has none.'

Shortly after Pu Yi's departure, I received new orders from Doihara. I was to resettle myself in Peking and report to the Secret Service Organ there to fulfil a new assignment. Major Muto's secretary in the Shanghai office would arrange my journey and accommodation and would forward my belongings from the villa. Wan Jung was upset but composed, she seemed resigned to being alone and said it would be better for me to resume my life before, like her, I forgot how to live it. She was happy that I would be waiting for her in Peking when she returned to the life fate had determined for her.

I said my goodbyes to Tada, who was sure that we would meet again, but I did not think we would. I would miss him a little, not just for the relief of his company, but because he admired me both as daughter of Japan and of China. Apart from Tamara, none of my other lovers had accepted me quite so completely as Tada had.

On our last night together, so that I would always remember him with warmth, he gave me a gift of three unset stones. A diamond for luck, a deep red garnet to keep my blood warm and jade, the stone of heaven, for happiness. With painted eyes and bare feet I played his grateful concubine for the last time. I bathed and massaged him and after we had made love I slept across his feet. I would miss our games, but knew that my place in his bed would be taken by a series of small-boned, pearl-toothed Chinese prostitutes, who in their submissiveness would find him a good master.

I made Wan Jung a present of my dragonfly brooch, although I think she would have preferred my writing case, which she much admired. Used now to partings she remained calm, simply taking my hand and pressing it to her cheek.

'I don't believe that either of us will make old bones, Eastern Jewel, but for what time is left to us I would rather live your life than my own,' she said.

Her affectionate leave-taking brought a lump to my throat and with tears in my eyes I kissed her hands and said goodbye. I never saw her again, although years later I heard the legend that she was alive and living somewhere in the Long White Mountains. It wasn't true.

Fish Congee and a Duck Egg

I set up home in one of the spacious apartments on the first floor of the Hôtel de Pékin, which was situated a short distance from the pink walls of the Forbidden City. It was an elegant nineteenth-century building decorated in the style of the Belle Epoque, full of French furniture and foreigners. There was a ballroom with a hall of mirrors that imitated the famous salon in the palace of Versailles, and a busy international bar that never closed.

Peking was a city of walls within walls, built to keep out the dust and deaden the clamour of its busy citizens. As wood was scarce, the houses were built with brick and wattle and had shapely roofs and slender windows. In the streets there were mules and donkeys pulling carts and on my first day I saw camels swaying along the broader avenues carrying coal and coconuts. The streets were narrow unpaved alleys where pedestrians vied for space with bicycles and wheelbarrows. After the modernity of Shanghai, I felt as though I had stepped back into the old century. Although the city had water, electricity and trams to ferry its citizens, it was still at heart the capital of ancient China. Its opium dens, known as 'swallows' nests', had inky carbon walls smudged by a hundred years of smoke, a unique darkness that powdered your clothes when you brushed against it. Peking's scent was of dung and toil and, for those who recognised it, the faintly gassy smell of corruption.

The office of the Special Service Organ was a ten-minute walk from my hotel. On my way there I ate a breakfast of pancakes cooked in the street on a charcoal burner. As I looked around me at the old buildings, at the solidity of the Forbidden City with its myriad roofs and gates, I was surprised to discover that nothing in the city of my birth seemed familiar to me.

My superior in the Peking office was Colonel Sumida, a cunning man in his late sixties who loved his work in the secret service. He had what looked like a fencing scar below his left eye, which he had a habit of tracing with one finger. He was of medium height with cropped white hair that contrasted with his iron-grey eyebrows, giving him an owl-like appearance. In certain lights he could look brutal, but I discovered him to be a man of culture with somewhat dainty tastes. Sumida was a snob, not as intelligent as Tanaka, but nor was he as narrow-minded as Muto. He was lazy but good at delegating and had Tanaka's attention to detail. Although I sensed that he liked women well enough, I think that in general he preferred the company of men.

He told me that I had been brought to Peking to make friends with influential foreigners and to infiltrate the ranks of the wealthy and upper-class Chinese. I was to ascertain who amongst them were secret Chiang Kai-shek collaborators, so that they could be brought to justice and made an example of. He said my task would not be easy, as Chiang's creatures took a perverted pleasure in showing a smiling face while stabbing us in the back. Japan, he said, was doing well in its bid to consume China, but the Chinese weren't without their successes and we couldn't rest on our laurels. He had been told that I was expert in gaining the confidence of foreigners, and that I spoke good English, assets that he said were sorely needed in Peking.

'Become well informed and keep me informed, Yoshiko,' he said. 'If you live up to your reputation I will be more than pleased.'

After our first talk the Colonel gave me a box of papers that Muto's secretary had forwarded from Shanghai. Amongst the accounts and files there was a letter from Jack, enclosing the print of his last photograph of me. It was dated two weeks after our parting and said that he had returned to New York as his father was gravely ill. He gave me the address of where to find him and said that he would be waiting for me. If I needed money for the fare I could get it from Teddy Black, the reporter from the *Chicago Tribune*.

I cursed Muto for not sending it on to me in Manchuria. It would have saved me months of pain and perhaps altered the course of my life. But I had already let Jack go in my mind and I wasn't sure that I wanted him back in my life. Yet just the sight of his handwriting made my heart race. Trembling even though the day was warm, I sat on my bed in the Pékin reading the letter over and over again. My body felt light, as though it were shedding the rust of years. I looked at the photograph of the girl in the blue dress and wondered if she still existed, if she had ever truly existed.

I wrote Jack a few brief lines explaining what had happened to his letter. I said that I loved him, that I had to stay in Peking for the duration of the posting and I asked him to write to me. His reply was quick but matter-of-fact, as though he too had reservations and did not wish to expose his hurt on paper. He wanted me to come to him and said that America would be the safest place for me. He was sure Japan would not be able to hold China, and that when it fell I would be in danger of falling with it. So there it was again: Japan was the essence of what divided us. I was torn, but as ever in my life I chose Japan. On the Pékin's thin notepaper I wrote him four words. 'You come to me.'

There was familiarity and comfort as well as pain in choosing Japan over Jack. I thought then that Japan would always come first with me, but I was wrong in that. I went to work with a heavy heart, but not entirely without hope that one day Jack might just turn up in Peking.

Colonel Sumida set me to work right away. He had contacts amongst the more prosperous Chinese in the city and knew an aristocratic second cousin of mine, Li Ching-yu, who was a Japanese sympathiser prepared to take me under his wing and introduce me to the right people. Li was a tall, good-looking man with soot-black hair and eyes as round as coins. He was the lightest-skinned Chinese I had ever met and I found the contrast between his dark hair and white skin quite shocking. Sumida told me that it was a pity Li had been born Chinese, because he was as loyal to the Japanese cause as any samurai. He could be totally relied upon to put Japan's interest above not only that of his business but also those of his friendships.

Li said that he was delighted to meet the famous daughter of Prince Su, a man whose reputation had lived on after his death. 'Your father, like mine,' he said, 'was a man of good instincts. He understood that Chinese nobles have more in common with their Japanese equals than with the peasant classes of their native lands. You and I were born with rare blood in our veins, Eastern Jewel. We must work together to ensure that our lines are not swept away by the envy of commoners.'

It didn't surprise me that Li held my father in such high esteem. Prince Su had always been admired by his peers as someone who lived up to the superior inheritance of his ancestors. In retrospect, even I, who as a child had been permanently angry with him, could applaud his strength of character, his recognition of Japanese intelligence and his disregard of what others thought. I believed that not only my father, but also Kawashima, would have accepted Li as one of his own. He would have warmed to Li's certainty, his sureness of his place in the world.

Li was married to Precious Pearl, a beautiful modern woman, who dressed in the western style and took her friends from amongst the most talented actors and artists in Peking. Preferring the pleasure of a man in his bed to that of a woman, Li had no concubines or children in his house. This state of affairs suited Pearl, as it allowed her the freedom to live the life she wanted, not only as a patron of the arts but also as the long-term mistress of

Baron Matsuyama, a Japanese aristocrat and businessman living in Peking who was not only amongst Peking's richest citizens, but also its most influential.

Despite their unconventional marriage, Li and Pearl had a close friendship and an intimacy that felt very excluding. Their large house hosted luxurious parties, where interesting foreigners were to be found in the company of opera singers, artists, and visiting members of the Japanese Royal Family. Pearl told me that there were at least twenty princes connected to the Imperial Family who stayed as her guests on their visits to Peking. Sumida, a man of bohemian nature himself, was often to be seen at Li's parties. He had a wife and a geisha in Japan, but in Peking his charming returned émigrée mistress, Madame Kim Yee, frequently accompanied him to social engagements.

Kim Yee owned two beauty shops in the city named Madame Kim's, one of which was in the Hôtel de Pékin. She had become rich by exporting Chinese antiques to dealers in America, where she had lived for ten years before returning home to China. As well as her export business and the beauty shops, she also had an income from some well-timed investments she had made in America. She was still officially married to an American-born Chinese, but they had been separated long before she chose to return to China.

Kim was more than pretty, yet not quite beautiful. She usually dressed in western clothes, but occasionally she wore exquisite hand-embroidered cheongsams, her long hair twisted into a gleaming rope at the base of her neck, her eyes smoky with kohl. In this style she looked so delectably Chinese that General Tada would have found her irresistible. I approved of Sumida's taste in mistresses and as it turned out, I made a good friend of Kim. Her capacity for loyalty outshone any man's that I have ever known, and once she had accepted you as a friend it was unconditional and without judgement.

Kim had no children herself but told me that Sumida had three, two daughters who had married into respectable military families and a son who was a pilot in the army air force. He never spoke of his wife, but I expect that she was the usual loyal and obedient type who stayed at home and didn't question her man. I knew his kind well and was at ease in his company, for he could have been a template for the men that Kawashima had sent to my rooms. I worked well with Sumida and enjoyed Kim's friendship too much to court her Colonel. She was a possessive woman who, unlike most mistresses in China, was independent and protective of what she considered hers. In any case, I thought then that Jack might seek me out and I wanted him to find me without ties.

Sumida told me that I was Japan's most special of spies. 'You are that rare thing, a well-connected Chinese aristocrat with a Japanese heart,' he said. 'You were made to succeed in Peking.'

Regardless of how Sumida viewed it, it took me longer to feel at home in Peking than it had in Shanghai. I was a smaller fish in a bigger pond, and since knowing Jack, I had somehow acquired the desire to be liked, even loved, not an asset for a spy. It was months before I settled and reverted to type, which in the end we all do, for all that we may wish otherwise.

I told Kim about Jack, every detail. The way he made me feel, how in his company I seemed a better person and how he despised the Japanese. Strangely, she said that sometimes she despised them too and that she thought I should go to Jack. I had, she said, the sort of ambition that drove most Americans and I would do well there.

'Go to him, Yoshi,' she said. 'Who knows what will become of any of us in China?'

Although I denied it even to myself, I knew deep down that Jack would not come to me. His nature, like mine, would not allow him to be the one to bend to the other's will. I was a fool, I should have gone to him then when our countries were not yet at war, while that passageway of time was open to me.

But I stayed, and I stuck to the rules of the job so well that Tanaka would have been proud of me. I made the right contacts, listened to what they said, learnt to read the subtext of their words. I reported to Sumida everything I thought he should know. I used my influence for those I liked and I promoted the Japanese cause in every way possible. Peking society, snobbish and fawning under the Japanese, opened its doors and welcomed me in. Within two years I had become the filter through which the wealthy Chinese community made contact with their all-powerful Japanese occupiers.

My social life was good. I never wanted for a party or a dinner to go to, although often my preference was to wander the streets finding my own entertainment. I was not as well known amongst the populace as I had been in Shanghai, yet still Li advised me against my unaccompanied outings, on the grounds that it was foolish to take chances. I frequented the opera with Pearl, went to the cinema with Kim, and as always found myself drawn not only to the establishment figures of the community, but also the more interesting of those who lived the demi-monde life in the city.

Amongst my contacts was a man called Jin, who made his livelihood from selling guns to gangsters and to those Chinese families who recognised that they were living in changeable times. Jin introduced me to his group of bodyguards, an ill-assorted bunch drawn mostly from the peasant class and from the armies of the old Chinese warlords. Some relied solely on their strength and menacing appearance, but there were those who studied the martial arts and took a pride in their profession. Jin was always shadowed by one of the latter kind and advised me that I should be protected in a similar fashion. Although I didn't feel the same hostility that I had done in Shanghai, Jin's voice, added to that of Li's, decided me. Petty street crime was rife and no one was immune from the robberies and even the murders that were regular occurrences in Peking. In any case, Sumida himself had also suggested protection and had offered to increase my allowance to cover the expense.

With my usual excess, I chose a pair of twin brothers born in the Year of the Monkey. They were secretive by nature, short in stature, but with muscular bodies and powerful hands. The older of the two by eight minutes had taken the professional name of Faithful; the younger twin was simply called Chou.

After I hired them I went to drink tea with them in their house on the riverfront at the poorer end of the waterway. It was little better than a shack and so cluttered with objects that there was hardly room for its occupants. Every available surface of its one dusty room housed a muddle of delicate china ornaments that would not have looked out of place in an English drawing room. A collection of lace fans hung on the walls, so covered in dust that they all looked the same colour. Throws of mouldy velvet covered the low seating, while the floor was carpeted with grime and the stains of past floods. For good luck, the brothers kept an ugly fire-bellied toad in a glass tank on the sideboard. The wart-covered creature croaked before rainstorms and consumed the ever-present mosquitoes, which were one of the hazards of living on the riverbank.

Faithful and Chou lived cheaply off muddy fish congee, the smell of which impregnated the walls and furniture of the hovel with a stale, watery fragrance. The brothers had never known their father, and their mother had died before their fifteenth year from the strain that chronic malaria had put on her frail body. I suspect that it was more from inertia than respect for her memory that her sons had preserved the house exactly as she had left it.

Their previous employer, a brothel keeper, had retired to his home village after making his fortune, leaving them without a provider. Not everyone wanted to take on the expense of the two, but they assured me that I would not regret my decision to do so, as they were loyal and strong and would never let me down. I could tell they thought that protecting a princess would enhance their reputation.

Jin advised me to always pay them on time and to give them a regular bonus. That way, he said, they would be encouraged to look on me as a good employer. I did what he suggested and was overly generous in my payment to them. The twins accompanied me everywhere and I slept easier on my visits to the opium dens of Peking, dreaming my sugared dreams, knowing I would only have to open my eyes to find them nearby. For all the time that Faithful and Chou guarded me, Kim, who neither liked nor trusted them, never relented in her view that they were bad news. It worried me a little, because her instincts in such matters were good, but I thought that where the brothers were concerned she was wrong. Although they spoke little, they seemed content in their work, and apart from occasional visits to their home by the river they were hardly ever out of my presence.

I cannot say that I was as happy as I had been in the good times in Shanghai, but life was interesting enough and I had my successes. I was made president of the China Gold Mining Company as well as of the Association of Manchurians in Peking. They were prestigious roles, of great use to Japan, and my future seemed secure.

In 1941, the year that Japan bombed Pearl Harbor, I completely abandoned the idea that I would see Jack again. Our countries were at war with each other. He could not come to me and I could not go to him. I no longer had the hope that I might catch sight of him, see him turning a corner or getting out of a car. Love, like everything else, grows old and we adapt.

I was in touch with Tanaka, who had been recalled in disgrace to Mukden by Doihara for failing in his battles to secure Mongolia for Japan. He had lost face by not sharing the hardship of his regiment of Mongolian horsemen, whom he had left to retreat on their own to the Japanese territory in the east, on the borders of Manchukuo. I could not bear his disgrace and I wrote to him telling him of my disappointment. My intention in writing was to spur him on, to encourage him to fight to restore himself in Japan's eyes, but I couldn't disguise my anger enough. He had always taken my criticisms hard and he replied promptly, reminding me that it was he who had opened his world up to me and that I owed my success to him. I let him have the last word on the subject, but I felt as though he had betrayed my faith in him.

My posting in Peking was going well. Sumida was more than pleased with my work which he often said was of great value to Japan. But my depressions were increasing and I relied on opium more and more. I pushed the fears of ageing and loneliness I had suffered since the loss of Jack to the back of my mind and dulled myself with alcohol and the sweetness of the precious poppy. I carried on as though I was still in love with life. I took the occasional lover, but without much enthusiasm. There were no lovers capable of ridding me of the awful emptiness I felt.

As in the past, I found that my allowance from the Special Service Organ was too small to support my lifestyle. Even though the China Gold Mining Company allowed me generous expenses, I was spending well above my income. So I set about getting my share of the huge amounts of money that circulated as bribes and indulgences in the capital. I let it be known that for a price I would intercede with my Japanese contacts to save the lives of those accused of collaboration or sabotage. More money than I could ever have anticipated came flowing in. A father will pay a high price to redeem a beloved son. A wife, if she loves her husband, will release his fortune to come to his aid. Those families, with their special needs, became my bankers, their money given willingly, for without me their causes were hopeless. To be fair to myself, I fulfilled for those families all that I promised and everyone did well out of it. Loved ones were returned to their homes and took care not to offend the Japanese again. Those merchants with hidden gold handed it over and were imprisoned, rather than given the more usual death sentence. Despite what some might think, I know that in their time of need those desperate people thought of me as their saviour.

The atmosphere at that time in Peking had become tenser than ever, mostly due to dissident Chinese challenging Japan's occupation in countless underhand ways. The citizens of Peking never knew from one day to the next who would end up in charge of their city, so they tried to please all sides. Those with money used it to gain favour and to protect themselves as much as they could. They paid their servants generously, hoping that, should China ever win back the capital, they would be loyal and keep their secrets. I would have been considered just another business expense, a sort of life insurance policy.

I gave generously to Pearl's charities, which were mostly for the support of artists and poets. I was always buying Kim expensive presents, and I ran up huge bills in Peking's nightclubs. My account at the Hôtel de Pékin was enormous, as I often entertained there, giving banquets for visiting Japanese royalty and parties in private rooms for my less salubrious acquaintances. As I hurtled through those last years in Peking I spent on clothes and jewellery, gambling and opium, fortune-tellers and beauticians who promised to make me look younger than my years.

Without Jack to give me ballast or Tanaka to reassure me, it was hard to know what to plan for the future. I lived my life as though nothing would ever change, while closing my mind to the knowledge that all things do eventually. I felt protected by the elite circle I moved in and did my part to sustain those connections. I saw Kim through two abortions, both of them more easily achieved than my own had been. I arranged for a lover of Li's, a handsome but mendacious young man, to disappear when he took to blackmailing Li with the threat of exposure of his sexual preferences. Most of Li's friends and family already knew where his desire lay, but in China it is not so much what you know but what you speak that counts. I helped Pearl through a difficult time when she fell in love with a young artist who courted her to his bed, before moving on and breaking her heart. So bereaved by her loss was she that she contemplated suicide. She had given up her lover Baron Matsuyama, and Li, although sympathetic, had no real idea of the pain she was in. She told me that without my support she would have had no one to turn to as her blood family lived in Nanking, and Li's mother would have taken pleasure in condemning her. I had made good and true friends of Li and Pearl, but it was Kim whom I loved and admired most. Her constancy and honesty were as sustaining to me as she said mine were to her.

It was only when Sumida's son died in a kamikaze attack on the American naval force in the Philippines that all of our lives suddenly seemed less secure. In the year that followed his death, Japan was pushed by the Chinese to discontinue operations in the interior of China. To my disgust, our troops were being withdrawn from Kwangsi province and sent home to reinforce defences there. To us Japanese who occupied Peking, ideas of failure were unthinkable and we put them from our minds. Not believing that we, the greatest warriors in the world, had suffered more than just a temporary setback, we danced the nights away in Peking, pretending that the rhythm of our lives was as constant as ever. But as though it knew better the city seemed to be holding its breath, waiting perhaps for the inevitable, while in subtle ways everyone around me seemed to be preparing for flight. The Chinese, second-class citizens in their own capital, sensed change and became less subservient, less willing to work for Japanese families.

Pearl and Li stopped giving parties on the excuse that, like the Japanese royals, they had other more pressing matters to deal with. Sumida did his best to bear the loss of his son in true Japanese style, but the ambition in his nature had deserted him. He was no longer exciting to be around and because I did not seek his company, I did not notice that he was avoiding mine. Kim, listening to the chatter of the Chinese, worried that Chiang would soon enter Peking. Through a neutral consulate she tried to reclaim her American citizenship, but they would not have her. She said that she was going to suggest to Sumida that she accompanied him when he was recalled to Japan. But for some reason she never broached the subject with him. I think she knew that he would have refused her. She told me that she thought that a Chinese mistress was a fine thing in China when you occupied her country, quite another in Japan when you have been seen off. I told her not to worry, that Japan would always succeed, but she wasn't comforted. A few months after Kim's failed attempt to regain her American citizenship, Sumida found out about it and dropped her. I think that she was pleased to be rid of him, but she said the damage to her reputation with the Chinese had already been done.

Around the same time, Jack's friend Misha Salmonov arrived in Peking. Sumida told me to contact him and rekindle our friendship. He thought the *Pravda* correspondent was spying for Russia and wanted me to feed him misinformation. Although he had never mentioned it to me, Kim had told me that Sumida knew of my affair with Jack. Like most Japanese men I suspect that he would have thought less of me for it, especially now that we were at war with Jack's country. But he was pleased enough to use my contacts from that time when it suited him.

I asked Misha to dine with me at my hotel and he accepted with enthusiasm. He told me that he would soon be on his way to Chungking, where he expected to see Jack who was on his way there to interview Madame Chiang Kai-shek.

'Jack's in China?' I asked quietly.

'Yes, but of course he can't come to you in Peking, Yoshiko. He would be arrested as an enemy agent, just as you would be if you went to Chungking.'

'Would he come if he could?' I asked.

'I honestly don't know, Yoshiko. He says that you love Japan and he hates it. He is still angry with you for choosing Peking over him.'

It wasn't so much that Misha stirred memories of those intense days in Shanghai, or that his quiet style reminded me of Jack that made me drink too much and end up in his bed. It was more to obliterate the pain I felt knowing that Jack had returned to China about his own business, which did not include me. When I said to Misha that we had both betrayed Jack, he bruised me by replying that he didn't think so. In his company I had sought unsuccessfully to find the girl in the blue dress, the one who smelled of musk and had slept with Jack on boats named after her for the voyage. But she was Jack's girl, not Misha's, so we did not lie together again. I saw Misha a couple of times after that night. We had a drink or two and spoke of old times, but being in his company only made me sad. He said he thought Chiang would succeed over the communists and would also rid China of the Japanese. I did not agree with him, but I liked Misha and didn't feed him the misinformation that Sumida had asked me to.

A few weeks after Misha left Peking, America dropped its cowardly atom bombs on Hiroshima and Nagasaki. Within days of those events my world, like those tragic islands, disintegrated.

I woke one morning to find Kim banging at my door. She told me through sobs that the Japanese Emperor had capitulated to America. She had heard him on the radio surrendering in a stilted voice. She said that Sumida had already returned to Japan and that she and I had been left to face the revenge of our countrymen. I thought that she had got it wrong and tried to console her, but she would have none of it.

'Don't be a fool, Yoshiko,' she sobbed. 'This is not a tactical withdrawal – Japan is crushed. You don't have Japan and you don't have China. If you are found by Chiang's men you will be executed as a traitor.'

I gave her a shot of the Russian plum brandy that Misha had left in my room and she calmed down a bit. She told me that she hoped to bring together a plan she had been working on for months, and that she would do her best to help me if she could but that for the time being she was going into hiding and that I should do the same. I left her in my bathroom at the Pékin repairing her ravaged face with cold water.

I caught something of her panic when, with a pounding heart, I visited the officers' mess and found it deserted. All Japanese soldiers were confined to barracks and were pulling out as fast as

270

they could. They had been ordered not to show their faces on the streets of Peking. I didn't fully panic until I called on Li and Pearl and discovered that they had left for Japan at the same time as Sumida. Their newly emboldened maid attempted to shut the door on me but I put my foot in her way and insisted that she look to see if Li had left a note in my name. She took pleasure in telling me that he had not. A chill began to creep through me. I knew without doubt that I was in serious trouble. After all I had done for them Li and Pearl had left without the slightest thought for me. For all their noble blood, they had turned out to be worms in the end.

I drove out to the airfield with Faithful and Chou to discover that, apart from a couple of pilots who were loading their plane with what looked like boxes of official papers, the place was deserted. They said that everyone who had been on the official list had already been flown to Japan. I asked the younger of the two to fly me back with them but he said it was against their orders to carry civilians. I told him that I was a commissioned officer in the Japanese Army and he laughed. Japan, it seemed, had forgotten my existence, and my heart ached with the betrayal of it. Just as my father had given me to Japan, so Japan had cruelly returned me to China. Overnight I had become a refugee in fear for my life, with no country or family of my own.

In a panic, I attempted to radio Japan from Sumida's office but the airwaves were deserted, silent as snow. While I was there I took the opportunity to destroy any papers that had my name on them and I burnt the meticulously kept invoices of payments to me. In a futile act of revenge I shredded the photograph of Sumida's dead son, which, in his hurry to be gone, he had forgotten.

That night in the Pékin I slept badly and dreamt that there was an earthquake that crumbled the hotel to dust. At dawn next day I visited my one-time friend and informant Jin. He offered me money, but said it was dangerous now for him to have his name linked with mine.

'If I am asked I will claim never to have known you, Yoshiko,' he said.

I took the money and his advice that I should attempt to change my appearance and get out of the city as quickly as I could.

When I looked for Kim she was nowhere to be found. Both her shops were open but her staff hadn't seen her for days. I couldn't hang around, hoping that she would turn up. Wherever she was I guessed that she would be experiencing the same panic as me. Time was running out and so I began my own hastily put-together plan. I oiled my short hair back from my face and added a twist of false hair to the back to give me the traditional look of a conventional Chinese woman of the middle classes. I threw away my jodhpurs and evening dresses and wore only plain cheongsams and low-heeled embroidered shoes. I tried to find lodgings with those Chinese families that I had helped in their hour of need, but none of them wanted to know or to help me. A man I had saved from ruin hissed at me to go away and die. They may have had troubles of their own, but it was hard to excuse their treachery.

Within a few days of my airport visit there were Chinese troops in Peking. I saw them swaggering in the streets and thundering down the narrow lanes in their jeeps, looking triumphant. The peasant Chinese welcomed them with open arms and the wealthy, fearing an uprising of the common man, managed false smiles of welcome.

The twins offered me lodgings in their shack and, much as I hated the idea of it, I knew that I had to accept. The Hôtel de Pékin was already filling with Chinese officers and I didn't trust its staff to keep my identity from them for long. I moved out quickly, taking only what I could carry with me. I took my precious writing case with its sentimental contents, my jewellery and a bottle of good sake and settled myself in the twins' hideous hovel. I had a fair sum of money with me, but not as much as I could have hoped for. The safe in Sumida's office where I had always kept enough for a year's good living had been looted. At first, out of habit, I suppose, I

272

found it hard to believe that Sumida had taken my money. I searched around in the drawers and cabinets hoping that he had hidden it for me in some other place. It was true that he had left me in the lurch, but to cut off my means of survival seemed too low an act for a Japanese officer. But as only the two of us had known the combination of the safe it was hard to retain my faith in his honour, or to believe that he had ever thought of me as Japanese. Perhaps he had known that I would never be sent for by Japan, that whatever I believed myself to be, I was nothing more than a colourful but expendable Chinese spy to them.

Depressed and panicked, I could only think of getting back to Japan. I still loved it and I played a game with myself of sometimes being angry at my abandonment and at others believing that there had been a terrible mistake, that Japan had not knowingly relinquished me. Even though it might only be to share Japan's defeat, I longed for home.

The thought of being captured by the Chinese was hateful but I was confident of avoiding that fate. I needed time to plan my escape and, although I loathed the mean little hovel, it was a place of safety that would do well enough for the time being. But as I settled into the damp shack it was with the worst possible timing that I discovered the unmistakable signs of the French Pox on my body. Brown sores appeared on the palms of my hands and the soles of my feet, I developed a throat so raw that I could not swallow. I had been feeling below par for some weeks and had suffered a rash on my chest and back, but it had disappeared and I had forgotten about it. Syphilis is a terrifying illness. I knew that it could make you blind and cause a slow death and I was very frightened. I went from feeling sorry for myself to believing in my strong survival instincts. I hoped that the signs of the illness would disappear without effect as they often did. At one and the same time I both cursed and felt sorry for Misha Salmonov, who must have passed it on to me without knowing.

Faithful said that he knew someone who could help me, and brought to the shack a man who believed that he could entirely rid me of the disease. He was not a doctor but called himself a healer. He earned his bread by removing warts and moles from his patients and from bloodletting with leeches. Syphilis, he said, could be cured with a new drug that had been specially developed for it called penicillin. He had seen it work on more than one occasion and due to its efficacy he had entirely lost the fear of the disease himself. Penicillin was hard to come by unless you were rich, but he had contacts at a hospital that used it and, for the right price, he would get me some. He was a slimy creature with boiled goose-berry-like eyes and a mean mouth, but I had no choice other than to deal with him. If I was to get myself out of China and home to Japan I needed to be well. We bartered until I had to part with over half of the money I had left, which he complained allowed him little, if any, profit for himself. As I didn't trust him to return with the medication, I sent Faithful with him to ensure that he brought me back the treatment.

Miraculously, within a couple of weeks of taking the drug, the sores on my hands and feet disappeared along with the raw throat and high fevers that I had been running. One moment there had been a sword at my stomach, the next I was reprieved. My good fortune turned my mood to optimism and to hope for the future. It felt wonderful to be better, but the cost had been high and I was finding it hard to keep up the payments to the twins for my protection. I could not eat their terrible congee and sent them daily to the market for fresh meat, fruit and sake, which seemed to increase in price at every visit. I decided not to indulge in opium until I was in a safer position, and so I slept badly, suffering dreams of drowning in the dirty water of the river that the twins caught their horrible fish in.

I dispatched the brothers to the city to try and find Kim, in the hope that we could be of use to each other. Worryingly, they stayed away for two nights and I couldn't sleep for concern at what their absence meant. But eventually they returned with the good news that Kim had become the mistress of the Chinese merchant Chi

Ming, who, due to his secret financial support of Chiang Kai-shek, was now in favour with Peking's new masters. I remembered the man from my early days in Peking, when Li had introduced him to me as someone who gave excellent business advice. I recall that he had liked the Japanese well enough then. Kim had been wiser than me, she had suspected what might happen and had made her plans. I had been blinded by my belief that Japan would always succeed, and that trust had been my downfall.

Chi Ming was older than Sumida, with thin hair and rotten teeth, but he had long desired Kim, who I knew would weigh his ugliness against his power to protect her. I shuddered at the thought of her sweet firmness in his thin old arms. She was set up in a small house on the road between the zoological gardens and the Five Pagoda Temple, a popular district with the mistresses of the rich.

Faithful told me that Kim had said that she would do her best to help me, but I must not go to her house until she sent a message that it was safe to do so. At Chi Ming's insistence she had signed her properties and shares over to him and it wasn't easy to get money out of him. But she promised that she would find a way to help me and urged me to be patient. I was elated that my prayers had been answered. With Kim under the guardianship of the old merchant my chances of escape had suddenly increased. I was relieved that she was safe and I trusted her to be as good as her word. Life in the shack was so dreary that I knew it would be hard to be patient, but I had no option, I had to live off what I had and wait for her to contact me.

Faithful said that Chinese troops were everywhere in the city, and that those Chinese who had been obliging to their Japanese masters had been harshly dealt with. They were either dead or suffering at the hands of their victorious countrymen. Apparently, the Hôtel de Pékin had become a dull place, full of sour-faced officers who had no sense of fun or any idea of how to enjoy their victory. He added spitefully that nobody missed the Japanese.

It wasn't long before I had to sell my jewellery to live. As I couldn't take the risk of being recognised I had no option but to trust the twins to sell it for me. One bangle fashioned from almost pure gold brought so little money that I suspected Faithful and his brother of keeping most of the profit for themselves. They knew the money was running out and were debating whether they should go on harbouring me. I promised them that when I got back to Japan I would send them enough gold to live on comfortably for the rest of their lives. I am sure that it was only that promise that kept them in my service at all.

Thoughts of escaping Peking and getting back to Japan were constantly on my mind, but the Chinese had secured every exit and everything I thought of seemed doomed to failure. I wondered about stealing a plane and flying myself to Japan, but the airfield was heavily guarded and even if I managed it the plane would have been shot down anyway. All boats and trains were inspected and had Chinese guards on them. I no longer enjoyed the friendship of those with influence, nor had I enough money to bribe my way out of my problem and China. It was against my nature not to act, but I believed my best chance of escape lay in Kim's hands.

Soon the good food and drink that I enjoyed became too expensive for my purse. I had no choice but to live on the same muddy fish and poor quality rice as the brothers. As my funds diminished, Faithful and Chou became rude and reluctant to follow my orders. They would disappear for hours, leaving me alone to fear what they might be up to. With the gift of familiarity I no longer smelled the peasant smell of congee or noticed the dirt in the shack. But it had become my prison, a hateful damp place that brought out the worst in me. When not angry at my fate, I was in misery at the treachery of those I had considered to be my friends.

Faithful told me that there was a rumour in Peking that I was being harboured and that there was a reward for my capture. He said I was referred to as the spy and war criminal responsible for the murder of Chinese babies and their mothers.

'They call you Japan's whore,' he laughed.

Despite my notoriety, I was surprised that I was being actively hunted. The thought of it so terrified me that I stopped going out in the hours of daylight, even to sniff the air. I made do with as little sleep as possible and developed a habit of listening for unexpected sounds. I was ready for flight, but to where I didn't know. Sometimes at night I would walk along the riverbank, thinking of my past and longing for a future. In the moonlight, without the sun's cruel exposure of its shabby banks and slum dwellings, the river looked deep and mysterious. On those night walks I could pretend that the world was still beautiful. For an hour or two I would breathe in the marshy air, my thoughts unpolluted by the horrible fear that usually invaded them. Despite the fact that I had heard nothing from Kim I still trusted her to help me, and it was that trust that kept my spirits up.

I often thought of simply continuing my night walk, going from village to village until I reached the sea, where I might stow away on a boat to Japan. But I knew that to be an unlikely means of escape. I had a small amount of money set aside for extreme emergencies and I considered paying a forger to make me an American passport and papers. With a new identity I might bluff it out with the authorities, go to America and become Jack's girl again. But as I no longer trusted the twins to organise it for me and did not dare be seen in the capital, it was hard to know how to enact the idea. In any case, no plan that I thought of came with any guarantee of success. Those that had the best chance needed more money than I had at my disposal. I never stopped thinking of ways to escape but I always returned to the plan of waiting for Kim.

Five weeks after first hearing from her she sent news with a trusted servant that she had money enough to pay for my escape. She said that she had contacts who would help me and that I must do exactly as she said. I should wait a week before going to her as her lover would be away on business in Canton then and our chances of success would be greater in his absence. I should come at night when the dark would better disguise me and she was longing to see me, her true friend. It hurt to hear her words of friendship and I wept like a child. I had been without affection for so long that I hardly knew what to do with the emotions her words had inspired in me. Kim, my loyal friend, had come to my aid; she was my hope, my compass, and I thanked the gods for her.

But bad luck haunted me and on the morning of the day I was due to go to Kim, I woke suffering a violent stomach bug brought on by bad fish. I was vomiting every few minutes and the pains in my stomach were so bad that I couldn't stand. I decided that if I were not better by nightfall I would have to sleep one more night in the shack and leave the following evening. Faithful and Chou were poor nurses and left me alone with my sickness. They said they had to get word to Kim that I would be delayed and that they would return for the dusk meal at the usual time.

I had sewn my emergency money into a pocket of my dress and had a bag packed with my few possessions ready at my feet. I longed to go but was too ill to move. My ribs ached with retching and, when I finally had nothing left to vomit, I slept. I had a dark dream where Mari and I shared the riverbed with strange ugly water creatures. They floated through our hair and nibbled at our bodies as we swayed with the rhythm of the current. Mari seemed oblivious to the creatures as she smiled a hollow smile.

I woke in a panic and listened for the footsteps of Faithful and his brother, which I had trained myself to recognise. The night was still and I heard only the lapping of the water against the river's bank. The darkness that was beyond dusk had fallen while the air was cloyed with the wetness that was usual between midnight and dawn. The brothers' absence concerned me, but I felt too bad to do anything about it and fell once more into a deep sleep.

I was woken by the sound of whispering outside the shack, then, before my eyes could adjust to the gloom, the door was kicked in and Chinese troops surrounded me. As I lay in the foetal position on the dirty bedding, a full sick bowl at my side, I was shouted at hysterically, pulled to my feet by my hair and dragged from the hovel. My own bodyguards, those fish-eating twins born in the Year of the Monkey, had betrayed me to Chiang's police. Not for money, as I later found out, but to ingratiate themselves with the new police force who were looking for recruits to keep law and order in Peking. I felt ashamed of how I was found and thought that the least I could have expected from the brothers, considering I had employed them at their time of need, was that they might have allowed me to be captured with some dignity. But I shouldn't have been surprised, for history is littered with such betrayals.

During my first year of incarceration in Peking Number One Prison, the Soviet Red Army moved into Manchuria and Pu Yi abdicated as Emperor of Manchukuo. He fled to the Korean border from where he hoped to escape to Japan. Instead he was seized by the Russians and flown to Siberia.

Wan Jung, abandoned yet again, was left terrified and fearful for her future. Yet I suspect that she was relieved that she no longer starred in the drama of the deposed Emperor's life.

In that same year General Okamura Yasutsugu surrendered all Japanese armed forces in China to General Ho Ying-chin, completing Japan's humiliation, as well as mine.

Three years have passed since that time and I am still in Number One Prison where I never know in what spirits I will wake. Sometimes, whatever the awful reality of my situation, I am filled with the certainty that all will be well, but mostly I am without optimism. I have adapted to my poor surroundings and these days I hardly notice the damp walls oozing lime or the drowned mice sometimes found floating in the urine of my night pot. There are times, though, when I am overwhelmed with rage. Caged like Miura's little canary, I have too much time to think of the past, to regret how many wrong roads I took in pursuit of an interesting life.

I have used up what few possessions I had left to barter for cigarettes and sake, which for a while I thought I could not do without. Now, like my fellow inmates, I survive on the weak vegetable broth which is a constant in this place, and the dusty drinking water that is rarely insect free. My night guard Suk-Ping is kind and sometimes gives me cigarettes. He never leaves me without a pencil and paper and once he brought me a duck egg, which I ate raw, hoping to take the sting out of my dreams.

In my second year of captivity I was brought before one of Chiang Kai-shek's military tribunals and tried for treason and espionage. The chief prosecutor said that I deserved death because I was a traitor, but most of all because I, a mere woman, had flown over my homeland in Japanese aircraft and looked down in contempt on the good earth of China. It was no surprise to me that the highest court found me guilty and sentenced me to death. China is run now by Chiang's so-called 'elite' who share his animosity towards anyone connected to the Qing dynasty. I expect no more from them, for how can those from rural farmlands understand the ties that bind the high-born together?

I bore up well, I think. My captors have never seen me cry, but if they could share my dreams they would enjoy the torment I have endured. No matter how many times I have insisted that I am Japanese and cannot be considered a traitor to China, the court will have none of it. They refer to me as the 'Arch Traitor', as though I had no given name. As I do not trust the advocate the court has assigned to me, I have spent this third year of my imprisonment working on my appeal. If I can prove myself to be a Japanese citizen I will be returned to Japan and not have to suffer execution at the hands of the Chinese. With this in mind I wrote to Kawa-shima, asking him to send the documents of my adoption to the court. In his letter of reply he said that he did not consider me to be his daughter, that I had never officially been adopted by him and that there was no mention of me in his family's registration records. He added that I had come to live in his household at the age of eight and he supposed that, as the majority of my years had been spent in Japan, most people might regard me as Japanese. The county commissioner in Tokyo had stamped the letter officially as being true and correct. As it failed to prove that I was Japanese and only stated that I might be regarded as so, Kawashima's cold missive had signed my death warrant.

I remembered clearly the day that Kawashima told me that he had adopted me and that I was now officially his and Japan's true daughter. I celebrated the occasion with Sorry by eating rice and red beans. We lit a starry firework and sent it to the heavens.

It may be that Kawashima himself is afraid of being accused of war crimes. It is the case that many Japanese are under suspicion by the allied victors. I have heard that Tanaka is in Sugamo Prison in Tokyo accused of such transgressions. I cannot forgive Kawashima for his cowardice, though, and am finally convinced that I am less than nothing in his heart. Yet I can't quite expel him from my own.

Amongst those who did speak up for me were my half-sisters Xian Qi and Xian Wo, whom I had not seen for many years and hardly knew. They said that I had always been clever, but that I was not capable of being a spy. Qi said that my beauty had been my downfall and that I had been corrupted by the Japanese. Wo said that I was not a bad person and that the tragedy of my life had been my adoption by Kawashima, which she remembered clearly my father, Prince Su, telling her about. I was grateful to them, although the court showed no interest in their opinions.

It was a foregone conclusion that I would lose the appeal, as the Chinese had decided my fate long before allowing it. As I write I am waiting to be told the date of my execution. Strangely, although I do not welcome it, I am not sad at the thought of my death. I think I always knew that I would not die with old bones, that I am only capable of enjoying the world's beauty if I am myself beautiful. There is no mirror in my cell, but I can tell by my guards' and my fellow prisoners' reaction to me that I am no longer beautiful. They say that physical beauty is no currency in the new China, but while men live I will never believe that.

It is odd, though, how everything in the world looks splendid to me now that my time in it may be limited. I see perfection in the simple cup of my rice bowl, the sweet symmetry of my rolled sleeping mat and the light, soft as moss, that filters through my cell window. These everyday sights touch my heart in a way I have never experienced before and bring me close to tears.

I have noticed too that memory comes to me so clearly from the past that I hear voices and remember the smells from my childhood as though they were present in my cell. The tender music of my blood mother's voice is heard, I see the way her hair grew from the delicate peak of her forehead and remember the look in her eyes softening at the mention of my father's name. How lovely it would be to start my life again now that I know the path not to take. But I fear there is too much blood in my past for me to make amends, too much grief and pain to heal even myself.

As Japan had seen fit to give me a military rank I requested of the court that I be granted the military honour of a firing squad. My request was denied and I know that I face beheading by the sword. I am more scared of the sword than of the gun but I try to put the thought of it from my mind. It comes to me, though, in dreams, where I have been beheaded on numerous occasions. In those dark imaginings I am always dressed as Shimako was on the night that she hung herself above the Buddha shelf in the shrine by the carp pool. I am afraid in the dreams, and sometimes I wake crying to find the gentle guard Suk-Ping at my side comforting me.

Suk-Ping brought me a letter from Kim, which by its delivery into my hands put his job, if not his life, at risk. It was simply signed 'your true friend' but I knew it was from her. She had scented it with her rose perfume, which was as good as her signature. She said she was working on my behalf and that all was not lost, that I should be brave and not give up hope. I am amazed that despite the danger to herself, Kim has been the most loyal of friends and thinks of me as a sister. If our situations were reversed would I have been so true to her? I have experienced most of love's repertoire and only now know that loyalty is the most precious thing. Her constancy and Suk-Ping's unexpected kindness have restored my faith in friendship.

I could not think of anything that Kim might do that would save my situation, but in her second letter she said that, with the help of a trusted friend, she had bribed the poverty-striken parents of a consumptive daughter to let the girl take my place at my execution. Kim said that I should not feel guilty because the girl was so ill that she would die soon anyway and was happy to know that her parents would not starve.

Suk-Ping knew a way to smuggle the consumptive girl into my cell, which he would do on the night before my execution. He would escape along with me and be well paid for his part in my rescue. Kim said that although he was scared he was determined to do it, and that I should trust him. I knew that Suk-Ping harboured a bitter grudge against Chiang Kai-shek, whom he held responsible for his wife's and child's death. They had died when, without warning to the locals, the Kuomintang had blown up the dykes on the Yellow River. Suk-Ping's village had been flooded, and with nothing but earth to eat his wife and daughter had died of starvation.

Kim wrote that my escape would be such a loss of face to China's new leaders that they would never let it be known that I had evaded their retribution. They would go ahead with the execution and it would be said that a false daughter of China had met a just end. After I had read the second letter Suk-Ping set fire to it with a lit cigarette, crushing the ashes into the floor with his heavy boots until nothing remained of it. I would not let him do the same to the first note, because I wanted to keep it as a talisman. I promised him that if things didn't work out I would eat the letter before my accusers could get their hands on it.

'Our plan will work and we shall leave this place together, Eastern Jewel,' he said, touching my cheek with his rough hand.

'You were not meant for such a cruel end. I could not save my family but I will save you.'

Despite the horror of the means of my would-be escape, I was at first elated at the thought that I might fly Number One Prison. Under a new name I could go to America, find Jack and seek out my dear friend Tamura Hidari. I reasoned that the girl would die anyway, that the sword might be a more merciful end than the consumptive drowning that I have seen to be truly terrible.

I could still have a long life ahead of me to enjoy all the things I have been deprived of in the last three years. The thought of freedom seems suddenly to be a realistic one, and I do so long for freedom. I long for more than a yard of sky above my head, long to live without the low moan of fear that hums through my body in the dark reaches of the night.

In the north of China they say that 'he who emerges with his life from great perils will have a happy and prosperous future'. I admit that the thought is appealing, but waiting each day as I do for news of my execution date, I cannot settle to a decision. Despite what I have done in the past I find myself turning away from this latest and most ugly path. Is it possible to take such a path and live happily? I fear the frail face of the consumptive girl that I picture in my mind will haunt me and spoil what I have left of life anyway. Her death by my sword would confirm the supremacy of the darkness in my nature.

And what would be the views of those that I have set up as my true judges? My mother would rather I join her than sentence this girl to such an end. Natsuko might urge me to go against my nature for once and choose kindness to another over myself. Sorry would not judge me, no matter which way I chose, but Jack, I think, would find the whole dark business unbearable. I am sad to discover that I do not know if he would urge me to redeem myself and go to the end that has been prescribed for me, or whether he longs for me enough to encourage my flight.

Soon the light through my window will turn to the colour of sea glass. A short twilight will come before the darkness that in this prison is the blackest I have ever experienced. I will unroll my sleeping mat and lie with my back against the wall in the habit I have carried with me since childhood. I do not know whether I will grasp my freedom and live a stolen life or go to a clean end, accepting my fate.

I will sleep, and if I wake with an urgent need for life then the decision is made. We are only animals, after all, and the instinct to live is paramount in us.

If I wake full of pity I will accept the sword and ask Kim to give the money to the consumptive girl's family anyway, in the hope that my last act may gain me approval in the next life. There is no more to be said, dawn will come, the decision will be made and either way I will be free.

The following report was published in the *Peking Daily* on the 26th of March 1948. 'At 6:40 on the evening of the 25th of March 1948, the woman known as Eastern Jewel was executed in Peking Number One Prison. Eastern Jewel was the fourteenth daughter of Su Qin Wang, a direct descendant of the younger brother of the first Qing Emperor of the Qing dynasty.'

The World of Eastern Jewel

1906: German neurologist Alzheimer identifies a new brain disorder.

1906: Eastern Jewel is born a Manchu princess, the fourteenth daughter to Prince Su and his fourth concubine. Prince Su was one of the eight princes of the Iron Helmet in the old Imperial Court of Peking, a direct descendant of the younger brother of the first Qing Emperor of the great Qing dynasty.

1912: The Titanic *sinks.*

1912: Empress Dowager Longyu issues an imperial edict bringing about the abdication of Emperor Pu Yi and the end to the almost three-centuries-old Qing dynasty. Eastern Jewel's distant cousin Pu Yi loses his throne and China becomes a republic. Pu Yi is confined to the Forbidden City where he plays Emperor.

1914: The First World War breaks out.

1914: Eastern Jewel is caught spying on her father, Prince Su, and is banished to Japan to live with Prince Su's blood brother Kawashima Naniwa.

1919: America adds an 18th amendment to its constitution, outlawing alcohol. This leads to bootlegging and the meteoric rise of the American Mafia.

1919: Eastern Jewel is adopted by Kawashima and renamed Yoshiko.

1921: Einstein receives the Nobel Prize.

1921: Eastern Jewel is seduced by her adoptive grandfather, Teshima.

1922: James Joyce writes Ulysses.

1922: Eastern Jewel is seduced by her adoptive father, Kawashima.

1925: Pu Yi flees the Forbidden City under the protection of the Japanese.

1925: Eastern Jewel married off to Mongolian prince.

1926: Laurence Olivier makes his acting debut at the Birmingham Repertory Company.

1926: Eastern Jewel escapes Mongolia and arrives in Japan en route to Shanghai.

1931: The Empire State building, one hundred and two storeys high, is completed.

1931: Eastern Jewel is recruited as a spy for the Japanese and Pu Yi goes to Manchuria.

1935: The FBI National Academy is established.

1935: Eastern Jewel is sent to Peking to work for the Japanese secret service.

1936: The Spanish Civil War begins.

1936: Eastern Jewel parties in high society in Peking.

1939: The Second World War breaks out.

1939: Eastern Jewel is still the partying princess in Peking.

1941: The Japanese bomb Pearl Harbor.

1941: Eastern Jewel is made president of the China Gold Mining Company and of the Association of Manchurians in Peking.

1942: Fermi conducts the first controlled nuclear chain reaction.

1942: Eastern Jewel makes friends and enemies in Peking.

1945: America drops an atomic bomb on Hiroshima and Nagasaki.

1945: Eastern Jewel is arrested in Peking by Chiang Kai-shek's forces and sent to Peking Number One Prison.

1947: The first supersonic flight.

1947: Eastern Jewel is brought before a military tribunal and found guilty of spying for the Japanese against China.

1948: The State of Israel comes into existence.

1948: Eastern Jewel loses her appeal against the guilty verdict and is executed by beheading on March 25th in Peking Number One Prison.

Acknowledgements

So many thanks to Rob Herman for getting the book launched and to the wonderful Stevie Lee for helping it on its way. A heartfelt thank you to the brilliant Robert Caskie, who is all that an agent should be and more. To Clive Lindley for so many things, but in particular for his fearless corrections and enthusiastic wielding of the red pen. Huge thanks to my editor Alexandra Pringle and her great Bloomsbury team who make things happen. Thank you, too, to Melanie Silgardo for her astuteness and her inspired touch. And to Julia Gregson, friend and writer – thank you for tough love and for kick-starting me when I wobbled. Also thanks to Tom Kinninmont for giving me that first most necessary flush of confidence. I am truly indebted to Jenny Parrott, for all the handholding and support she gave me along the new-to-me paths of publishing. And thank you to all my dear friends in the shed's club who sustained me with their interest and fine dinners – you know who you are. And a very special thank you to my gifted reader Richard Gregson.

A NOTE ON THE TYPE

The text of this book is set in Linotype Sabon, named after the type founder, Jacques Sabon. It was designed by Jan Tschichold and jointly developed by Linotype, Monotype and Stempel, in response to a need for a typeface to be available in identical form for mechanical hot metal composition and hand composition using foundry type.

Tschichold based his design for Sabon roman on a font engraved by Garamond, and Sabon italic on a font by Granjon. It was first used in 1966 and has proved an enduring modern classic.